THE PILGRIM

THE PILGRIM

Journeys

JOHN K DUXFIELD

iUniverse, Inc.
New York   Bloomington

The Pilgrim Journeys

iUniverse books may be ordered through booksellers or by contacting:

iUniverse
1663 Liberty Drive
Bloomington, IN 47403
www.iuniverse.com
1-800-Authors (1-800-288-4677)

Because of the dynamic nature of the Internet, any Web addresses or links contained in this book may have changed since publication and may no longer be valid. The views expressed in this work are solely those of the author and do not necessarily reflect the views of the publisher, and the publisher hereby disclaims any responsibility for them.

ISBN: 978-1-4502-2165-8 (sc)
ISBN: 978-1-4502-2166-5 (ebook)
ISBN: 978-1-4502-2167-2 (dj)

Printed in the United States of America

iUniverse rev. date: 4/21/2010

For those who journey

ACKNOWLEDGEMENTS

Again, this book would not have made it into print without the ongoing support and encouragement of my wife and family. To Sally and Emma: thank you.

Mum, you prodded me along when other things threatened to take over. Pat, your patient and careful editing was priceless. Thank you both.

AUTHOR'S NOTE

I have not yet had the privilege of visiting South Africa — having not made it south of Kenya. I hope to be able to rectify that one day soon. But the challenge of writing convincingly about somewhere you have not actually been is now largely offset by an information-rich cyberspace, and, of course, modern visual media.

That said, this second novel in the series, and its setting, remain entirely fictional. Any apparent similarity with actual people, places, organisations (armed forces in particular) or real events is entirely coincidental.

PART 1

DEPARTURES

CHAPTER 1

It was past what should have been the end of the dry season, but the rains were late, and the late afternoon sun rendered the featureless country a dull grey monotone. Any larger animals had moved to the slightly richer pastures further south, and little moved under leaden skies. Paul dozed fitfully, as best as he was able. On the last stage of his long trip back to the High Veldt, he was jammed inside the noisy cab of a heavily laden truck as it ground its way over the rough, unformed track that led into the valley of the Impala. The muted tones and quiet order of the Episcopal seminary in California were a distant counterpoint to the dust and noise.

Almost exactly twelve months before, Paul Tradour had left South Africa, and his work with the Royal Impala Tribe, with a real sense that he had accomplished his mission. For the best part of a decade he had laboured faithfully with Esther amongst the remnant people of one of Africa's great tribal nations, as teacher, doctor, and pastor. As the years progressed, they had become part of the community in all but the technicalities of their passports and missionary credentials. But in those last traumatic days before his sudden recall to the United States, he had buried his wife and soul mate under the giant kiaat tree in the front garden of their cottage. Everything lost, but so much accomplished.

For him, all signs had pointed to a new start, a new beginning. Indeed, the first few weeks of his university appointment had been rich and rewarding; travelling around California sharing his missionary adventure, encouraging continued support for the wider work of the church across the African continent.

Then he had settled into the little campus flat, and his teaching duties. The faculty did their best to support and encourage him through the transition that many of them understood only too well, but each day became more of a struggle that the one before. Until late one night in the faculty lounge a wise old friend said to him, 'Paul, Africa is a place of wonder, a place of great beauty, richness, and pain. It always has been, and always will be. You carry a burden for her people that will haunt you, one way or other, for all your days. You are hers, and she will always call you back to her.'

So he was returning. He tried to free a cramped leg from around his case, stuck fast against the feet of the other occupants of the severely overcrowded cab, but anything was better than riding on the back where breathing was almost impossible in the clouds of fine dust. Just another few hours, he consoled himself.

For not the first time that afternoon, his thoughts turned to Elizabeth. Apart from Sarah Dortmus, her mother, the only other white face in the valley — refugees from the nation's darker political forces. Strong, capable, and beautiful. At first Elizabeth was Esther's friend, then, as Esther's disease progressed through the later years, she became a shared confidant and refuge through the dark times. *What would her reaction be to his return?*

He tried to separate out his motives for going back — the man, and the missionary — but was unable to. Perhaps he was not supposed to. In one of those rare moments of insight, he realised that one of the things that he had learned over the last couple of years was to hold his missionary calling, and indeed the direction of each part of his journey, very lightly. At the end of the day, his God was big enough.

Somewhere off to the left, a lion roared. A family of warthogs momentarily danced in the dust ahead, and then vanished into the scrub that defined the limits of the track. *Racing towards or away from danger?* wondered Paul. *Like me.*

Africa.

A spontaneous cascade of joy erupted within his heart, and he thumped the dash and allowed the laughter to rip its way from his chest.

Africa.

But the truck driver looked across the cab with a face that had stilled a thousand songs, and Paul was silent, again. A little embarrassed, he resorted to an examination of the dusk out through the grime of the passenger window.

And what about Daniel? The former Sergeant Daniel Rutter, South African Special Forces sniper. Daniel, who had seen too much. Sent on one final mission from which he was never supposed to return. Ordered to hunt down and kill Pieter, Elizabeth's father.

Pieter Dortmus, persona non grata with sections of the South African ruling elite. Friend and mentor of the Impala, where he and his family had taken refuge after their home and business premises were systematically torched one terrible night. Pieter who died unknowing on a far-away beach, at the hand of a man he would never meet. The man who would return to the Impala with details of Pieter's legacy, a fortune in diamonds, accompanied by Pieter's faithful companion, Marcus, the giant of a dog.

Perhaps it would have been best if Daniel had not felt so compelled to make the long and difficult journey back to the valley — and Pieter's death had remained a mystery. Elizabeth would have been spared the almost simultaneous double trauma that took her to the very edge of her sanity. She would certainly not have fallen for the tall, decisive soldier who had taken her father's life.

Should I have stayed? thought Paul, when Daniel was forced to return to barracks to face the military charges against him. *Or would that have forever compromised my friendship with him?* Having lost track of Daniel's fraught appeal process, he assumed that his friend was still confined to barracks. All he could do was trust that events would unfold in their time. He knew there was a risk he might find he was, in fact, not needed — even not welcome. Much could happen in twelve months, but it felt right.

Home.

The vehicle crested the last rise and he got his first view of the valley laid out in front of them, the lake still visible in the last of the daylight. There was the main town, just a little to the right. He knew the tall column of dust that seemed to be tied to the back of the truck would have announced their approach several hours ago. Already the townspeople would be gathering in anticipation of the goods and supplies piled high on the hardwood timbers of the flat deck behind the cab. And of course the truck carried the only mail that came in, or out, of the valley. Paul was reasonably confident that his arrival was going to be a surprise.

In fact, Daniel Rutter sat on the porch of the little lodge not too far distant, and watched the evening flight of the waterfowl to their roosts. At the periphery of his vision, just short of the big old kiaat tree, was Esther's simple grave, carefully tended by the villagers as a sign of their enduring respect for her love and sacrifice. Much of the furnishings inside still technically belonged to Paul, although there was no practical way of ever being able to get it to him.

God, how he missed his friend.

Everything should have been well with the world, but he was increasingly troubled. While he was ever mindful of his debt and obligation to the Impala for funding his defence against the very serious charges he had faced, he was finding the hours in the classroom not that different from being confined to barracks, or worse. Never much of an academic, even explaining simple concepts to his students was difficult, while he had yet to find a way of focusing the children on their studies for even relatively brief periods — something that apparently came quite naturally to Elizabeth.

For her part, Elizabeth did not seem able to understand why he so quickly became frustrated with both his own, and his students', lack of progress.

Increasingly Daniel longed for freedom across the wide spaces of the High Veldt. He'd not yet been able to free himself from commitments here in town to seek out the Bushman, Dktfec. Perhaps that old warrior, Tshakai, would be able to help. He would speak with Elizabeth tomorrow — but even the fact of having to consult with her just made him feel more trapped and frustrated.

He was rescued from his misery by the tell-tale column of dust from a distant truck, as it ground its way over the last few kilometres into town. Daniel reached for his boots.

Elizabeth had joined Swabi for supper a little earlier in the evening, but their conversation had been difficult. Elizabeth had not been prepared for Swabi to apparently side with Daniel, when she voiced her frustration at the lack of progress in the classroom. Whether this was also a symptom of where her relationship with Daniel was going, she was not yet prepared to address.

'What am I doing wrong?' Elizabeth asked her friend.

'About what?' came the reply, as Swabi feigned innocence; not at all sure she was ready for this conversation.

'Don't play simple with me, Sister, for I know you are not,' Elizabeth scolded in mock tones. 'What am I doing wrong with Daniel?'

'Oh, that,' but Swabi's thoughts were with another soldier, deployed many days journey to the north. Her distraction was obvious.

'Roos will be all right, you know,' prompted Elizabeth.

Swabi glanced across at her friend, guiltily. 'I am sorry Elizabeth. I just can't get him out of my mind. There are reports of heavy fighting with the rebel groups, and Roos is up there in the thick of it.' She paused, and then got to her feet. 'But your problem man is right here.'

Elizabeth got to her feet, and walked across to join Swabi in front of the window. 'Yes, he is. But then again, he is not. He seems lost, somehow. He's a very different person — withdrawn and moody — without some battle to fight.'

'Perhaps he just needs more time to adjust,' offered Swabi.

'Maybe,' was the distant reply. Elizabeth's eyes settled on a painting of three figures seated under a giant willow on the lake shore. One of the faces was very familiar. 'I wonder how Paul is getting on in California?' she asked, giving voice to the question without thinking.

She endured a sharp glance from Swabi for her honesty. 'I would be careful of where you allow your thoughts to drift, sister. The last thing that Daniel needs right now is for you to revisit your affection for Paul. Daniel deserves far better than that!'

The words stung as if she had been slapped, but over her friend's shoulder Elizabeth was the first to notice the column of dust from the approaching truck. Rescued from the need to continue an increasingly fraught discussion, they both reached for their brightly coloured wraps as protection against the cool of the evening air, to join the festival throng moving towards the far side of the town square. There, the truck would stop to unload its cargo into the large warehouse at the front of the markets. Many carried torches in readiness for the onset of the dark African night.

Elizabeth looked around for Daniel, but he was nowhere to be seen. Soon the crowd was thick enough that he might have been standing alongside them and she would not have noticed.

The truck laboured its way up the main thoroughfare, and into the square itself. Along with its cargo, everything was a uniform shade of pale brown as the dust clung to every exposed surface. As the big vehicle came to a halt and fell silent, the crowd pressed around to the extent that the occupants of the cab had difficulty getting the doors open. Finally, a couple of the village constables pushed forward and began to restore order so that the truck could be unloaded.

Elizabeth and Swabi were on the opposite side of the truck as Paul climbed down, but he was immediately recognised by those around him, and the chant of *Misser Paul, Misser Paul* raced across the crowd like an electric current.

At first the women were confused, but then Paul came into view atop the shoulders of an impromptu guard of honour, and Elizabeth's heart missed a beat. She allowed the crowd to surge past her, and reached out to a handy fence post for support. Swabi had to work hard to get back to her.

'It's Paul,' was all that Elizabeth could manage through the dust stirred up by the crowd. Swabi just nodded and escorted her friend around the side of the crowd and into the quieter shadows, as the remaining light faded.

Daniel picked them out as he came up from the lake shore. 'I almost missed you, sisters,' he remarked. 'What is wrong, Elizabeth? You look like you have seen a ghost.'

Elizabeth just shook her head, so Swabi answered for her. 'It's Paul. He was on the truck, but the crowd has taken him down to the Royal Lodge.'

'Really!' exclaimed Daniel. 'That is wonderful news.' He immediately turned in the direction of the royal quarters, and called back over his shoulder; 'It will be great to have him around again — perhaps he will rescue me from the classroom.' It was the most animated Elizabeth had seen him since he had returned to the valley, and he quickly left them behind.

'The old Daniel,' Swabi commented.

'I should have seen it,' remarked Elizabeth sadly, and they picked up the pace so as not to fall further behind.

The evening passed in a blur of noise and celebration. Elizabeth, Daniel and Swabi found themselves very much on the outside of a community outpouring of joy at the return of 'Misser Paul'. The young Queen Ngashi, who rose to the Impala throne after her Uncle's mysterious death during the earlier troubles, formally welcomed Paul back to the valley, the giant dog Marcus at her side, and declared the following day a holiday.

It was not until much later in the evening that Paul managed to detach himself from the crowds of young people, and make his way across to where they were seated against one of the overhanging willows. Daniel was the first to recognise the opportunity, and met him half-way in a huge bear hug. 'Paul, my brother, it's great to see you.'

'Daniel!' Paul gasped through crushed ribs. 'I had no idea that you had been released. This is great news.'

Daniel picked out a particularly noisy group intent on claiming back their prize, so led the way through the fringe of the crowd. 'Quick. The girls are over against the tree. If we stay here the party will catch up with you again.' He had to shout to make himself heard over the ongoing din of celebration.

'Right,' laughed Paul, and followed.

At their approach, Swabi rushed forward and wrapped the slightly embarrassed young man in a sisterly embrace. 'Paul. This is incredible! Why didn't you tell us you were coming back?'

'It seemed more efficient to deliver the good news myself,' he replied with a broad smile, and then detached himself to greet Elizabeth. She was standing slightly apart, obviously uncomfortable. *More lovely now than I ever remember,* Paul thought, unsure how to cross this first bridge. He glanced across to Daniel, but got no cues there.

Swabi finally broke the tension. 'Is this really how two friends greet each other?'

Realising that it was up to her to make the first move, Elizabeth finally stepped forward and kissed Paul gently on the cheek. On the edge of her vision she could see Daniel watching but could read nothing on his face, so, acting on an impulse, she threw herself into Paul's arms and held him tight. A dam burst inside her and she wept great tears of joy and pain.

Swabi reached across and laid a gentle hand on Daniel's arm, observing that even his eyes were a little moist. 'We've missed him greatly.'

'We all, Swabi. Haven't we all,' he replied, with a wry smile. He wiped his left eye self-consciously. 'Tell Paul that there is a hot brew on at home, when he is ready.' He slipped away. Swabi watched him go, unable to read the set of his shoulders for any clue of how he was feeling.

Daniel moved his few belongings into the spare room of the lodge, and was enjoying the first cup of rich bush tea when Paul knocked on the open door.

'No need to knock on the door of your home, Paul.' Daniel put down his cup and got to his feet. 'Here, let me take your bag.' He picked it up off the porch and dropped it on the bed in Paul's room.

'Are you sure?' was all the other man could get out.

'Didn't like the mattress,' came the reply, and they both burst out laughing and slapped each other on the back. 'It's very good to have you home, Paul.'

They settled down over a deep black pot of tea and spent the rest of the night catching up, as if only a few days had elapsed. Daniel took Paul through the trauma of endless investigations, and then being forced to leave behind everything that he had worked for, just to stay a free man. Paul's tale was remarkably similar in many ways.

Eventually their stories arrived in the present.

Daniel stood and took his cup to the window, allowing the night breeze off the lake to tease the loose folds of his shirt. 'I've made a bit of a mess of being a school teacher, Paul. Your shoes were much bigger than I could ever hope to fill. To be honest, I am itching for wide open spaces and the sound of the bush at night.'

The rich silence between them was framed by the constant hiss of the kerosene lamp just outside the door. Paul looked into the dark liquid of his tea. 'And Elizabeth?'

Daniel turned back to the room. He took in the candles burning dimly on the table and the few simple furnishings. 'She doesn't seem to understand — or perhaps she doesn't want to. Given the long absences of her father, perhaps that is only reasonable. Anyway, for whatever reason, things have not exactly worked out as expected.' He looked out the window into the black African night, where distant storm clouds hung silhouetted against a new moon. 'It might have been better for her if you had stayed ... and I had not come back.'

Paul was struck by the heaviness in the last comment. 'I could not stay, so that is not an issue — for better or worse.' The chair protested as he rose to join his friend at the window. 'It's in the past, Daniel. The question is — what next?'

A remarkably similar conversation was taking place in Elizabeth's lounge, except that it was accompanied by substantially more emotion — at times bordering on a flat-out argument. 'What would you have me do now, Swabi? You seem to claim to know my heart better than I do!'

Swabi turned away, not prepared to allow Elizabeth to see her tears, and then replied in carefully measured tones. 'I would have you treat them both with the care and respect that they have earned, sister. God only knows that I love them both almost as dearly as you.'

But Elizabeth just mocked her. 'Really!'

Swabi spun around with her eyes blazing. 'I will not see you dishonour their friendship with foolish women's tricks.' But it was overdone, and Elizabeth crumpled. At first Swabi was a little suspicious of her friend, but soon realised that the reaction was genuine.

Elizabeth's grief was so full that it left her gasping for breath between bouts of incoherent sobbing. All the other could do was hold her tight.

Much later, Swabi slipped across the alley to her own empty room, and cried herself to sleep.

CHAPTER 2

The elderly truck that had brought Paul back to them carried provisions for the next few weeks, and a rough leather bag of mail. That mail was taken to the strong room in the Police Station for overnight storage, and then a clerk collected it first thing in the morning. He sorted it by addressee and passed it to an eager band of small boys, who fanned out across the town with the packages and envelopes. It was all part of the natural rhythm of the community, made more significant because it was a holiday, so all the recipients were enjoying a slow start to the day. But very quickly the holiday became irrelevant.

'Misser Daniel, Misser Paul!' came the urgent little voice from the doorway.

'What is it, Nathan?' replied Paul from his seat on the porch. He'd been dozing in the early morning sun, allowing the sounds and smells of the lakeshore to wash away the fatigue.

Nathan was the very picture of urgency. 'Queen Ngashi need to see very soon please.'

'What time is it?' asked Daniel as he walked onto the porch, carrying a steaming cup of tea for them both.

'Very soon, please!' The little boy wailed.

'OK, Nathan, OK, we are on our way,' acknowledged Paul. The two men glanced at each other and hurried to dress, now worried. Something was very wrong.

Swabi was still asleep when Elizabeth banged on the door. She rolled sleepily onto her feet, wrapping her house-robe around her as she made her way from the bedroom. 'Who is it?'

'Swabi, it's Elizabeth. Ngashi needs us, quickly.'

'Elizabeth?' She opened the door. 'What on earth is going on?'

'I wish I knew, but there is quite a panic. Get dressed quickly. I'll wait for you out here.'

Without need of further explanation, Swabi rushed back into the bedroom and threw on the clothes that lay across the cane chair at the end of her bed, where they had been dropped not many hours before.

As they hurried up the road, they met Daniel and Paul coming up from the lake. Dispensing with the normal courtesies, Paul found his voice first. 'What is happening?'

Elizabeth shrugged. 'We've no idea.' They rounded the corner and found a section of police taking post around the perimeter of the royal lodge.

'That is not a good sign,' commented Daniel, glancing at Paul. They were ushered through the gate and into the courtyard to join a group of the town councillors already assembled on the broad porch, with Ngashi off to one side. She waved them towards seats and then began without formality.

'Friends, I have dreadful news.' She put down the letter she had held in her hand and took a deep breath. 'Early last week, our loyal solicitor Mr Johansen and his wife, were abducted.' She held up a tired hand to prevent the obvious questions, and continued. 'Their bodies were found in the harbour the following day. Apparently, they had been tortured.' She paused to gather her strength, fighting a wave of nausea.

After the reactive noise of the gathering subsided a little, Swabi voiced the obvious. 'Who would want to do such a thing?'

'Who is a mystery, but the motive, sadly, is not,' Ngashi replied, fighting for control, her eyes fixed on the headland across the lake. 'The Bank where Pieter's papers were kept for safe storage, along with a fortune in diamonds, was burned to the ground the following night. We have to assume that the details of his claim are compromised.'

'Along with Pieter's will, and Elizabeth's inheritance,' Daniel added, grimly, looking across to the ashen young woman.

They were all stunned, and apart from a few murmured prayers there was little to be said. Finally, it was the senior member of the Impala Council, Ambassador Ngassi, who stood. 'Then we must do everything in our power to secure the claim, and the mine. We are already the best part of two weeks behind the criminals who are responsible for this.'

'Yes Ngassi,' Daniel stood, grateful for the cue, 'I agree. I can leave immediately for Cape Town. We must know who's behind this.' He looked around the worried faces. 'Certainly there are a few likely places to start, from our earlier investigations.'

Ngashi smiled through gathering tears. 'Thank you Daniel, but Inspector Petronas is already on his way down there to take care of that. Ever since Pat's role in our troubles resulted in him being removed from command of the Police special tactics team, he's been looking for an opportunity to even the score sheet.' She got to her feet and came across to where he was standing. 'What I need you to do is much harder to ask. Would you lead a party across to the coast? Secure the mine before it is too late. Pat suspects that whoever is behind this will almost certainly attempt to establish a presence at the mine, with or without a legal claim.'

Finding her rhythm, she next turned to Elizabeth. 'Sister, the Inspector has agreed to meet you in Cape Town. We must secure title to the mine. Apparently, as Pieter's sole heir, you are the only one who can gain access to the duplicate documents held by the Ministry of Lands and Resources. I've asked the truck to wait a little, to allow you to get a few things together.'

'I am not sure that I can, Ngashi,' Elizabeth whispered. 'It is years since I have been out of the valley. How do I get to Cape Town?' Swabi reached out to steady her.

There was an awkward silence until Daniel broke the tension. 'Paul still has his suitcase packed?'

Ngashi turned to Paul. 'It is a lot to ask, but Elizabeth has a point. In any case, it would be unwise for her to travel all that way by herself.'

Paul nodded, desperately trying to control a soaring mix of emotions. 'Of course. If you will excuse me, I will go and sort out what I will need to take.' Ngashi nodded gratefully and Paul jogged out through the gate.

'Sister, I will help you pack,' urged Swabi. 'The truck driver will be anxious to get on his way before the heat of the day.' They hurried back to Elizabeth's lodge.

Queen Ngashi reached out to Daniel. 'Daniel of the Tall Trees, I have no doubt as to the danger of your mission. These people have demonstrated that they are entirely ruthless.' She knew that he had hoped to leave that part of his life well behind him.

'This ongoing tragedy is largely of my own doing, Ngashi.' Daniel replied grimly. 'It's the least that I can do.'

She squeezed his hand, urgently. 'You take too much on your own shoulders, my friend. I've sent a runner to Tshakai ahead of you. He will have a section of his finest warriors waiting to depart.'

'Thank you,' he replied. 'I will look forward to a few hours with him before continuing to the west.' He bent down and kissed her on both cheeks, and then jogged down the path.

Just as he was about to disappear through the gate of the palisade, Ngashi called out, 'You are forgetting something, Daniel.' She reached down and whispered into the ear of the huge dog that was constantly at her side. Marcus licked her hand and trotted handsomely across the courtyard.

'Take care of each other,' Ngashi whispered, as they disappeared from sight.

Paul was just coming out of the door as Daniel jogged around the corner. They spared time for a brief embrace that said more than words could ever convey. *See you*, and, *God speed*, was sufficient.

A little to the east, Swabi carried the small case as the women hurried up the road to where the truck was waiting. Paul intercepted them half way across the dusty town square. The big vehicle was already backing around so it could retrace its path through the town. 'Have you seen Daniel?' Elizabeth asked.

'Briefly,' Paul replied. 'He was rushing in to the cottage to pack. Knowing him, he is already out of town and heading up the valley for his rendezvous with Tshakai.'

Confused, Elizabeth shook her head at the fickleness of men, and took Paul's offered hand to assist her up into the cab of the truck. No sooner had Paul joined her than the truck driver released the air brakes and they headed out of town, belching black smoke as the old diesel engine warmed up.

Emerging from the town gate, Elizabeth had a fleeting glimpse of a man and a giant dog heading up the hill through the scrub, on a more direct route to the village of Tshakai of the Veterans at the top of the valley.

Daniel was free, and thrilled to the movement as he jogged across the low ridge and back down to intersect the winding road, Marcus trotting happily beside him. Totally focused on the mission ahead of him, he had not even briefly considered that Elizabeth might have expected some farewell. Settled into the old rhythm of travel, his mind was already on the practicalities of the forced march over the High Veldt, the climb over the escarpment to reach the coast, and the defensive arrangements necessary to secure the mine. By the time the walls of Tshakai's village came into sight, he had most of the details of both requirements sorted in his mind.

A section of Tshakai's impi was almost packed and ready to leave. The old warrior himself was working his way up and down the line of tall, athletic men, ensuring they were well prepared, but not carrying any surplus weight. He knew that Daniel would be travelling fast, and light, able to set a gruelling pace across the open terrain for days on end. They would spring from waterhole to waterhole, and live off the land. The chances were that at least one or two of his men would get left behind on the way, but time was now the enemy. Tshakai only wished that he was twenty years younger, and able to join them.

Daniel jogged through the gate, breathing heavily.

'What took you so long, Daniel of the Tall Trees?' Tshakai asked in the dialect of the bush people as they embraced.

'My boots still have a mind of their own, Great One,' Daniel countered, in the same tongue, delighting the old man with his quick wit.

'Well said, my friend. Well said.' He pointed the way to his lodge. 'Come. Have some tea while Shadz completes his inspection.'

Daniel looked down the line and nodded his approval, before following Tshakai to the porch of his lodge. He accepted a steaming cup, along with a few nuts and dried fruit. Marcus dropped to the dust beside them, panting.

Daniel was keen for any information the northern outpost might have. 'Have your hunting parties noted any unusual activity up on the High Veldt in, say, the last week?'

'Nothing,' replied Tshakai. 'We had a group of hunters return to camp only last night.'

'Good.' Daniel took a seat on the step. 'Even though the location of the mine may be compromised, it is another thing to cross the escarpment without any directions. We may still be able to beat any ground party out there.'

'Ground party? You sound as if you think they might attempt to fly?'

Daniel shook his head. 'The challenge, for even the best bush pilot, is first the almost continuous poor weather over the escarpment at this time of year, and second the lack of a practical landing strip on the other side. I also think it is too far from a fuelling point for anything but the largest helicopter. And I am working on the fact that that would draw too much attention for their comfort.'

'Good,' said Tshakai.

'Not quite.' Daniel absently drew the outline of a small ship in the sand in front of him. 'If it were up to me I would come in from the sea. While the coast is pretty exposed, it is only a few hundred miles from the nearest fishing port. Something not much over a day in one of the larger vessels.'

Tshakai nodded. 'They could well be there already, then?'

'Yes, and that is good reason for us to be moving.' Daniel stood up. 'I intend to call in to see Dktfec on the way. We may have need of his skills if they have, in fact, opted for an overland route.' He moved across to where the warriors waited.

He greeted their commander, Shadz, formally, recognising the young warrior who had intercepted his little party on their first arrival in the valley, and then been roundly scolded for his rudeness. 'Shadz, I am honoured to have you and your men with us. Are you ready to fly like the little Bushmen?'

Shadz danced lightly from foot to foot, delighted to have the opportunity to prove himself. 'We will be as light as tick birds on the buffalo's back, and as swift as the cheetah hunting for her cubs,' came the reply.

Daniel slapped the man's rawhide shield hard with an open hand, and the report echoed off the surrounding hills. 'Then let us hunt as the leopard hunts, my warrior brother.' He led them out of the gate to the sound of the tribal songs of war, feeling more alive than he had for years. Quickly they climbed out of the valley, heading directly west.

There was a good moon, and they made full use of the natural light and cooler temperatures to force the pace. In less than two days they were at the hill where Marcus had attacked the rogue lion; saving Daniel's life, almost at the cost of his own. Daniel used it to orient his advance, hoping that the Bushmen were not far away at this time of the year. He knew that the little people would be aware of the rapidly-moving column of warriors long before there was any chance of coming across one of their seasonal camps.

When he was confident that they were in the right general vicinity, Daniel called a halt and told Shadz to have his warriors drop their armament against a large rock, and withdraw a little to wait. At first the warriors protested, but Daniel stood firm. He knew that the little ghosts would not normally approach such a heavily armed group. As the dust settled around them in the late afternoon light, off to one side he thought he heard an almost imperceptibly high whistle, followed by an answer slightly further to the south. He imitated it perfectly, and sent Marcus off into the scrub. A few moments later the great dog appeared with a solitary little man at his side.

Dktfec of the whispering grass pulled himself up to his full stature. 'Big brother should know better than to go jumping around in the middle of my hunt. My family will go hungry tonight.'

Daniel bowed formally. 'I am very sorry, little brother, but I had great need to find you, and could not spare the many moons it would have taken to search out your hearth.' He tried to look as contrite as possible.

'Something must be very wrong that you fly toward trouble rather than away from it?' Dktfec looked up at him quizzically.

'You are as wise as you are handsome, little brother,' continued Daniel, trying to preserve as much of the protocol as possible, without delaying more than was absolutely necessary.

'I have missed our hunts, big brother,' said the little Bushman, now standing directly in front of Daniel, tears coursing down his dusty cheeks.

'As have I, Dktfec. At each breath of the evening breeze.' Daniel picked up a stick and drew an empty circle in the dust between them, to indicate a potential new phase to their shared journey. 'We would travel much faster if I knew where to find the best waterholes.'

Dktfec drew a figure inside the circle. 'That would require a guide.'

'Yes, little brother.' Daniel scratched a few more lines in the dust.

'A man must take leave of his family,' observed the little man.

'I understand,' nodded Daniel. 'It would also be rude not to leave behind enough food for the period of sadness.'

'That is true,' Dktfec smiled, and Daniel produced a calf-skin pouch full of the finest dried antelope.

Dktfec took the gift with a little bow. 'I will meet you under the great divided rock that weeps, about a day's run after the sun?'

Daniel nodded. 'We will wait there for you.'

'Only if you are very fast, big brother!' Dktfec responded, and vanished into the scrub behind them.

Daniel briefly explained the situation to Shadz, who immediately challenged his warriors with the need to beat the Bushman to the meeting place. For a while, even Daniel had to work hard to keep up. He eventually called a halt for just four hours rest sometime after the moon began to slip towards the distant horizon, and they ate a little more of their precious supplies, splashing their remaining water around inside parched mouths.

It was midday, under a fierce African sky, when they finally dropped down into the little rift that protected one of the few permanent springs in the region. Although it was at the very limit of their hunting range, Shadz and his warriors were amazed, completely unaware of its existence. But they were flabbergasted as they rounded the final corner to find the little Bushman squatting on his haunches to tend a discreet hunting fire, looking well pleased with himself.

As they approached, Daniel touched the big man on the arm. 'Remember that these little people have been running before the breezes of the veldt for longer than any can remember. I fully expected Dktfec to be waiting for us. He probably also took a more direct route to get here.' Shadz reluctantly agreed, more prepared to believe in some form of witchcraft at that point.

Daniel stopped a few paces back from the fire and feigned exhaustion. 'Little brother, I see that you did not take long over your farewells?'

Dktfec rose and clapped at the humour. 'My sisters understood the importance of making sure that you did not get lost again.'

'Your sisters are very wise.' Daniel noted the freshly cooked leg of antelope keeping warm in the embers. 'I see that your arrows are as sharp as I remember.'

'Even though game has been scarce through the dry grasses of this season,' Dktfec replied as he picked up the meat and passed it ceremonially across the fire.

Daniel bowed slightly. 'We are very grateful. This is much better on the tongue than our dried meat.'

'And you will need less of the precious water to chew it.' To emphasise his point the little Bushman smiled and squeezed a little of the juices from the meat to show how expertly it was cooked. By then the warriors, waiting respectfully for an invitation to drink from the spring, would have crawled across hot coals for a portion. 'I am sorry. I am forgetting my manners. Please, drink your fill, and help yourself to a Bushman's humble offering.'

Over the simple meal, Daniel brought Dktfec up to date. After a moment's consideration, and some more scratching in the sand, the little man asked the obvious question. 'After we have crossed the plains, would it be reasonable for a Bushman to cross the great hills and view the mighty expanse of waters?'

'It would be reasonable, and big brother would value a Bushman's company — as would Marcus,' Daniel remarked, looking at the big animal that had not strayed far from Dktfec's side since they had arrived. 'But let us see how the crossing looks when we get a little closer.' The little man nodded, sagely.

Four long and hard days later they paused at the last waterhole, facing the climb into the mists ahead of them. As Tshakai had expected, two of their number had been left to find their own way home, unable to match Daniel's pace as the superbly fit ex-Special Forces soldier drew on all his training and reserves to force their progress to the very limits of human endurance. Even Marcus was exhausted.

Daniel called Shadz and Dktfec over. 'We will rest here for a full day, as the next two days will be far tougher than the last.' Neither of the other two flinched. 'Shadz, you should ask your men if they're carrying any injuries. We cannot afford to be held up at altitude in this weather.' To emphasise his point, Daniel placed his hand on the warrior's shoulder. 'There would be no shame, as the cold is a killer just as sure as your spear.'

Shadz met his gaze. 'We are ready, brother.'

'Good. Then let us allow the view to restore our souls.' The morning sun climbed in all its splendour over the rich purple hues of the African High Veldt laid out at their feet, and the warriors lifted their voices as one in a song of praise and thanksgiving for the new day, before breaking into the ancient songs of battle.

Truly these are men, Daniel thought. He suddenly realised that he had not thought of Elizabeth since the climb up the hill away from town.

CHAPTER 3

The big vehicle laboured its way out of the valley and settled into the long process of eating up the miles towards Springbok. Although it was not the most direct route to the south, that was where the truck was going, and Paul was confident that they would be able to catch a bus from there.

It was too noisy in the cab for any conversation, and so they were left to their own thoughts, as the seemingly endless hours of dust, and ruts, passed beneath the wheels.

Elizabeth could not get the image of Daniel powering up the hill with Marcus out of her mind, and mentally replayed the events of the last twenty-four hours over and over again, very aware of the man beside her. Paul, on the other hand, was trying to sort out the ethics of his current situation. Neither had resolved very much by the time the driver pulled off the track, and announced that this was as far as they were going for the day.

They were, quite literally, nowhere. A veteran of the trip into the valley only a couple of days before, Paul knew that they were on their own to make themselves as comfortable as possible, and that the driver expected them to vacate the cab to allow him to rest. The next best place was on the back of the truck, under the tarpaulin to protect them from the cool of the night, as comfortable as possible amongst the boxes and loose goods.

The driver handed Paul a rifle as he stepped down into the long dry grass off the side of the track, with nothing more than a grunt by way of instruction. Elizabeth cast him a *do you know how to use that?* glance as she joined him, but Paul simply led the way around the back of the truck, and then helped her to climb up.

'Not quite the Hilton, but the company is OK,' he observed with a smile.

'After today, I think that I could sleep anywhere,' she answered, reorganising a few boxes to clear them a flat surface. That done, she sat down, motioning him to join her.

'I … er … I will keep first watch,' Paul said clumsily, suddenly embarrassed. Elizabeth was too tired to protest, so just shrugged and was almost immediately asleep.

Paul soon found a reasonably comfortable seat that afforded a decent view in all directions, and settled down to watch out the night, not exactly sure how he would respond if anything large and nasty wandered along. Blessed with the same moon that had allowed Daniel and his party to make such good progress, he wondered again at the providence that had carried him from a dusty university library to this very real place in the middle of an African night. Sitting there, with a rifle cradled awkwardly under his arm, and the sounds of the wild around him, he realised that he was the most at peace he had been in many years, and whispered a simple prayer of thanksgiving.

In the small hours of the morning, Elizabeth stirred, now sore from the caress of the lumps in her makeshift bed. She slipped out from beneath the tarpaulin and joined Paul under the great firmament of the heavens. 'They say that there is nowhere else on earth where the night is more beautiful,' she whispered reverently.

Paul shuffled across to make room for her beside him. 'On a night like tonight, that must certainly be true.'

Elizabeth paused to tease out the heavy canvas covers underneath her before answering. 'Tired?'

'Too alive to be tired,' came the reply. 'Besides, I can sleep through tomorrow.'

'How much longer?'

Paul stretched out a cramped knee. 'Another night in the bush, and then about half a day.'

She pulled her jacket closer around her. 'I don't actually remember much of the city. It's nearly fifteen years since the fires that destroyed my father's business, and our home, forcing us to leave.' Elizabeth shivered. 'There was never any reason to go back.'

'Hopefully we wont have to stay any longer than necessary,' noted Paul. 'Big cities are not my favourite places. I will definitely feel more comfortable when we are able to link up with Pat.'

Elizabeth simply nodded, her hair reflecting the moonlight, and they sat quietly as the night weaved its magic around them.

Finally Paul broke the gentle silence between them. 'I missed you dearly after I left, Elizabeth.'

'Me too,' she said and briefly leant her head on his shoulder.

But if Paul had hoped for some assistance with this conversation, she was not ready to give it, so after a while he continued. 'It took me some time to even begin to sort out the mess of emotions between what seemed a civilized period of mourning for Esther, and how I really felt about us.'

Elizabeth rested her hand gently against his bare forearm. When Paul chose not amplify this further, she picked up the theme. 'I have loved you for many years, Paul. At first it was just friendship, but, as I think you know, I was unable to keep it in that box — besides, you had the advantage of being the only white male that I knew.'

Paul chuckled.

'Then Daniel came into our lives, just after I had lost mother.' Paul made to interject, but Elizabeth cut him off. 'I am genuinely not sure how I feel about him now. Was I just carried away by the drama and romance of the situation? Since he came back to the valley we seem to have gone backwards, if anything.' She paused. 'Did he say anything to you?'

Uncomfortable at the directness of the question, Paul feigned innocence. 'About what?'

Elizabeth turned to face him. 'You men are all the same, the same rules. This .... this sense of honour that you constantly measure yourselves by!'

Somewhere off in the distance a hyena barked, and Paul leant forward. 'I count Daniel among my closest friends, Elizabeth. I would never deliberately say or do anything that might prejudice that.'

'I'm sorry. I expected you to understand.' She lifted her hand and stared out into the night, but Paul chased her hand with his.

'Elizabeth, this is what little I understand.' He took a deep breath, wanting to say it right the first time. 'I was not aware that Daniel was free, and so had expected to come back to the valley to you, and for you. I care for you now as much as ever.' There was another, longer pause before he could continue. 'But it would seem wise to allow a little space to work out which of us you would, or should, choose.'

She nodded, quiet for a moment, then continued. 'What would Daniel want?'

Paul's answer seemed to take a long time. 'Only he can answer that.'

She gave him back his hand. 'Did he not say something, anything that might help me?'

The hint of rejection was enough, and Paul relented, a little. 'He did tell me that he was finding life in town rather difficult. He's a wanderer — a man of action. It sounded to me as if he wasn't at all happy.'

Elizabeth's hand returned to his. 'And now he is racing for the coast, and goodness knows what, while we're on our way to Cape Town.'

'And goodness knows what,' Paul repeated quietly.

CHAPTER 4

It was Dktfec who noticed the column of dust first, and slipped around the boulders to wake Daniel carefully. 'Big brother, we are not alone.'

Instantly fully aware, Daniel followed him to the edge of the low ridge that formed their cover. 'That is what I feared, little brother. Wake Shadz.'

How many are there of you? Daniel wondered of the dust rising in the distance. About 10–12 miles away; perhaps three hours.

'Hunters?' asked Shadz a few moments after he crawled forward.

Daniel considered that for a moment. 'Possibly, but it is the wrong time of year to be pushing this far west. I think there are two vehicles — you can just see a split in the dust cloud.'

'There are three, big brother, and one is a small truck, well-loaded by the looks of things,' corrected the big warrior.

Daniel smiled, still getting used to the phenomenal long range vision of these people who had for centuries relied on their acute visual skills for a successful hunt. 'They will be looking for a good site to camp. It will be interesting to see if they know where the water hole is.' *That, in itself, will tell us a bit about who you are and what you are doing out here*, Daniel continued to himself.

They spent the next two hours observing the approach of the small convoy, until it stopped about half a mile from the foot of the escarpment. The occupants climbed out to establish their camp.

'I count eight?' Shadz whispered.

'Good odds,' Daniel smiled. 'They don't look as if they are expecting company, and that should work to our advantage.' He crawled back from the ridge-line. 'As soon as it's dark, I will get a little closer and see if we can find out who they are, and what they are.'

Shadz nodded.

A little closer was a relative term — Daniel could have helped himself to tea. The men had not posted a picket, or even allocated responsibility for a lookout, so getting inside the camp amongst the dark shadows cast by the gas lamps was too easy. From beneath one of the big SUVs Daniel listened to the banter around the camp fire, as they prepared, and then ate, their evening meal. But he had no real clue as to who, or what, they were until there was a high pitched ring from inside the vehicle.

'Yes. This is Karl. Right, two days, we will be there.' There was the sound of a couple of switches being thrown, and the generator pitch dropped as the equipment was turned off. The vehicle moved on its suspension as a man got out and went over to where the others were grouped around the fire.

'Everything OK?' asked another voice.

The first voice replied. 'The weather could be better, but we will rendezvous with the trawler in two days.'

'So we cross the escarpment tomorrow,' offered a third voice. 'We had better organise our packs tonight so we can get away at first light. It will take us at least thirty-six hours to get through to the coast.'

The next voice was Karl, again. 'Jacques and Rolfe will stay here with the vehicles and await instructions.' Without further comment, they tidied up from their meal, and began to unload equipment to establish a more permanent camp.

Daniel slipped away into the sounds of the night, undetected.

He gathered the others behind the ridge, leaving one of the warriors to watch the activity below. 'We are going to have to move now if we are to have any chance of getting to the coast before our enemies. There is another group coming in on a fishing boat, now less than two days away.'

'And what of this group?' asked Shadz, running his finger along the blade of his spear.

Daniel shook his head. 'We are only lightly armed and can't afford to delay.' He then turned to Dktfec and switched to the Bushman dialect. 'Little brother, I need you to get a report back to Tshakai as fast as possible.' Dktfec looked at the dust at his feet. 'Tshakai must establish a rear-guard so that if we fail, these men are prevented from getting back to their big towns beyond the eastern sky. It is very important. Then return to your hearth and watch for our return.'

The little Bushman looked up. 'I will not be the first of my people to gaze upon the great waters?'

'I promise to return for you, little brother.' At this, Dktfec brightened a little, drew the customary picture in the sand that showed his intended path and how it intersected with Daniel's again, and then disappeared into the shadows. As the moon rose over the horizon behind them, Daniel led the warriors up the narrow ravine, and deep into the first row of hills.

It was a cold, miserable trip. The change in the seasons was well overdue, and the contrast to the heat of the plains behind them was profound. Daniel drove them relentlessly, knowing the risks of stopping in those conditions. He even passed a number of sites where he might have otherwise set a trap for those following, simply to keep moving.

Just over twenty-four hours later they finally dropped out of the mist and caught their first glimpse of the South Atlantic, as the moon rose over the hills behind them. In the middle of the bay they could plainly see the lights of a small ship.

'We are too late?' Shadz asked from the vantage of a line of scrub.

'Not necessarily. They must have only just arrived, and will probably wait for the ground party. I spent a good week searching for the track up here,' observed Daniel. 'We must get as much as possible from the cabin up to the mine. A handful of people could hold off an army up there.' They set off down the slope, and dropped into the top of the hanging valley, just behind Pieter's small cabin. Daniel mentally ticked off each landmark as they went.

He approached the cabin alone, apart from Marcus at his side, but as he expected it was unoccupied. They were alone in the valley, for now. He gave a short, sharp, whistle, and a moment later was joined by Shadz and his warriors.

After a brief meal they loaded the Army packs that Daniel had stored at the end of his last dramatic visit, and worked their way to the head of the valley, then up the naked slopes that led to the mine. They crossed the lip of the natural ledge that hosted the inconspicuous-looking cave entrance just as the first glimmer of the dawn was becoming obvious across the eastern sky. Always cautious, Daniel went in first, relieved to find everything just as he'd left it. He disarmed the claymore mine that protected the deeper access to the mine proper, and called the other men inside. Shadz smiled when he saw the piles of stores neatly arranged against the dark walls.

'Drop your packs and get some rest,' said Daniel. 'I don't want to risk moving back down into the valley in the daylight, and we should be at least a day ahead of the ground party.' Shadz's men did not need any urging.

About noon, Daniel and Shadz stirred and moved to the cave entrance. Daniel took a powerful optical sight off one of the weapons he had left in storage there, and focused on the vessel that sat quietly in the bay. It was one of the larger ocean going trawlers that worked out of Cape Town, and one or two of the larger fishing ports on the western coast of the great continent. He knew that Shadz could see almost as much with the naked eye.

'Nothing much doing,' Shadz muttered.

Daniel agreed. 'They really have no reason to come ashore until the ground party locates the route off the beach, unless they want to stretch their legs.'

'We could always pay them a visit?'

'I was thinking about that,' replied Daniel. 'We could dramatically improve the odds by spoiling their plans to get to the beach. How are you in the water?'

'I doubt any of us could get even half way out to there.' Shadz smiled. 'There is not much interest in swimming with the crocs and hippos in the lake.'

'That I can understand, my friend. It is probably one of those jobs that is best done alone, anyway. The moon will be a little later tonight, which should give me enough time to get on board, unnoticed. I doubt that they have much of a lookout here in the bay.'

'What will you do?' the big man asked.

'Well — they are going to need their boats. Best to make it look like equipment failure rather than sabotage.' Daniel grinned. 'No sense in advertising our presence.' Let's get this gear sorted. Time for your warriors to learn how to use one of these rifles.' He indicated the military weapons behind him.

Daniel spent the rest of the afternoon drilling the warriors with the automatic weapons, until they could do it blindfolded. 'Unfortunately we cannot afford to actually fire them until we need to do so in anger, but you will find that the recoil is less than the rifles that you have fired in your training with Tshakai. Remember the important thing is to fire short bursts — just single shots, or two or three rounds — or the weapon becomes very inaccurate.' The men nodded. Daniel knew that they were all hand-picked for this mission, and that Tshakai took considerable pride in the calibre of his impi. They would not let him down.

As the late afternoon shadows groped across the landscape below them, they moved back down the mountain in single file. First stop was the cabin, and here they cleaned out the storehouse of everything that was remotely of value. Then Shadz led his men back up to the mine, while Daniel moved off down the valley to check out the state of the narrow track down to the river valley below. He felt alive with the familiar anticipation of action.

The night was, by now, fully dark and Daniel had to tread carefully, with only the starlight and Marcus to guide him. A casual observer might just have noticed a slight change in the shadows as they passed. At the top of the narrow defile that led down to the river below, Daniel paused to check his orientation, before following Marcus down. It was not long before he confronted the pile of logs that had nearly taken his life, and where his assailant was still entombed. Was there a way around? Just off to one side he heard a whine from Marcus, and moved over to see what he had found. He got a good fright when one of the logs unexpectedly moved underneath him, almost flipping him over the edge.

But Marcus had found a hole beneath the pile of debris, carved out by the seasonal rains. It led back onto the track below the log fall, and soon Daniel was standing on the edge of the river below. A river that had nearly claimed his life. He put the memories of that horrendous night trapped on the waterfall to the back of his mind, and set off down-stream. No risk of a flash flood at this time of year.

It was almost totally dark in the narrow valley, and Daniel had to resort to holding Marcus around the ruff of his neck so that the big dog could guide him. About thirty minutes later they came to the entrance of the natural pool where Marcus had recovered from the encounter with the hyenas, but did not tarry. Daniel was keen to get out to the trawler before the moon rose, and it was another thirty minutes to the beach. The same beach where he had killed Pieter Dortmus.

They heard the surf well before they broke cover. Daniel made a pile of everything that was not going into the water with him, told Marcus to stay, and slipped across the beach.

There was a good surf running, but Daniel was a powerful swimmer and was soon out beyond the turbulence. With the trawler's anchor light bright against the blackness of the night, it was no problem to orient his progress, and it was only a few minutes before Daniel was resting quietly on the anchor chain.

The big chain was tempting, but likely to leave him exposed on the foredeck for too long, so he moved towards the stern, looking for other options. On the seaward side, he found that the crew had left a couple of lines in the water, and in no time he was on deck, and tucked in behind one of two inflatable boats that were still lashed to the fish-processing platform. Not far in front of these he could make out a couple of darker shapes nursing the glowing tips of whatever cigarettes they were smoking, and the murmur of their conversation was just audible over the slap, slap of the chop against the side of the vessel.

Keeping a boat between him and the two crewmen, he slipped underneath the big outboard with a screwdriver and drained the oil from the lower crankcase that drove the big stainless steel propeller. Helping himself to more tools from the chest lashed conveniently between the two boats, just for good measure he removed the locking pin from the big nut that secured the prop, backed off the nut a couple of turns, and then replaced it. He then repeated the exercise on the other boat. There was a good chance that after a couple of accelerations between here and the shore the crankcase would either seize, or the prop would fall off, or both. Daniel was not fussed which happened first. A casual check would not notice the motors had been tampered with — at least not until the damage was done, and then the first accusations would naturally be targeted at a member of the trawler's crew.

Fifteen minutes later, Daniel was back with Marcus, working their way back up the stream, now enjoying the benefit of light from the late-rising moon. Marcus growled a warning and a couple of shadows disappeared back into the scrub, while overhead the monkeys began to chatter amongst themselves. 'Easy boy,' Daniel counselled the big dog.

They stopped for a drink at the cool, clear waters of the secret grotto, and then continued up to the log fall. Daniel noted that a couple of well-placed explosive charges would bring the whole structure cascading down into the valley below.

Shadz was drilling his warriors when Daniel arrived back at the mine. They had spent the balance of the evening sorting and stowing the final haul of equipment, so that each man knew where everything was, and everything had a man responsible for it. It was time to plan the defence of the mine.

'What I hope to avoid is a shoot-out,' said Daniel to the assembled men. 'What we will do is use our knowledge of the terrain, and our ability to move quietly from point to point, to confuse and disorient our enemies. Remember, above all else we must not lead them back here.' The warriors murmured their understanding. 'We are playing for time. Time for our friends in Cape Town to secure legal title to the land, and the claim over the mine.'

CHAPTER 5

The bus rumbled down the highway that led into the city of Cape Town from the north, while Paul and Elizabeth tried to get as much rest as they could in the cramped seats. Eventually they arrived at the central-city terminal, and were relieved to see a familiar face waiting on the platform.

'Pat, it is so good to see you,' said Paul, arm outstretched, as he stepped down from the bus.

'Likewise,' replied the burly inspector, greeting them both. 'Grab your bags and follow me out front. I have a car sitting in the car park.'

They were soon on their way across the city, with Pat catching up on events back in the valley of the Impala since he had left. 'Daniel back all right then?'

'Yes,' replied Elizabeth. 'Although I might add that he is not the best school teacher in the country.'

Pat chuckled. 'That I can understand. He was, after all, one of the most respected members of the Special Forces community.' But then he adopted a more serious tone. 'They have not treated him well, but I guess that is politics.'

Paul leant forward from the back seat. 'Are you any closer to finding out who is behind all this?' Pat just shook his head in frustration.

'Whoever it is, they are very well connected, and have been extraordinarily careful. Every lead that we've had concerning the murder of your solicitor and his wife has come to nothing.' Pat glanced across to Elizabeth. 'You must realise that there is some risk in coming forward at this stage to protect your inheritance?'

She leant forward from the back seat. 'You mean from my father's enemies?'

'No, at least not that I am aware of.' Pat swung into a hotel car park. 'More from the criminal underworld that seem to be behind the events last year, and who are obviously still intent on getting their hands on the diamonds — and the mine itself. From what I understand it could be the last major diamond prospect yet to be exploited. Anyway, let's get you inside, and you can clean-up and grab a bite to eat. As soon as the Office of Lands and Resources, just along the road a little, is open, we'll walk down.'

The shower was heaven itself, and they both felt refreshed after a hearty breakfast in the hotel dining room. At 9 AM they gathered in the lobby. 'Time for Miss Elizabeth Dortmus to reappear,' commented Pat with a smile, and he led the way out the door to their first appointment.

Elizabeth found the traffic and noise of the city quite disorientating, after so many years in the bush. It occurred to her that this was also a part of Daniel's world that she had no appreciation for at all. Perhaps it was no wonder that their relationship was foundering before it had even really got started. She was still tossing the issues around in her head when Pat led her through two immense revolving doors, and showed her to the counter.

'Can I help you, Miss?' a young clerk on the other side of the counter asked, without as much as a glance in her direction.

'I hope so,' was all that came out, but the tones of her voice caught the young man's attention. 'I am here to confirm title to a parcel of land that my father left me in his will.'

'Do you have a certified copy of that will?' he asked.

Elizabeth looked inside her shoulder bag. 'I have the will itself.' She handed over the letter that Daniel had brought back from the coast.

The clerk's eyes went straight to the bottom of the page. 'This ... er ... letter is not witnessed.'

'That was not possible,' replied Elizabeth.

'Do you have any proof that this is authentic?' The clerk glanced at the clock on the wall. So close to his break. 'You must appreciate that we need more than just a letter to confirm titles of deceased estates.'

Elizabeth looked confused, and turned to the men waiting behind her.

'Would it be sufficient to have a solicitor's stamp on the document?' offered Pat.

The young man glanced at the clock again. 'I would still need confirmation of a number of matters, but that would certainly help. Meantime if I could have the details of the title, and proof of identity for Miss?'

'Dortmus. Elizabeth Mary Dortmus. Here is my birth certificate.' Elizabeth handed over the well-worn document.

The clerk took it and made a copy at the machine in the back office.' There you are, Miss Dortmus. I can research the other details while you are validating the letter. I presume you would like to have the prospecting rights transferred under your name as well?'

'Why ... er ... yes, thank you,' replied Elizabeth.

Paul told the clerk that they could be reached at the Plaza hotel, and they made room for the man waiting in the queue behind them.

They didn't notice the office manager in the back room, looking through the interior window while waiting for his call to go through.

After five rings, a female voice across town answered. 'Yes?'

The manager glanced at the three individuals leaving his branch. 'I need to get a message to Franz.'

'Who is speaking, please?' asked the voice.

'Mr Robertson, at the office.'

There was a brief delay, a click, and then a terse male voice. 'This had better be important.'

'Does the name Elizabeth Dortmus mean anything to you?'

'No,' came the impatient reply.

Mr Robertson continued. 'Apparently the daughter and sole heir of Pieter Dortmus?'

'So?'

'So, a woman claiming to be her was just in the office seeking to have title etc to her late father's lands transferred into her name.'

'Really.' The other man paused only briefly. 'Find out where she is staying.'

'But —?'

The line was already dead.

Paul, Pat and Elizabeth worked their way slowly back to the hotel through the early morning pedestrians. Once upstairs in their room, they worked through their options.

'I know a good solicitor, who should be able to help,' offered Pat. 'If you like, I will give him a call to see when he can see us.'

Elizabeth smiled. 'Thanks, Pat.'

Paul reached across the coffee table and took Elizabeth's hand. 'Not the best start, but I guess it was to be expected.' She just nodded, looking out the window. You could just make out Table Mountain between the tall grey buildings across the road.

Pat hung up the phone and turned towards them. 'The best that we can do is 9:45 AM tomorrow morning. Meantime I have a couple of calls to make, and I need to get back to the Police offices here, to see what progress they have made on the other investigation. You might as well do some sightseeing?'

'I agree,' replied Paul for them both. Elizabeth shrugged noncommittally, her thoughts miles away.

The rest of the day past in a blur. Paul managed to find a reasonably inexpensive half-day bus tour of the 'must-see' tourist highlights of Cape Town. Elizabeth had been reluctant to get back on a bus so soon after the marathon trip down, but allowed herself to be persuaded. In the end she actually quite enjoyed the day amongst a very cosmopolitan group of people from all around the world. *Maybe travel was the answer to her current personal difficulties,* she mused.

Later, after a quiet meal at a little Asian restaurant across the road, Elizabeth finally excused herself and went up to her room, to get an early night. The men sat over a beer, and continued to try and solve the riddles that confronted them.

Early the following morning Paul stepped out of the shower, refreshed after the first decent sleep in a week. He dressed, made a cup of tea for them both, and knocked quietly on Elizabeth's door. No reply. Unsure what to do next, he decided to give her another half an hour, and sat down to read the morning paper.

He had just about finished reading the front page news, when the phone went. 'Hello?'

'Paul?' came a voice that he thought he recognised.

'Yes. Who is this?'

'Paul it is Peter. Peter Hogan from Bloemfontein.'

'Hello Major Hogan.' Paul recalled the tall cavalry officer, longstanding friend of Daniel, who had been so instrumental in resolving the crisis in the Impala homelands of just over a year ago. 'It is good to hear your voice.'

'How is everything going?'

'Fine at this end, although it is slow going. Only to be expected, I guess.'

'Yes. How is Elizabeth?'

'Pretty good, considering. Although I have not seen her this morning.'

'Paul, I know this sounds strange, but would you mind waking her up. I need to talk with her urgently.'

'OK. Hold the line.' Paul went and knocked on Elizabeth's door. Again, there was not reply so he tried the door. It was locked. 'Elizabeth? Elizabeth? Are you awake?' Still no response.

A little concerned now, Paul thumped on the door. 'Elizabeth. Please open the door!' He went back to the phone.

Peter heard the noise, and then the sound of the handset being lifted off the table. 'What's going on, Paul?'

'I am not sure. I can't wake her. I need to get the hotel staff to let me into her room. Do you have a number that I can get back to you on?'

'I'm about to leave for work. I will call you back in an hour or so.'

'OK. Hear from you then.' Paul broke the connection and called the front desk. It seemed an age before there was a knock on the external door.

'What seems to be the problem, Sir?' asked the hotel manager.

'I cannot wake my friend in the other bedroom, and the door is locked.'

The man, now sharing Paul's concern, produced a master key and hurried across to the bedroom door. He soon had it open and stepped back to allow Paul to enter.

The room, and the adjoining bathroom were empty. The bed didn't look as if it had been slept in, and Elizabeth's bags and personnel items were gone. Paul was confused. Where had she gone and why?

'Can I be of any further assistance?' the manager asked. It now seemed to him as if he was in the middle of a lover's quarrel, and the young man before him had simply been stood up. Not that unusual in his establishment.

'Can you call the night staff, and see if they saw anyone leave last night.'

'What did the lady look like, Sir?'

'Young, attractive, with red hair,' Paul explained.

'Well Sir, I am sure that if anyone by that description left the hotel overnight, my staff will have noticed. Leave it with me.' He let himself out the door.

Very concerned, Paul picked up a sheet of paper off the coffee table and rang Pat.

'Inspector Petronas.'

'Pat, it is Paul, Elizabeth has gone! She was not in her room this morning, and it doesn't look as if she came back to the room last night.'

'I am on my way over. Don't go anywhere, and don't touch or move anything!'

Too late, Paul thought, through the mists of advancing misery. *Too late.*

CHAPTER 6

Daniel and Shadz watched as six men moved up the valley to the cabin. Through a set of binoculars, Daniel studied each individual: what he carried, how he moved, what sort of condition he was in after the march over the escarpment. The man leading them looked like any one of the many hunters who made a living guiding tourists across the vast African interior — quite likely hired just for the trip. He moved easily, placing his feet naturally and without apparent effort, on the uneven terrain.

But the rest of the party weren't in good shape, moving painfully under their packs. *Welcome to the bush*, thought Daniel. *Take out the hunter, and the others won't know which way to crawl.*

'They move like three-legged cattle,' observed Shadz at his side.

Daniel grunted. 'But they will run like wart hogs when the lion is on their scent.' The warrior at his side made a passable imitation of a lion's roar, and Marcus growled. Daniel gave him a pat, and continued. 'I think that we should take out their guide, as soon as possible. That way they will not have an opportunity to establish their base.' He led the way to another pre-prepared observation point, just up behind the cabin, and they were comfortably in place when the party arrived.

'Careless,' commented Shadz, as the men simply walked up to the door and went straight inside.

Daniel finished the old bush saying. 'Then scared, then dead.'

They watched as the group stripped off their loads and sorted themselves out a meal. From the body-language of the guide, he'd already had enough of their company. It was not long before he picked up his rifle, and moved off down the valley. 'So, the hunter becomes the hunted,' observed Daniel, as much to himself as to Shadz, and they moved off.

It did not take long for their quarry to drop one of the little antelopes that were plentiful in the valley, and he was bent double with his knife buried in the bowels of the kill, when he felt Shadz's spear rest against the small of his back. 'Don't move.'

Lester Rushton was old school. He prided himself on his bushcraft, kept himself in good condition, and would back himself against most of his competitors at any one of his many hunting skills, including a fist fight if it came to that. He raised his free hand from the carcass slowly in order to gain the necessary balance for the pivot that would knock the spear to one side, and put him in a position for a counterattack. But Tshakai had trained his men well, and Shadz was the best of them. With lightning speed, the spear flew around and the heavily weighted end cracked hunter Rushton just behind the temple. He dropped like a stone, and Daniel moved out of his hide.

'Well done,' said Daniel. 'You saw him move for the offence.'

Shadz smiled. 'I would have attempted the same.'

They dragged the hunter into the shade, relieving him of a pistol and a handy-looking knife, and tied his wrists to his ankles. Shadz finished cleaning the antelope while Daniel tended to the nasty bruise on the man's head. 'You are going to have a headache when you wake up, my friend.'

At that moment the other stirred, and immediately went to test the damage to his temple. 'What hit me?'

'The other business end of an Impala hunting spear. A very effective weapon,' replied Daniel.

'Apparently so.'

'You are?'

'Rushton. Lester Rushton, of *Upington Guiding*.'

'And you?'

'Daniel Rutter, lately of the South African Special Forces.'

The other man swore under his breath. 'And now?'

'Shall we say I am freelancing: taking care of the interests of my friends, on whose land you are currently trespassing.'

'I was not aware that there were any tribal lands on this side of the escarpment.'

'It is a long story, but we will have plenty of time to explain.' Daniel released his ankles and helped the man to his feet. He turned to the big dog at his side 'Marcus, watch,' and then looked at Lester. 'Attempt to escape, and the dog will kill you.'

'Just like that?'

Daniel nodded. 'Just like that.'

'Right. Where are you taking me?'

'Well, I have a problem,' replied Daniel. 'I could kill you now and leave you for the hyenas — or take a risk.'

'I like the risk bit,' Lester replied, rubbing his temple.

'Thought you would.' *This guy could grow on you*, thought Daniel. 'So, here are the rules. Make a sound, or attempt to attract attention, and I will break your neck. Run away, and Marcus will do it for me. Questions?'

'Will I get antelope for dinner?'

Daniel cut the rope that bound the hunter's wrists. 'If you get to dinner, you will.'

'That will do nicely. I was getting very tired of my clients, anyway.' Daniel just held a finger to his lips in the universal sign for quiet, and led the way back to the mine with Shadz acting as scout. They gave the cabin a wide berth, and arrived at the cave without incident.

'Very cosy,' said Lester, as he was ushered into the cave in the gathering dusk. The warriors that were not allocated to the early watch were gathered inside, tending a small hunting fire that was well hidden.

'Wait here,' said Daniel, and left to use the last of the daylight to check the initial defensive positions. Lester tried to open a conversation with the big warriors, to no avail. He might as well have been talking to the rock wall behind him, so set himself the task of building a mental image of the piles of stores that took up a fair proportion of the cave. Of course he had no idea what was down the narrow passage off to his left, which appeared to lead nowhere in particular.

Daniel came back into the cave. 'Comfy?'

'Yes, thank you. The bar service leaves a bit to be desired, but all-in-all it's very comfortable.' Lester grinned, his best, engaging, client-winning grin. 'Still antelope on the main course?'

'I believe it is the starter, entre, main, and desert. The market was closed today, so fruit and vegetables are in short supply.' Daniel moved across to where the meat was roasting, filling the cave with rich, gamey aromas.

'Remind me to ask for a refund.'

'Certainly.' Daniel cut them both a good sized portion of meat and took a seat. He tossed the man his knife to attend to the stringy bits.

The hunter caught the knife in an easy fluid motion, that did not go unnoticed. 'Thank you.'

'Just don't make me regret it.' The menace was unmistakable, and Lester decided not to push the point. At least not tonight.

After they were settled over a steaming cup of bush tea, Daniel decided it was time to even the odds a little further, by giving his guest a canned version of the story thus far. He just left out the fact that they were about five metres from a fabulously rich vein of diamond-bearing material. *No sense in testing the man too much.*

'So you are telling me that I have brought over a bunch of criminals, probably with international backing, certainly responsible for a number of murders.' Lester shrugged. 'So what is the big attraction?'

Daniel had anticipated the question. 'Diamonds. At the head of the canyon.'

Lester Rushton thought about that for a moment. 'That actually explains a few things.' He paused and then amplified his comment. 'They seemed happy to pay well over the odds, and were just a little too anxious to get here. I guess the other question is whether or not they ever intended to allow me to return?'

'On past performance: probably not.' Daniel allowed that to sink in.

'In the movies, it's about now that the hero changes sides.'

Daniel nodded. 'In the movies.'

Lester nodded quietly. 'OK. I guess I do have something to prove. Maybe tomorrow I can make myself useful.'

'We will see.' Daniel settled down against the stacked equipment, and was promptly asleep. The hunter realised that Marcus had not taken an eye off him since they began their trek up to the mine, and opted to get some rest himself.

The following morning was misty, and cold. After a hot porridge and honey, Daniel gathered his party for a brief. 'I will drop down the mountain with Marcus and Shadz, to see what is going on. The hunter will stay here, as our guest. If he does anything foolish, kill him. Oh — and try to avoid gunfire if you can.' Daniel looked around the assembled warriors, and then stopped at Lester. 'Questions?' There were none.

On the way down, Shadz voiced his concern. 'Big brother should have left the man at the bottom of the waterfall.'

'Perhaps. But then again, his divided loyalty might yet come in handy.' Daniel looked across at the big man. 'Remember that sometimes the best course is to confuse your enemy. The rest of the party will be wondering what happened to their guide. When they start going missing they will suspect him, as long as we can hide our presence.'

Shadz clapped his hands quietly.

The sun was well up when they slipped carefully into their hide, just above the cabin. There was no-one around, as far as they could tell. Then from further down the valley came a volley of three shots. 'Sounds like they are trying to find our friend,' observed Daniel. 'Let's give them something to run to.' He lifted his rifle, slipped off the safety, and fired off the same pattern. It was immediately answered.

The black man at his side shook his head. 'So much for the hunting today.'

Leading the way up through the scrub and dropping in behind a small spur, Daniel grinned. 'For now, we are the game!'

They outflanked their pursuers, and dropped in behind the last of the party struggling back up the valley. The hapless man had no idea what hit him. Shadz lifted him effortlessly over one shoulder and they melted into the bush. Now there were four — a useful morning's work.

Back at the cabin the situation was going downhill fast. Recruited in the cities far to the east, none of them had got any sleep while waiting for their guide to return. They were lost in the bush, and now Vizha was missing. Behind them the radio burst into life.

'What is going on Rex? Answer me man!'

A man with a huge scar on his face picked up the radio. 'We have problems, Baas. The bluedy guide has done a bunk, and now Vizha is missing.'

'Well pull yourself together and get down to the beach, so I can get some more men on shore. We have the boats in the water right now, and will check out the beach this afternoon.'

'Yes Baas.'

'And Rex, the weather forecast is not good. The skipper does not want to be caught in the bay when it arrives. I am relying on you to sort out your end.'

'Understood Baas.' The man called Rex took the radio with him outside and looked at the horizon. It was already dark with ominous-looking clouds as he turned to the remainder of the group. 'Right. We need to find a way down to the beach, so we can link up with the guys on the trawler. We will work our way down the edge of the canyon. Keep your eyes pealed.'

Daniel, Marcus, and Shadz watched them go. They had left their most recent captive bound and gagged in the same grove where Daniel and Marcus had fought to a standstill, over a year ago. If the hyenas found him it would not be pretty, but they had little option if they were going to stay in touch with what the rest of his party were up to.

'They are looking for something,' commented Shadz.

'The way down to the beach, which is blocked. Marcus managed to find away around the log-fall, but I would be surprised if this crowd get anywhere near it.'

From their vantage they also had a view out into the bay. The trawler was teasing her anchor as the wind began to pick up ahead of the squall line approaching from the South Atlantic. The breeze carried the sound of powerful outboard motors to them. *This will be interesting*, thought Daniel. They watched the two boats appear from the other side of the trawler and accelerate across the bay, chasing each other in a game of water-borne cat and mouse.

'About now,' Daniel remarked. Right on cue there was a loud bang and the lead boat stopped dead in the water, only to be swamped by the stern wave. The driver of the second boat did very well to avoid a collision, and was turning hard when the gearbox on his motor seized. Without the thrust and torque, the following wave picked up the stern quarter of the boat, and drove the bow under the rising chop. The boat went straight down.

The rapidly rising pressure crushed the inbuilt buoyancy of the alloy hulls, and the boat settled onto the sandy bottom a couple of fathoms down. Daniel allowed himself a moment of celebration, and flashed Shadz a winner's smile.

Shadz nodded, impressed. 'That will give them something to think about.'

The two men on the first boat had recovered sufficiently to begin desperately bailing, and managed by a hair's breath to avoid it sinking. Those on board the trawler could only watch helplessly.

'Come on. Let's see how our friends are getting on.' Daniel led them carefully down the valley. They picked up the balance of the ground party grouped around one of their number who was busy on the radio.

'What do you want us to do now, Baas?'

'Find that way down to the beach. I will swim ashore if I have to, to get off this bluedy boat!'

'Yes Baas.' They moved off along the edge of the canyon, still looking for clues as to the way down into the river they could just make out through the treetops below them.

But they were making slow work of it. With the advantage of knowing the exact location of the top of the narrow defile leading down the precipice, Daniel decided they had plenty of time to circle ahead of them, and arrange a surprise. When he got there, he dropped straight down until he came to the log fall. Salvaging a piece of rope from the edge of the chaos, he looped it around the loose log that had given him the fright the night before, then ran it back up the cliff and into some dense scrub. They then cleared some of the regrowth at the top of the track to make it more obvious, and retreated into the scrub to wait. It took about another thirty minutes before the men appeared and immediately started down the track, bunching protectively. *Some people never learn*, thought Daniel, waiting. He knew that there was a chance that at least one of them would notice the rope when it pulled taut. A necessary risk.

When they got to the pile of logs, the last man held back a just little, perhaps a little more sensitive to his environment than his fellows. The other three scrambled around the back of the chaos, just as Daniel had done. He waited until he judged that they were totally reliant on the loose log for support and gave Shadz the word. They pulled as hard as they could.

The rope was well positioned, and, right on cue, the log broke free. Two of the men went straight over the edge, screaming. The third just managed to grab a protruding branch, but the log proved to be a pivot for the whole structure. With a huge roar it fell out from underneath him, and he followed the others down.

The sole remaining member of the ground party missed the only cue that mattered — the trigger rope. It had all happened too fast, and, as luck would have it, he was facing the wrong way. Dumbfounded, he just stood, and looked down at the barely visible pandemonium below him, as a huge column of dust was lifted by the developing breeze and blown back up the cliff into his face. Coming to his senses, he turned to make his way to the relative safety of the top of the cliff, only to find himself staring into the barrel of Daniel's rifle.

'It appears that you have been left alone,' announced Daniel, without a hint of a smile.

'But at least you are alive,' said Shadz, stepping into view from behind a tree to one side of the top of the track.

The barrel of the rifle motioned him up, and he complied, still dazed. The wind picked up another miniature dust storm around his boots as he struggled to the top on all fours.

'Put your rifle down, and then walk slowly toward me,' instructed Daniel, and the man obliged, carefully. 'Search him Shadz.' The big man moved forward and frisked him expertly.

'Nothing. Not even a knife,' Shadz reported.

'So ill prepared,' agreed Daniel.

The man finally found his voice. 'Who are you?'

'Who are we Shadz?' Daniel smiled, enjoying the moment. 'Well, we just happen to represent the legal owners of this little piece of paradise.'

The man shook his head in disbelief. 'That is impossible. We were told that there was no way that you could get here ahead of us.'

'You are very poorly advised,' noted Daniel. 'We were here a full thirty-six hours ahead of you, in force. I just hope that you can keep up on the way home.' Their captive just looked at his boots, resigned to whatever fate was coming his way.

'Look after him Shadz. I just need to check whether it is possible to get down to the river — or up for that matter.'

Five minutes later he was back, shaking his head. 'It will take a team of engineers a week to reconstruct that. The logs have scraped the face of the cliff clean as a whistle.'

'The others?' the man asked.

Daniel grimaced. 'They wouldn't have stood a chance. The first two to go down will be buried under tons of debris. The last will simply be part of the pile of vegetation that was dragged down on top. Best we go and see how your friend back up the valley is getting on. In retrospect, he is lucky he was enjoying our hospitality rather than being with the others at the bottom of the cliff.'

'Looks like we might have some more company,' Shadz observed, pointing to the side of the trawler where a makeshift platform was being loaded.

'Very determined, aren't they,' agreed Daniel. They watched as it slowly made its way to the shore and was pulled up on the beach. 'Not that it is going to do them any good.' Thinking them distracted, their prisoner made a couple of paces towards the nearest set of trees before he was confronted by the biggest, and angriest, dog that he had ever seen.

Daniel told Marcus to stay. 'Sorry about that. I should have mentioned that the really dangerous one of us has four legs. Come on then.' He led the way up the valley.

They found their first victim where they had left him, well attended by a host of little stinging ants intent on creating their own particular form of misery, but otherwise unharmed. Shadz untied his ankles, and removed the gag, after a nod from Daniel. The two men did not seem particularly glad to see each other, but Daniel put it down to a sort of misplaced macho embarrassment at being reduced to their present state.

'Where are the others?' the first asked.

'Dead at the bottom of the cliff,' the second replied. 'They were in too much of a hurry to get down to the beach and triggered a landslide.'

Daniel shared a secret glance with Shadz. 'Lucky for you we detained you before you could join them.' But the man did not seem at all grateful.

Moving back up the valley to the empty cabin, Daniel retrieved a radio and spare batteries from the table, secured the balance of the packs and equipment inside, and shut the door securely. There was one other thing that caught his eye. Leaning in the corner of the porch was a .308 calibre semi-automatic rifle with a telescopic sight. It was a beautiful weapon, and Daniel could not resist slipping it over his shoulder. *You never know,* he thought.

Shadz called out from the far side of the front porch. 'The trawler is leaving.'

'They were worried about the weather,' obliged the second man they had detained. 'Something about a lee shore.'

'And well they might be worried,' said Daniel, looking out to sea. 'We had better get up to the cave before the storm breaks.'

He led the way, monitoring the radio, but apparently there was no reason for any further traffic. Perhaps the group from the trawler, now frantically seeking shelter off the beach, had assumed that the shore party were all at the bottom of the cliff. Daniel decided there was no reason to dispel that assumption, for now.

It was a long and frustrating climb, their prisoners still suffering from the trip over the escarpment. The rain was coming down hard by the time they scrambled over the lip of the platform, and they were all soaked to the skin and growing chilled.

'Inside, everyone,' Daniel called out to the reception committee. 'No-one is crazy enough to be out in this weather.'

Once inside he quickly organised fresh clothes, and in no time they were gathered in two groups — the two prisoners, looking very sorry for themselves; and Daniel's party, listening attentively to Shadz's account of the days hunting, only slightly embellished. Lester Rushton was careful to include himself in the latter. He eventually moved to where Daniel was cleaning his new weapon.

'You will find that she shoots slightly to the left at three hundred yards.'

Daniel raised an eyebrow. 'Yours?'

Lester nodded. 'My father's, actually. He gave it to me just prior to his death.'

'That explains the initials: *R.R.R.*'

'Rory. Rory Reginald Rushton, originally of Sussex, and then Rhodesia, and finally Upington on the High Veldt.'

Daniel shook his head, in mock sadness. 'Careless of you to leave it lying around?'

'In hindsight, yes. But then I was not to know that you and your 'impi' were going to waylay me.'

'But then the company that you were keeping was not exactly trustworthy!'

'True enough,' Lester agreed.

'Well, I guess that you will have to trust me to look after her until I can trust you.'

The hunter grinned. 'You look like a trustworthy type.'

'Maybe. Just maybe,' came the enigmatic reply, and Daniel went to check on the weather. It was pitch dark.

'So what now?' Lester asked when he returned.

'Their move. I am reluctant to leave here with the party on the beach.' Daniel resumed his seat. 'Given enough time they will find a way up to the valley. Ideally what I need to be able to do is simply persuade them to get on that boat, and go back from where they came from.'

'I might be able to help there.'

'How?'

'Well. I could stage a miraculous reappearance and state the obvious — there is no way up, so the only way back for them is by sea.'

Daniel considered that for a moment. 'Has some merit, but might need a little refinement. I will think about it.'

CHAPTER 7

Back in Cape Town, it took Pat just ten minutes to get across to the hotel. Paul was waiting for him in the lobby, talking with the night manager who was just about to go off duty.

'So you saw no-one fitting that description leave?' asked Paul.

'No. I am sure of it,' responded the night manager.

Pat picked up the questions, flashing his Police ID. 'Inspector Petronas. What time did you come on duty?'

'10 PM, inspector.'

'And you were at the front desk the whole night?'

The off-duty manager shrugged. 'Some of the quieter hours I was in my office over there. It has a good view of the reception area and, lifts and stairs.'

'Did anyone come to the front desk and ask for Miss Dortmus.'

'No. It was a very slow night.'

'Thank you. That will be all for now.' Pat turned to the hotel manager. 'I will need to talk to the staff that were on duty earlier in the evening — from about eight when Miss Dortmus left the dinning room.'

'Of course,' replied the manager, and went into his office.

Pat turned to the uniformed constable behind him. 'Get up to the room and secure it. The forensic team will be here any minute.' The young woman nodded and headed for the stairs.

'Anything else that you can recall, Paul?'

'I went straight to bed after you left.' Paul stepped through the events of the previous evening. 'Elizabeth's door was shut so I assumed she was asleep. It was not until Peter rang this morning that I became concerned.'

Pat nodded, only half listening, as he scanned the lobby for anything, or anyone unusual. If he had stepped outside, he just might have picked up the man standing in a shop door across the road.

'Peter sounded very concerned, almost as if he knew that something was wrong, before I tried to wake Elizabeth.'

'I am not sure,' replied Pat. 'He asked me to get to a secure phone, and the closest one is back at Central. That will be my next stop.'

Paul shrugged to indicate that he did not understand. 'A secure phone?'

Pat placed a hand on Paul's shoulder. 'Sorry, I can't tell you anything more.'

At that point the forensic team arrived and they all went upstairs. Pat led the way into the hotel room, and got Paul seated at the small table in the middle of the lounge. 'Stay there while the team has a look around. We will need to take your fingerprints, just so that we can eliminate yours from all the others that will be scattered around the inside of a hotel room,' Pat said grimly. He was interrupted by a call from one of the specialists on the patio outside the external door.

'Inspector, I think I may have found something.'

Pat moved across the room. 'What is it?'

'Here, around the lock.' The man pointed to direct his attention. 'The door hasn't been forced, but there are some fresh scratches around the lock mechanism. I think this lock has been picked.'

'Fingers,' Pat called out. 'Get over here and see if there are any prints.'

The fingerprint man dusted the area around the lock carefully. 'Nothing useful. Actually looks as if the area has been wiped.'

The forensics man turned to Pat. 'This is beginning to look like a professional job — made to appear as if the victim was never here. No signs of a disturbance. No signs of a struggle.'

'And no body,' added Fingers.

'We are not at that stage yet, I can assure you,' snapped Pat. 'Go over this room inch by inch. There must be something.' He went back inside to where Paul was waiting. 'Let's go and see if the manager has managed to dig up any of the other staff.'

Downstairs, the manager had the evening porter on the phone, and Pat took the handset. 'Inspector Petronas here. With whom am I speaking?'

'Andre. Andre Short.'

'You were on duty last evening'

'I was, Sir. Through until just after ten.'

'Good. Did you notice a red-haired, attractive woman go in or out of the hotel?'

'Miss Dortmus went straight up to her room after dinner. She did not come down again,' came the reply.

'You are sure.'

'Quite sure. I was in the lobby the entire evening.'

'And you are sure that it was her?'

'Absolutely. She is quite an attractive woman, and said goodnight to me as she passed my station.'

Pat mentally ran through the standard list of questions, but found nothing of relevance at that stage. 'Thank you, Mr Short. You have been most helpful. I assume that you will be on duty tonight, just in case we have any further questions?'

'That is correct, sir.'

Pat handed the phone back to the hotel manager. 'Well, that confirms that Elizabeth did go up to her room, and that she did not leave by the front door.' He looked at the lifts, and then to the stairs. 'Do you have a service entrance?'

'Yes, of course. There is a lift on the rear of the hotel, and a door that goes out the back onto the side road.'

'It is secured at night?'

'Of course.'

'Best we have a look at it,' instructed Pat, and they followed the manager to the rear of the hotel.

The door was closed, as advertised, and Pat couldn't see any obvious damage to the lock. *Maybe they just did a better job of this one*, he mused. He glanced up into the lens of a closed-circuit TV camera. 'Security?'

'Yes. There will be 24 hours of tape in the hotel security office.'

'Where else is covered?'

'Just the lobby.'

The inspector grunted. 'I will require the tapes for a forensic review.' He forestalled the obligatory protest. 'I could go to all the trouble of getting a search warrant. But that would require a number of big-footed policemen to execute it.'

'Of course,' the man relented. 'I will get onto it right away.' He hurried away. *Better call the owner,* he thought.

Pat and Paul stood and looked at each other. 'We will find her, Paul. I will turn this town upside down if necessary.'

'This could be the same people that murdered the solicitor and his wife,' worried Paul.

'I am not so sure.' Pat pointed above them. 'It is a very clean job upstairs, whereas the criminals that abducted those two left a trail of destruction behind them.'

'Is that good, or bad?'

'Something else I don't know, at this stage. Come on, I could do with a coffee.' Pat led the way back to the front of the hotel. As they stepped into the lobby, his mobile phone rang.

'Yes?'

'Hello Peter.'

'Nothing as yet, I am afraid.'

'I will head over there now. Give me thirty minutes.' Pat turned to Paul. 'Peter is pretty keen to get me on the end of that phone, so I had better get across town. Best if you stick with me, for now.' Taking their coffees they went outside to the unmarked car waiting for them on the street.

As he walked around the back of the vehicle, Pat noticed a man standing in the doorway of a shop across the road. Trusting his instincts, he turned and walked boldly across the road.

The man slipped inside the shop. Pat swore, dropped his coffee, and charged across the pavement. Struggling through the revolving door, he looked around the piles of multi-coloured cloths. The man was nowhere to be seen.

Pat arrived back at the car five minutes later, in an even darker mood.

'What was that about?' asked Paul.

'We were being watched, but I was not quick enough. Waste of a good cup of coffee.' He straightened his jacket. 'I have a feeling that today is going to get quite interesting.' They joined the heavy morning traffic.

Finally reaching the downtown Police Headquarters building, Pat parked in the secure underground carpark, and led the way to the lift. 'Paul, I regret that you will have to wait in reception while I make the call. I won't be long.'

'That's fine. I am as keen as you are to see what it is that has Peter so concerned.'

Pat nodded. 'And what it is that requires a secure phone to talk about. That is assuming, of course, that I'm able to talk my way into the Intelligence Section.' They stepped out of the lift at reception, and Pat went through the security barriers and up the stairs. Paul found himself a seat, and a magazine, in an attempt to take his mind off Elizabeth's mysterious disappearance.

Upstairs, Pat was already frustrated with the process of getting himself through the inner security barrier. A young uniformed officer was sticking to his guns. 'I am sorry, Inspector, but only accredited personnel are allowed beyond this point.'

Pat tried to think laterally. 'Is there another secure phone in the building?'

'Not that I am aware of, sir.'

'Then this is what you are going to do, Constable. You are going to ring the section head and tell him that I am out here, before I climb over this counter, and let myself in. Is that clear?'

'Perfectly, Sir.' Still the young man hesitated.

'Then pick up the phone and call him. Now!' roared Pat.

The constable went one better, and pushed the security alert. Suddenly Pat was joined by two very earnest-looking chaps. 'Is there a problem?' the bigger of the two asked.

'Inspector Petronas is insisting on coming through into the secure area. He needs—'

'Inspector Petronas needs to use a secure phone. Very urgently,' interrupted Pat.

'Then the Inspector should stop being a nuisance, and come in,' came an authoritative voice through the open door and the deputy section head poked a balding head around the door frame. 'Let him in.'

'But Sir,' challenged the Constable, still intent on his duty.

'Constable Peterson. Your diligence is admirable, but your situational awareness needs a lot of work, if you get my drift.'

'Right Sir.' The door swung out of the way and Pat was ushered through.

The Deputy put out a hand. 'How are you Pat. Good to see you, although I suspect that you are not causing my constable grief on a social call.'

'True enough, Ken. I would be happy to bring you up to play when I have made a call to Bloemfontein.'

'By all means. This way.'

Alone in the communications office, Pat dialled the number. It was answered by a clerk at the other end, who immediately went to find Major Hogan.

Peter came on the line. 'Hello, Pat?'

'Yes Peter.'

'How are things at your end?'

'No leads, I am afraid. Looks like a professional job, and I just missed picking up their surveillance on the way out of the hotel.'

'Interesting. Best we go secure,' Both men turned keys and pushed buttons on their panels, and then listened to the computers underneath the counter exchanging information. It was not exactly state-of-the-art, but it was effective. As far as they were aware, neither the Americans, nor the Russians, had been able to break the encryption code.

'Are you there?'

'Yes Peter. And I have a green light at my end.'

'Me to.'

'So what is up?'

'Earlier today a very good friend gave me a call and I took a little drive in my car. He works in one of those organisations that no-one talks about.'

'OK.'

'It appears that a phone call was made last night between two parties that the intelligence agencies have been watching for some time.'

'Go on.'

'Nothing specific, but the analysts have been constructing a pretty detailed picture of their relationship over the last eighteen months. Very sensitive, and I suspect that there is a lot that he was not able to tell me, but it does provide a link between the events of last year, the recent murders, and Elizabeth's disappearance.'

'More and more interesting.'

'Correct. Now the real reason that I was tapped on the shoulder is to warn you, and steer us clear of a very sensitive, I repeat, very sensitive operation.'

'So what are we supposed to do?'

'Continue with your scene investigation and initial enquiries, but keep Ken informed. Apparently he is in the loop. We agreed that it would appear suspicious if you just dropped things where they stand, but we will not be allowed to compromise a much larger operation, if you get my drift.'

'I understand, Peter. What am I allowed to tell Paul?'

'Nothing. Absolutely nothing. I know that will be hard, but it is for the best.'

'Roger that.'

'That is all I have for now. Stay close to Ken, and you may find out a little more.'

'I agree.' The line went dead, and Pat noticed that Ken had come in and shut the door behind him.

'How much more can you tell me, Ken?'

'Not much. We are all out on a limb with this one. But I will stress that we are drawing to the culmination of one of the most important international investigations in recent years.'

Pat voiced his concern, and frustration. 'That doesn't tell me anything, Ken. Somewhere out there is a terrified woman in the hands of God only knows. Don't forget that for a minute.'

'I won't, Pat. I won't. I can tell you that we have information that suggests she is still alive, and should remain so.'

'Little comfort.' Pat suddenly twigged. 'You know where she is don't you?'

'We know that she has not been taken out of Cape Town. That is all.'

'Bluedy hell. That is not much use.' Pat looked at his watch. 'Her friend is waiting downstairs. I will take him back to the hotel and get him checked into a new room. You have my mobile number?'

Ken smiled. 'We have everyone's mobile number.'

CHAPTER 8

The trawler slipped quietly back into the picturesque bay, having weathered the storm safely out to sea. From the vantage of the mine, Daniel and Shadz watched it slip gently closer to the beach, and then drop anchor. Marcus enjoyed the sun at their side, sound asleep.

The radio at Daniel's side burst into life. 'Welcome back Hans. Good of you to come back for us.'

'Good morning Baas. What are your intentions?'

'We will spend the day trying to find an alternate route up onto the escarpment behind us. It appears that the ground party are all dead, killed in the log fall that has also blocked what we assume was the normal route up from the river.'

'And if that does not work out?'

'I am not about to go back empty-handed. How long until you need to head back for fuel?'

'About a week, assuming that the weather doesn't pull anything nasty again.'

'OK. We will either be rich, or rotten, by then. Next sched at six tonight.' The reply was simply two clicks from the handset.

Daniel turned to Shadz. 'We may need a contingency plan.'

The big warrior nodded. 'Just eight of them?'

'I think I counted nine,' replied Daniel. 'It sounds like one of the shore party is the leader.'

'Can we get down into the valley below us?'

'With our ropes, from the top down it is not a problem. Much more difficult from the bottom, trust me.' Daniel thought back to his earlier experience on the waterfall, when a flash flood came very close to being the death of Sergeant Daniel Rutter.

As he was sorting out the gear in the back of the cavern, it occurred to him that there might be an easier route down into the valley — the sink hole that had formed the secret grotto on the edge of the canyon. It was certainly worth a look.

Daniel led an augmented party down the valley, stopping where he judged the top of the sink hole should be. After thirty minutes of careful probing on the edge of the canyon, he abseiled over the edge on a rope, and was soon standing on the sandy beach that had played host to Marcus, and himself, many months before. Releasing the rope, he gave it two firm tugs, and it obediently snaked its way back up the sheer wall, while he did a quiet recce around the side of the pool. Moments later, Shadz joined him. 'Is there an easier way back up?' smiled the big man. Daniel just shook his head, listening. He thought he heard a voice. This would not be a good time for the party off the trawler to discover the secret water supply. They would be caught like rats in a trap.

There. Closer this time. Daniel motioned Shadz back into the pool behind them, and led the way under a ledge. Almost totally submerged, and in deep shadow, they were effectively invisible.

One of the shore party off the trawler dropped through the opening and waded across the shallows to the beach. It was only a matter of time until he noticed the boot marks in the sand at his feet.

'Baas,' he called out. 'I think you should have a look at this.'

A huge man with a heavy beard slipped easily through the opening. Daniel noted the way he moved — with the grace and power of a prize-fighter. *Mark that man*, Daniel thought.

'Two of them, I think,' remarked the Baas. 'Look over here — they dropped down on a rope, so there will be more at the top.'

'Our guys?'

'I don't think so.' The Baas looked around the interior of the grotto, eyes probing the shadows. 'This explains a few things, Jack — the guide going AWOL, the log fall, even the mishap with the boats. Both boats!'

'But how?'

'One man, Jack.' Baas spat at his feet. 'One very dangerous man.'

'You know this man?'

'I know of him. Apparently he was responsible for the failure of the first expedition to secure title to this valley, and find the mine. I thought that he was rotting away in some dark place. We need to get back to the beach and warn the others, and break out every weapon you can lay your hands on. From now on we stay in two groups. Shoot at anything that moves.'

Daniel gave them a good five minutes and then slipped out of the water. Shadz was shaking uncontrollably. 'Cold, eh?'

'Yep.'

'Let's get back up that cliff. That will warm you up.' Daniel gave a couple of quiet whistles and the rope came snaking back down.

'You are not going to follow them?'

'I know everything that I need to know. Time for plan B.'

'You have a plan B?'

'I always have a plan B, Shadz. Now, up you go.' With remarkable agility for such a powerful man, Shadz climbed the rope and disappeared out of sight. The rope jumped in his hands twice and Daniel started his climb. He was almost over the edge when a shot rang out from below. The bullet ricocheted of the rock just in front of his hands, and he froze.

'Up and you die. Down and we will see. What is it to be, Sergeant Rutter?' The big man chuckled at the rhyme, but it was lost on Daniel.

He started back down.

'You will stop there please and drop your weapon.'

Daniel did as he was told.

'Good. I can see that we are going to get on just fine.' He motioned Daniel to one side with the barrel of his rifle, and turned to the man standing next to him. 'Jack, grab the rope before they pull it up.'

'I wouldn't do that if I were you,' warned Daniel.

Jack paused at the bottom of the rope. 'Why not?'

Daniel smiled, and leant toward the man. 'It is not a good rope.'

'Grab the freeken rope, Jack!' commanded his boss. Jack did as he was told.

Daniel just shrugged and moved out of the way as a heavy log crashed down from above, tied to the other end of the rope. Jack had a choice — jump left or right. He favoured the right and was wrong, although at least he knew what hit him.

Daniel moved to use the chaos to his advantage, but his opponent was one step ahead of him and remained back out of reach, using the advantage of his rifle to full effect.

'Stay where you are, Rutter.' The menace was clear.

You know your business, whoever you are, thought Daniel.

'Move over there and lay down. You know how.'

Only when Daniel was prone did the man move forward. 'You will place you hands behind your back, please.' Daniel complied, and the man moved over and applied the full weight of his knee on Daniels' neck while he tied his hands tight enough to cut off the circulation.

'Much better.' He stood up. 'I am Anders. As you know, my men have taken to calling me Baas. What you will have already observed, is that I know what I am doing, right?'

Daniel nodded.

'Right. Now we will go down to the beach, where I will introduce you to the others.'

'I am sure that they are dying to meet me,' interjected Daniel, looking at the dead man at his side as he got to his feet.

The man on the end of the rifle scowled. 'We will see how long your sense of humour holds out.' He paused, and then drove home his advantage. 'You know, of course, that we have your Miss Dortmus?'

Daniel spun around, but for a moment could not frame the question. 'Where?'

'Maybe later, but don't worry. She is safe enough, for now. But that will depend on how both of you behave.' Daniel simply nodded, his mind racing.

That changes the rules, he knew.

Daniel was given no chance to escape on the way down to the beach. He was pointed in the direction of the make-shift camp, just inside the first line of bush, and immediately tied to a tree. 'I know that you like my company, but can't have you creating your normal mayhem,' said Anders.

Daniel decided to play ball for now, given the potential risk to Elizabeth. 'You have her, you have me.'

'Exactly. Make yourself at home.' Anders went across to a pile of equipment, and picked up a satellite phone. He punched in a long sequence of numbers, and waited for the line to connect.

Dispensing with any formalities, he made his report. 'We have Rutter. I now expect to get up to the mine in the next day or so.'

'Right Sir, I understand.' He broke the connection and turned to Daniel. 'Good. Things are proceeding according to plan. With you and the woman we hold all the cards.'

'A temporary state of affairs, I can assure you.'

'We have certain, shall we say, insurances in place. Every night I check in, and so Elizabeth stays alive. If I fail to make the call, plan B is put into effect.'

Daniel tested his bonds. 'And what might that be?'

'Your woman is forced, uncomfortably I expect, to sign over her inheritance. After that — well I could speculate, but that would be crass, wouldn't it.' Anders looked at his watch and moved to the radio. 'Come in.'

The speaker came to life. 'Nothing to report.'

'Roger.' The speaker clicked twice and was silent.

Anders called the men together and allocated watches through the night. 'Two on watch at any time, positive handovers, and keep your eyes peeled. And if you have to go for a leak make sure the

pickets know you are going. We don't want any stupid accidents.'
There were nods around the group.

Daniel looked at the seven tired men, more used to the smoke-filled bars of the cities. Nine hours to dawn was going to make it a long night. Adjusting his seat to relieve the inevitable pressure-points, he decided to get some rest.

There was just the first hint of the moon on top of the escarpment behind the beach, and the night breeze was rustling the tree tops, keeping the pickets jumpy. Back in the deep blackness of the bush an owl hooted, and Daniel began to work his muscles to get the blood flowing again. Moments later he felt the pressure on his wrists relax as the bonds were cut in one smooth motion. A knife was placed in his left hand.

He waited, knowing that Shadz and his men would have worked this out to the millimetre. The last thing they needed was him stumbling around, alerting his captors. He thought he felt a brief hot breath on his cheek.

Abruptly there was a yell from one of the pickets that turned into a terrible gurgling. At almost the same time there was a long burst of automatic fire from the other corner as the guard panicked, firing blind into the shadows. When his magazine ran out, there was a thud, and then quiet. Daniel felt Marcus at his side. 'Hello boy. Good to see you.' He gave his ears a rub. The silence was deafening.

Off to one side a hyena barked, and Daniel answered. He went across to where he knew there was a torch. Hooding it carefully so as not to affect his night-vision he went around the camp and counted the bodies. Five men that never woke up. Including the two pickets that made seven. Where was Anders?

Shadz came to his side, carefully. 'Not as quiet as I would have liked. The trawler will know all about it.'

Daniel nodded. 'Send a couple of men to the tree line to watch how they respond. Any casualties?'

'One. Got in the way of a random bullet. Just a flesh wound.'

'Good.' Suddenly there was a shout from sharp eyes closer to the beach. They both hurried out onto the beach just in time to see a figure plunge into the phosphorescence of the surf.

Already barefoot, Daniel raced down the beach and dived in after the retreating figure, knife between his teeth. Ahead of him powerful searchlights from the trawler were already sweeping the bay, but there was still a good swell rolling into the anchorage so it was proving difficult to hold the powerful beams steady in one place.

Anders had a twenty metre lead and the trawler was about two hundred metres off shore, but Daniel knew he had to get to him before they came within effective range of the weapons already barking in his general direction. Then again, they would have to stop shooting for fear of hitting one of their own.

Quickly catching his man, Daniel simply swam over the top of him, seizing him in a choke hold that kept the other man's hands where they could not get to a knife. It was a very uneven fight, and soon they were back on the beach.

Daniel was careful to keep his captive between him and the sporadic rifle fire from the trawler, as he dragged him up the beach. Shadz raced down the beach to help. When they got back to the camp site, Daniel tied his prisoner to the same tree that he had spent the last night getting acquainted with, and stripped him unceremoniously to his underwear. He then went and picked up the radio.

'This is Rutter. Are you receiving?'

'What is going on? Who are you?' a voice replied.

'That does not matter, but I am going to take care of your Baas from here. At first light I will send the survivors from the overland party down to the beach for you to pick up. You can then return to port.'

'What about Anders?'

'He will remain here with us. We have a little negotiating to do.'

'And the rest of his group?'

'Bring some shovels to bury what the hyenas don't dispose of.' Daniel turned the radio off.

They searched the crates of equipment, and took anything that might be of use, including the satellite phone. They then used the moonlight to good advantage, returning to the mine via the rope ladder that Shadz and his men had fashioned to get down from the valley above.

CHAPTER 9

The Major General responsible for South African Defence joint operations hollered through the half-open command centre door to the watch commander. 'Get me Major Peter Hogan! Right now.' His ears were still burning from the angry phone call he had just concluded.

'Yes, Sir.'

'Send a car and an escort to get him in, if that would get him here faster.'

'Right Sir.' The duty officer looked across to the watch desk staff. *Bluedy hell. What has stirred up the old man?*

Major Peter Hogan was sound asleep when the phone rang, but beat his wife to the handset.

'Hogans.'

'OK.' He rolled out of bed and slipped into the bathroom.

When he came out his wife was sitting up with the bedside lamp on. 'What is going on, Pete?'

'Some flap with the Impala. Daniel is in strife again, it appears.'

She glanced at the bedside clock. 'So why do they need to wake us up at this ungodly hour?'

Peter picked up the grab bag from the closet. 'It seems they need me to get out there and sort things out. I might be away for a few weeks.'

'But it is Andre's birthday, tomorrow,' she reminded him gently.

'I know, honey. But there is nothing I can do.' He came round to her side of the bed, kissed her, and was gone into the night. Again.

Just under forty minutes later he slipped through the multiple layers of security at the base, eventually arriving at the outer door of the command centre. He was met by one of the staff and taken straight upstairs. They ran into the General at the coffee machine just outside the inner sanctum. 'Major Hogan.'

'Good morning Sir.'

'No, it is not, unfortunately. Come into my office.' He led the way. 'Shut the door behind you.' The tired officer pointed to a seat. 'What I am going to tell you now does not go outside this room. Do you understand me?'

'Absolutely, Sir,' acknowledged Peter.

'Right.' The General perched on the front of his desk. 'We, along with a number of other intelligence and security agencies, both here and overseas, have been working to uncover, and then counter, a major international arms smuggling ring for nearly two years.'

'I see,' commented Peter, not at all sure where this was going.

'The, er, trouble that you became involved in earlier last year is linked to this group.'

'Sir?'

'We now believe that the underlying reason for the attempt to gain access to this supposed diamond mine, is cash. Cash to fund a major arms deal.' The General walked around behind his desk and looked at the map pinned on the wall. 'The weapons are bound for rebel forces operating out of Southern Namibia.'

'Russian, then.'

'You are well informed, Major.'

'Perhaps, Sir.'

'Anyway, we have been holding back from any direct action while internal security tries to uncover who is sponsoring this. We do know there are very powerful political forces involved, but so far they have been extraordinarily careful, or lucky, or both. Each time there is a lead, it comes to nothing.'

Peter leant forward in the seat. 'Why would anyone here be supporting arms trafficking to the rebels?'

The General turned away from the map, hands clasped behind his back. 'That's what galls me. Potentially, just to promote instability and keep the emergency provisions in force.'

Peter shook his head. 'Sure, I had heard about it, but thought it was just cynical speculation.' He paused. 'But where do I come in?'

'We have received more information — highly sensitive.' The General looked at some papers on his desk in a brightly coloured folder. 'From what we can piece together, after they murdered the Impalas' solicitor and his wife in Cape Town, these people put together an expedition to get across to the coast and plunder the mine — using the information obtained from the bank vault.'

It all fell into place. 'That information must have been quite specific.'

'Agreed. But they ran into trouble: Rutter's particular brand of trouble. Now they may be forced to abandon the mission. It seems, without the diamonds, their backers will not deliver the shipment.'

Peter nodded. 'The whole thing would fall apart.'

'Along with the best part of two years of surveillance and planning, with international involvement from the CIA, and sister agencies. We have units in the field right now, enroute to what we believe to be the delivery point.' The General turned again to the map on his wall. 'But we are going to look like amateurs if it falls apart under our noses.'

Peter knew the conversation was getting close to the punch line. 'So what do you need me to do, Sir?'

'Get yourself out to the Impala, further if necessary, and get Rutter out of it. Any way you can, before I divert some very mobile resources to dump on him from a great height.' The General came around the table to stress his point. 'And Peter, that is not out of the question. We must stop these weapons getting to the rebel forces, and we must uncover who is behind it in the Government.'

That revelation got Peter's attention. 'Government level?'

The General nodded. 'The highest.'

'Sheez,' exclaimed Peter; then suddenly a list of hitherto unanswered questions had an answer. 'Sir, with respect, you knew all along. It was you who ultimately prevented Daniel Rutter spending the rest of his life rotting in prison?'

'Partly,' came the careful reply. 'Rutter's little crusade last year actually provided a couple of important clues. I could not just stand by and allow him to bear the brunt of political reaction to a little war that he walked in to the middle of. It was bad enough to see him treated like he was.'

'I will see to it that Daniel appreciates your intervention.' Peter stood up. 'Any chance of a lift out there? It is a minimum of four days to the Impala from the nearest airfield.'

'I can get you to Springbok by tonight. I will have vehicles waiting there. You have until 1000 hours to pick your team and get to the airport.'

'How many pax?'

'Eight. Three SUV's.'

'Understood, Sir. If you will excuse me.' Peter stopped at the door. 'Have we an update on Miss Dortmus — the woman who was kidnapped a few days ago?'

'We believe that she is still alive, but her usefulness to these people finishes the moment the operation is called off. I would not rate her chances very highly after that.' Just at that moment there was a knock and the General opened the door. 'What?'

The watch commander stood uncomfortably in the doorway. 'Sir, you had better see this.' He handed across a signal message.

The General read it in silence and handed it over to Peter. 'Captain Veork was one of yours, wasn't he?'

Peter nodded.

'I am very sorry, Peter. I will see to it that the necessary arrangements are made while you are away. Did he have a family?'

'A brother in my unit. Roos was to marry a lady who I will see in five days time.'

'I see. Please convey my deepest sympathy to both of them. I understand he was a fine young officer.'

'Too fine, Sir. Too fine.' It was now 0700, so Peter dropped in to an empty office to see if he could get through to Pat.

The burly inspector was in his car, getting across Cape Town ahead of the morning rush hour, when his mobile phone went. He punched the little green button and held the bulky handset up to his ear.

'Yes?'

'Morning Pat, Peter here.'

'Peter. Good to hear from you.'

'Likewise. How are things at your end?'

'Nothing further. Just another crime scene to process and no leads to speak of. It all takes time. Paul is just about beside himself with worry.'

'I can understand that.'

'Yes.'

'Listen, I have just been called back in to work, and am now on my way out to the Impala. Can't say much over the phone, but Daniel has been busy out on the coast, and carefully laid plans could be at risk, if you understand my drift.'

'I do. That would not be good for Elizabeth.'

'Correct.'

'OK. Anything that I can do at this end?'

'Not really. Just try to keep a low profile on the investigation.'

'As things stand, that is not going to be a problem. When will I hear from you again?'

'Good question. As you know, communications out of the Impala homelands are almost non-existent. I will try and get messages through by radio to your base station.'

'OK, Peter. I will keep my ears to the ground. Good luck.'

'Cheers, Pat.' The line went dead.

After a moment's consideration, Pat checked the rear vision mirror, hit the lights and siren, and did a U-turn across the heavy traffic. It was only fair to bring Paul up to date as much as possible.

Paul was having breakfast in the hotel dining room when Pat walked up to the coffee machine, and then came over to join him. 'Inspector Petronas,' Paul said with mock formality.

Pat threw it back at him. 'Mr Tradour. How is the coffee this morning?'

'Same as ever, given the import restrictions.'

'Right. The price of liberty, apparently.'

'Or politics,' smiled Paul.

'One and the same thing, are they not?'

'Careful, or you will have to arrest us both.'

Pat chuckled, relaxing. 'That would be one for the morning papers, wouldn't it?'

'Yep.' Paul patted the morning issue that he had been using as a distraction from the real issues of the day. 'Any progress?'

'No. But I do have some news.'

Pat nodded, and sat forward in his seat so they could keep their voices down a little.

'Peter Hogan has been sent to the Impala.'

'Why?'

'Apparently Daniel has been busy over on the coast — too busy. Peter is supposed to rein him in, before things get out of control.'

Paul scratched nervously at the paper. 'Could that impact on Elizabeth's safety?'

'It might.' Pat nodded.

'If only we had a lead, of any kind.'

Pat felt a twinge of conscience. 'Peter did say that the authorities believed that she is still alive, and being held as insurance by whomever it is that is trying to get their hands on the mine.'

Paul played with this coffee. 'How do they know this?'

'I can't say. Sorry, you will just have to trust me.'

'Right. Doesn't seem to be much that I can do, anyway.'

Pat leant a little closer. 'Just pray, brother. Just pray.'

'Every waking moment, Pat. Every waking moment,' replied Paul.

The inspector glanced into the huge picture mirror across the room, and saw a man move in the shop doorway across the road. *Maybe the morning was looking up*, he thought. Pulling out his phone, he hit a speed-dial number.

'Control, sir,' announced the female voice on the other end.

'I want a patrol in the alley backing onto Fesham, now, but no siren. Suspect in hotel abduction case is likely to use the alley to avoid pursuit. May be armed. Detain, repeat detain for questioning. Call me when in position.'

Paul looked across the table, questions across his face.

'Carry on with your breakfast, Paul. I am going to slip out the side way, and see if I can surprise this guy. Give me five minutes and then make a fuss in the lobby — knock over a pot plant or something. OK?'

'OK.' Paul was relieved to finally have something to do. Anything was better than sitting around waiting for a phone call that might never come from Elizabeth's abductors. He studied his newspaper, trying to behave as if Pat had just gone to the toilet and was expected back at any moment.

As soon as he was out of sight, Pat moved across a block so as to come up the road behind the surveillance. Right on cue there was a crash from the entrance to the hotel, and pottery and earth scattered on the pavement. Paul was doing a very good imitation of someone in the grips of a massive heart attack, and drew all eyes to the little pantomime.

The phone went in his pocket, nearly giving the game away. Pat dived into a handy doorway.

'Yes? Good. I am on the move. Keep the line open.' He slipped along the shop frontage, and then launched himself across the gap at the other man, who was still focused on events across the road. But at the last moment his target picked up the movement reflected in the window alongside him. Spinning round to meet the threat, he drew a knife.

Pat was already committed, and hit him low and hard, driving the wind from the man's lungs. He rolled clear onto the pavement, opening up the shop door if his target chose to run.

The man did, gasping for air that would not come into his tortured lungs and broken ribs, but only got as far as the revolving door, and then collapsed.

Pat got to his feet and went for his gun, only to find that his right arm was not responding. He looked down and saw a rapidly growing pool of blood on the ground at his feet. His blood. He jammed his foot in the door to ensure that his opponent wasn't going anywhere, and fought to stay conscious as sirens began to wail in his head.

Out in front of the hotel, Paul staged a dramatic recovery and raced across the road to where his friend was propped against the door, only semiconscious. A uniformed policeman appeared on the other side of the door, inside the shop, and threw the lever that locked the doors in position. Paul eased Pat onto the ground and frantically tore at his heavy clothing to find the source of the bleeding.

'Get an ambulance! Quickly.' His voice carried over the open phone line to the Police control centre, and the fact that the line was still connected probably saved Pat's life. A handful of blocks away, an alarm started ringing.

But Paul was losing the fight to stem the bleeding from a deep stab wound right at the top of Pat's arm. He turned to a couple of the men standing around. 'Quickly. Help me get him onto his side. We must stop the bleeding!' In the distance he could hear the wail of the ambulance as it worked its way slowly through the choked traffic, at times having to get up onto the pavement to make any progress. Fifty metres short of the shop door it became completely blocked, so the paramedics debussed and sprinted up the road, carrying their triage kits.

Approaching the scene, they saw three blood-soaked men struggling to turn over another larger man, who was ashen and unconscious. One of the men shouted, 'Stab wound at the shoulder radius, severe blood loss, we are losing him!' The senior paramedic sent his partner back for the plasma, while the rapidly increasing police presence tried to clear the crowd, and the traffic, so the ambulance could get closer.

When the plasma arrived, the paramedic found a useful vein and got the life-preserving fluid flowing. 'My name is Karl.' He inspected the wound and ripped a field dressing and surgical tape from his kit. 'Didn't think I would be doing combat medicine downtown.' The stretcher came up, and together they move the patient onto it. Pat's blood pressure was dangerously low.

Paul leant over. 'I am a doctor. We are going to lose him if we can't get hold of the end of that artery, Karl. Do you have any retractors?'

'Yes — in the ambulance.'

'Feel like a little combat surgery?'

'Let's do it.' Karl replied. They got Pat onto oxygen and then rolled him onto his side, while police moved the crowd back a little further and formed a protective screen.

Paul took a scalpel and amplified his qualifications. 'I did a surgical internship at John Hopkins. This should be relatively straightforward. I am simply going to make an incision far enough to get hold of the end of the artery, and clamp it. The bleeding should show us where to go.' The paramedic nodded.

With no time to waste, Paul exposed the arterial canal and worked his way deeper into Pat's shoulder, until the end of the artery itself came into view, pumping blood into the soaked dressings. It took three attempts to get the clamp securely in place, but the bleeding stopped as advertised, assisted in part by the critically low blood pressure.

'Well done,' acknowledged the paramedic.

'Cheers,' replied Pat, as they both worked to dress the wound to reduce the risk of infection from the pavement surgery. Then it was time to get their patient into the ambulance, and off to the nearest accident and emergency department. Paul climbed in the back with the paramedics, and just registered the other man being taken away by the police as the doors closed behind them. *I will need to pay the hotel for the pot plant*, he thought.

Paul managed to get into theatre to observe the surgeon's work. At one stage the gowned and masked figure turned to him and nodded, 'Nice job, Doctor. Any time you want a job, just let me know. Almost certainly saved his life.' The surgeon then turned to the intern standing alongside him. 'Get him stitched up. It doesn't look like there is any permanent structural damage, but he is going to be sore for a while. Call me if you have any problems.' Turning away from the operating table, he asked Paul to join him for a coffee.

'A friend of yours, I understand.'

'Yes. And a very good man. It would have been tragic to lose him.' Paul was a little shaky as the adrenalin worked its way out of his system.

A reassuring arm steadied him. 'Been quite a morning, then.' They rounded the corner and ran straight into a uniformed police officer coming up the corridor. 'Morning Superintendent.'

'Hello, Hans. Busy morning?'

'Yes.' They shook hands. 'Good of you to come down, sir. I expect your man to make a full recovery.'

'That is good news. When can I speak to him?'

'He has lost a lot of blood. We will keep him under for the next twenty-four hours to reduce the trauma. I can have Intensive Care give you a call when he wakes up.'

'OK. The sooner the better.' The Superintendent turned to Paul. 'Mr?'

'Mr Paul Tradour. Inspector Petronas has been looking into the abduction of my friend, Miss Dortmus.'

'Right — so you were with Pat this morning.'

'Yes, we were having coffee in the hotel when Pat picked up the surveillance and went to investigate.'

The surgeon interrupted. 'We were just about to get a brew. Care to join us?'

'Thanks. I need to catch up with events this morning as soon as I can. For some reason this has gone straight to the top.'

Over coffee Paul brought the Superintendent up to date with everything that he knew. 'Hmmm,' came the reply. 'Doesn't explain the flap up the line. I will make a few calls today, and see what else I can dig up.' He turned to Paul. 'I would appreciate it if you would stay in town, Mr Tradour.'

'I am here until we get Miss Dortmus back, Superintendent. And I will be with Inspector Petronas when he comes around tomorrow,' Paul replied, getting to his feet. 'Will you arrange for someone to let his wife know he has been injured?'

'Of course. And thanks for your assistance earlier.' The Superintendent reached out his hand. 'Sounds like Pat was lucky to have you there.'

The three men shook hands. Paul was left alone to the last of his coffee. With nothing better to do he got a cab back to the hotel and went up to his room, to shower and change into a fresh shirt. The hotel staff had cleaned up the shattered remains of the pot plant, and there was a note at reception asking him to contact the manager when convenient. Later, Paul decided. From the vantage of the balcony it was possible to look out over the harbour. As he watched a large container vessel leaving port, his thoughts turned to Elizabeth.

CHAPTER 10

Having left Paul and the Inspector to their deliberations, Elizabeth had wasted no time settling between the fresh linen sheets of the most comfortable bed she had ever laid in. But she was not fully asleep when a quiet scratch, and then the soft click of a lock, intruded into her subconscious. Something was not right. She turned on the bedside lamp and flooded the room with light. Everything was as she left it, but there was a draught on her face.

She slipped a bathrobe over her shoulders. The door to the lounge was open, so perhaps Paul was back and had opened the door out onto the terrace.

'Paul?' Nothing.

She moved to the door and looked around the lounge of the hotel suite. Across the room, the curtains were blowing in the breeze coming through the open door, and she could hear the noise of the traffic on the street a couple of floors below. That must have been what disturbed her. Perhaps the door just blew open. She went to investigate, but only got two paces before a cloth bag dropped over her head, and she was thrown roughly to the floor. The bag was soaked in chloroform, and her futile attempts to call out simply accelerated her loss of consciousness.

An indeterminate time later she gradually became aware she was in a cold steel cell, tied hand and foot, and dumped on a mess of stinking canvas. Her system grappled with waves of panic, and then she promptly vomited.

A couple of decks above her, in much more comfortable surroundings, Colonel Victor Krakovsky of the Russian Secret Service was putting a call through on his mobile phone, mindful that it was not particularly secure.

As the connection was made, he passed his message in clipped, heavily accented tones. 'We have her.'

'Was there any problem?' came the voice through the handset speaker.

'No. It will be morning before anyone notices.'

'Good,' came the reply.

'How is the operation going?' he asked.

'Fine. We will be ready by the end of the week.'

Krakovsky looked down at some papers on his desk. 'I will need a few days to prepare departure formalities, assuming that the delivery address for your goods has not changed.'

'Make the arrangements. I will arrange for reception at the other end.'

He paused. 'And what of my guest?'

'Take her with you, for now,' was the non-committal reply, and the line went dead.

He took a cigarette, lit it, and then left the room. Half way down the corridor, he grunted and reversed his direction. 'Bring our guest up to my stateroom, Alexis,' he said to the man who waited motionless outside his door.

'Yes, Colonel.' The man dropped down the companionway and out of sight.

A few minutes later there was a knock on the door. 'Enter,' Victor called out. He allowed Elizabeth to hit the floor heavily before turning around. She stank of raw fear, and vomit.

'Where am I?' she whispered, struggling to frame the words.

'Nowhere,' came the reply. 'At least that is all you need to know.'

Elizabeth struggled to orient herself. 'Who are you?'

'Right now, as far as you are concerned, I am the most important man in the whole world.' The Colonel took a long drag on his cigarette, followed by a mouthful of neat vodka.

'Why are you doing this?'

'My dear. So many questions.' He bent down close to her, and she smelt the alcohol on his breath. 'I would have thought that you would be grateful to be out of my cells.'

Elizabeth decided not to respond, too weary and confused for games. Victor bent down and untied her legs, allowing her to struggle into a low seat, head spinning. From across the room he tossed her suitcase — the kidnap team had grabbed it on the way out, just in case it contained any documentation that might have been useful.

'Just to show you that I am not an unreasonable man.' He paused, and looked at her huddled in the hotel bathrobe. 'You should get dressed — the bathroom is through that door. I regret that I cannot allow you to lock the door, however.'

Elizabeth scowled, and offered him her wrists. He considered that for a moment, and then cut the bonds, observing how delicate her hands were compared with the rough world that he was forced to operate in. She picked up her case and slipped inside the small room.

The Colonel walked across to his desk and picked up a small family portrait, allowing himself a moment of tenderness. Two years. Two years stuck here on the other side of the world, with just the odd letter that managed to get through the complex chain of false addresses and redirections. His sons would have grown — how he longed to be back in the forests behind their home just outside of Kiev, teaching them to fish and hunt. Nina's last letter was the typical letter from a good military wife: they were all well, the boys were doing fine in the early years at school, the house needed a little maintenance but she had his parents close by and his father was looking after those things. All those things that a husband should really be there for.

But between the lines were those coded messages that can only pass between a husband and wife. Where are you? Why has it been so long this time? Are you alright? I love you. I need you. He poured himself another drink, promising no-one in particular that this would be the last for the night, and then ran his hand down the long line of books that were carefully arranged in shelves on one side of the stateroom, looking for a distraction from his current reality. While he knew that his men in their cramped quarters on the other side of the vessel, and one deck down, would be pouring through their collection of dog-eared magazines, he preferred the Russian classics. He had even managed to find a couple that were currently unavailable in the bookstores in Kiev, presumably because those guardians of the Soviet mind — the KGB political commissars — considered them heretical.

There was a thump as the door to the bathroom opened, and the woman stepped out. Yet another complication. 'You are refreshed?' he asked.

'Cold showers tend to do that,' came the testy reply.

'Ah yes. Russian plumbing. Even the Captain endures that from time to time. But fresh water is precious, so it keeps the crew from washing unnecessarily.'

'I noticed.'

He grunted. 'I can have your clothes washed. Leave them in the bathroom.'

'That will not be necessary,' Elizabeth replied. 'I am not planning on staying that long.'

It had been a long day. The Colonel put the tumbler down on the desk just a shade too heavily and spilt his drink, which did not improve his mood. 'Please appreciate that by rights you should still be sitting in your own vomit, down in that stinking cell. If you wish, that can be arranged!'

Elizabeth quickly sat down on the nearest seat, and began sorting out her clothes. But she was unable to stop the tears.

Angry at himself for losing his temper, her captor poured a drink and brought it across. 'Here. It will help.'

She refused, so he left it alongside her.

'It really does help,' he said, picking up the photo again. He showed it to her. 'My family. Wife and two sons. It is over two years since I have been home.'

Elizabeth glanced at the glass alongside her.

'Vodka. A very Russian drink.' He raised his glass to the photo of Lenin on the wall behind her. 'It may not be to your taste, but it comforts the inner man.' He bowed to her. 'Or the inner woman, as the case might be.'

Finally, desperate for something to take the taste of bile from her throat, Elizabeth reached for the glass and took a sip of raw liquor, gagging as it tore at the sensitive tissues in her throat. But he was right, she did feel better. 'Thank you.' She placed the empty glass at her feet.

'My pleasure.' He replied formally.

'Who are you?' she asked, for the second time.

'Everything in its time. For now you can take the spare cabin and get some sleep. I have a busy day tomorrow.' He showed her the door.

The following day they made ready for sea. The Colonel did not like using the mobile telephone. It was far too easy to intercept. He was also wary of the local direction finding capabilities — probably not as good as his own, but still to be respected. He kept his call as brief as possible.

'Everything is arranged for the delivery on Sunday week,' he advised.

'Good,' came the reply. 'Payment will go through overnight — half in advance.'

'Fine.' He hung up. Even if that was intercepted, all it told the local authorities was a time. The place could be anywhere between here and Gibraltar. He looked at the timer on his desk — connected for twenty-three seconds — far too short to localise.

He left the shelter of the bridge and walked aft along the rail. The woman was where he had told her to wait.

'It is not too cold for you?'

'Any fresh air is good, cold or not,' replied Elizabeth, wearing a shapeless pair of overalls that were several sizes too big, and an equally ill-fitting beret in order to keep her striking head of hair out of sight of casual observation.

'Thank you for respecting the risk I have taken bringing you on deck.' He meant it.

Elizabeth smiled, desperate to continue to build his favour. 'You have been far more reasonable than I might have expected in the circumstances.'

What woman's games is she playing? thought her captor. 'Time to go below.' He took a final glance at Table Mountain and then led the way back to his stateroom, where Elizabeth went back to the book she had been reading. Almost immediately the Colonel left to attend to other duties.

Elizabeth closed her eyes and ran every detail of her situation over and over in her mind. There was no sense in it, nor, more importantly, any indication of how this might end. She was still prowling around like a caged lioness when he returned.

'You will wear out my carpet,' the Colonel remarked, stepping into the room.

Elizabeth looked down at the threadbare floor covering. 'Too late.'

'You will join me for the evening meal?'

'Thank you.'

'Good. Excuse me.' He disappeared into his cabin. Elizabeth was left to retreat into the pages of her book.

As usual it was a simple, and characteristically Russian, meal. Elizabeth had decided there were only a couple of variations to the menu. But she had found their evening conversations genuinely interesting, and, for his part, the Colonel had enjoyed talking of home and his family. Tonight, however, the comfortable truce between them seemed absent, and eventually Victor Krakovsky confronted it head-on.

'You are not yourself?'

'Neither are you.'

'Yes, I am.'

After a pause, Elizabeth pushed her chair away from the table and stood up. 'What are you going to do with me?'

Victor avoided the question. 'What do you mean?'

'You know exactly what I mean.' Elizabeth got to her feet, took a pace away from the table, and turned to face him. 'Obviously this cannot continue forever. You will return to Russia. What will become of me?'

Victor got to his feet, suddenly weary of the whole mission. 'We have a delivery to make. For now you must stay down here, so that you have no idea where that is. The logical place to put you ashore is somewhere on the Ivory Coast.'

'What! And then I should simply walk home?'

His tone changed abruptly. 'The expectation is that you will disappear, permanently. It is only the method that has been left up to me — is that understood?'

'Yes.' But the defiance was missing in her voice.

'Good. Then I would be pleased if you would play your part in our little charade. You will be pleasant to me, and I will do whatever is in my power to spare your life.' Victor moderated his tone. 'That is all I can promise, Elizabeth. Do you understand?'

'Yes, Colonel,' she replied, the formality hitting him as if she had slapped his face.

'I am not a monster,' the Colonel replied tiredly.

'No. I know you are not. But you are my enemy, Victor. And that you will remain.'

'Good. I am glad that we have clarified things. You will retire to the cabin and allow me to enjoy some privacy.' Elizabeth picked up the book from where she had put it down on the seat, and left.

That night, Colonel Victor Krakovsky got very, very drunk.

The following morning, Elizabeth was reading on her bunk when she heard the sound of the anchor chain running through the fairleads. Opening the door to the stateroom, she found it empty. The deck tilted subtly under her feet, and she knew that the vessel was finally leaving harbour and heading for the open sea.

The Colonel came into the room with a folder of papers, and placed them on the desk. He looked terrible. 'These were dropped off early this morning. I must ask you to sign them. I will act as witness.'

She stood her ground. 'What are they?'

He handed them across. 'Read them for yourself. They are simple declarations that you forfeit all rights and privileges to your father's land and prospect on the western coast.'

'Why on earth would I do that?'

Victor sat down behind the desk and put his head in his hands. 'To stay alive, Elizabeth.' He looked up and there was something much deeper in those dark Russian eyes, but she could not pick it, or perhaps she just chose not to notice. 'Just to stay alive.'

'They will kill me anyway, won't they?'

He shook his head, slowly.

'Won't they!' Her face was a strange mix of fear and determination.

'Not on my ship,' he sighed. 'But they are demanding that I hand you over when we offload our cargo. I cannot refuse. If they do not get title to the land, and access to the mine, my Government will not get paid. If that happens, my career will be over, and my family will be left to beg on the street corners of Kiev.' He smiled at her. 'It is really that simple. Nina and my sons, or you. Who do you choose?'

Elizabeth sat on the bench seat as the first of the Atlantic Ocean swells lifted the ship. She tried to stop the tears, but they came anyway. Her words were very carefully enunciated. 'I choose life, Victor. I choose life.'

The KGB Colonel left her. Alone.

She woke from a fitful sleep, to the sounds of the ship coming to anchor. For the last four days they had steamed slowly in circles just outside of South African territorial waters, wallowing uncomfortably in the swells coming up from the Southern Ocean. Elizabeth had been miserably seasick, and the stillness as the ship took up the tension of the anchor was a welcome relief. Opening the door into the stateroom, she found the Russian eating a hearty breakfast.

'Ah. Miss Dortmus. Would you care for some?'

'Just some toast, thank you.' Their relationship had become difficult, both trapped in their own particular miseries, with little opportunity for distraction. Her trauma was amplified by the very real fear that she would die here, soon. His anguish was due to the fundamental conflict between his duty, and his humanity. He looked at the photo on his desk. *How would he live with himself, if he handed this innocent woman over to the thugs he was forced to work with,* he asked his wife. *How?*

The toast arrived, and Elizabeth sat down at the table. 'Where are we?'

'Back in Cape Town.'

'Why?' she asked, confused.

Victor shrugged. 'There have been some delays, again. We were wasting fuel running around in circles, and it is much more comfortable to wait in the relative shelter of the harbour, as you have already noticed.'

She nodded, still weak from four days unable to hold anything in her stomach.

The Colonel leant back in his chair. 'You have thought about signing those documents?'

'Yes, but I cannot.' They ate in silence for a few minutes.

Finally, unable to shackle his frustration any more, Victor leant over towards her. 'Is your inheritance really worth your life?'

'No. Not as such, but it is much more than that. My father left the land and the mine in trust to me, but it is for the benefit of my people. It is not so much if I die, for the Impala will then be the sole beneficiaries of what the mine produces. But if I were to sign away their heritage, I could never live with myself.' Elizabeth pushed a second piece of dry toast away from her, deciding that her constitution was still a little too fragile to handle it. She decided to change the subject. 'If we are back in port, you may get a letter away to your wife?'

'Yes. At least I hope to,' he remarked. 'Even better, to receive news from home. It has been too long.'

'You are not able to make a long-distance call?'

Victor shook his head. 'Security.'

'Oh, I see.'

'Nearly two years away from home, without hearing the sound of her voice. Right now, that in itself would be a treasure.'

Acting on impulse, Elizabeth reached across and covered his hand with her own. 'Victor. You have been very kind to me in the circumstances, and, whatever happens, I will always remember that.' They sat for just a moment, enjoying the strange companionship. There was a knock on the door.

'Yes?' Victor called out.

'Call for you upstairs, Sir.'

He got up from the table, again a Russian KGB officer, pulled on his heavy coat, and left without a word. Elizabeth buried her head in her hands, and wept.

Up in the radio room, the operator was sorting out incoming messages into priority order, before attaching them to a wooden clipboard. When the Colonel entered, he stood up and handed it over. Victor scanned them from the bottom up. Just routine until he got to the one at the top. In terse, clipped tones it advised him that he was to use every measure to conclude the sale and delivery of his cargo, within the next ten days. In any event he was to return to the Black Sea port of Sevastopol, without delay. Apparently the vessel was required for other tasks.

Whatever, he was on his way home.

About noon, the ship's boat bumped alongside the Customs steps. Colonel Krakovsky jumped across the gap, and disappeared into the crowds of the busy port. Slightly behind him, two of his men followed. Their job was to make it very hard for him to be tailed without it becoming obvious. He moved confidently towards a line of taxis waiting for tourists off a cruise ship the Russians had watched dock earlier that day.

As he approached, the driver of the taxi fourth in line got out of the cab and placed a seaman's cap on his head. Victor picked up the pre-arranged signal and dropped into the back seat. In seconds they were out in the traffic.

'Good morning, Colonel.'

'Good morning, Joseph. How are things at the Consulate?'

'Rather quiet, to be honest. The Consul is expected you.' They narrowly avoided a bus coming the other way, and Victor decided that he would be quiet and let the man drive.

91

'Very good.'

Arriving at the allocated meeting by a roundabout route, Victor was across the pavement and through the doors before the taxi had come to rest. It accelerated into the lunchtime traffic.

Just inside the door, he paused to check for obvious signs that he was being followed, but nothing looked amiss. Then the inner door was opened for him, and he moved inside the dim, smoke-filled room. Apart from two body-guards positioned at either door, there were only two others present, as expected.

The Consul was a large, portly man who had extensive business connections with the Russian Mafia, Victor knew. It was a practical arrangement: he looked after Russian interests in Cape Town, and the KGB looked after his interests in Moscow.

Victor knew the other man even better, or knew his dossier, and despised him. This was the man who was prepared to keep his country in a state of virtual civil war, for entirely his own ends — the worst kind of treason. There were no lofty revolutionary goals, or noble quests for freedom. Victor despised him, and loathed every contact, every minute spent in his presence. The room had suddenly got smaller.

The Consul got up and greeted him the Russian way. 'Colonel.' Releasing him from the embrace, he turned to the other man. 'You know the Minister, of course.'

'Of course.' Victor extended a hand. 'Minister.'

The other man did not get up, but just waved him to a seat. 'Do you have the documents?'

Victor sat down, and responded carefully. 'No. She would not sign them.'

The Minister, well-known around political circles for his very short fuse, leaped to his feet, standing over Victor. 'What do you mean?' He turned his attention on the Consul. 'Why do I have to continue to deal with amateurs?'

'Minister, please, sit down,' urged the consul. 'I am sure that this is only a temporary setback.' But all this achieved was the demise of one of the table lamps as it flew across the room.

'This is all I seem to hear of — setbacks!' He turned back to Victor. 'Incompetence, that is what it is. Incompetence.'

'I am sure that the Colonel will be able to resolve this, er, this difficulty?' interjected the Consul.

'It is too late. I will have to do it the hard way.' The Minister pulled out his mobile phone, and punched a number. 'Get me Rathson.'

Apparently whoever Rathson was came on the phone.

'File those papers with the High Court today.'

'No. There has been a problem.'

'Yes, I will talk to the Chief Justice myself. He owes me a favour.'

'No! You do not understand. That is too late.' Victor was sure that the phone was going to go the same way as the table lamp.

'Unacceptable. Get hold of the Clerk of the Court and get a hearing scheduled next week, yes? As soon as possible!'

The connection was broken, and the Minister moved to the door. 'In light of your failure, Colonel, I presume that the delivery will now be made in advance of payment. Seven days from now. I will have the precise location passed through to your ship, after you are on your way up the coast.' He paused. 'And give the woman to your men for a bit of sport. They have been cooped up on the ship for a long time. Feed whatever is left to the sharks.'

Victor was close to that point in a man's rage where it becomes blind and irrational. The Consul intervened, quickly, and saw the Minister out of the door. He was a far better judge of Russian psyche. He poured two large tumblers of his best vodka and slid one across the table. Without a word the Colonel took it, downed it, and left.

Joining the early afternoon pedestrians, for a few minutes Victor was comfortable to allow the crowds to carry him along. It was a fine winter morning, just a little chilly, with a brisk wind off the vast expanse of ocean to the South. His counter-surveillance team moved easily down the busy road on either side of him. For just a moment, the world was good. He even contemplated doing a little bit of shopping so that he could surprise Nina and the boys when he got home. Ironically, what he really needed was for his prisoner to guide him through the minefield of trying to buy clothes for his wife.

Walking around the corner, he was brought back to reality with a thump. It was a trap.

'Colonel Krakovsky, so nice of you to join us.' There were three of them, no weapons visible. He looked for his men, but they were still out of sight, around the corner.

'Please, step inside. We understand the coffee is very good.' He was bundled through the door into a deserted shop, with a *For Lease* sign on the front.

'Very neat,' said Victor.

'Always helps when the team plays,' said the largest of the three with a grin.

So you are local secret service, thought Victor.

'Exactly,' said the Brit.

Victor tried to visibly relax. 'You have me at a disadvantage.'

'Just as we like it. We have learned the hard way to respect the KGB.'

'I am sure that they would be flattered to hear it. How can I help you gentlemen?'

'It is actually how we can help you.'

'Really? How kind.'

'Let's get to the point, Krakovsky.'

The impatience of the Americans, thought Victor. So predictable. 'Yes, let's. I still have some shopping to do.'

'We have a fair idea of what you are doing here.'

'If that really was the case, we would not be having coffee,' smiled Victor.

'A fair idea,' the American repeated. 'We do know, for example, that the KGB has been supplying weapons to at least one of the guerrilla movements operating in the northern border region. We have recently come to suspect that your ship may be running arms through the blockade.'

'So why don't you just come and see for yourselves.'

'Well, you know the delicacies of the international situation as well as we do. It would not be, shall we say, productive,' said the Brit.

'Very astute.'

'Thank you. But this is the issue. We will not allow you to offload your cargo in South African waters. Period.'

'That sounds like a threat.'

'My Russian friend. That is a promise,' said the American. Victor knew that he was not bluffing.

'So what would you propose that I do?'

'Return to Sevastopol. Tell your KGB masters that it was not possible to make the delivery without compromising Russian involvement in this dirty little war.'

'I will consider it. If you will excuse me please?' They moved out of the way. As he opened the door, Victor decided it was time to play his trump card. 'You don't know who you are dealing with at this end, do you?'

'That is not relevant,' responded the South African.

'It should be.' He threw them a mock salute, and slipped out into the crowds.

CHAPTER 11

Not much later in the day, the Superintendent called in at the forensics lab on the way up to his office. 'Morning Zach. Anything yet on the Dortmus abduction?'

'Very little, Sir. Either the lady was never in the room, or her abductors did a very thorough job of sanitizing the crime scene. We think they got in off the patio — there were fresh scratches around the lock — but it would have been almost impossible to leave the same way.'

'Back exit?'

'Logical. But there was no sign of the door being forced, and unfortunately the security tapes were degaussed, somehow.'

'Someone in the hotel knows more than they are letting on.'

'Certainly,' agreed the forensics man.

'Anything else?'

'Not really. We had one half-print that had been missed when the place was wiped down. Didn't come up on any of our databases. We were asked to fax it through to Military Intelligence in Bloemfontein, but have heard nothing.'

'Unusual,' commented the Superintendent. 'Chase it up, just in case they forget to come back to us. I will be in my office.'

He had barely sat down when the phone on his desk rang. 'Yes? Right away.'

When he arrived down in the operations centre, he was taken to one side by a man that he did not recognise. The security pass that the grey-suited man flashed was generic enough, but the code on the bottom indicated that this individual was cleared to know things that the Superintendent would not even dream about.

'In here, please, Superintendent.' They went into one of the small briefing rooms off the side of the watch room. There were two other men seated around a small table, just closing up their briefcases.

He was not introduced, so he introduced himself and shook their hands. 'Good morning.'

'Busy, anyway,' the taller of the two remarked in an American accent. They all sat down, and the first man led off.

'Is Inspector Petronas going to pull through?'

'Yes, thanks to the quick thinking of a friend.'

'Good. You are aware of the investigation that he is currently running?'

'Yes. I have just come from forensics,' the Superintendent replied.

'Any developments?'

'Nothing substantial.'

The three men looked at each other, and the American spoke. 'We might be able to help you there, on the understanding that this information is for your ears only, and that the Police investigation is shut down immediately and left in the hands of certain other agencies.'

'I would have to be the judge of that.'

'This is very serious, Superintendent.'

'So is the attempted murder of one of my officers!' He pushed his seat back from the table. 'I currently have a man in custody, and I intend to prosecute him to the full extent of the law.'

The third man found a voice, obviously a Brit. 'Please Super, we understand your obligations, I assure you. But we must also protect a much wider operation that is currently at a very delicate stage.'

'OK, I am prepared to listen. So what is this information?'

The American spoke. 'The half print that your lab faxed through earlier is a probable match with a known KGB operative, on file with my agency.'

'KGB? Involved in what is apparently a simple abduction.'

'Unfortunately for Miss Dortmus, and Inspector Petronas, it is a long way from a simple abduction. You will, of course, be aware of the connection between this case and the twin murders of Mr and Mrs Johansen. And then the probable link to the robbery and arson of the Central Bank?'

'Yes, only a hypothesis at this stage.'

The South African took the lead. 'Certain other sources have confirmed the links.'

'Right, so you know where she is being held?'

'Not specifically.'

The Superintendent looked long and hard at the other man's face. *Perhaps,* he thought to himself. 'So what do you want from my department?'

The man who had led him into the room, leant forward. 'Hand your prisoner over to us. We very much want to talk with him, in private, if you get my drift.'

The Superintendent went to protest, but then thought better of it. 'OK. I would only be postponing the inevitable. God only knows how I am going to explain this to Pat when he wakes up tomorrow.'

'Probably not as hard as you think,' said the local man. 'He is already aware of much of what we have just told you, through, shall we say, informal links with Defence sources in Bloemfontein. You can tell him that having one of these guys in custody is a real bonus, and we intend to make best use of it.'

'All right. On the understanding that you will do nothing that will further prejudice Miss Dortmus's safety.'

The Brit answered. 'We will do what we can, Sir, but in all probability she is unlikely to make it through this.'

The Superintendent got to his feet. 'Well, I am not prepared to accept that, just yet. But I will put our investigation on the back-burner. No sense in putting her at any more risk.' He turned to the door. 'You will, of course, keep me informed of any significant developments?'

'Of course,' replied the American.

'Fine.' *Like talking with the proverbial three-headed man*, the Superintendent thought — you never know which head is going to reply. He went back up to his office, stopping in at the front desk to sign over the prisoner. 'How is he, anyway?'

'Pretty sore. Pat clobbered him good and hard,' replied the duty sergeant.

'Good,' grumped the Superintendent, and stomped off up the corridor. He had a feeling that the day was not going to get any better.

Paul decided that he had had quite enough of the midday crowds, as he made his way on foot back to the hospital to check on Pat's condition. He desperately needed to talk to someone. Anyone. But Peter was out of touch on his way into the Impala, Daniel was somewhere over on the coast, and Pat was in intensive care. It was difficult to think about Elizabeth's situation at all. For the moment, he was on his own.

He crossed the road and went through the main doors into the hospital, looking for the internal map to get him up to the Intensive Care Ward. In the end he went across to reception and asked at the desk.

'Good afternoon, could you direct me to Intensive Care?'

The receptionist smiled. 'I am sorry, Sir. No visitors are allowed out of normal hours.'

Paul nodded. 'I understand, but my friend was admitted this morning. I really need to know how he is doing.'

'I could ring through to the ward for you and ask the charge nurse?'

'Thank you.'

'Please take a seat over there. I will let you know when I have got through.'

Paul took a seat, as directed, and settled down to wait. *Today is full of waiting*, he thought. About five minutes later the receptionist caught his eye and he went over.

'Your friend's condition is unchanged, Sir. He is heavily sedated, and unlikely to regain consciousness until tomorrow morning.'

'Thanks. I appreciate that.' He turned away from the desk just in time to see the surgeon who had operated on Pat earlier in the day heading out for some fresh air.

The surgeon spotted him at the same instant. 'Hello Doctor, I trust your day is proving to be a bit less dramatic than earlier.'

'So far so good.' The two men shook hands.

'How is your friend doing?'

Paul shrugged. 'No change, apparently. The ward is closed to visitors, so I have not been able to get up to see him.'

The other man grinned, looking at his watch. 'I can fix that. I have a few minutes before I am due in theatre. Come with me.' Ignoring the glare from the receptionist, he led the way up the adjacent stairs. After transiting the normal maze of hospital corridors, they came to the desk that monitored the entrance to the Intensive Care Ward. A flash of the surgeon's hospital ID, and they were directed down the corridor.

As they rounded the corner, they noticed a man in a hospital gown duck into the room. Next two men came out, and moved down the corridor away from them in a hurry. Initially just curious, the surgeon called out. 'Excuse me,' but the men accelerated away from them.

Leading the way into Pat's room, the surgeon banged the security alarm on the wall. There was a syringe still hanging from the drip line, and the ECG monitor was all over the place. Paul punched the emergency button on the wall as the surgeon grabbed the syringe and looked around the room for any clues as to what might have been in it. Nothing. The ECG alarm went off.

Racing to the door, the surgeon bellowed down the corridor at the charge nurse. 'Resus. Stat!' Paul heard the sound of the trolley and running feet racing down the long corridor towards them. The emergency team went to work with smooth efficiency, and Paul could do nothing but stay out of the way.

A nurse picked up the syringe, and the surgeon pointed down the corridor. 'Get that down to the lab, fast.' Pat was responding, but they could not establish a stable cardiac rhythm. 'Wish I knew what was in that syringe, Paul,' said the Surgeon from the other side of the room.

'I know,' replied Paul. 'I might take a walk down the corridor and check out anywhere that a vial might have been discarded'

'Good idea.'

He slipped out the door. The security alarm was still howling overhead. Through just two of the fire-stop doors, Paul got lucky. Dropped behind a water cooler was a drug vial. He grabbed it in a paper towel, and sprinted back to where the emergency team was fighting to keep Pat alive.

'I've got it! This is what they gave him.' He passed it across to the leader of the emergency team. 'OK. This shouldn't be a problem, and there is still half of the vial left.' He turned across the bed. 'Nurse, given him ten mil of NSRS.'

'Ten mil of NSRS.' She held up the syringe for the cross check. 'Going in now, doctor.'

Their patient quickly stabilised, and a few minutes later opened his eyes. 'Good to see you, Inspector,' said the doctor. 'Don't try to move. You have a nasty injury to your shoulder.'

Pat mouthed, 'OK'.

The surgeon returned to the room after a brief conversation with hospital security. He turned to Paul. 'No sign of the culprits, but it is pretty easy to get lost in a hospital wearing a white gown. I have suggested that security gets hold of Superintendent Smuts. He will be interested to know that they have had another go at one of his men.'

'Presumably he will be posting a guard on this room?' asked Paul.

'I would think that goes without saying.'

It took about twelve minutes for the Superintendent to get across town, with a uniform car leading the way. He was directed straight up to Pat's room. 'How is he?' he asked of the assembled medical team.

'Not bad, considering. It was a near run thing,' answered the Hospital Registrar.

The surgeon nodded. 'If the good doctor here had not turned up the vial that allowed us to identify the drug they used, the result may have been very different.'

'Twice in one day, Paul.'

'We got lucky, this time,' noted Paul.

The inspector turned back to the Intensive Care Registrar. 'These guys are pretty serious. Obviously I will be posting a uniform guard outside this room.'

'By all means,' he replied. 'We would obviously prefer not to have people like that floating around in our ward.'

The Superintendent looked across to Paul. 'Would you have a moment?' Out in the corridor he continued. 'Something about this does not add up at all, but right now all we have to go on is the fact that the bad guys just attempted to murder a police officer, something I take a very dim view of. Is there anything that you have not told me?'

Paul shook his head. 'This is as much of a surprise to me as it is to you, Superintendent.' He went back over the story since the murder of the solicitor and his wife.

'Nothing new,' confirmed the Superintendent. 'OK, I need to get back to the office. Keep your head down; I would not put it beyond this crowd to have a shot at you.' Up until now, that hadn't really occurred to the young missionary doctor.

Paul spent the rest of the afternoon with Pat, bringing him up to date with events since he tackled the man in the entrance to the shop, and then reading hospital magazines while the patient dozed. Late in the afternoon the Registrar came back on his rounds.

'Still here?'

'Yes. Nowhere else to be right now, and to be honest the Superintendent managed to put the wind up me about who might be next on the list.'

'Understandable. Stay as long as you like.' The registrar moved around the bed. 'I can arrange for a cot in one of the empty rooms, if you like.'

'Thanks, but I should get back to the hotel and check to see if there are any messages. How is his shoulder doing?'

'Fine.' The Registrar checked the charts. 'He was lucky. There is no structural damage. I dare say there will be some discomfort, and he will need a bit of physio to ensure that he regains full mobility of his arm, but he should heal nicely.'

'Good news.'

'Certainly is.' The young doctor turned on his way out the door. 'The story of how you saved his life with your pavement surgery is the buzz around the place today. Good effort.'

'Right place, right time.'

'Always is.' With a friendly wave he was gone, and Paul was left to his riddles as the sun set on the day.

CHAPTER 12

Daniel watched the last of Ander's men make their way off the beach, and turned to the man himself. 'Much as I would prefer you to join them, I am going to have to insist that you take the long way back, with us.'

Anders scowled, but Daniel continued. 'You are my insurance that this little adventure is over. You see, I really don't trust you to go away and stay away.'

'I don't intend to be with you when you get over to the vehicles,' the man challenged.

'Then, you will be dead. I promise you that.' Daniel called Marcus to his side. 'You might just be able to fool me, but I can absolutely guarantee that you will not be able to fool Marcus.' This appeared to make the man reconsider.

'Shadz. We will depart for home tomorrow at first light. We will take it a little easier on the way home, so tell your men that they can take a few trophies with them.' What with the kit that Ander's ground party had brought over, and the equipment that had been dropped off by the trawler, each of the warriors would return to the village a rich man. Most prized were the knives and the fire-arms.

Noticing Lester out of the corner of his eye, Daniel thought for a moment and then moved over to where the hunter was polishing the blade of his skinning knife.

'A nice touch,' offered Lester.

'You are welcome to do likewise, Lester. I am assuming that you are not going to get paid the other half of your fee, which will leave you significantly out of pocket.'

'Thanks. It will certainly help pay the bills.'

On an impulse, Daniel took the .308 from over his shoulder. 'This is rightfully yours.'

Lester got to his feet, a little overcome. 'I am in your debt, Daniel. I can assure you that you will not regret it.'

'If I thought there was any chance of regretting it, it would still be over my shoulder.' They shook hands, warmly, and then turned to watch the trawler raise her anchor and slip out of the bay into the South Atlantic.

'Wouldn't want to be in their shoes when they get back to port,' commented Lester to no-one in particular.

At the same time the next day, Daniel kept them going in the fading light, keen to find somewhere with a bit of shelter from the cold drizzle, and biting wind, blowing in off the Atlantic. The only one complaining was Anders, but Daniel was not about to pay him any mind. They dropped off the side of the ridge they had been climbing, and found a rocky ledge that provided some relief from the weather.

'Make yourself at home,' said Daniel. 'We will stop here until the moon is up, and then see how much light we have through this crap.'

Lester came up. 'Good to see that our friend is enjoying himself.'

'Yes. I don't think that he is carrying enough. What do you think?'

'Depends on how much complaining you can put up with before you decide that his company is really spoiling your day.'

Daniel grinned. 'I reached that point when we left the cabin.'

'So why not just leave him to his own misery in the wilderness?'

Daniel glanced at Marcus. 'Because he is just like me, Lester. He would hunt us down, without remorse, until one or other of us was dead.' Lester caught the cold, hard edge of his voice, and shivered. They ate from their packs and made themselves as comfortable as they could.

In the early hours of the morning Daniel got them up and moving. They were all wet and cold, but there was a reasonable amount of moonlight seeping through the overcast, so they toiled across the broken ground. Anders was unusually quiet. They were picking their way across a swollen stream, when he made his move.

Using the noise and distraction of the cascade, he just dropped into a deep pool, and slipped around the back of a boulder. Gone. Even Marcus was fooled, and the noise and the water negated his extraordinary canine sensory suite. It was Shadz who noticed he was gone.

'Daniel, the man is gone!'

Daniel shared a meaningful glance with Lester. 'OK. Lester, you take the lead. Carry on up the stream and through the saddle. It is downhill from there. Get out of this weather, and wait for me at first light.'

'And if you don't catch us up?' asked Shadz.

'Run for all you are worth.'

'Right,' said Lester. 'Good hunting, then.' He turned and led the way out of sight.

Daniel patted Marcus, good hunting, indeed. He checked his rifle, moved the safety to 'off', and patted his knife. Aware that his quarry could not have gone far, he moved up to a useful vantage, hunkered down under his poncho, and waited. He knew that Marcus would spot anything that moved below them.

Below him in the pool, Anders was cold to the core, but he had trained in the depths of Finnish winters on the Russian border. Cold was his friend. He waited for a full ten minutes, then very slowly allowed the current to carry him into the shallows, using the turbulent water as cover. Making for the dark of the shadows, he was certain he was being hunted. As it happened he was lucky, ending up on the same side of the ravine as Daniel, hidden from observation by the rocky slope.

He stripped off, wrung as much water as he could from his clothing, and put it back on. The woollen layers quickly began to trap the escaping body heat. He did a series of quick squats to get the circulation going again, and then began to move upstream, very carefully, keeping to the darkest shadows and moving slowly and smoothly, so that if he did momentarily break cover the movement would be almost imperceptible.

Nothing. Daniel was now worried. Would the man go back toward the coast, or would he attempt to follow Shadz and his group returning overland? He knew what he would do, and moved off up the narrow valley, Marcus at his side. The balance had shifted in his enemy's favour.

After an hour or so of moving carefully up the watercourse, the stream had reduced to a trickle. A fickle eddy of the wind moved down in their faces, and Marcus growled quietly. Daniel patted his shoulder, and the big dog slipped into the lead. They were approaching the saddle — broken, irregular, and strewn with giant boulders that had rolled down from the peaks to the left and the right. An ideal ambush. Clambering over the rocks, Daniel knew that his rifle was of little use here. The other man would be upon him before he could react effectively.

Marcus however, was a different story, and Daniel decided it was time to apply some pressure. 'Speak up, Marcus.' The big dog roared fit to wake the dead.

But all it did was pinpoint their position for their opponent. Many years before, Anders had killed a giant timber wolf with his bare hands to prevent discovery, while on the wrong side of the Russian border. He respected, but was not at all afraid of, the big dog. He continued to circle around behind his quarry. *Just a little further, my friend.*

Daniel had let Marcus get a little ahead of him, and so Anders let the dog go by. Hidden in the dark shadow, confident that he was invisible, he could now clearly make out the man silhouetted in the moonlight. He allowed Daniel to cross in front of him, only metres away, and launched his attack from behind. In his hand was a wickedly pointed rock, heavy enough to crush his opponent's skull. He was in mid air when the .308 bullet entered his chest, and was clinically dead before he hit the rock at the end of his natural trajectory.

Daniel heard the thud behind him at the same time as the shot, and dived for cover. There was a deathly quiet, and Marcus appeared at his side. 'Nice shot,' Daniel called out.

'Lucky,' replied Lester, jumping down to join him. 'Bit close to be sporting, but he appeared to be about to rearrange your skull.'

Daniel got to his feet. 'Lucky that you were around, that I will give you. Thanks.'

Lester shrugged. 'He was beginning to get on my nerves. The others are hunkered down just on the other side. One or two weren't looking too good, so I called a halt. Should have a tent up and a brew on by now.'

Daniel's estimation of the man went up another couple of notches. 'I knew there was a reason why I gave you back your rifle.'

'Exactly.' Lester motioned towards the body. 'What about that?'

'Leave him where he fell. He deserves no better.'

The sun was well up and warm on their faces as they arrived at the place where Daniel had farewelled Dktfec. Daniel led Shadz and Lester up the low ridge, explaining to the latter that his party had been under surveillance as they prepared to cross the escarpment. When Shadz recounted how Daniel had got right into the camp, Lester was suitably embarrassed.

'Lucky for you, as it turned out,' said Daniel. 'That was how we knew where your party was headed, and about the rendezvous with the trawler.'

'Right,' replied Lester, begrudging him the point. 'Looks like they are still being careless.'

'They have no comms with the outside world?'

'Not as far as I am aware. We took the satellite phone with us.'

Daniel cast him a glance. 'Radio?'

'Too primitive for these guys.'

'Then we should be able to walk right into camp,' suggested Daniel. 'They will likely think that I am off the trawler.'

'A bold approach, but no reason why it shouldn't work.' Lester got to his feet and brushed the dust from his bush shirt. 'Shall we?'

Daniel got to his feet. 'Stay here with your men, Shadz. Three shots when it is safe to come in. Marcus will have to stay with you, for now.'

Shadz watched as they made their way down the hill and across to the camp. There was something not quite right, but he could not put his finger on it. Marcus rested comfortably at his side.

Daniel and Lester walked into the camp site as if they were meant to be there. The three vehicles had been organised to form part of the perimeter, and a large awning was slung between the knob thorn trees to provide some relief from the midday sun. There were a few dishes on the portable table, and a cloud of bush flies was making a meal of a piece of meat that was sitting on a tin plate.

It was the smell that Daniel picked up first, a smell that he would recognise anywhere. He looked at Lester and they both took their rifles off their shoulders. Daniel motioned for Lester to go to the right and outside the vehicle on that side, while he went the other way. They met at the centre of the middle SUV. Nothing.

Another whiff of putrefying flesh. Daniel allowed his eyes to follow the breeze. On the other side of the thicket there was movement. Black wings and bald heads. Vultures. Sweeping their sides for any threats, they moved around to what they already knew. As far as they could make out, there were two bodies. The hyenas had already been in and had their fill. The vultures were finishing the job before leaving the insects of the dust to tidy up.

'Leave them,' said Daniel quietly. 'I don't think we should announce our presence until we know what went on here.'

Lester nodded, taciturn as ever.

A good man, Daniel thought to himself. The sight and smell would have turned the gut of most men. He led the way back to the camp and they scanned the area for clues.

'Looks as if they were surprised,' observed Lester. 'Nothing disturbed.'

'But anything of value taken,' replied Daniel, looking at a series of empty boxes. He opened up the hood of the closest SUV. The diesel injector manifold was smashed beyond repair.

Lester asked the obvious question. 'Why didn't they take the vehicles?'

'No fuel where these guys come from.' Daniel thought for a moment, looking around. 'This could also be a message.'

'To?' asked Lester.

'You,' Daniel replied.

'Right. The sort of 'go away and stay away' message.'

'Correct.'

'Been at least a day,' Lester observed.

'One day too long. I would really love to know where they were headed from here.' Together they walked a big circle and it was not long before they picked up the inbound spoor, and a little later, the outbound spoor, these made heavy by the increased load the intruders were carrying. Their track took them directly east, towards the Bushmen's range. 'Not good.' Taking a calculated risk, Daniel fired three times. 'I hope we are not too late.'

It took Shadz and the other warriors just six minutes to arrive, but they were the longest six minutes of the day, by a good margin. Daniel met them just outside the camp, doing his best to curb his impatience.

'Quickly. Drop your kit in the vehicles; it should be safe enough there until we can get back for it. Just keep your weapons, and all the ammunition that you think you can carry. Then get back here.'

Daniel sat on his haunches, drawing in the sand, waiting. When the men were back, he quickly brought them up to date. 'The men who were left here are dead — left to the vultures, over there.' All the heads turned and followed where Daniel pointed.

'Who?' asked Shadz.

'Rebel guerrillas, from what I can tell.'

One of the other men leant forward. 'This far south?'

'Unusual, I know. But they are barefoot, at least forty or fifty strong, travelling light, and making themselves unwelcome.' Daniel shrugged. 'Right now, I can't think of another explanation.'

'They are tracking straight towards the Bushmen's camp,' observed Shadz.

'Yes, and they have at least a day's head start on us. But first things first. I want you all to be absolutely confident that you can fire your weapons effectively. These guys will be combat veterans — they have been fighting regular Army troops for a number of years.'

For the next thirty minutes Daniel and Shadz drilled and drilled the men until they were completely happy each could load, fire, and clear any stoppages in their weapons. Each man was then told to fire twenty precious rounds, five rounds single shot, five double-taps, and a final automatic burst — just to show them how inaccurate it was.

Their confidence boosted, they gathered around, full of fight. 'OK,' said Daniel. 'Here is the plan. We run like we have never run before. Dktfec and his tribe depend on us to run the enemy down before they reach his hearth. Shadz, I want your two best men as scouts. Marcus will run ahead — he will warn us when we get close. When he barks fall back on me, immediately. Likely as not we will have a fight on our hands.'

Daniel turned to the hunter. 'Lester, I am afraid that we will quickly leave you behind.'

Lester held up his hand. 'I will follow you at my best pace. You will not be that far ahead of me when you run into trouble.'

'Good man.' Daniel looked around the men in front of him. 'We are well outnumbered, but they march on our homes. By the setting of the sun two days hence, you will all have taken a life.

Make sure that you hold yours close.' The warriors turned to face each other and Shadz stepped up to them. He uttered the ancient call to arms.

His men embraced the challenge, roaring their response to the bush around them, causing the vultures from the carrion behind the vehicles to rise into the air, in a cacophony of protest. Shadz picked up the drama of the picture. 'The vultures will feast upon the bones of your enemies.' The tight skins on the shields thundered under the hammering of hands. Shadz turned to Daniel. 'Lead us to our enemies, Daniel of the Tall Trees.'

Without another word, Daniel turned and led the way out into the heat of the day at a steadily building trot. Shadz detailed off the two strongest to run ahead as scouts, as Marcus stretched out ahead at an easy lope that he could keep up for days on end. They gradually built the cadence until they were covering ground at pace, and each man slipped into a carefully trained zone of endurance that insulated them, to a certain extent, from the pain and hammering of limbs on the tortured earth.

Sensibly, Lester settled into a quiet jog.

CHAPTER 13

They ran, and they ran, as their ancestors had run from battlefront to battlefront to protect the borders of their homeland from multiple enemies. Today, there were just two: exhaustion, and the rebel troops well ahead of them. Daniel ran them to the very edge of the first, in search of the second.

When the light ran out, they rested while they waited for the moon to light their way. Lester caught them up just as they were about to move off, but was at the end of his endurance. They left him, and one of the warriors who was nursing a strained knee, to follow as best they could. In the moonlight, Daniel pulled the scouts in and had them running in an extended line, with Marcus leading the way. It was much easier in the cool of the evening, and mile by mile they closed the distance between themselves and their quarry. But they were also running out of time and territory, as Daniel began to recognise the familiar landmarks that indicated they were now inside Dktfec's home range. His heart sank as they crested a small rise. There were fires in the basin a few miles ahead.

Forcing his emotional response deep within him, he brought the warriors in. 'You have run like the cheetah. Now you must hunt like the leopard. We must keep surprise on our side.' He looked around, meeting the eye of every man. 'Check your weapons again.'

They did so. 'OK. A hunting line on me as the pivot.' They moved off into the first light of the new day.

Marcus walked beside Daniel, and the man watched every cue and nuance of his motion. When Marcus stopped, they all stopped. When he went forward, they all went forward. Yard by yard they covered the ground between themselves and the bright-burning fires still visible through the low scrub.

It was quiet. Too quiet.

Soon they could hear the crackling, as the dry timbers protested against the flames that devoured them. Then they stood in the middle of catastrophe. In the early morning light that still allowed the flames to throw wickedly dancing shadows against the edges of the clearing, they picked their way through the horribly disfigured bodies of the Bushman tribe, lying where they had fallen, surprised in the middle of their rest.

One by one, Daniel moved from corpse to corpse, recognising the faces of the little people that he loved.

Shadz came over, quietly. 'This is only a portion of the tribe. Could some have escaped?'

They stood in the clearing in the middle of the remains of the camp and assessed the carnage. Daniel broke the silence, a sense of hope in his voice. 'You are right. I should have seen it. Most of these are the elderly or the very young.'

'Did the others flee, or were they somewhere else when the village was attacked?' asked Shadz. Daniel called Marcus and they worked their way around the site. On the far side, Marcus became interested, and the men could see a faint spoor in the dust.

'Just a small party,' observed Daniel. 'Perhaps they left the rest of the tribe somewhere safe and came to investigate.'

Shadz stood up and drew a mental map of the terrain. 'But these go in the wrong direction — towards the village of Tshakai.'

They hurried back to the camp, where the others were arranging the bodies on a makeshift funeral pyre. Desperate to continue the chase, no-one would contemplate leaving their little friends to the carrion eaters of the bush. But every man now knew exactly where the rebel force was headed, at speed — their village.

Just as they set a torch to the dry timbers, Marcus barked from a little outside of the ruined camp. Daniel and Shadz looked at each other. 'Stay here,' said Daniel. 'Get your men ready to move out. I will see what he has found.'

Following the sound of the dog's gentle whining, he moved into the low scrub that surrounded the clearing. Around the back of a termite mound, Marcus was worrying the edge of a big patch of thorn bush. 'What is it fella?'

Marcus would not be distracted, so Daniel got down on his hands and knees to peer underneath the thick matting of spines. There was just enough light to make out two brown shapes tucked away as far out of reach as they could get.

'Little ones, do you not remember the big dog that you would play with around your father's hearth? Do you not remember Daniel of the Tall Trees who would make play things for you?' From inside the thicket he could just make out a gentle whimper.

'We remember. Have the bad men gone?'

'Yes, little ones,' Daniel sighed. 'They have. It is safe to come out now.' Moments later the two children were nestled in his arms, trembling. Marcus licked them, tenderly.

With trembling lips, the older of the two spoke, still traumatised. 'We watching them kill everyone. I took sister and we ran hid in our play place, like father taught us.' Daniel wondered at the foresight of their parents, that such a refuge was prepared so close at hand.

'You did well, little warrior.'

'I could not save mother.'

'But you did save your sister. Come, we must be leaving here. It is not safe.' Daniel slung his rifle over his shoulder. 'We have a long way to walk.'

But Daniel now had a problem. He was desperate to overtake the rebel force, but was slowed by his new charges. Shadz had the solution.

'Two of my men are lame, Daniel. We could leave them to follow us with the children.'

Reluctantly, Daniel agreed, and turned to the boy at his side. 'I need to chase the bad men, and prevent them hurting anyone else.'

The little head nodded, wisely. 'You will pay back?'

'Yes. I will pay back,' Daniel replied grimly.

The boy stood as tall as he possibly could. 'Then fly with the feet of the little people, Daniel of the Tall Trees.'

He recognised the words. The last time he had heard those were from Dktfec — it was his personal blessing. Daniel bent down and drew a new circle in the dust, with three crosses inside, a sun and a moon. The little boy led his sister forward until they stood inside it. He then held out a clenched fist, as he had watched his elders do many times. Daniel touched his knuckles with his own, and turned away to lead his depleted force out into the early morning heat.

Just four of them left. Daniel, Shadz, and two ragged and weary warriors. And Marcus. Knowing that they had to keep something in reserve for the fight, they moved a little slower, allowing their bodies to recover a little.

'Do you think that Dktfec got your message back to Tshakai?' asked Shadz.

'I am sure that he would have,' Daniel replied.

'Then there is a good chance that the valley will be well defended.'

'Yes. But it is a huge perimeter to cover,' worried Daniel. 'Our advantage is that we are tracking them. At least we know where they have been.'

'And they are running a straight line to the covered saddle,' observed one of the other warriors.

Daniel slowed a fraction. 'They know exactly where they are headed.' He looked over to Shadz. 'Their presence down here is no coincidence.'

'You mean they might be connected with the men who attempted to steal Pieter's lands?'

'We will see, my friend. We will see.' Daniel picked up the pace again. He knew that they were probably not covering the ground much faster than those that they pursued, and on a straight run there was no opportunity to use their knowledge of the terrain to any advantage.

They were about half way to the outer defences of the valley when the little ghosts of the high veldt appeared among them.

Running out ahead of the party, Marcus was the first to notice that he had company as Dktfec of the whispering grass gracefully bounded over his shoulder and effortlessly took up station alongside him. Daniel was the next to notice their arrival as he caught the briefest glimpse of a fleeting brown shape slip and bound through the long grass just at the periphery of his vision.

Shadz then called out from out on the other flank just as the bush seemed to come alive with surreal racing figures, that seemed to float across the ground without effort. Daniel knew it was the legendary hunting run of the ancient Bushmen, and challenged the others to renewed efforts as Dktfec momentarily dropped back to give him the hunter's salute, and then moved ahead to join Marcus. There was no happiness in his greeting, and every touch of little feet with the ground cried out for vengeance.

It was late on the same afternoon when Tshakai's picket was overrun. The two men were on the far Western flank of the village's defensive line, and only had time for a couple of hurried shots before they died. But it gave the village vital warning.

The buffalo horn sounded the alarm, and the women and children hurried inside the protective walls. Tshakai immediately sent two sections of his men out to reinforce his forward lines, holding the other two back as a reserve. It was not long before the first runner arrived back, bloodied and exhausted. 'Many men with rifles and machetes. They have broken through the first line and the second line is under much pressure.' It was time to deploy his reserve, and the old warrior turned and looked at his village, tears in his eyes, before leading his men out to the cadence of the ancient battle hymns.

They followed the directions given by the runner. The scene on the battleground only a mile northwest of the village was mayhem. The rebels had formed a rough wedge and charged the middle of the defensive line, machetes swinging. The first section had given at the middle and then collapsed inward in an attempt to surround the enemy, who had been stopped by the stout line of the second section. It was close quarters, hand to hand fighting, machete on shields and spears — the two forces now approximately equal.

Without a pause, Tshakai led his men into the thick of the fighting, his war-club swinging in great soaring arcs.

The enemy saw the danger, and turned to face the new pressure. One or two looked around for a way of escape, but the impi were well trained and flowed around the flanks and rear as the fresh warriors poured into the fray, eager to avenge their fallen brothers. Their blood was up and there was no mercy in their eyes.

There was one thing that Tshakai had not foreseen, however. The enemy had split into two groups before the opening engagement, and the second group, equal in strength, had moved around the flank, using the terrain and low scrub to stay just out of sight. As soon as Tshakai's reserve section was fully committed to the battle, the second rebel group attacked from behind. Tshakai was forced to pivot his formation to face the new threat, allowing the enemy to renew the pressure on two fronts. The balance dramatically shifted in the rebel forces' favour.

The sounds of battle carried out across the hills, and Daniel picked up their pace, fanning out into the loose hunting formation that came as second nature, each providing cover for the other. Over the low familiar saddle, and then down through the thinning bush, they raced. When they broke into the open, it was obvious that Tshakai and his men were in imminent danger of succumbing to the enormous pressure from both sides of their formation, and without hesitation Shadz and the two remaining warriors charged into the fray. Daniel, however, rushed across to a low rise that overlooked the fight, and began to coldly and methodically pick off the rebel leaders with his rifle. Marcus stayed to watch his back.

But it was the Bushmen who turned the tide of the battle. The little warriors slipped into the ranks of the rebels from behind, appearing to lack form or substance, razor sharp blades slashing and stabbing, moving in and out of the melee with apparent impunity while uttering an eerie howl.

The rebels thought they were being attacked by spirits, and panicked. Those that were able tried to flee, but did not get very far before being run down by the Impala warriors.

As suddenly as it had started, it was done. There were no enemy left standing, or willing to fight. Already the vultures were circling overhead. Daniel and Shadz joined the remnant of the impi moving across the clearing, sorting through the wreckage of bodies. Blood and water were mixing and running down into the small stream that drained the field. Shields and weapons lay where they had fallen.

Daniel had seen it before. The horror setting in after the rush of the battle had subsided, with the survivors confronted by the carnage wrought on their fellow men — friend and foe alike. Many already dealing with guilt to have survived, while friends died to their left, and their right. Had they done as much as they could? Why were they alive and their sister's husband, or their brother, or father, dead?

Something much deeper was wrong, however, and Daniel had a very bad feeling as he walked over to where a group were preparing a litter for one of the fallen. They moved aside to allow him through.

His heart fell — lying very still on a litter made of shields already lashed together with rawhide was Tshakai the Veteran, Hero of the Impala. One of his captains was leaning over him, praying softly, and looked up as he sensed Daniel's presence.

There were tears in the young man's eyes, but they were tears of awe and pride. 'He turned the battle, leading the reserve into the thick of the fighting. He saw us to our victory, but then his heart —'

'He has died a hero,' interrupted Daniel. 'As he lived. It is fitting.' Daniel turned to Shadz through the driving rain, and spoke quietly to his friend. 'My brother, I believe that you are now the senior one here. I know that of all men your grief will be long and deep, but the impi need your leadership and direction. You must take over here before the trauma overwhelms them.'

Shadz looked down at prone form of his spiritual and tribal leader and mentor for a moment, before lifting his face to the heavens, allowing the rain to cleanse his spirit. He then turned and mustered the impi into line in the gathering dark. 'You are the warriors of Tshakai the Magnificent. Who are you?'

At first the response was muted and lacking commitment.

Shadz danced down the line and roared in their faces. 'You are the warriors of Tshakai the Magnificent. Who are you?' The second reply was better. Shadz stepped back and smacked his spear hard on his blood-spattered shield. 'You are the warriors of Tshakai the Magnificent.' He paused, looking down the line. 'Who are you?'

'We are the warriors,' came back the reply, echoing off the hills around them, accompanied by a bang from the many shields that was so perfectly timed it sounded as one.

Shadz pranced in front of his men, spear held high above his head. 'Yes you are. Yes you are!' He posted a picket to protect the dead from carrion eaters, and led the way back to the village, supporting the wounded, carrying Tshakai the Fallen between them. Daniel and Marcus gathered the Bushmen, still with the haze of battle lust in their eyes, and followed the procession.

The community was awash with grief. Husbands, fathers, brothers: there was no family that had not paid a very dear price for their safety. That was evident in the steady procession of carts that went in and out of the gate, in the driving rain. Out to collect the battle's grim harvest, in to confirm the unthinkable.

With Daniel's support and guidance, Shadz had quietly, but firmly, organised the resources of the village to deal with the aftermath of the catastrophe. A runner had been sent down the road, carrying the tragic news to the capital. Preparations were in place to convey Tshakai's body to town for a funeral fitting to his rank and status, while a row of dead warriors was growing in the centre of the village square, attended by mourning family members. They would be sent into the heavens together, as they fought and died, before the dawn. The rain was making that difficult, and an awning was being built to protect the funeral pyre until it became established. There would be no sleep for the villagers tonight.

Daniel went to check on the rebels that had been taken prisoner — just two survivors from a force that he now assessed as somewhere close to sixty. 'All secure?'

'Yes,' answered the two warriors on duty outside the cage, which would normally hold the town goats during the night.

'Have they had anything to say for themselves?'

'Nothing.'

Daniel decided that he had no stomach for further mystery that night, and returned to the village square. Shadz was doing well, keeping the momentum going against the weather and the raw emotions of the night. Daniel went across and told him so.

'Thank you big brother. But I would be lost without your steady hand.'

Daniel shook his head, sad to the core of his being. 'Much of this is my doing.'

'What do you mean?'

'I set in train the events that led to this.' Daniel swept a tired arm over the bodies that were still gathering in front of them.

'It was to be, big brother. It was to be,' reassured Shadz.

'Maybe.' Daniel wondered at the quality of a faith that would lead to that level of trust. He looked around the square. 'Where are the Bushmen?'

'Around the side of Tshakai's lodge. They could not be persuaded to occupy one of the vacant lodges,' grinned Shadz. 'But we have offered them food, and a few blankets.' He looked around at the weeping village. 'We owe them a great deal — without them, who knows how this would have ended?' Daniel placed a brother's hand on the big man's shoulder, and then turned to seek out Dktfec.

The Bushmen were sitting together under a shelter normally used for cooking, working quietly on cleaning and then restoring the razor-sharp edges of their prized weapons. It was a sombre moment — a long time in the stories of the tribe since a group of hunters like them had sat down to cleanse themselves of the blood of their enemies. Marcus sat with Dktfec, seeming to understand their trauma.

Seeing Daniel, Dktfec placed his weapons to one side carefully and stepped out into the rain to greet him. Daniel was shocked at the appearance of his little brother — his normally plump and cheery face was drawn and haggard.

'The south wind has brought the chill of the plains,' Dktfec offered formally, but could not complete the greeting.

Daniel replied. 'The north wind will soon bring the rains to refresh the earth.'

'But the happy feet of the little people will not dance before the stars this season.' The tears streamed down the cheeks of the little man.

'There will be many stories to tell of the bravery of Dktfec of the whispering grass, of how he, and his hunting party, saved the village of Tshakai the Magnificent.'

Dktfec sat on his haunches. 'But there are no women, or little ones, to hear of such stories. For what purpose might they be told?'

Daniel knelt on one knee. 'Not all of the heritage of the tribe has been lost? There were some that survived the raid on your village?'

'Not many — maybe not enough to ensure that our stories will continue.'

Marcus gave a little bark and got to his feet, padding off around the corner. He returned moments later with the two little children that had survived the attack on their village, just arrived after the long walk.

The effect on the little warriors was profound. They gathered around the little ones in a frenzy of excitement, everyone talking at once. Dktfec looked up at Daniel, almost beside himself with joy. 'This is a gift ... a gift to surpass all gifts. My brother has returned to us our stories. We will not forget his place around our campfires for many generations.'

The glow on the Eastern horizon indicated that it was time for the funeral ceremony to begin at the top of the valley of the Impala. Daniel joined Shadz, and the other villagers, gathered around the huge pyre that was now waiting for the torch.

A little earlier the Bushmen had made their farewells, anxious to return to what remained of their families. Daniel had, however, persuaded them to leave the children in the relative safety of the Impala community for a time, at least until they knew there were no other marauding rebel groups crossing their territory. The little ones were soon sound asleep in the corner of Tshakai's porch, cuddled in close to Marcus, who was as protective of them as a mother lion of her cubs.

A short distance off to Daniel's right, a lone voice began with the opening verse of the tribal song of ascents, clear and pure. They listened in rapt silence as the ancient song swelled and soared around the inside of the walls that surrounded them, and then escaped heavenward. Next the chorus was picked up by the surviving warriors, rich and pure. Then the women picked up the theme, and the dance began. Slowly at first but gaining purpose and momentum, until it seemed that the walls would not contain it.

Daniel had never experienced anything like it. He was very much a spectator until a group of youths took him by both hands to lead him into the centre of the twisting and turning lines. The entire gathering became a unified entity that seemed to draw energy from some primal source, as the celebration and commemoration of so many lives, and such sacrifice, rose to a crescendo.

Abruptly there was total silence. After a moment of suspense, the sacred horn sounded from the hill behind them, and torches were passed forward through the crowd to the line of warriors. As the dead had gone in battle, it was their privilege and responsibility to light the funeral pyre. For a few electric minutes there was complete and perfect silence, then, as the first ray of sunlight fired across the valley and touched the far hills with its promise of a new day, the sacred fire was lit. The hymns began again, surrounding and supporting the journey into the heavens.

Daniel knew that the fire would be tended carefully until there were only ashes remaining, ushering in three days of mourning. But that would have to take place at the same time they took Tshakai home.

CHAPTER 14

By midday the procession was assembled. An honour guard of Tshakai the Fallen's Impi went ahead of the simple cart that bore him on his last journey. The balance of the warriors followed, including Daniel and Marcus. The big dog had been very reluctant to leave the two Bushman children, who would be brought through to the Impala capital when they were more rested. Many of the villagers joined in behind them. Together they sang the tribal hymns to lighten their way.

About an hour out of town, they were met by the cavalry of the Royal Battalion, in full regalia, led by Queen Ngashi herself. It was a slight breach of protocol, but she would have it no other way. They swung around to lead the way into the capital, as the sun broke through the overcast for the first time that day.

Entering the gates, the entire town was silently lined up on either side of the wide avenue. The hymns died, and the rest of the journey was completed in virtual silence, as the Impala dealt with the enormity of their loss. A wave of grief swept across the town that would build towards the release of the night-long celebration, and farewell.

On arrival in the town square the crowds dispersed, while the bearers carried the body of Tshakai into the great hall of the Impala Council. A steady procession of mourners passed by and threw small branches of the kiaat tree onto his corpse as a sign of respect.

Queen Ngashi took the opportunity of the break in proceedings to send for Daniel and Shadz. Given the situation, she opted to receive their report in her lodge rather than the formality of the offices in the centre of town. Included were key members of the council, including Swabi.

The two men had stopped in at the cottage to wash and change, so were running a little late by the time that they were let through the gate into the compound. The other council members met them halfway across the lawn, before stepping aside to allow them to climb the steps to where Ngashi and Swabi waited. Marcus was already asleep in one corner of the royal porch.

Both men were on the edge of exhaustion. 'Welcome back Daniel, Shadz,' said Ngashi as they came forward for her embrace. 'You both look like you could do with some food and rest.'

They both just smiled and Daniel moved across to where Swabi was waiting, trying to control her emotions. 'You look terrible!' she said quietly as they kissed formally on the cheek.

'Just need to rest for a day or so.' Daniel tasted the salt of her tears, reading pain in the depths of her eyes.

'I missed you, my friend,' Swabi whispered.

'It is good to be home, Swabi. Thank you.'

Daniel took the seat that was offered, and began his story, leaving out a few details that he didn't consider important, but making sure that he did justice to Shadz's contribution. His audience only interjected to clarify a couple of issues that were not particularly clear, until he got to the rebel guerrillas.

'Extraordinary,' interjected Ngashi. 'The guerrilla forces have never come this far south. There is no reason for them to do so.'

'They seemed to be hell-bent on destruction,' added one of the council members.

Daniel was almost overcome with emotion as he recounted the trauma of what they found at Dktfec's camp. For a while there was silence as each one present processed the information.

Then, as if ordained, one of the guards came down the path and informed them that there were some people to see Daniel, if they might be received, or should they be told to wait. With a glance at Ngashi, Daniel got to his feet and made his way to the gate, not sure who to expect. Outside he found Lester, along with the two warriors who had been left behind at Dktfec's camp, and the Bushmen children.

The children were completely overawed by the town, the crowds and strange buildings. Daniel knew that, in other circumstances, he would have spent some time with them out in Tshakai's village, before bringing them into the claustrophobic environment of the capital. He gave a whistle for Marcus, and moments later the big dog appeared through the gate.

'Here is your friend, little ones.' They immediately wrapped themselves around the delighted animal. Daniel shook Lester's hand. 'The little cottage you passed just back around the corner?'

'Yes.'

'Make yourself at home. I will be back there as soon as I can.'

'Thanks. I could do with a good brew.'

Daniel nodded. 'I will take the children with me. We won't be long.' He turned and led Marcus back to the porch, the two children still attached to the shaggy ruff around his neck.

Swabi was the first to react, and came down the steps to meet them. Ngashi stood up. 'Who do we have here?'

'Allow me to introduce the children of the whispering grass. They are almost certainly the only children of the tribe to survive the massacre.'

'They are truly beautiful,' whispered Swabi through her tears, bending down. The little girl allowed herself to be lifted up into Swabi's arms. Her brother was far too proud for that, and took Daniels hand, standing as tall as he could. He did not know what was being said in this strange language that had no clicks to separate out the words. But it did seem a rather important occasion, so it was up to him to represent the tribe with dignity. Daniel introduced Queen Ngashi in his own tongue and he did his best to find a reply that fitted the honour, just a little amplified by Daniel in the translation.

Ngashi laughed and clapped at the reply, but there were tears in her eyes. She looked at Daniel with the obvious question in her eyes.

'I have a son, and a daughter, for now' Daniel replied simply.

'So you do, Daniel of the Tall Trees. So you do.'

'Shadz could continue with the report, if you would excuse me?'

'By all means. Take Marcus with you. I will see you at the funeral celebrations this-evening.'

'Of course.' Daniel turned to go, but the little girl would not be parted from Swabi.

'I guess I am coming too,' she replied with a smile, and led the way out of the gate.

It only took Daniel, Swabi, and Marcus a few minutes to walk back to the cottage with the little Bushman children. The two warriors had already slipped away to join the survivors of Tshakai's Impi, and catch up with all the action that they had missed. Lester was resting on the porch, not really comfortable with making himself welcome. Daniel introduced him to Swabi, and then scolded him for his reluctance to accept their hospitality.

'I was much more comfortable having a quiet nap on your porch,' Lester replied. 'The view is breathtaking. I had heard stories of this place, but always dismissed them as romantic exaggerations.'

Daniel smiled. 'All real, I am happy to report.' He led them inside, but the children were reluctant to follow. Daniel knelt down, switching effortlessly to their tongue. 'This is my hut. It is a little bigger that you are used to, but I am sure that we can find a corner where you will feel safe, with Marcus to look after you?'

His little charges looked at each other and then nodded, shyly, and followed Marcus inside. Five minutes later they were sound asleep in a shady corner of the lounge, wrapped around the big dog.

Swabi smiled, and touched Daniel's arm. 'Good recipe.'

'One step at a time. It will take them some time to adjust. They have been wrenched out of their culture, and witnessed things that would haunt most adults for a long time.'

Swabi turned away from the restful scene. 'I am here, any time they need me, Daniel.'

'Thank—'

'Daniel, it looks like you have visitors,' interrupted Lester, his head through the doorway. Daniel made it to the doorway just in time to see three military vehicles pulling up on the road outside the fence. For a moment he was apprehensive, and then Peter stepped out of the lead SUV.

'Peter! What timing, as usual.' Daniel trotted across the lawn and vaulted over the low fence, wrapping his oldest friend in a huge embrace.

'Daniel. Great to see you.' Peter stepped back and looked his friend up and down, immediately noting how much weight Daniel had lost. 'I was expecting that you would still be over on the coast?'

'A very long story,' Daniel replied. 'But first things first. Shake off the dust, and come and get a brew. Your team can make themselves at home in the shade.' He pointed to the area under the bushwillow trees.

Lester retreated to the cool of the rear of the cottage. Swabi excused herself, and went to check with Ngashi. Daniel and Peter spent the rest of the afternoon sprawled on the porch catching up, Daniel with events that Peter was aware of, and vice versa. The resulting picture was not encouraging.

'This is pretty complex, particularly when you throw in the guerrillas operating this far south.'

Daniel nodded. 'We have two prisoners. I haven't had a chance to question them yet. Not sure how much they will know, anyway.'

'Probably not much. I need to get through to Pat and find out what is going on in Cape Town.' Peter stood up. 'Daniel, I am really sorry about Elizabeth.'

Daniel got up, looking at his watch. 'Thanks. I need to tell Ngashi and Swabi. They will be pretty upset.'

Peter checked him by placing his hand on Daniel's shoulder. 'I have other news, Daniel, tragic news. Captain Veork was killed in action few days ago. I found out just as I was leaving base.'

Daniel did not know what to say. 'Swabi will be devastated.'

'Yes. He was a fine young officer. There is no easy way to break the news.'

'Let me tell her, Peter?'

'If you think that would be best.'

'Who knows what is best with these things, but somehow I think I should.' Daniel climbed stiffly down the steps and headed out of the gate, suddenly mortally tired.

He found Swabi with Ngashi. They were still trying to come to terms with the shock attack on Tshakai's village.

Ngashi scolded him. 'Daniel. Don't you ever rest?'

Daniel paused at the bottom of the steps, suddenly unsure of how to break the news. The women came down to meet him on the lawn in front of the porch. 'What is it?' asked Ngashi, sensing his struggle.

'Peter has arrived, with some news you should be aware of sooner rather than later.'

Ngashi took a deep breath. 'Yes?'

Daniel decided to deal with perhaps the lesser of the two shocks, first. 'Elizabeth has been abducted from the hotel in Cape Town.' He held up his hand to forestall the question. 'As far as we know she is OK.'

'But who would —?'

'We know very little,' interrupted Daniel. 'Peter is going to try and get through to Pat on the radio for an update. In fact, when I think about it, I can do one better. I have the satellite phone we picked up over on the coast.' The two women looked at each other, fighting the natural tendency of their minds to jump to horrible conclusions.

Daniel did his best to reassure them. 'Paul and Pat will be doing everything possible to get her back safely.'

'She will be alright, won't she?' Ngashi's hand went out to Daniel. He nodded, trying to look more convinced than he felt.

'Of course she will,' said Swabi with a confidence that she didn't really feel, putting her arms around the other two.

Daniel waited for a moment for the initial crisis to pass. 'Swabi, Peter had another message that I have to pass on.' He looked very uncomfortable.

'What it is, Daniel?' Swabi asked, taking a pace away from him, raw fear already filling her throat with bile.

'I don't know how—'

'No, don't.' Her face pleaded with him as she backed away across the lawn, her hands travelling to her face. 'No!' But she read the answer on his face as surely as if it were written in the clouds behind him, and she turned away to try and shield her soul from the body blow.

Daniel went to follow her, but Ngashi held him back. 'It is Roos?'

Daniel pushed his hands through his hair. 'He was killed in action a few days back, just before Peter left base to come out here.'

'Are they sure?'

'Yes. It is an official report. There will be no mistake.'

'Dear Lord, have we not had enough tragedy for one day?' She looked up at Daniel and then gave him a sisterly hug. 'I will look after Swabi, there is nothing more that you can do, for now.' Then, sensing the man's need for action, she gave him a job to do. 'Go and get that satellite phone working. We desperately need to know what the situation is in Cape Town.'

Arriving back at the cottage, Daniel found the two little children playing with Marcus, the three of them taking turns to chase a couple of sticks. It was a happy little pantomime, and for a few moments he leant against a big willow in the shade from the afternoon sun, and just watched. Peter was just across the road organising his camp, and compiling his initial report back to the command centre. Lester was doing something that he was apparently quite good at — sound asleep in the dappled shade of the huge bougainvillea that grew over the porch. Shadz was nowhere to be seen, probably across with his impi getting ready for the funeral to be held that evening.

Ambassador Ngassi and his wife came around the corner. Spotting Daniel, they joined him in the shade.

'Ambassador, Sister, great to see you,' said Daniel. They embraced warmly.

'It seems yet again we owe you a debt.' The Ambassador held up his hand to prevent any interruption. 'Without your intervention, we could well be facing a much more serious crisis.'

'Although, as you know Ngassi, I still feel that I am largely responsible.'

'I disagree. The diamonds were inevitably going to bring their particular breed of trouble. Just as they have everywhere else on the continent.'

'Perhaps,' allowed Daniel, without any real commitment.

The Ambassador's wife gave her husband an impatient nudge. 'Anyway, that is not why we are here.' He smiled at the lovely middle-aged lady beside him, as beautiful as the day they were married. 'Mguni was concerned about the little children, and wondered if we could help out in any way. As you know, I can get my tongue around just a little of their language.'

Daniel turned back to the happy scene in the garden. 'That is a very generous offer.' He paused to gather his thoughts. 'I consider them to be my children, at least until they are able to return to the high plains. The fact of the matter is, however, that I know very little about raising little ones.' Daniel bent down and picked up the stick that his right foot had been playing with.

'It is no small task,' acknowledged the Ambassador. 'Daniel, we count you as family. We owe you our lives. It would be our joy to bring these precious children into our home, for as long as they might need to stay. We are well able to care for them.'

Daniel sought the balance of the stick in his hand, and then tossed it in the air. 'Then you should come and meet them.' He chuckled. 'They are more attached to Marcus than anyone else, right now.'

Daniel marvelled at how pragmatic and adaptable children are in the face of catastrophe. After just a few minutes of play, the Ambassador and his wife walked off down the road with the two little ones either side of Marcus. Daniel was actually a little hurt, expecting just a little more drama.

He went looking for the satellite phone, and it dawned on him that, of course, it was locked in the sabotaged vehicles, three days march back across the High Veldt. He suddenly realised just how tired he was, and decided that he should follow Lester's example.

Peter finished compiling his report, and then left it with the radio operator to see if they could establish a reliable link with the communications centre hundreds of miles to the east.

It was good to be out in the bush again, where his heart was. The seemingly endless days of staff work in the headquarters were slowly grinding away what remained of his enthusiasm for Army life. He longed to be back in the saddle, and leading a company of men out on their survey and reconnaissance duties across the vast South African hinterland. That had come to an abrupt end after he had run square into the politics that surrounded this valley and its people.

Major Peter Hogan had barely survived a difficult investigation into the circumstances surrounding his intervention in a joint operation between the Police, and officers of the Native Commission. That might have saved the Impala, but it resulted in the death of the local Commissioner. He had also contributed to the then-Sergeant Daniel Rutter's continued absence from duty. One day he would find out who was behind it all, and why.

The radio operator called from the back of the communications vehicle. 'Just gone through, and been receipted, Major.'

'Well done, Corporal. Thank you.' Little to do now but get some rest, before the funeral of the old warrior.

As the last of the light of day left the valley of the Impala, the funeral celebrations for Tshakai the Fallen began in earnest. The eldest son, Shadz had the principal role in the night-long ceremony. Supported by two specifically chosen members of Tshakai's Impi, he moved across town and uphill to the natural amphitheatre that was the focus of the valley. Most of the local people were already there. Thunderheads over the distant ranges flashed and rumbled in the night.

A hush fell over the assembly as the three men paused in respect of their elders at the edge of the gathering. Then from across the other side an elderly woman stepped forward into the last shaft of sunlight, lifted glistening eyes to the western sky, and sang the first soaring cadence of the royal song of ascents. The tone was so pure that it appeared to gain its source from the very heavens that framed her, as she raised her hands in rapture. Next every female voice joined her in exquisite melody — the cadence soaring for the required seven questions of the heavens — before the male voices rose to the challenge with the answering phrases of praise, in rich and cascading harmonies.

With this opening scene complete, Shadz followed his escort up to where Queen Ngashi and her court were assembled. At a respectful distance from the group of elders, he paused with eyes downcast. The silence was electric. Ambassador Ngassi came forward, clothed in the simple rags of mourning. 'My son, your loss is our loss, your pain is our pain,' he rumbled. His wife responded softly from beside him. 'Your hope is our hope; your joy is our joy.'

'My life is your life, Imbabwe,' Shadz responded, and they embraced, while below them the little valley filled with the mellow and subtle tones of the tribal requiem, as the bearers brought up Tshakai's corpse to his final rest.

The simple stretcher was held aloft by those who had fought alongside the great warrior. They moved slowly through the crowd, until finally arriving alongside the waiting pyre. The stretcher settled easily onto the waiting supports. Shadz was joined by the council as they moved down from their vantage to pay their last respects, reaching out to grasp outstretched hands, or pausing to embrace someone special.

The funeral pyre was arranged at the top of a small earthen mound inside the focal point of the amphitheatre. The children who had gathered in close now moved back in respect of their elders, their feet kicking up the dust and mixed grains that had been placed earlier in the day. They knew that the dust represented the substance to which we must all return, while the grains represented new life and hope. Much later in the ceremony they would sprinkle the precious water that would unite the ashes, dust, and the grain again in life, as the first light of dawn illuminated the eastern sky.

Flanked by his escorts, Shadz moved across the open ground to place on the stretcher the bloodied shield and war club that Tshakai had carried into his last battle. He was followed by a long line of mourners. Next, as the torches flared and the battle pennants of the Impi and the Royal Regiment danced in the evening breeze, the speeches of record began. The old and young, great and small, stood before the pyre and declared the merits and achievements of Tshakai of the Veterans, Great of the Great, Hero of the Impala. Each testament brought a fresh revelation, or confirmed an earlier. Many included Shadz as the wisdom of the ancients had established, so as to reinforce the informal and formal fabric of the tribal lineage.

The final testament was that of Ambassador Ngassi. Ngassi began with the formal greetings, and acknowledgement, and then rehearsed the life and history of one of Africa's great men. His words were reinforced with murmurs of agreement and affirmation, before he finally took his place alongside his Queen at the edge of the funeral mound.

As they withdrew, from one corner of the crowd the drums began to pulse and dance as only they can in Africa. From the other corner the dancers appeared — first the warriors, tall, and handsome. Then the women, beautifully adorned. They rehearsed the tribal myths and stories, many adapted for this occasion to reflect the impact that Tshakai had had on their individual and collective lives, understanding that it was important for a full and accurate record to be established, before the arrival of the dawn.

Through the deepest part of the night the majority of those attending slipped away to a few hours of rest, in order to be fully prepared for the climax of the ceremony and the celebration breakfast. They left the continuation of the watch in the hands of a small cadre of warriors.

The town was woken by the drums calling the assembly from its rest. Moving through the streets and up towards the mound each voice joined in a simple unison five-tone chant.

Arriving solemnly before Tshakai's final resting place, Shadz took a torch of pitch, and lit it from the brazier to one side of the mound, that had been providing light for the vigil of the night watchmen. As he lifted it high above his shoulder the valley was hushed, waiting for confirmation from the hilltop of the arrival of dawn's first light.

It was only a matter of moments before a shout rang across the valley from the nearest ridge. It was picked up by those nearest and rippled around the crowd rank upon rank, file upon file, swelling in volume and intensity as it circled the valley, descending with each circuit until it finally cascaded to where the official party stood, slightly to one side and in front of the other elders and guests. On its arrival, Shadz moved forward a couple of paces and touched the flame to the dry tinder at the base of the pyre. The flames quickly took hold and enveloped the shrouded corpse just as the first sunlight of the new day touched the tops of the mountains behind them.

The pyre was arranged to collapse inward. As it did so a shower of sparks roared into the sky. The little pieces of fire were caught in the rotating updraft of a huge thunderhead that had formed overhead, that flashed and roared its own tribute.

'Truly my father was a great warrior, and a great man,' remarked Shadz, in awe of the display.

'Yes, he was Shadz,' Daniel agreed. 'But he leaves that greatness in very good hands.' The two men embraced as the celebration of the life, and release, of Tshakai the Fallen began in earnest around them.

PART 2

RETURNS

CHAPTER 15

Paul sat in the dining room of the hotel, picking at the meal in front of him. All around was the happy hum of conversation, mingled with the other sounds of hotel patrons enjoying their evening meal on a fine Cape night. But he felt totally at a loss, quite disconnected from the whole rich cinema of life around him.

It had been two days since Pat had nearly died. The Inspector was making good progress, although the compulsory bed rest, along with the pain from his wound, were not exactly improving his disposition. He was proving to be a very reluctant patient. But there had been no further attempts on his life.

On the other hand, they appeared to be no closer to finding Elizabeth. She had disappeared off the face of the earth, although 'sources' apparently kept suggesting that she was still alive. The specific reason for her abduction remained a mystery — there had been no ransom demand, or communication of any kind. Without her they were no closer to securing title to her father's lands, or to the mine. The Superintendent had promised to keep Paul up to play with any developments, but it had gone very quiet.

Paul wondered how Peter was getting on. If the Army party had pushed through into the nights on the trip over, they should just about be dropping down into the Impala homelands. Whether Peter would be able to get a message out by radio, and then to Pat through the Police command system, was uncertain. Paul was also unsure what Peter was supposed to achieve. How would he prevent Daniel inadvertently escalating the situation, when the latter was out of contact, over on the coast?

All in all it was not going well, and he was very, very, lonely. At what point did he just give up and go home? For that point, where was home? He got up from the table, leaving most of his meal behind, and went up to his room.

He opened his bible, looking for some sense of things. But tonight the words were cold and lifeless on the fine paper. He thought back to the euphoria around his return to Africa, and his mind questioned the wisdom of it. Lost.

There was the slightest scratch at the door, as if something brushed against it. Paul's immediate reaction was fear, recalling the Superintendent's warning. Had he locked the door? Heart pounding, he looked around the corner. It was shut, and on the safety chain, but there was an envelope on the floor.

He considered checking the corridor, but thought better of it. The envelope had his name on the front, nothing else, and he recognised Elizabeth's handwriting immediately. He sat down on the floor where he was and tore open the envelope.

My dearest Paul.

I truly hope this letter gets to you. I wanted you to know I am not being ill treated, and that this thing will be resolved soon. It may take a little while for me to make my way home, but please do not attempt to find me, as that would put all our lives, and others, at risk.

All my love, for always,
Elizabeth.

Paul read the letter again, and again, searching for some hidden meaning. Nothing.

Realising he should ring the Superintendent, he knew he should have been much more careful how he opened the letter, if indeed he should have touched it at all. The Police would not be impressed.

Best he approach that difficultly through Pat, first thing in the morning.

He walked across to the window of the suite, and looked out across the harbour at the ships working the busy port. 'Where is she?' he asked of his reflection in the window.

Elizabeth was, in fact, standing on the upper deck of the rusty, non-descript, freighter, looking back at the lights of the city. The Russian Colonel was standing beside her. 'I will do everything in my power to get you home safely, Elizabeth.'

After a moment, Elizabeth replied into the evening breeze off the mountain. 'I wish that I could believe that.'

'Have I done anything, so far, that would put you in any more danger?'

'Not that I am aware of.' She turned to face him. 'Was my note actually delivered?'

The Colonel caught the inflexion in her voice. 'Yes it was.' He was tired of this, and longed for home. There was an edge to his voice. 'Elizabeth, you need to be aware that I am under some pressure to hand you over to the same bunch of thugs who murdered your solicitor and his wife not long ago.'

Her reply was harsh, and unexpected. 'So why not just get it over with?'

So much like Nina, he thought, and softened his tone. 'I am not a criminal. We are here doing a job, supporting the guerrillas in their fight against oppression. The Western powers are doing exactly the same, on the other side. I am not at all happy with the people we have to deal with along the way, and Moscow is aware of my concerns. It is very unfortunate that you have found yourself caught in the middle.'

'I am not even sure that I know why,' Elizabeth observed, sadly.

'Well, I can answer that for you. It is very simple. War is an expensive business, and your enemies need control of that mine.'

'It must be more than that. What we have seen is a deliberate and callous attempt to destabilise the Impala homelands.'

'Well, I am not an expert on your local political situation, but I would hazard a guess that this is about power. Power on a scale that brings unbelievable wealth. Certainly that is the pattern in most other places I have been.'

Elizabeth considered that for a moment. 'I think I understand. Above all else, Victor, I must do what I can to ensure the safety of the Impala, and the preservation of their homelands.' She turned to face him and smiled. 'When do we sail?'

'Later tonight. I want to be well clear of South African waters by daylight.'

'And where?'

'Home, Elizabeth. We are going home.'

'But not mine?'

'You have my word, that I will release you as soon as I am able. But I am sure that you would agree that it is not safe for you to stay here in Cape Town, for now.'

She nodded. 'I was considering doing some travelling. Your offer sounds like the best one going, for now.' Taking one last look at the Cape Town lights, she turned and followed her Russian captor. Or was he her protector, or both?

Paul pulled himself away from the view, and folded the single page letter, placing it back in the envelope. He hoped that if there was any forensic evidence, it remained intact. Looking at the time, he decided against ringing the Superintendent. It was well he didn't because the phone went about two minutes later.

He picked up the handset. 'Hello?'

'Paul, it is Pat. What's happening?'

'Hi Pat. Have you been bullying the nurses again?'

'Yes. They think that I might behave myself if they gave me access to a phone.'

'How is your arm?'

'Sore. Very sore. Every time I move it. I get to see the physio tomorrow morning, and I am not looking forward to that.'

'Rather you than me.'

'So have there been any developments in our case?'

'Just one. About an hour ago a note was slipped under the door of my room.'

'Ransom?'

'No. Nothing like that. It was from Elizabeth. Pat, this confirms that she is OK'

'That is great news. Rather unusual. Normally, if we have not received any demands within the first twenty-four hours, there will be a body somewhere.'

'Well, not in this case.'

'We need to get the letter to the lab. I will ring and get someone over to the hotel to pick it up. What does it say, exactly?'

Paul recited the letter from memory.

'No hints there,' replied Pat.

'No.'

'Our best approach might be to do exactly what it says.'

'You mean?'

'Nothing, for now at least.' Pat paused, apparently gathering his thoughts. 'I am beginning to think that we should let things take their natural course until we have more information, a solid lead, or some reason to intervene.'

'What should I do then?'

'We just need to close off the loose ends. I talked to my solicitors earlier in the day, and they suggested that we go to the High Court and get something called a *stay of process,* or something like that.'

'What would that do?'

'It would prevent the court making any judgements, either way, on the disputed title and prospect, until Elizabeth's interests can be properly represented.'

'I see.'

'My solicitor suggested one thing that the other party may try is to get a non-competence ruling.'

'What is that?'

'The court would rule that the title and the claim are null and void on the basis that there is no competent authority to hold or administer it.'

'But that is nonsense!'

'All that needs to happen is that the court is convinced, on the balance of the evidence before it.'

'That would certainly explain why they were so keen to establish a presence over on the coast.'

'Exactly. If the court made a no competence ruling, it would then be easy to lodge a clear application for title, and to have a prospecting license issued in their name.'

'And there would be nothing the Impala could do.'

'Nothing.'

'Then I had better talk with your solicitor in the morning, and get those papers filed.' Paul got up and walked around the small room.

'He is expecting you. But Paul, this will not be without risk. These people are very well connected. As soon as the papers are filed with the court, we can count on them knowing.'

'It has to be done. I am up for it, but what about your solicitor?'

'He will draw up the papers for you, and help you get them to the court officials. After that you are on your own.'

'OK.' But his voice didn't sound like he was.

'I will talk with the Super in the morning, Paul. Let's see if he is prepared to assign a constable to hang around with you.'

Paul sat down. 'Thanks. That would make me feel a lot better.'

'Right, I will get someone over to pick up the letter.'

'Sure. I will be here.'

They both heard the click on the line, as if a third party had disconnected. 'Did you hear what I just heard?' asked Pat.

'That click?'

'Yes.'

'What —,'

'Paul, get out of the hotel, right now! Leave your things in the room. Walk to within a couple of blocks from the hospital, and then find a cab. Get over here, understood?'

'You think —?'

'I might be wrong, but we cannot afford to take any chances. Get out of there, now!'

Paul didn't waste any time. He was now seriously scared, and only started to unwind a little when he was in the cab, and heading back to the hospital by a roundabout route. Somehow Pat had managed to persuade reception to let him in without a fuss, and Paul walked the deserted corridors, every nerve firing, until he came to the Intensive Care ward.

There was one bad moment when, of course, Paul discovered that Pat was no longer in the ward. The charge nurse checked her records, and found that Pat had been transferred into one of the general surgical wards, earlier that afternoon. Five minutes, and a couple of wrong turns, later, Paul finally spotted the uniformed policeman outside of Pat's room. He was expected.

'Paul. Good to see you. Have a seat.'

'Thanks. Don't mind admitting that this is beginning to really put the wind up me.'

Pat touched the bandages on his shoulder with his good hand. 'That goes for both of us.'

'I was thinking on the way over, would these people know who your solicitors are?'

'I don't think so, but I have warned him out, just in case. He is going to work out of home for a few days.'

'Wise.'

They passed the rest of the evening talking themselves around in circles. Pat had a look at the letter from Elizabeth, and agreed with Paul that it appeared genuine. They came up with a plan to get the paperwork filed with the High Court, with a minimum of risk, and then settled down for the night. At about the same time, Elizabeth lay awake listening to the familiar sounds of the ship getting ready for sea.

CHAPTER 16

Colonel Krakovsky was in the radio room, reading through the latest round of messages. Many were of no immediate relevance, but there was one just coming off the teletype that was the reason for his presence.

The duty operator passed it across, before logging it in. 'Here it is, Sir.'

'Thank you, Corporal.'

The Colonel skimmed over the header and transmission details. His eyes settled on the key elements of the message and he swore a very unpatriotic oath. It was inconceivable, did they not understand the position he was in? How did they expect him to offload his cargo, when his mission was compromised by the Western security agencies? For all he knew there was someone in the US watching his progress out of port on a satellite, right now. He knew his ship was tagged in their surveillance systems, so it was suicide to even attempt to get to the rendezvous. Their only advantage was the darkness, and the weather forecast that was typically foul, even for this time of year.

He stepped out of the radio room, and up to the bridge. The Captain, a bear of a man that had spent the best part of his life at sea, greeted him cautiously. Victor watched as the ship worked its way to sea. After ninety minutes they were clear of the coast, and the officer of the watch took the ship.

Victor asked the Captain to join him in the Navigation room. He was still carrying the message, and showed it to the other man without comment.

'It cannot be done. Not in this old tub,' came the reply.

'I agree with you Captain, but those are my orders. First we must lose ourselves in the weather. When we are sure that we have broken any surveillance, we may have a chance.'

'Colonel, even if I could make my ship invisible, I could not close the coast again unobserved. They know within 50 miles or so where the rendezvous must be.'

'What if we could change that?'

'That would certainly shift the odds a little in our favour.'

Victor looked at the map, moving his finger slowly up the coast. 'How about here?'

The Captain shook his head. 'Too exposed, and the beach shelves too quickly.'

Victor's finger searched the contours of the coast a little further north. 'So, how about here?'

'Not ideal, but it might do if the weather played ball. You could get our friends to agree?'

'We will not give them the option,' replied the Colonel. 'They are desperate for the ammunition, in particular.'

The Captain marked the location on the chart. 'So be it. We will run under the cover of the weather systems, and look to sail the eastbound legs of our course at night. Let's see how good the opposition is.'

'Good. I will inform our customers. How long?'

'Let's give ourselves five days to be safe,' the other man advised. 'If necessary we can wait out to sea for the right weather, to cover our approach.'

'That makes it July 24. Yes?'

'As good as any other day, Colonel.'

Victor moved across the ship to the radio room, and drafted an urgent message to Moscow. It had to work. For Nina, it had to work. Outside there was a hint of grey on the eastern skyline.

Prone on the floor of the bathroom, Elizabeth was feeling very sorry for herself as the ship rolled uncomfortably with each caress of the South Atlantic swell. Another wave of nausea overcame her, but her stomach was completely empty.

The spasms eventually passed. She knew that she must try to get some fluids into her system, so made her way slowly across the stateroom to the little fridge where there were a few bottles of dry lemonade. This time she had to hold it down, she told herself, lying on the floor.

She woke with a start as the Colonel came through the door. He looked terrible — tired and haggard from the combined effect of lack of sleep, and too much vodka.

'Are you feeling any better?' he asked.

'A little.'

'We should be able to turn and run with the swell for a while tonight: that will allow us all to get a little rest.'

'I wondered why we were wallowing out here.'

He waved his hand at the small porthole. 'The weather. Our friend that hides us from prying eyes through the day.'

'Of course.'

Victor went to his desk and sat down, playing with the portrait of Nina and his sons, something that Elizabeth noticed that he did more and more as the days accumulated.

She rolled over to look at him. 'You look more worried than usual, Victor.'

He leant back on the chair, and ran his hands through his greying hair. 'I will be honest with you, Elizabeth, I am very worried. We have been ordered to deliver our cargo, regardless of the fact that our mission is compromised, and the South African authorities almost certainly know the general area where we must run our containers ashore.'

'They will be waiting for you?'

'I would be, if I were in their shoes,' he said with a wry smile.

'What will they do, arrest you?'

He laughed. 'It is likely to be much more dramatic than that.'

'How?' probed Elizabeth, but Victor's mind was elsewhere. He glanced at his watch as men do when they need an excuse to end a conversation, and went up to the bridge.

The Captain was in the navigation room, working with his charts. 'Course change in half an hour or so. We are now well off-shore, thanks to the weather. It should be safe to turn and parallel the coast through the night.'

'Good. My men are still getting their sea legs. They need to be in good condition before we make the run in-shore to deliver your cargo.'

The Captain was not at all sympathetic. 'I understand that, Colonel. But it is not much good if we are intercepted before we get anywhere near the rendezvous.' Victor was about to respond, when they were interrupted by a call from the bridge.

'Radar has a contact, Captain!'

Both men raced up the ladder to the radar station.

'Where?' asked Victor, breaking the protocol between his command of the mission, and the Captain's command of the ship. He got a warning glance for his trouble.

'165 degrees at 10 miles, closing. He has been out there for a while, but must have finally got a decent return on us.'

'Maritime patrol?' asked Victor.

'We will find out soon enough,' replied the Captain, and raced out onto the starboard bridge wing. The rain was coming through in black squalls, and it was growing dark. He turned to the Colonel, who had followed him out. 'Another ten minutes, and it will be dark!'

Victor shook his head, and pointed out to sea. 'Too late!' They could now clearly make out the grey outlines of the aircraft, as it manoeuvred to fly close alongside them. The big radial engines could be heard pushing the stubby airframe against the turbulent air of the South Atlantic. Then, it was gone, climbing into the overcast.

'I hope they are as uncomfortable as we are!' shouted the Captain, and led the way back inside.

He was right. It had been a long patrol for the crew, checking and plotting shipping west of Cape Town, while being bounced around mercilessly by the weather. They were almost at the limit of the aircraft's endurance when their radar picked up an intermittent contact, just off the edge of their patrol area.

The Navigator in the rear of the aircraft came up on the intercom. 'Skipper, I think we should go and check that one out. It could be the Russian cargo vessel mentioned in the intel brief.'

'Roger, Nav,' came the reply. 'How is the fuel?'

'We have another twenty minutes out here to get home with full reserves, and the weather forecast, and latest report, looks good.'

'OK,' noted the pilot. 'Heading?'

The Navigator used the track ball on his control panel to position the electronic cursor on top of the radar contact. 'Turn on to 345 degrees. It is up on the tactical display.'

'345, got it.' The aircraft turned slowly onto the new heading. 'Crew, Pilot, we are on our way down for one last contact. Should be a port side run.' The Pilot called for the descent checklist, and the crew worked their way through the familiar procedures that set the aircraft up for the drop to low altitude.

'200 feet set on the radar altimeter,' replied the Co-pilot.

'Descent checks complete,' confirmed the Nav.

The radar operator took over responsibility for directing them onto the target. 'Pilot, Radar, come left fifteen degrees onto 330.

'330, roger.'

The Nav cued the required altimeter check. 'Through 5,000 feet on 996 millibars.'

'996 set Pilot.'

'996 set Co.'

'Pilot, Radar, range 15 miles.'

'Thanks Radar.'

'Through 1,000 feet,' checked the Nav.

The Pilot checked his harness one final time. 'Passing 1,000 for 200 feet.' The aircraft was really getting bounced around now it was down in the turbulent layer close to the surface.

'500 for 200.' The co-pilot was peering out the front of the aircraft, searching for a glimpse of the water below. 'What did you expect the ceiling to be, Nav?'

'Looking at the forecast inside this front I would say 300 feet and visibility anything down to 2000 metres in rain.'

'I just love it when you are funny,' joked the co-pilot.

The radar operator interjected. '10 miles.'

'Thanks Radar,' replied the Pilot.

'Bit of wind sheer here, Pilot. Come further left on to 300 degrees.'

The Pilot leant forward and reset the marker on the tactical display in front of him. '300.'

'250 feet for 200 feet,' prompted the Co-pilot. 'I have just got the swell running underneath us, but the visibility out the front is almost nil.'

'Three for two, Pilot, roger.' The tension in the crew increased as he levelled out the aircraft just above their minimum safe altitude of 200 feet. At this altitude, there was little room for error. They were punching in and out of the scudding overcast.

'Pilot, Radar, 5 miles. You are clear either side of the contact.'

'Roger, Radar. Bring me down his starboard side.'

'Radar acknowledged. Turn right now onto 355. Contact is now 4 miles.'

'355, roger. Coming back to 100 knots'

'Altitude!' warned the Co-pilot, as they dipped below 200 feet.

'Pilot, roger.' He was working hard to slow the aircraft, while holding altitude and heading in the continuous turbulence.

'Contact! Slightly left, 2000 yards.'

The Pilot acknowledged. 'Got him, thanks Co.'

'Nav, Co, we have a group four cargo vessel, stack aft, estimated 10,000 tons, heading 360 at 8–10 knots. Grey hull and white superstructure. A number of containers on deck. I can't see any flag or identifying markings.' The ordinanceman gave him a thumbs up from the other side of the cockpit. 'And we have the photos.'

'That will do me, Pilot,' acknowledged the Nav.

'Let's go home,' replied the Pilot, applying power and gently turning the aircraft towards base. As they climbed back to their cruising altitude, the radio operator was already busy sending the contact report back to the communications centre just south of Cape Town. From there it would be turned around and sent through to the command centre, as top priority traffic.

They had not even settled into the cruise when they were called and asked how long they could stay on station to shadow the ship. The Nav conferred with the Pilot, and they decided that they could stretch things for a further hour by eating into their fuel reserves for the arrival back at base. They set themselves up in a lazy racetrack that allowed the radar operator to plot the course and speed of their target over the next hour, while they talked of their plans for the weekend.

Below them, the operator monitoring the sophisticated communications suite on the ship had intercepted the radio traffic. The Captain and the Colonel were in the middle of a conference in the chart room.

'I take it that we have been identified?' asked the Captain.

'Almost certainly,' replied Victor. 'And now we have a shadow.'

The Captain was studying the chart on the table. 'Do they have enough aircraft to keep a twenty-four hour cover on us?'

'Probably not, but you can be sure that there will be surface assets on the way to intercept us.'

The Captain marked off their distance out of Simonstown, the Naval Base just south of Cape Town. 'If they don't have anyone currently at sea, we are ten to twelve hours out.'

'Not far enough,' Victor sighed.

The Captain had to agree. 'If we are going to break contact we will have to do it well before we are within radar range of their patrol boats. There is no chance of outrunning them.'

'Our electronic surveillance will tell us when the aircraft goes off station,' remarked the Colonel.

'And warn us when we have company.'

'Always the optimist, Olav,' Victor joked.

The Captain stretched to his full height, pushing against the ceiling of the compartment. 'All these years at sea, what do you expect?'

They went around to the radio room, technically part of Victor's domain. 'Let us know as soon as the aircraft goes off station, Corporal.'

'Yes, Colonel. Immediately.' The two officers went back to the bridge, where the officer of the watch had just gone to red lights as the last of the daylight disappeared after the setting sun.

CHAPTER 17

Half a continent away to the east, the communications staff officer rang through to the command centre, alerting the watch commander to the fact that there was a high precedence message on the way up for the personal attention of the General. Moments later, the duty officer knocked on the door of the Commander's office.

The General read the report from Peter quickly, and turned to the map on his wall. 'They made good time getting out there, but the damage may already be done.' He turned to the tall officer standing behind him with most of the weight on his good leg. 'Rebel guerrillas that far south — flag that for the brief, and pass it to Intel.'

He pondered how best to support the small team out there in harms way, without disclosing what they already knew about the operation in the wider context. Certainly the Impala troops had acquitted themselves well, by all accounts. Perhaps if they could keep the bad guys' attention elsewhere for just a while.

The duty officer cleared his throat. 'Just a reminder, Sir, that we have an Operation Thunder brief with all agencies involved at 1900 hours.'

'Thanks.' The General looked at his watch. Thirty minutes away. 'I know it is asking a lot of the briefing team, but this needs to be in the picture.'

'Got it, Sir.' The door closed, but the General was a long way away already. Keep the pressure on the bad guys; that was the key. Perhaps this time they could flush out the politicians that were playing both sides against the middle. He got up and went into the watch room to where a young communications operator was sitting at her desk.

At precisely 1900 hours, the General walked into the briefing room and took his seat, after acknowledging the other agency staff present.

The brief commenced with an intelligence update. 'Sir, gentlemen, intel update for Operation Thunder. This brief is classified secret. Over the last twenty-four hours there have been a number of developments, and I will deal with these by location, rather than by time.' The briefing officer glanced at the General, and received a confirmatory nod.

'The Russian cargo vessel, that we believe to be carrying weapons and ammunition for the rebel forces, sailed from Cape Town at approximately 1730 last night. We lost radar contact with them at 0130, steaming pretty much due west at 15 knots. Today we launched a maritime patrol aircraft down that track, tasked to clear a box between their assessed position, and the west coast. Right at the end of the sortie they investigated a radar contact, which we believe to be the vessel concerned. The photos should be through by about midnight.' He paused for a breath. 'We were able to divert an aircraft from another task, and it is currently on station. The most recent update of the vessel's position is marked on the chart.' An aide turned on a view foil of the South Atlantic off the west coast. 'Questions to this point, gentlemen?'

'You are confident that this is the Russian ship?' asked the General.

'Almost certain, Sir. But the photos will confirm it.'

'Good. How long will we be able to keep up the surveillance?'

The briefing officer glanced at the one of the senior Air Force staff. 'Assuming that the aircraft don't let us down, for the next thirty-six hours,' came the reply.

'Surface assets?' queried one of the other senior staff.

'We have a patrol corvette getting ready for sea. She should sail within the hour.'

The General picked up on the line of questions. 'Intercept time?'

'About twelve hours later, assuming the vessel continues on roughly her current course and speed.'

'I can guarantee that will not happen, General,' advised the Brit from the second row. 'We know these guys, and they are good. They will have communications intercept equipment onboard, as well as electronic sensors, which will almost certainly have alerted them to the fact that they are being shadowed.'

'Understood.' The General turned to the watch commander. 'Make sure that information gets through to our guys in the air, and on the corvette. Two can play at that.'

'Wilco, Sir,' came the reply.

The General got to his feet and turned to face the assembled staff. 'So here is the game. We shadow the vessel, playing with their minds a little with some creative use of our sensors. Provided they continue northwest out into the shipping lanes we have no quarrel with them.' He surveyed the room. 'Right?'

'On the understanding that we anticipate them to at least attempt to put their cargo ashore, somewhere up the coast,' noted the Brit.

'We do. But by that time I plan to have a very well armed ship just off their stern quarter.' The General turned back to the briefing officer. 'Is the target vessel likely to be armed?'

'She has a hold full of rocket propelled grenades, and the like,' offered the American.

The General nodded. 'Make sure that the Navy is aware of that.'

'Aye Sir,' replied the Navy liaison officer.

'Naturally, I expect them to respond in kind.'

'With pleasure, Sir.'

The briefing officer continued, looking to keep things moving. 'Moving on to the situation out in the Northern Cape province. Sir, gentlemen, I think that you have all read the recent report, so I will keep this brief.'

There was a nod from his boss.

'After the sea and ground parties were neutralised by local forces, the trawler has returned to port. We have alerted the local Police, but at the moment there is little to warrant further action without disclosing what, and who, we know.'

The Brit leant forward. 'By all accounts your people did a great job, General.'

The General glanced at the briefing officer, and decided that for now he would get away with the bluff. 'Thank you.' He glared at the man behind the lectern who was about to die of a coughing fit. 'Carry on.'

'Sir,' said the young man, desperately attempting to control the spasms in his throat. 'The intervention by ANC guerrilla forces is a significant development. There are two prisoners, who have yet to be interrogated. We agree with initial on-site assessments, that this was a deliberate attempt to destabilise the Impala homelands.'

'Motive?' asked the General.

The intel chief stepped in. 'We are still working on a number of different scenarios, Sir. At this time we would not like to speculate.'

The General turned the question to the audience. 'Any thoughts?'

'Well General,' replied the local secret service man. 'We suspect that there is an unhappy connection between the Impala, and the arms smuggling. Events on the coast would seem to confirm it is connected to lands they have title to, and a licence to what some believe to be the richest untapped diamond mine left on the continent.'

'Cash,' concluded the General. 'The connection is cash to keep the other side of our nasty little war going.'

'But that does not explain the direct attack on the homelands, surely?' asked the watch commander.

'Yes it does.' The General nodded to himself. 'Yes it does. Under emergency legislation it opens the door for intervention, and ultimately for confiscation of tribal assets.' He moved to the door. 'Back here at 0700 tomorrow morning. We have a busy night ahead.'

On the way back to his office one of the watchkeepers poked his head out of the door. 'Sir, I have the CIB Section Head in Cape Town for you, on the secure line. He says it is urgent.'

'Always is,' muttered the General. He walked into the busy operations room, and crossed to the corner where the red phone sat on the cabinet housing the encryption equipment.

'Evening Ken, what keeps you at work so late?'

After a slight pause, the other end of the connection replied. 'You do, as it happens, General.'

'Well, don't keep me in suspense, what is it?'

The other man continued. 'I am loosely aware that you guys are at the business end of a certain highly sensitive operation.'

'We could be,' said the General, code for *yes, but I am not about to tell the Police.*

Ken knew better than to take offence. 'We have been bumping along on a double murder, and abduction, apparently connected, neither making a lot of progress. In fact certain other parties have been trying to get us to back off, apparently so we do not complicate your, er, problem.'

'Really.' The General took the seat that was offered to him. 'What leads do you have?'

'Well, that is just it. Our only information at this stage points to a rather interesting mix of organised crime, and KGB.'

'Not unusual bedfellows,' observed the General.

'No, but their political connections are.' Ken knew by the pause at the other end, that he now had the General's complete attention.

'Tell me more.'

'Just by complete fluke, a surveillance team on another job caught one of our ministers leaving a rather shady meeting with the

Russian consul, and an unknown person, who we have now been able to identify as a Colonel in the KGB.'

'When?'

'Two days ago. We even have photos.'

The General was not in the mood to be generous. 'Nice to know so early in the piece.'

'We only just got the second ID through from friends offshore.'

'Sorry, Ken. It has been a long day.'

'No problems, General. But we have reason to believe that the KGB are holding the woman who was abducted. Possibly on a Russian-flagged ship moored in the harbour.'

'How on earth did you make that connection, Ken?'

'The key piece came from a communications intercept, through a friend of a friend, if you know what I mean.' Then Ken decided to come clean. 'Actually, my source was a member of your staff, who was speaking with one of my inspectors, who just happens to be working the case.'

A number of loose ends suddenly connected. Well-known for his short fuse, the General's blood began to boil. 'Ken, thanks for this. I have to go right now, but I will be back to you very soon. I have some re-educating to do.' Without waiting for a response, the big man slammed down the phone. Everyone in the watchroom tried to become invisible, but this time they were not the target.

The General managed to catch the three secret service guys having a coffee in the crew room. 'You three. My office, right now!'

'I think, old chap, that our cover has just been blown,' said the American as he got to his feet.

'I just knew that I could trust you, Randy,' replied the Brit, following his lead.

'We are screwed,' noted the local man.

He was closest to the truth. The General ushered them through the door and closed it behind him, blocking their exit. It was a very effective way of gaining the high ground.

'When were you going to think it necessary to pass on to me, that the KGB are holding a South African national, on that vessel?'

'In the big scheme of things, it did not seem particularly relevant,' replied the Brit, apparently the senior member of their little community.

'In any event, it is a criminal act, and therefore a police issue,' added the South African.

'And, if I decide to send that ship to the bottom of the ocean, whose issue is it then.' The General moved across the room and crowded them uncomfortably in the corner of the room. 'You tell me that!'

'You would have been protected in making that decision, by not being aware that the woman was onboard,' noted the American.

'Incredible. Just incredible,' raged the General. 'Do you really think, if this thing goes down to the wire, the Russians will not play the hostage card?'

'It is hard to judge.'

Back to the Brit again, the General noted. Like dealing with the three stooges.

He decided to take a more conciliatory tone, and see what other information he might be able to get out of them. 'What else might you have concluded that I should be protected from?'

'In view of the likelihood of a confrontation, it might help your intelligence chaps to have a backgrounder on Colonel Victor Krakovsky, KGB. He is widely respected as a very resourceful, professional officer.'

'Know your enemy,' replied the General. 'Very good. Anything else?'

The South African looked at his colleagues. 'We now have a good idea who is behind this, and why.'

CHAPTER 18

The same dawn found the Russians working their way further to the northwest, trying to stay under a frontal band of weather that was moving up off the cold waters further south. With the ship riding the ocean swells much easier on this course everyone on board was in better humour. Elizabeth had apparently decided to stay in her bunk, and after a brief breakfast Colonel Krakovsky went up to the bridge.

The Captain was sitting in his seat, brooding over the grey Atlantic waters that slowly pushed under his ship and then moved out ahead of him in a majestic procession. 'Good morning, Colonel.'

Victor moved across the bridge. 'Good morning, Captain. What is our situation?'

'Interesting.' The Captain stepped down from the high seat, leading the way down into the chart room. Victor followed.

'We are currently here.' The Captain pointed to a triangular mark on the chart. 'Still being shadowed. Our South African friends must have had another aircraft handy. As far as we have noticed, there was no clear break in the surveillance.' He looked up from the chart and grinned. 'They do try to fool us now and again by turning their radar off, but cannot risk losing our track. It is all pretty obvious.'

'So the Navy knows exactly where we are?'

'Every turn of the propeller, comrade Colonel.'

Victor looked at the ship's chronometer on the wall. 'Ten hours since we were spotted. Not long until we have more company, then.'

'Not long.'

'What then, Captain?'

'I was going to ask you the same question, Colonel. I assume that it is too early in the piece to simply blow them out of the water?'

Victor could smell the alcohol on the other man's breath. 'Just a little. The chances of us making it home would reduce dramatically at that point.'

'I agree.'

The Captain was halfway back up the ladder when he paused and half-turned back to Victor. 'Do you think that they know about your guest?'

'What do you mean?'

'I mean, Colonel Krakovsky,' said the Captain, completing his turn, 'Will they fire on this vessel knowing that there is a South African hostage, a woman, on board?'

Victor's voice reduced to barely a whisper. 'I don't know, and I am not planning on finding out.'

'That may become unavoidable.'

'Until it is, it is not. Understood, Captain?'

'Yes, Colonel Krakovsky: I understand perfectly.' The Captain turned and climbed up to the bridge.

50 miles east of their position, a very bored aircraft crew turned yet again towards the electronic marker that oriented their seemingly endless orbits in the morning sky. The weather made it uncomfortable, and difficult to move around the aircraft to ease muscles complaining from being too long in one position.

'How long until we are off station, Nav?' asked the weary radio operator.

'Another ninety minutes.' They were flying the co-called dog-watch. Briefed at midnight, and airborne at 0200 hours. It completely messed up their body clocks, and now their eyes felt as if they were full of gravel. A steady stream of coffee and bad jokes kept them awake, and sane.

'How far behind are our Navy friends now?' asked the Pilot.

'50 miles, give or take a couple. At a closing speed of 10 knots, another 5 hours.' *Somebody else's problem,* thought the Nav.

'Have we seen an airborne report for our relief?'

'Not yet, Skipper.'

'Late, again.'

'Looks like it.' At that moment the teletype machine burst into life. The radio operator groaned as he read the words appearing in front of him.

'Our relief aircraft is hard down with engine problems. Weather is good. Ops wants to know how long we can extend.'

The Pilot swore. There goes golf this afternoon. 'Do the numbers, thanks, Nav. Watch the weather en route. That depression to the south is deepening.'

'Wilco, Skipper.'

After a few minutes of work in the aircraft performance manual, the Nav had a figure. 'Pilot, Nav; conservatively, we can hang around out here for another three hours.'

'Fine by me. That should just get the Navy within radar range of our Russian friends. Pass it to Ops.'

'We should warn them out,' suggested the Nav. 'They might be able to pick up a little bit of time.'

'Good idea. Your comms.' The Pilot flicked a couple of switches on his side panel, so that he could listen to the conversation with the Navy corvette below them.

A few minutes later the Nav checked back. 'He seems happy. They should hold the vessel on radar in an hour or so.'

'Good. We may be able to go home then.'

'Yey,' exclaimed one of the other members of the crew.

Victor and the Captain were looking at the radar display on the bridge. 'Nothing yet,' said the Captain.

'No, but our sensors are picking up an E/F band surface search radar, coming up behind us.' Victor looked at the time. 'They are behind schedule?'

'Probably using the air cover to allow them to take it easy and conserve fuel,' replied the Captain. 'Certainly what I would be doing.' He stretched. 'It will be interesting to see whether they keep up the air surveillance, once the Navy is on station.'

'Could that present an opportunity, Captain?'

'Yes, absolutely.' The Captain looked down at his hands, noting the heavy calluses from a hard life at sea. 'We still can't outrun them, but we just might be able to outfox them.'

The Colonel went below and checked on his men, now masters at passing time doing nothing. But today they had their weapons out on the floor, and were cleaning and checking each part before reassembling them and checking their functions.

One of the men looked up. 'Would be really good to be able to fire a few rounds, Colonel?'

Victor nodded. 'Good idea, Sergeant. I will talk with the Captain. We may have company in a couple of hours, so we will need to do it before then.'

'An escort?'

'Yes, Sergeant,' he observed. 'But not one of ours.'

'Target practice, then,' offered one of the others.

'Aren't all grey boats?' countered another. Victor decided that his men were in good heart. Probably better than him, he had to acknowledge, making his way back to the bridge.

The Captain saw the wisdom of checking the operation of the weapons, and passed the authorisation over the ship's intercom. It also served to warn out the other crew members that there was going to be a live firing practice.

A few minutes later Victor was called over to the radar display. 'There they are.'

Victor looked at the little smudge on the scope. 'So if we can see them.'

'They can see us.'

'Apparently our airborne shadow has left already. We have a very small window, but it is worth a try.' The Captain walked over to the helm and dialled a new course into the autopilot, pushing the engine telegraph up to maximum revolutions. 'What they don't know, is that this old girl was designed to run a North Sea blockade. By turning away from them and speeding up, we might just be able to break contact. Especially if we can find a good, heavy shower at the critical time. Just like that one there.' He pointed to a shadow on the radar about 20 miles ahead. It was a good time to be running with the sea.

At first the radar operator on the corvette was not overly concerned, but then realised that it had been a dozen or so sweeps without a return of the target.

'Operations Officer from Radar, we appear to have lost radar contact.'

'What do you mean, Radar? A ship of that size does not just disappear!' came the reply from the plotting table in the middle of the cramped room.

'I am not sure, maybe there is a bit of weather in-between us. He has just dropped off my scope.'

The senior rating in charge of the combat team came over and checked the radar settings. 'Radar looks good, but I can't see him.'

The Operations Officer picked up the handset in front of him, and pushed the transmit switch. 'Executive Officer, Operations.'

'This is the XO. Go ahead Ops.'

'We have lost radar contact with the target vessel. I repeat, we have lost radar contact.'

The XO addressed the senior rate. 'What do you think, Chief?'

'I think that he has picked his moment, with us just on the limit of our radar, and the air cover having to leave.'

'I agree.' The XO called across the bridge to the young seaman on the helm. 'Helm, bring us up to flank speed. We need to run him down before he gets too far away. Hold your course, for now.' The XO was about to drop down to the Captain's cabin, when he appeared at the top of the ladder.

'Captain is on the bridge,' called out the Coxswain.

'What's up, XO?'

'Was just on my way down, Skipper. We have lost radar contact. This guy is slippery.'

'Just as we were told,' the young Lieutenant Commander replied. 'Shame the Air Force had to go back to the bar.'

'Should we tell Maritime Ops?' asked the Ops Officer as he arrived on the bridge.

The Captain picked up his binoculars and stepped out onto the bridge wing. 'Let's give it a couple of hours to see if we pick him up again. No sense in creating a flap unnecessarily.'

'Aye, Sir.'

The corvette picked up her skirts and charged across the surface, with the wind behind her and a following sea. The Coxswain took over the helm as she became difficult to steer, surfing down the face of one swell, and into the back of the one ahead.

Down in the operations room the radar specialist was trying every trick in the book. The Israeli sourced equipment was among the best in its class: they just had to get lucky.

Just over the radar horizon, the Captain was pouring over his own tactical display in the chart room. An unusual fit for a freighter, but then this was no ordinary freighter.

'They have switched the search mode of their radar,' remarked the Captain.

Colonel Krakovsky stepped forward. 'That would indicate —?'

'We may have broken their cover, for a little while at least.' The big man thumped the table. Underneath their feet the hull was singing in sympathy with the big marine engines running at full power.

'How do you plan to take advantage of that?' queried Victor.

'They will initially try to run us down on our original track.' The Captain moved across to the chart table. 'That is a race they will eventually win. We need to step to one side and get them into a two dimensional problem. Then the empty ocean becomes our friend.'

'When?'

'Before they think we might try it.' The Captain leapt the steps back up the bridge two at a time. He glanced at the weather on the radar, checking the swell patterns. 'Helm, come left two-zero degrees.'

'Helm aye, Captain. Left twenty. New course 335 degrees.'

'Good.' The Captain turned to his KGB associate. 'We cannot afford to turn too sharply, or they will quickly overtake us.' The new course also put the ship at an optimum position to surf the big ocean rollers, and she picked up another couple of knots. The Captain went out onto the Port side bridge wing and allowed the biting cold to invigorate him. They did not have him yet!

With every passing minute, the tension on the bridge of the corvette was increasing. Their quarry must be out their somewhere.

'I can't believe that he was able to keep ahead of us,' muttered the XO.

'Well, short of some newfangled Russian stealth device, that is what he has done,' his Captain replied. 'XO, I am beginning to think that we underestimated this guy. What if he has more to play with than just a navigation radar?'

'You mean —?'

'Even a rudimentary radar sensor would give him our bearing.'

'And would have told him we had lost contact as soon as we went to a sector search.' The XO moved back to the bridge radar display.

'Exactly.' The CO got down from his chair and led the way down to the operations room. 'Radar, I want you to drop back to your normal all-round scan, and gradually wind down the gain over the next 15 minutes.' He turned to his officers, now gathered on the bridge. 'I want our friends to think that we are falling behind them.'

'Aye, Sir,' responded the Ops Officer.

'Now let's put ourselves in his shoes.' He led the way down to the Operations Room. 'He knows that he will not outrun us, so what would you do, XO?'

'Look to shift the game as soon as I had the opportunity. Particularly if he could get outside the limits of our sector search.'

'Exactly. Nav, I want a plot thirty degrees either side of our last fix.' They braced themselves as the ship rolled over the face of a particularly large wave, and got lucky as it lifted them high on its crest.

'Radar has a contact!'

'Radar down!' ordered the Captain. 'Plot that contact.'

The Navigator transferred the electronic marker to his tactical display.

The CO thumped the table. 'Got you. He has turned left, away from the coast.'

'And into the thick of the weather,' remarked the XO. 'Course and speed?'

The Nav plotted the two fixes on the chart. '335 at 28 knots.'

'Not bad for a rusty old tub,' commented the XO.

'I would say this ship is only rusty on the outside.' The Captain grinned across the Nav table. 'Right, next move by him?'

'He will be looking to open up the side step,' offered the Ops Officer.

The idea was picked up by the XO. 'So he must turn away from us, but he won't want to get too far away from his rendezvous on the coast.'

'I agree.' The Captain hunched himself over the plotting table. 'So the question is when, and by how much?' He took the ruler and pencil from the Nav. 'The max I would risk turning is another 30 degrees, or he increases the chances of us picking him up as we overtake him along his original course.' He extended the track line, and then drew another line 30 degrees further to the left. Finally he used the dividers to step out position estimates for each hour. 'Agree?'

'Aye, Sir.'

'So we go direct to this position, radar down. From there we should be able to pick him up, no matter what he has done.'

The XO stepped back and looked at the big picture on the chart in front of him. 'Unless he makes an early radical move back to the coast.'

'Which he will not do as long as there is a chance that we are between him and his rendezvous. With our radar down, he is as much in the dark as we are.'

Victor came back onto the bridge from checking on a very ill Elizabeth. The Captain wondered for a second what was really going on there, but decided to stick to just one set of problems, for now.

'Intriguing, Colonel. Our pursuers have gone off the air.'

'What do you think that means?'

'I am not sure.' The big man took off his hat, and scratched his unkempt mop of hair. 'We appear to have drawn a little ahead of them, then lost their radar signal altogether. But that would indicate it was turned off.'

'Why?'

'If I were a cunning old fox, I would think that, having lost contact, they decided not to broadcast their position any more.'

Victor peered out of the rear bridge windows. 'So?'

'So we are both guessing what the other should now do.'

He turned back to face the other man. 'And if you were in their shoes?'

'I would be concerned about us changing course towards the coast, and our rendezvous. So I would attempt to position myself inside our current track.'

'Which actually takes them away from us.'

'Correct.'

Victor leant back against the bridge superstructure. 'Your intentions?'

'Go the other way. Make it 300 on the helm.'

'Helm, aye. New course is 300 degrees, Captain.'

The Captain grinned at his comrade. 'If I am right we will pick up their radar signal in about 45 minutes, from out in this sector. We will be well below their radar horizon.'

'And then?'

'We go right around them, to your new rendezvous.'

'Fair enough,' said Victor. It was going to be a long forty-five minutes, on both vessels.

The bridge team on the corvette strained their eyes into the late afternoon gloom. 32 knots and no radar, with the visibility dropping to less than 2000 metres in the squalls, was not something that any seaman enjoyed.

'One hour since we took the radar down,' remarked the Navigating Officer to the XO.

'Correct,' said the CO as he walked into the confines of the room. 'One sweep, all round scan on low power please Radar.'

'One sweep, Radar aye.' Everyone in the room held their breath.

'Radar has a contact, 045 at 8 miles!'

'Battle stations!' roared the CO, thumping the table.

The next two minutes were organised pandemonium as the Off Watch crew raced to reinforce their duty stations. One by one the reports came into the operations room. The Captain and XO were out on the starboard bridge wing peering through powerful gyro-stabilised binoculars.

'Ship is at battle stations, Captain,' came the report from the Officer of the Watch.

'Very good.' Instinctively the CO looked at his watch. Not bad, but still could be better. He looked across at his young Executive Officer. 'Knock another 20 seconds off, yet.'

The XO moaned, inwardly. 'Aye, Sir.' He avoided his CO's hard gaze by fixing his eyes to the binoculars. There, on the top of the swell, now dropping out of sight, and back again. 'Contact, 045 at 6 miles, closing.'

The CO leant into the bridge. 'Helm, hard to Port. Make your speed 20 knots. Roll out on 330 degrees. Officer of the Watch, darken ship.' The CO looked across at his XO. 'They may not have noticed us yet. We will see if we can sit off their stern quarter and track their wake.'

'The Weapons Officer might be able to use the laser rangefinder on the fire control system to hold position without bringing up the radar,' suggested the XO.

'Good idea. Make it so. And have someone break out the night vision goggles.' He watched the much larger vessel through the driving rain for any indication that they had been spotted. They were running parallel to it, and slipping back quietly so as not to throw up any unnecessary bow wave or wake. It would take a sharp pair of eyes on the bridge of the freighter to pick them out of the angry grey seas.

In the chart room of the freighter the Captain was glued to the tactical display when the Colonel dropped down the ladder from the bridge.

'Anything?' asked Victor.

'One sweep only, relatively weak.'

He moved around the display. 'Bearing?'

'That is what doesn't make sense. It was out here.' The Captain pointed to the line on the plotter, and tapped his pen on the side of the table.

'How?'

'And why, comrade Colonel?'

'Guess at the range, Captain?'

'Going by the signal strength, 30 or 40 miles, assuming they are transmitting at full power.'

'What now?'

'Well, inexplicably they seem to have left the door open for us to turn back towards the coast, so we will do exactly that.' The Captain did a couple of quick calculations on the plotter; then picked up the intercom handset. 'Helm, make your course 045.'

'045 on the helm, Captain,' replied the seaman at the helm.

The Officer of the Watch came in from the bridge wing. 'He is turning. Helm, starboard thirty. Make your speed 25 knots.' The deck tilted under his feet at the same time as the coxswain replied.

'Weaps, XO do you have a range on him yet?'

'Weapons, aye. 6 miles and opening slowly.'

'XO roger. Keep the ranges coming every five minutes until we have worked out what speed he is sitting at.'

'Weaps, aye.'

Half an hour later they were comfortably sitting a steady 6 miles dead astern. The XO picked up the handset and called down to the Captain's cabin.

'Captain.'

'XO, Sir. Request permission to stand down from Battle Stations.'

'Certainly, XO. Could be a long haul from here.'

CHAPTER 19

It was certainly a long haul for the two men on the ground in Cape Town. Pat's shoulder was healing well, but it would be at least a month before he would be fit enough to return to duty, after a painful rehabilitation. About the same time that the dawn rose on the grief of the Impala, Paul and Pat shared a sparse hospital breakfast and planned the day's activities.

Pat put down his toast and reached for his lukewarm cup of tea. 'My solicitor is coming here first thing, so we can sort out how best to get these papers filed in the High Court.'

'Do you think that I should go and get my things from the hotel?' asked Paul.

'Yes. But if I can convince the surgeon to let me out of here today, I think we might go and stay at my sister's place. She is overseas at the moment, so I have been keeping an eye on her apartment.'

Paul perked up. 'Probably better than another night on one of these cots.'

There was a knock on the door. 'Come in,' Pat called out.

'Good to see you so perky, Inspector.' It was the Superintendent, accompanied by the Deputy Section Head.

'Sir, Ken. This is a surprise.'

The Superintendent led the way into the room. 'Had to make sure that you weren't abusing the hospital staff, Pat.'

'Shocking patient. That's what I heard,' laughed Ken.

Paul chimed in. 'That is not the half of it.'

'OK, OK, so I get a bit grumpy being cooped up in here, while you guys are having all the fun.'

'Well, fun would be a rather generous term,' counselled the Superintendent. 'I haven't been home in 36 hours.'

'And that doesn't look like changing for a day or so,' Ken amplified.

Pat was now intrigued, and sat up a little further in his bed. 'What is going on?'

A uniformed policeman popped his head in the door. 'Both rooms either side are empty and locked, Sir.'

'Thank you Constable. No one comes in until you hear from me.'

'Understood, Sir.'

The Superintendent moved across to the window, looked outside, and then took a seat on the window sill. 'We have been receiving phone calls from some very interesting people, including the boss of a friend of yours at the Joint Operational Command Centre in Bloemfontein. Some want us to do more. Some want us to do less. Some, in fact, want us to forget we ever launched this investigation.'

'Hard to just ignore a double murder, and then an abduction, apparently linked,' observed Pat.

'Our point, precisely. But we have had to hand over your assailant to military intelligence. They have agreed to let us know if anything relevant to your case turns up.'

Pat frowned. 'Military Intelligence? Will he eventually be charged?'

The Superintendent glanced down into the courtyard below. 'If we see him again, Pat.'

Ken chuckled. 'He might actually think he is better off with us.'

'What else don't we know?' commented Pat.

'Right first time.' The Superintendent began to pace up and down in front of the window. 'We know that we can tie the murders to organised crime here in Cape Town. Those involved have links with a prominent political figure. Pat, we also know there is a link with the abduction of Miss Dortmus.'

'But—?'

Ken leant forward. 'This sounds far fetched, I know. But the evidence is compelling. The connection is the need for cash. Cash to fund the ever-increasing costs of operations against the Army up north.'

'The diamonds, I assume?' asked Pat.

Ken nodded. 'The diamonds.'

'So where are they holding Elizabeth?' asked Paul.

'We have had trouble getting that out of our friends who know these things,' replied the Superintendent. 'But we do know she appears to be safe.'

Pat tried one more time to get comfortable. 'So far. What are they holding her for?'

'We assume that they are still attempting to get their hands on the diamonds.'

'While they are also pushing an application through the High Court to have the title and claim put aside,' added Pat.

The Superintendent raised his eyebrows. 'We hadn't heard that, but it fits with the overall picture. Now, what you will not be aware of is that there has been trouble in the Impala homelands. Big trouble.'

Paul was on his feet. 'What?'

'It is all under control, but not without many fatalities, including a significant number of what we understand to be rebel guerrilla forces.'

'That far south?' exclaimed Pat.

'Yes, I know. But when you put that in the big picture, perhaps it is not that surprising. If the crimes here in Cape Town did not manage to secure access to the enormous wealth that is supposedly in that mine, the attempt to create instability in the homelands fits the picture.'

'How?' asked Paul.

'Under the recent emergency legislation, assets of the tribe can be frozen, or confiscated, if so ordered by the authorities.'

Pat nodded. 'Leaving the mine vulnerable to a counter-claim being lodged.

'Precisely.'

'Superintendent,' asked Paul. 'You mentioned there were fatalities?'

'Yes. A significant number of the tribal forces.'

'Any names?'

'No. I am sorry.'

'Thanks.' Paul looked at Pat. 'So where does that leave us?'

'It is now vital that we get that motion before the High Court today, Paul. That may be all that is standing between us and disaster. At the very least it will buy us time.' There was a knock on the door.

'This had better be important,' growled the Superintendent. 'Come in!'

It was the Constable. 'Regret the interruption, Sir, but the Inspector has a visitor who insists on seeing him urgently.'

Pat nodded, and his solicitor was ushered into the room.

'Good morning, gentlemen.' There were handshakes all around, finishing with Pat.

'Good morning, Luther. What do you have for us?'

The visitor opened a tatty briefcase and produced some papers. He looked around for a table, but ended up spreading them out on the foot of the bed. 'I have here a motion for a stay of process, until all parties are able to be properly represented. It has been used quite successfully recently, but is only valid for thirty days.'

Pat nodded. 'I think that will be sufficient.'

'Paul, you will need to sign as representing the interests of the Impala people. I will witness it as an officer of the court.' Five minutes later the solicitor was on his way.

'He will be alright,' Pat replied to the question on Paul's face as the door shut behind them. 'He will just lodge the papers at the court offices, and then go on holiday for a while.' Pat brought the Superintendent up to date with their concerns for Paul's safety, and then produced the letter from Elizabeth. 'We were going to bring this in today.'

'An interesting development. This tends to make me feel more comfortable with taking things slowly.'

Pat agreed and turned to his friend. 'I am beginning to think that you would be better out of Cape Town, Paul. If anything comes up we can handle it at this end.'

'If that is what you think is best.'

The Superintendent leant forward. 'I think he is right, Paul. The last thing we need is for you to go missing. I can arrange for a car: get you out of town and headed back to your Impala friends this morning.'

'Just need to get across to the hotel and check out.'

'We can drop through there on our way back to the station,' offered the Superintendent, gathering his jacket.

After their farewells to a very grumpy Pat, who had just been told that he would not be going home for another couple of days, the three men made their way across town through the mid-morning traffic. Ken got to stay with the car out in front of the hotel, while Paul went up to his room, accompanied by the Superintendent.

The big policeman stepped in front of Paul as they approached the door, and opened the door with a police-issue clean handkerchief, just in case. He asked himself why he was not totally surprised to find the house maid lying in a pool of blood just inside the door. It was not going to be a good day.

The hotel was soon crawling with police. Paul was downstairs having a very stiff drink, in the company of a very large and heavily armed uniformed officer. The Superintendent had raced away with Ken to tend to a couple of urgent things along back at the station.

The initial scene investigation of the ransacked room had revealed nothing extraordinary. Paul's few personal belongings were scattered around the suite. The intruders had appeared intent on doing as much damage as possible, without attempting to hide their identity. Forensics were having a field day. Tragically, it seemed as if the housemaid had just been in the wrong place at the wrong time. Her throat was cut from ear to ear.

'These are not the same people who abducted your friend Miss Dortmus, that is clear,' was all the comfort that the Superintendent could offer. 'But you will understand, Paul, that I am going to have to ask you to stay for a few days while we get this cleared up.'

Paul was still in shock. 'Stay where?'

'We have a safe house just outside the city. I will make arrangements to get both you and Pat up there. This thing is rapidly getting out of control.'

'Thank you, Superintendent. I don't mind admitting that this has got me rattled.'

'Quite understandable.'

It was not yet lunchtime, but Paul decided that another whiskey was in order. Right now he desperately needed a friend.

Eventually a car arrived, and he was bundled unceremoniously inside. They slipped through the lunchtime traffic and made their way out into the suburbs, eventually driving up a long drive to a villa set back on the lower slopes of Table Mountain. Neither of the two policemen turned out to be great conversationalists, nor were they great hosts, simply letting him in the door and then leaving him alone. Security guards and their dogs roamed outside.

Paul explored the inside of the house, and decided that its furnishings were closer to a prison cell than a residence. He was not at all impressed by the bullet holes in one of the kitchen walls, but there was food in the cupboards. He prepared a light lunch, immediately feeling better.

With one hand on a cup of coffee, he went back to the lounge and picked up the telephone, thinking that he might give Pat a call. It was dead. He turned on the television, only to find that it, too, was not working. Finally, in desperation, he thumbed through the good selection of books on the shelves in the study, eventually finding something that looked like it would take his thoughts away from his current situation. Exhausted, he was quickly asleep.

He was woken much later by someone coming into the room. It was one of the security guards.

'Sorry, Sir. I didn't mean to disturb you. We had not seen any lights come on, so just wanted to make sure that you were alright.'

'Must have dropped off,' replied Paul. 'Pretty tired, I guess.'

'Is there anything that I can help you with?'

'No, I am fine, thank you.' Paul's stomach growled. 'But hungry. Are you guys allowed to join me for something to eat?' He quickly went on to explain. 'I could do with the company — it has been quite a day.'

'There are three of us on duty tonight. We could come in one at a time for a cuppa.'

Paul led the way back to the kitchen. 'Great. Give me half an hour and I will have something ready to eat, as well.'

'Sure thing.' The guard picked up his torch off the kitchen table and went out into the twilight.

Paul immersed himself in the cooking therapy, and soon had a passable meal on the table. He had just poured the coffee when there was a knock on the door, and the guard stepped back into the room.

'All quiet out there?'

'Very quiet,' the man answered. 'The dogs can't even dig up a rabbit.'

'Just how I like it. Have a seat and get yourself around that coffee.'

'Thanks.'

Paul indicated the food on the table. 'Something to eat?'

'Maybe just a biscuit.' The guard got up and went across to the cupboards on the far wall. Outside one of the dogs started barking.

The guard paused, listening to its pitch and tone. 'Rabbit, I expect. Wait here.' Before going out the door, he went around and pulled the heavy blinds down, then shut the interior door behind him to prevent being silhouetted against the light on the porch. It all wound Paul up very successfully, and instinctively he looked around for a weapon. Suddenly the quiet of the Seminary Library was looking very good.

The minutes ticked by. The dog was still barking. Then there was one shot that echoed off the rock wall behind the house. Paul ducked, although he had no idea where the bullet went. Silence. It seemed to take an eternity until there was the sound of boots on the porch.

The door opened. 'Nice big rabbit. Save me having to feed them tonight. Mind if I borrow a knife?'

Chapter 20

Daniel went through into the kitchen and found a nice sharp blade for Lester to use preparing the antelope steaks. The Army patrol had set up a heavy steel plate over their fire, down by the edge of the lake. A big pot of vegetables, fresh from the town markets, was cooking on the other side, and the rich aromas were mingling with the evening breeze.

After having filed their evening situation report, the radio operator had just signed off, while the other soldiers were cleaning and checking their equipment and weapons. It was a familiar and comfortable scene for Daniel, and he felt very much at home. Picking up a beer out of the fridge, he sat down next to Peter. 'Only thing missing is your horses.'

Peter paused in the middle of cleaning the rifle lying in carefully arranged pieces on a groundsheet at his feet. 'Yes. Matty is getting fat and lazy down at Dad's. I don't get anywhere near enough time to keep him in proper work.'

'Did you get a chance to talk with your father about getting one of the young stallions out here, to complement the local breeding stock?'

'I mentioned it briefly the last time I was down. He seemed pretty keen. Something to follow up when we get on top of this latest crisis.'

'Another one,' remarked Daniel. He turned to his friend as the stars came out overhead. 'Peter, I really hope that this one turns out better than the last time I dragged you into a mess out here.'

'Well, we certainly need to stop having people murdered under our noses.' He touched his beer to Daniel's. 'You should know that I had a very interesting conversation with the Major General.'

'What about?'

'It now seems clear that it was his personal intervention that got you off the hook, and limited the collateral damage to my career.'

'Really?'

'He is very well connected. I know he is doing all he can to find out who is behind all this, but is under enormous pressure to prevent the weapons and ammunition getting to the guerrilla forces.'

'No surprises there.'

'No, but the size of the operation is.' Peter laughed. He dropped his voice to a whisper and leant closer. 'With your normal nose for trouble, you got yourself smack bang in the middle of one of the biggest combined operations for a number of years. If we can prevent this weapons shipment getting through, we dramatically shift the military balance in our favour. It is that important.'

Daniel looked into the firelight. 'So is getting Elizabeth back.'

After a latish breakfast the following day, Daniel left Pat and Lester swapping war stories and decided to go and check on how the little Bushman children were settling in with the Ambassador's family. It was one of those astoundingly perfect mornings in the valley. After a good night's rest and three meals crammed into the space of two, Daniel was feeling more like himself.

Walking along the track around the lake shore, he instinctively rehearsed all the events of the last couple of weeks, matching up what they knew, and looking for links with what they did not know. Peter had tasked his radio operator with trying to pry out of headquarters a situation report on progress with the investigations in Cape Town. They would all feel much more comfortable if they knew what was happening down there.

'Daniel!' It was Swabi, coming down off the porch of her lodge. Daniel tried to reorient his mental processes, but was only partially successful.

'Hello, Swabi,' he replied. 'Lovely morning.'

She came across the road to join him. 'I hadn't really noticed.'

'Right.' He looked at his feet. Anywhere else, in fact, than her face that still bore the angry marks of her loss.

'I am sorry,' she said. 'I didn't mean to interrupt your walk.' She looked out over the lake, but her eyes were too full of tears to focus.

Daniel struggled for words, and then finally managed a smile at her face. 'I am going to check on the children.'

'Why? Where are they?'

'With the Ambassador,' he replied. He turned to go and almost fell over his feet. Why did he feel so responsible for her loss, as if every bad thing that happened here was somehow his fault? After a few paces he looked back. Swabi was seated in the dust where he had left her, sobbing.

For a moment Daniel stood where he was, drawn back to his distressed friend, but not sure how to respond. Finally he slowly walked back to her, and sat down. Nothing happened for a moment, and then Swabi's hand emerged and settled on his forearm — stayed on his forearm. So he covered it with his free hand, not daring to move his captured arm. 'I am so sorry. If there were anything I could do, I would be out there doing it,' he whispered.

Swabi managed a nod, and then a shake of her head, and then buried her long hair deep in his shoulder as the grief took control of her. After a while, Daniel felt comfortable enough to place his arm around her shoulder.

Swabi eventually found her voice. 'We are quite a pair, you and I.'

Daniel looked at her. 'How so?'

'We seem to attract disaster, like a magnet of some kind.'

'Is a bit like that, isn't it?' he agreed.

'What will you do when this is all over, Daniel?'

'Haven't really thought about it.'

'Liar.'

He smiled and gave her a friendly squeeze. 'You know me too well.'

'Perhaps,' she said. 'I do know that you are not suited to domestic bliss and teaching class every morning.'

'Was it that obvious?'

'Painfully.' She paused. 'I think that Elizabeth was the only one who couldn't see it.'

'And now Paul is back for her,' added Daniel.

'Perhaps that is for the best. They were always very close, Daniel.'

'Even —?'

'When Esther was still with us. Yes. It was a delicate situation, which they both had to handle very carefully. We all assumed that after a suitable period of mourning, Elizabeth and Paul would marry and live happily ever after.'

'And then Daniel Rutter appeared on the scene, and upset things.'

'Saved us,' she corrected. 'And don't forget that Paul had to return to the States. He had no option there.'

Daniel began to draw in the sand, but Swabi decided that it was time to get it out in the open, gently. 'Elizabeth was in love with a romantic figure. But that figure was not real, could not be real. Ngashi saw it as well.'

'And me? Who was I in love with?'

'A beautiful, vivacious woman, who gave you hope and focus through a very difficult year after you were arrested and taken back to Bloemfontein. That is not wrong, at all, Daniel.'

There was no ready answer for that, so Daniel resorted to tossing a few pebbles that lay handy to his feet. They made a happy sound as they hit the mirror surface of the lake.

Swabi decided that she had given the poor man more than enough to think about. 'Come on. Let's go and see how those children of yours are doing.'

Both of their thoughts, however, were with Elizabeth, wherever she was.

They found the two Bushman children asleep in one corner of the porch, curled up against Marcus. It was a touching scene. Daniel and Swabi knocked gently on the door, and the Ambassador beckoned them inside.

'How have they been?' asked Daniel, quietly.

'Fine, Daniel. But they have not moved far from Marcus. I really think that he has adopted them as his own.'

Daniel smiled. 'Marcus has a very special relationship with Dktfec.'

The Ambassador embraced Swabi. 'Hello Sister. I am so sorry to hear about Roos. He was a fine young man.'

'Thank you, Ngassi.'

Mguni came into the room and embraced her, much as a mother would. 'If there is anything I can do, you only have to think about it and I will be there.'

Swabi smiled and sat down on the couch. Daniel realised that he had not been in the room since the traumatic ending to the siege of the village well over a year ago. The family had redecorated, probably to mute the impact of some very dark memories.

'Looks nice, Mguni,' said Swabi.

'Thank you. We needed a change.'

'How is your daughter?'

'She still won't leave the house by herself, and is terrified of strangers.' Mguni turned to Daniel. 'But she does seem taken by our little guests. Perhaps they will be part of the healing process.'

Daniel nodded, and shared a glance with the Ambassador. 'Both ways.' He paused to consider his words carefully. 'I did not have time for the details the other day. The children watched their mother die. They escaped by hiding during the confusion.'

It was Swabi who reacted first. 'Dear God!'

The men nodded.

'They are truly precious,' said Mguni. 'Do they have any other family that survived?'

'A few. Fortunately there was a hunting party away from the camp for a few days. Often a few of the younger women travel with the men.'

'Other relatives?'

'Outside of the few survivors, I am not sure. Dktfec's people were the only group that I have had contact with in that part of the country. But it is a good point. Eventually we will need to go back and see if we can find any other Bushman clans in the area. They are a very special people.' Daniel paused, digesting that thought.

They heard waking sounds from the porch, and Marcus appeared, framed in the doorway. Either side of him were the children. Daniel got down on his knees and greeted them formally, placing them within his world on this special day. The little boy responded equally formally, and then Marcus led them forward into a huge, doggy embrace with Swabi.

At the Ambassador's invitation they stayed and shared a light lunch, with Daniel interpreting and encouraging the children to eat the strange food. They were a little reluctant until the Ambassador's daughter joined them to show how it was done, child style.

In the middle of proceedings, they heard footsteps on the porch, and Queen Ngashi appeared in the doorway. She put her finger up to her lips to prevent a fuss, and dropped down to join them on the floor. Daniel explained to the new arrivals what an important person Ngashi was. Marcus made a rare exception to his total focus on his little charges, and gave Ngashi a friendly lick before returning to his supervisory duties. 'I think I have lost my dog,' laughed Ngashi.

'Such a loyal beast,' replied Daniel.

It was Swabi who turned their attention back to the current crisis. 'Any news of Elizabeth, or Paul?'

'Nothing,' Ngashi replied. 'I was looking for Daniel when I ran into Peter: and Lester, is it?' she looked over to Daniel.

'Yes. I apologise for not bringing Lester around to meet you earlier.'

'Don't be silly. If I insisted on meeting everyone who came in and out of town, I might as well shift down to the city gates!'

Daniel smiled at her grace. 'Thank you.'

Ngashi continued. 'Peter is still waiting for a report from his headquarters. Radio reception is not good, evidently. He is also thinking that he should get up to Tshakai's village, and bring back the two prisoners.'

'Much easier in his vehicles,' commented Daniel. 'Wouldn't mind going along for the ride.' He looked at his watch and got to his feet. 'Please excuse me. If we go now we can get there and back before dark, easily.'

Ngashi laughed. 'Always on the go.'

Swabi got up and accompanied him down to the gate in the low fence that surrounded the lodge. She gave him a gentle kiss on his cheek as they parted, that spoke of just a little more than friendship. 'Thank you for this morning, Daniel. It meant a lot to me.'

'Me too.' With uncharacteristic composure, he returned the kiss. 'Very much,' he whispered. There was a spring in his step as he marched up the road to his cottage.

Swabi watched him go, and then turned back to join the others inside. Ngashi was watching from the porch. She reached out her hands to her dear friend as Swabi mounted the stairs. 'Gently, sister.'

There was nothing gentle about the manner in which the two prisoners were extracted from the goat's cage, and handed over to Peter and his patrol. The men were not in very good condition after their cramped incarceration. When Daniel asked if they had seen any food or water, the response from the two warriors who had been guarding them was a sullen silence. Peter waited until they were on the way back to town, and then got one of his men to jump out and give them a canteen of water each.

'I have spoken with the Chief of Police,' said Peter. 'We can secure them in one of the Police station's holding cells. I am keen to get what information I can out of them.'

Daniel leant forward from the back seat. 'I might be able to help there.' Up until now he had been very careful to respect the internal command structure and dynamics of the little patrol, particularly now that he was a civilian. Peter had tried to insist that he ride up front, but Daniel would not hear of it. 'I think that I can make myself understood.'

'Thanks. Toby speaks the lingo of the northern tribes who make up the majority of the guerrilla forces.' Peter frowned. 'But if we do need to resort to a little persuasion, I will give you a call.'

Daniel shrugged and sat back in the comfortable seat. He dozed most of the way back into town, only waking up as they approached the fortified gates. 'I might get you to drop me off as we go past the turn-off to the cottage, Peter.'

'Sure thing. We will be down a little later, for another one of Lester's famous grills.'

The young soldier in the passenger seat looked around. 'What about food for our guests?'

'I am sure that the Police can look after that,' replied Daniel.

It appeared that nearly everyone was invited to the lakefront cottage for Lester's grill that night. It was a perfect African evening, and it did not take long for the story-telling to start, as it only can in what was still fundamentally an aural culture. The stories, old and new, were accompanied by much dancing and even more drama, which grew in scope and expression as more and more of the local beer was consumed and the townspeople filtered in from their own meals and chores to join in.

Well into the evening, Daniel noticed that Swabi had slipped away from the main group, and moved across the crowded lawn to join her. He was almost through the crowd when one of the soldiers who had come in with Peter appeared at her side from down at the lake. They embraced, warmly.

Daniel turned away, confused. He finally sought out Peter, down with the vehicles. 'How did you get on with your guests?'

Peter shrugged. 'They were happy enough to talk about everything they knew, which, as you know is often the case, was very little. The only thing of any real value was an indication of where they were based.'

'Should have left them to run away home.'

'We still might, but for a different reason.'

Daniel was intrigued. 'What might that be?'

'As you know, over the years we have had great difficulty tracking the rebel forces back to their base camps. They move all the time, in any case. There was a suggestion from headquarters just before that we let them go, and then track them as they head north.'

'That would require some pretty high-end tracking skills.'

'Which, as you know, I do not have with me. But we wondered whether you and Lester might be interesting in a bit of hunting up that way?'

Daniel was immediately enthused, and the apparently intimate scene he had just witnessed made the decision that much easier. 'For me, absolutely. I would have to ask Lester.' He threw his head over his shoulder. 'If he keeps cooking like this, he may not be allowed out of the valley.' They could see the great white hunter doing his best to imitate one of the tribal war dances, thoroughly part of the entertainment.

'Right.' Peter jumped up into the back of the vehicle to retrieve some of his personal gear. 'Either way, I will put an outline plan to headquarters first thing in the morning. Might as well make something out of my long trip to get out here.'

But Daniel's thoughts were miles away, and he drifted back into the heart of the party. However, he was unable to reconnect with the noise and laughter, so slipped around the back of the crowd and into the cottage. Within moments he was asleep.

He did not notice when Swabi came looking for him, and then left for her lodge to deal with her own ghosts.

Early the following morning, Daniel placed his pack onto the trailer behind the bigger of the Army vehicles. Lester was not far behind. They joined Peter in the lead vehicle, and moved quietly out of town, followed by the rest of the patrol. Overnight, the escape of the prisoners had gone as planned. Now it was time to pick up the trail.

'Won't seem the same without Marcus,' remarked Daniel. 'But it is too early in the piece to try and separate him from the two Bushman children.'

Lester leant forward from the back seat. 'Guess you will just have to put up with us.'

'Very poor company,' laughed Peter. 'What about your little Bushman friend?'

'I considered that, but he has his hands full with rebuilding his camp, and his tribe,' replied Daniel. 'Next trip.'

The easy banter kept up as they drove north past Shadz's village. They paused briefly to pay their respects at the site of the battle with the guerrilla forces. The villagers had cleared away the scattered weapons and gruesome remains, and then erected a cairn of rocks, as an enduring memorial to all those who died.

Peter looked back across at Daniel. 'Must have been quite a scrap.'

'It was. But I have a feeling there is at least one more to come. Let's go.'

CHAPTER 21

The ship was rolling heavily on her new course and Elizabeth was weak with continued nausea. Having trouble keeping any fluids down, she was gradually dehydrating. Prone on her bunk, she looked at her watch. Just coming up on 4 AM. She decided that she must try and get something to drink, and slipped into the stateroom.

It took a couple of attempts. Eventually she resorted to crawling on her hands and knees across the room. She took a bottle of fizz out of the fridge and broke the seal on the top, just as the Colonel entered the door.

'Still not found your sea legs?'

'Not exactly.' She forced a smile. 'How much longer are we going to roll around like this?'

'A while, I am afraid. We need to get back towards the coast, while your countrymen are looking for us out to sea.'

'What will they do if they do find us?'

'An interesting question.' The Colonel went and sat at his desk, reaching for the bottle of vodka. 'That could depend on a number of things.'

'Such as?'

'Well. If we were simply to steam over the horizon, they would probably let us go.' He slowly stretched back on his chair, folded his arms behind his head, and inspected the ceiling.

'And if you don't?'

'They will do everything in their power to prevent us landing our cargo.'

Elizabeth pulled herself onto a nearby seat. 'What is everything?'

'They may start with trying to signal us.'

'Yes?'

'If we don't comply, they will deliberately escalate their tactics until we do, or until we are stopped. Whichever comes first.'

'And what might come first?' she probed.

'A very interesting question.' The Colonel played with the portrait of his family. 'Elizabeth, I am going to ask you to do me a favour.' He took the photo from its frame and wrote something on the back. 'Whatever happens, please make sure that this gets to Nina. Would you do that for me?'

'Why yes. Of course.' She took it from him and slipped it into the pocket of her overalls. 'But you will see her yourself?'

'I certainly hope so.' His fingers drummed on the top of one of the books lying on his desk. 'But Russian history is full of tragedy.'

'Now you are being morbid,' she scolded. 'I liked it better when you were rude.'

'Perhaps.' The Colonel got up from his desk. 'Some fresh air might help. Come.' He led the way out on to the rail that looked out over the stern of the ship. They stood and watched the foaming wake disappear into the darkness behind them.

There was nothing to say. A man and a woman from very different worlds, but both prisoners in their own way. The moon came out from behind the clouds as they broke free from the edge of weather. It danced on the wave tops, and Elizabeth's eyes followed the water as the ship ran away from it, straight to the glistening foredeck of the corvette chasing their wake a few miles behind them.

'Wha—?'

Then it was gone.

The Colonel had been looking out to one side, and turned towards her. 'Yes?'

'What — were you thinking?'

'Of you.'

'Why?'

'Elizabeth. I truly hope that you get home safely. No matter what happens, you must trust me in this.' He turned and took her hands. 'Understand?'

'I think so.' Her voice caught in her throat.

'Yes?'

'Yes. There is a warship following us.'

Victor looked into the darkness behind them.

'In the moonlight, just for a moment on the top of a wave.'

'You are sure.'

She nodded. 'As sure as I am standing here, Victor.'

He led them inside, excused himself and raced up to the bridge. 'Captain!'

The Captain was dozing comfortably in his chair. 'What is it Colonel?'

'We are being followed.'

'What?'

Victor elaborated. 'I caught a glimpse of a warship in our wake as we broke out into the moonlight.'

'That close?'

'Yes'

How? The Captain was struggling to fit it into his mental plot, unless they had a radar that his sensors were blind to. He reached forward and turned on the inshore Navigation radar — low power, short range. There it was, dead astern at 6 miles.*Well, let's see how awake they are,* he thought. 'Helm: hard to port.'

'Helm is to port,' replied the coxswain.

The Captain knew that his vessel turned slightly better in that direction due to the rotational dynamics of the propellers in the water. It was a risky manoeuvre in the heavy seaway, but he knew the capabilities of his ship better than the contours of his face. Even so, throughout the ship equipment slid across decks and tables as the vessel heeled with the turn hard down the face of the swell. He watched the relative bearing of the other vessel change slowly. It was not long after 0400 hours, so the watch had just changed. They would be trying to wake up, even as they took over the various tasks of keeping the ship in position. He would know how alert they were in moments.

No reaction, yet. Just a little longer. 'Midships!'

'Helm is midships, Captain.' They had turned through 180 degrees, and at the closing speed of just under 60 knots in no time they were past and clear in the other direction.

Holding onto one of the rails bolted to the bridge superstructure, Victor wondered whether his containers were still attached to the deck. 'I wondered if you might have tried to ram them, Captain?'

'Too small a target, Colonel, in this old tub. Best we run and hide for now.'

Down in the operations room of the corvette, the weapons officer was trying to get the laser rangefinder to lock on again. Then it dawned on him there was another possibility.

'Bridge, Weaps, I have lost contact!'

The officer of the watch raced out onto the starboard wing and frantically got himself organised into the night vision goggles. The ocean was empty. Just on watch, it occurred to him that now was one of those times when careers are made, or not.

'Ops, Bridge, bring up the radar, full power, all round scan.'

The operations officer, slightly senior in rank, came up on the intercom system. 'You're sure you want to do that?'

But the young officer kept his cool. 'Ops this is the Officer of the Watch. Bring up the radar. Now.'

'Ops Aye.'

'And get the XO up here!'

'Radar is up.' The seconds ticked away as the aerial above them rotated slowly. 'Radar has a contact. 235 at 6 miles.'

The officer of the watch raced to the other side of the bridge. 'Helm: hard to port, flank speed. Battle stations.' The claxon alarm sounded through the ship.

'Rudder is to Port. Engines are coming up.'

'Very good. Roll out on 225.'

The yeoman on the other side of the bridge spotted the shadow on the ladder. 'Captain on the bridge.' The XO was just behind him, by virtue of having just a little further to run.

'I presume that there is a very good reason for rolling me out of my bunk?' demanded the Captain.

The officer of the watch stood as tall as he could. 'The freighter turned about, Sir. Contact is now 8 miles, dead ahead.'

'He must have got lucky and seen us.' His CO took his chair. 'Well done, Andrew. We could have lost him.'

'It was Weaps who picked up that he wasn't where he should be, Sir.'

'As he was supposed to.' He looked around his bridge. 'OK, let's get things squared away again. He knows we are here, so keep the radar up. Sooner or later he will turn north.'

Across the water on the Russian freighter, the Captain and the Colonel shared a glass of vodka in the Captain's cabin. 'We tried, comrade. For a moment there I thought we might have got away with it.'

'And now?'

'The north star beckons.'

CHAPTER 22

The Operation Thunder morning Intelligence brief was getting under way. The usual suspects were present, including the liaison officers from external agencies. Since the melt-down in the General's office over the probable presence of the South African national on the freighter, they had been going out of their way to be useful.

'Little of significance to report overnight, Sir,' advised the briefing officer. 'Navy reports that the vessel has been manoeuvring through the night to try and evade their surveillance, without success.'

The watch commander leant forward in his seat. 'We appear to have a stalemate, Sir. They know we are there, and vice versa. There have been no signals from them, and at present they are steaming slowly south, away from any rendezvous.'

The General nodded. 'The pressure will tell, sooner or later. How long can the corvette stay on station?'

The Navy Liaison Officer stood up at the back of the room. 'She used a fair amount of fuel achieving the intercept, Sir. About another four days.'

'Thank you.' The General got to his feet. 'Warn out Maritime Operations that they should anticipate the need for a relief. We will be looking for a hot swap — I can't afford to have them break contact now.'

'Aye, Sir,' replied the duty officer.

The General turned to his Air Force liaison officer. 'How are your aircraft?'

'We have one on stand-by, Sir. Another is doing some local training today, and could be diverted if required.'

'Very good.' The General finally turned to the men that he had come to regard as the three stooges. 'Anything to add?'

The local man replied for the three of them. 'Nothing, General.'

'Nothing? I was rather hoping that having us sitting on top of their shipment might have produced at least some reaction?'

'Not that we have picked up.'

The General turned back to the briefing officer. 'What about you, Int?'

'We agree with your assessment, Sir. The ship is going around in circles, while we have no indication of any concentration of forces for a rendezvous at this stage.'

'Our forces?'

'Ready to go.'

The CIA man leant into his Brit counterpart. 'Not letting much away there, are they?'

'Neither are we, comrade. Neither are we.' Everyone in the secret service community loved Brit humour.

Humour was in very short supply in the chart room of the Russian freighter. Between them they had finished the best part of a bottle of vodka. The Colonel had just brought up a very blunt message from headquarters. It demanded explanations. He had none that they would accept.

'So,' said the Captain. 'It is time. We turn north and proceed directly to our rendezvous. I have done all I can, short of making my ship invisible.'

Victor nodded. 'Agreed. It is time to see what our opponents are made of.'

'Your men are ready?'

'They are ready, Captain.'

The Captain paused, and then leant over the table towards the other man. 'Are you ready, comrade Colonel?'

Victor knew that there were only two possible responses to the challenge. The first was to hit the larger man, hard. The second was to walk away. He actually preferred the first, but chose the second, knowing that it was far from over. Trapped like a rat in a cage, he only needed one enemy at this stage. As he made his way down to check on his men, he felt the ship turn under his feet. So be it.

There was a knock at the door. 'Yes?' called out the General, gathering his thoughts.

It was one of the watchroom staff. 'The Russian freighter has turned north, Sir. He appears to be on a course direct for a rendezvous sometime early tomorrow morning.'

'Right. Make sure that gets out to everyone involved. Activate the next phase of Operation Thunder. I will see what stomach the politicians have for a fight.' He picked up the phone, and was soon through to the office of the Chief of Defence. After a short conversation with the obligatory gatekeepers, he was put through.

He began the typically one-sided conversation. 'Good morning, Sir.'

'I am fine, thanks Sir.'

'We think that Operation Thunder is going to come to a head in the next 24 hours.'

'Yes.'

'Affirmative.'

'No chance of anything more robust?'

'Understood. Self defence only until specifically authorised by Cabinet though you.'

'Thank you, Sir. I will await your call.' He slammed down the receiver and stormed through to the watch room.

'Good morning, General,' said one of his staff rather louder than required, to alert the other staff that their Boss had just stepped into the room.

'Wish it was. Where is the watch commander?' It was a rhetorical question, as the officer in question was sitting at his desk.

'Sir.'

'Get an amplification out to all Op Thunder forces. Do not, repeat do not escalate any tactical situation. Lethal force may only be used in self defence. Clear?'

'Very, Sir.'

'And before you ask, I have no idea what's going on in Cape Town, either. HQ will have an update later today. It appears that our political masters have been eating too many cup cakes!'

'Right, Sir.' The watch commander had absolutely no idea what that was supposed to mean, but he had worked for the General long enough to know that now was not the time to ask.

Cup cakes were, Defence HQ staff knew, the standard fare for morning tea in the Cabinet Rooms. Most of the Cabinet members were enjoying a coffee break, in the middle of their regular morning caucus. Many of their key advisers and staff were present, taking the opportunity to network with each other, and to update their ministers ahead of the next session. It was one of the oldest games on earth. With three notable exceptions, they were unaware of the drama unfolding off the Northern Cape. The first exceptions were obviously the Prime Minister and the Minister for Defence. But another of their colleagues knew a great deal more than he was prepared to admit.

The Prime Minister's Private Secretary called him across to the executive suite for an urgent call. It was the Defence Chief, who quickly brought him up to date with Operation Thunder's status, and then sought approval for a more aggressive response. The Prime Minister acknowledged the request, and undertook to put it to his inner Cabinet, at the end of the morning agenda. On returning to the Cabinet Rooms he had a word in the ear of his Defence Minister, who simply nodded. No change.

CHAPTER 23

Elizabeth was feeling a little better, helped by the more sedate behaviour of the ship on its current course. She was helping herself to another drink when the door opened and the Colonel stepped into the stateroom.

He was carrying a heavy seaman's jacket, and a life vest. 'Quickly. Get into these.'

'Why?'

'We are getting you off this ship. No time for questions. Hurry!' Elizabeth struggled into the bulky jacket, and the buoyancy aid, her heart pounding.

'Do you have the photo?' asked Victor.

She was confused. 'What?'

'The photo of my family!'

'Yes.'

'Good. Follow me.' There were two other men outside, armed with short, ugly weapons. They led her down a couple of decks and then along to where the superstructure of the ship met the much lower cargo deck. The swells were clearly visible, rushing along just below the side rail. A small inflatable dinghy lay in the corner.

'We are going to put you over the side,' Victor said into her ear. 'As soon as you are clear of the stern of the ship, light this.' He handed her a marine flare. 'The Navy vessel behind us is sure to see that, and pick you up.'

'Are you sure?'

'Yes.' He showed her how to fire the flare. 'Just remember to pull this tag, hard.' He hooked the lanyard on the other end through her life jacket.

'Thank you, Victor.' She kissed him on the cheek. 'I won't forget you.'

'Good. Let's go!' The two other men lifted the dinghy onto the rail, while Victor tied the mooring line to Elizabeth's jacket. 'If you get thrown out, don't worry about trying to get back in. Just fire the flare! The dinghy will make it easier for the Navy to spot you.'

Elizabeth nodded and moved to grab hold of the dinghy, but without warning a couple of shots rang out from above them. One of the pressurised bladders exploded in her face, knocking her off her feet.

The Russians dived for cover, but there was none.

From high up on the superstructure, well back out of sight, a voice shouted down. 'Don't even think about being heroes, comrades.'

The seconds ticked by as the three men on deck considered their options, first as a team, and then as individuals.

The Captain continued. 'Put down your weapons, and move across to the door — slowly. Colonel, you can help the lady.'

Victor reached down and helped Elizabeth to her feet. There was blood on the deck. 'You are hurt?'

'My hand, I think,' replied Elizabeth.

They moved to the door, and went inside. The Captain was waiting for them, accompanied by two of his sailors, heavily armed and looking murderous. 'Comrade Colonel, I am very disappointed.' He pointed up the companionway. 'The cooler, I am afraid, for all three of you.'

'The lady has done nothing,' protested Victor. 'Let her return to the stateroom.'

'I can't afford the manpower to guard the door,' replied the Captain. 'You should have thought of the consequences, before you embarked on your foolish attempt to get her off my ship. You realise, of course, that I have saved her life. Her chances of making it safely past the wash under the stern would be almost nil.'

'He is lying, Elizabeth,' countered Victor. 'I would not have even thought of attempting it, if that was the case.'

She nodded, and in the light of the corridor Victor noticed how pale she was, just before she fainted. He caught her, and turned to the Captain. 'She is hurt, and losing blood!'

'I am sure that you can find something to use as a bandage.'

'At least let me get one of our first aid packs.'

The Captain was in a hurry to get back up to the bridge. 'I will send someone down with it, as soon as you are safely locked away. Now move!' He was true to his word, and five minutes after they stumbled into the cold, empty room, the door opened slightly and the medic was allowed in, with his triage pack.

'Colonel, what is going on? Who is hurt?'

'Over here.' Elizabeth was lying on the life jacket. Victor had ripped up his shirt to bind her bloodied hand.

The medic quickly checked her vital signs, and then unwound the makeshift bandage. A splinter had neatly amputated her left index finger just above the second knuckle, and it was still bleeding readily. 'That would hurt, I can assure you. She has probably passed out through pain and shock, more than blood loss.' He bandaged the stump tightly. 'That will stop the bleeding, and I can give her something for the pain, if you agree, Colonel.'

'Of course. Go ahead.' Victor moved across to where the other two men were leaning against the cold steel wall. 'Alright?'

'Yes, Sir.'

'Good. We have been in worse situations than this. Kabul in 1982, remember?' They nodded. 'The Captain will have to let us out when we get inshore. He wouldn't dare attempt to get our cargo off, with us locked in here.'

One man asked, 'How far away from the rendezvous are we?'

'Less that twelve hours.'

'Might get some sleep then,' replied the other.

'Good idea,' said Victor.

The medic came over to them. 'That's all I can do for her, Colonel. She should come around in a few minutes.'

'Very good, Alex. Get back to the others. Tell them we are OK, and to be ready to move from 0300 hours.'

'Good luck, Sir.' The medic knocked on the door. A moment later it opened, and he was gone. Behind Victor, Elizabeth stirred.

He went to support her as she woke. 'Easy, Elizabeth. Your hand will be a little sore.'

'What happened?' she asked.

'A bullet must have ricocheted off one of the containers.' Victor kneeled down beside her. 'It took the top off your finger.'

Elizabeth looked down at her bandaged hand. 'Looks like just a little more than the top.' She began to cry as her emotions caught up with her situation. 'Dear God, that hurts.'

'The medic gave you something for the pain. It should kick in very soon.'

Elizabeth nodded. 'What now, Mr KGB Colonel?'

'Plan B.'

'What is plan B?'

He smiled and sat down beside her. 'Let's just say that it is currently under development.' It seemed the most natural thing in the world for her to curl up in the protective arc of his arms.

Back in Cape Town, Paul had endured a day of solitary confinement, with no visitors and no news. And no way of making contact with the outside world. This particular group of guards also seemed less inclined to provide him with company. He alternately read, prowled, cooked, and dozed.

He had actually given up on the day, when a vehicle came up the drive and there was a knock at the door. It was the Superintendent. 'Good evening, Paul.'

'Good to see you, Superintendent. Please come in.'

'Thanks. I am sorry for being very late, but it has just been one of those days. I was meaning to get up here, with Ken, earlier this afternoon. That obviously didn't happen.'

Paul's pastoral instincts kicked in. 'When was the last time you got home?'

'About this time last week.' The policeman took off his jacket. 'But there is very little at home to keep me there.'

'How so?'

'You know. Grown up family. Wife whose interests have developed in other areas. That sort of thing.'

Paul smiled. 'Tea?'

'Unless you have some scotch, tea will be fine.'

'Sorry. Just tea.' Paul filled up the kettle and plugged it in. 'Any progress with the forensic examination of my hotel room?'

'Yes, as a matter of fact. Fingerprints left in your room match those found in the solicitor's rooms. It seems certain that we are dealing with the same culprits. We are trying to find out where your phone was tapped, and how. The hotel switch board is electronic, and there is no indication of tampering.'

Paul sat down while the kettle boiled. 'So where does that get us?'

'Not a lot further, I am afraid. The fingerprints have identified a couple of thugs in the local criminal underclass. We will eventually pick them up, and they will be charged with all three murders, and the arson at the Central Bank, most likely. These people are not smart enough to stay out of sight indefinitely.'

Paul got up and went across to the bench, as the kettle boiled. 'And Elizabeth?'

'Nothing, Paul. Less that nothing.'

'So where to from here?'

'Well, I can confirm that the papers were filed with the High Court yesterday. The application was in order, and duly processed, so you are now protected from anyone attempting to push through a claim on the land, or the mine, for thirty days.'

'So?'

'So it is time for you to get out of harm's way.' The Superintendent got up. 'There is a car waiting at the edge of town to drive you north. I have tickets to get you to Springbok. From there you are on your own, I am afraid.'

Paul looked around him, and then shrugged. His nearest clothes were in the cottage on the lake shore. 'Let's go.'

CHAPTER 24

Getting moving was very much on the General's mind, as he walked along the corridor to the evening brief. It would be good to get Operation Thunder's final phase underway. He reflected on a frustrating afternoon of trying to get information in, and out, of the Defence Headquarters bureaucracy in Cape Town.

Apparently the Chief of Defence and his strategic staff had confronted their own problems securing an opportunity to brief senior ministers, so that Defence Headquarters could give the operational commanders the necessary executive orders. The whole process had seemed a little harder than it should be, and again the General pondered the level of political involvement on both sides of this whole business. He arrived at the briefing room door, and was ushered through by the security guard. 'Please gentlemen, take your seats.'

The briefing began without further formality. The room was full tonight, as all the liaison officers and the shift augmentees were in attendance. After a routine intel brief that outlined the track of the Russian vessel, the disposition of known ANC forces, then their own forces on land, sea, and air, the Watch Commander briefed the actual operation. The most important part, they all knew, was the commander's intent, and rules of engagement.

As was his habit, the General delivered his intent personally, standing at the podium. 'Our forces will act to prevent the Russian cargo vessel offloading weapons and ammunition to rebel guerrilla forces grouped in the Northern Cape Province and Southern Namibia. This will be achieved by the following action. Naval forces will continue to monitor the vessel's movements, and warn the Russian crew by all means available of the consequences of coming inside the three mile limit of our territorial water.

'If those instructions are ignored, Naval units are authorised to disable the vessel by whatever means are available to them. In the unlikely event of the cargo actually being offloaded onto the beach, air force assets will destroy the containers, and render their contents inoperative. If and when we have a location for the rendezvous, we will launch an air mobile operation against ANC guerrilla forces concentrating in the area.'

There were nods around the room.

'Your rules of engagement, gentlemen.' The General glanced at several key players attending the briefing. 'Offensive action and lethal force is authorised, if and when the vessel enters the territorial waters of South Africa, including Namibia. That includes the Russian security force when inside South African territory.' The last bit had caused a good deal of head scratching with Foreign Affairs, given the status of very sensitive bilateral negotiations with the USSR. 'Are there any questions?'

'Navy, Sir. Are we to fire on the vessel in any event, if we are fired on?'

'Self defence applies at any time,' came the reply.

'Air, Sir. I presume that we can go ahead and destroy the containers, even if Russian personnel are in the vicinity.'

'That is correct. I am not going to ask you to put your aircraft and crews at risk by announcing your intentions and allowing them to prepare a nasty reception.'

'Thank you, Sir.'

An Army officer in the middle of the room completed the script. 'Standing rules of engagement for us on the guerrillas, Sir?'

'Yes Colonel,' replied the General.

The brief then went into the detail of timing, communications, medical and casualty arrangements, and so forth. Some fifty minutes later the General stood to have the last word. 'This may not come to anything. They may just have a very un-Russian attack of common sense, and go away.'

'That would be one for the books,' said an American voice from the back of the room.

'But one that we should not discard, too early,' the General responded, firmly. 'Last comments or questions, gentlemen?'

There was quiet around the room from planning teams needing to get away and put their particular pieces of the puzzle together.

'Very good. Good luck.' The General turned and walked out, but remained just to one side of the door until his three stooges emerged. 'A word, please.' He led them to his office. 'Do you have confirmation or otherwise that the South African woman is still effectively a hostage on the vessel?'

'We are convinced that is the case,' replied the South African. 'You didn't mention it in the brief?'

'Exactly, and I would be pleased if you keep it to yourself. I don't want any of my forces thinking silly chivalrous thoughts in the middle of a fire-fight. Understood?'

The South African seemed to have been elected spokesman that morning. 'Understood.'

'One other thing.'

'What might that be, General?'

'You indicated the other day that you had a fair idea who was supporting this at the political level?'

The Brit stepped up to cover the embarrassment of his South African colleague. 'We know who it is. We are just having trouble exposing him.'

The General looked between the three of them. 'Treason is very strong poison. I am not keen to have good people dying up there because you people have not done your job. Keep at it.'

The Navy corvette was still locked in behind the freighter. 'Questions?' asked the Captain. He looked around the operations room team for cues. They were now just 6 miles off the coast, on a gradually closing track that left about 20 track miles to run to the point where the freighter would enter the territorial waters of South Africa, assuming that she kept to her current course. At that point all the rules changed.

'Right. Everyone on their toes. If they do decide to offer any resistance, we will not get a lot of warning. Ops Officer, battle stations, please.' The ship's address system carried the message around the vessel.

The Captain turned and called through the door into the radio room. 'Start hailing him, Comms.'

The radio operator began broadcasting. 'Russian freighter, Russian freighter, this is the Warship *Exetor* on Maritime Common. Do you copy?'

After five minutes, and radio calls on all regulation frequencies for international maritime traffic to be listening to, the corvette began to transmit the full message on the shorter range bands. 'Russian freighter, Russian freighter, this is the Warship *Exetor.* Be advised that you are not, repeat, are not permitted to enter territorial waters. If you do so we will disable your vessel. If you do so we will disable your vessel. Do you copy?'

Silence.

'Not unexpected,' said the XO.

'Right,' said the CO. 'Let's close up to 500 metres and bring up the searchlights. See if that gets his attention.'

'Aye, Sir.'

The Russian Captain had turned the bridge monitor from the radio room down so it was only just audible. *Predictable,* he thought. He looked at the radar to check their distance off the coast and then dropped down into the chart room. Twenty minutes until he must turn to parallel the coast, just outside the three mile limit of their territorial waters.

There was a call from the bridge. 'The Naval vessel is closing us, Captain.'

'Very good.' Time for that test of nerves that precedes any real action. 'Bring us up to maximum revolutions. We will at least force them to burn their fuel faster than they might like.'

For the next three hours the two vessels steamed up the coast like partners in some fantastic marine ballet. The corvette dropped back a little so as to make station keeping easier, and conserve just a little fuel. Soon there was a glimmer of light on the Eastern horizon.

Colonel Krakovsky looked at his watch. 0530 hours. He had picked the change in course and speed, so knew that they had passed the initial rendezvous, and were now making all speed up the coast to their alternate. It was a gamble of wind and tide and time.

But the Captain had nothing to lose. An hour later, it was time for the next move. 'Pump out all ballast tanks.'

'All ballast tank pumps are running, Captain,' responded his engineering officer.

On the corvette, the crew could plainly see the dirty ballast water being discharged overboard. 'He looks like he is pumping out his tanks. What do you think he is playing at, number one?'

'I would say that he is preparing to beach her, Sir.'

'But where?'

'There is only one spot that I would choose within a hundred miles,' said the Nav. 'Right here.'

The Captain and the XO turned to the chart behind them, looking at the contours of the beach, and its approaches. 'I think you are right. Get that information off to Marcom, flash precedence.'

'Aye, Sir.'

The XO tapped the map with his pencil. 'Will he get across the bar?'

'He obviously thinks so,' his CO observed. 'But I am not sure that we will.'

They looked at the contour of the coast and the orientation of the three mile limit. The Captain drew a circle with his finger out in the broad bay. 'When he does turn in we are not going to have a great deal of time to disable him.'

The XO agreed. 'Less than five minutes.'

'Make sure Weaps is on the ball. We are going to have to get this right first time.'

The radio operator passed a piece of paper forward. 'Weather report, Captain. We are running into the tail end of that system that went through here yesterday. It is going to get rough.'

The Captain read it and thumped the table. He could feel the building seaway under his feet. Circumstances were starting to turn against them. 'There is a good chance that after all our work, we are going to have to leave this one to the Air Force,' he remarked to no-one in particular.

The crews of both vessels counted down the miles, and the minutes, to the shallow entrance to the bay. About fifteen minutes out from the point where he would turn and make his desperate run across the sand bar, the Russian Captain sent the first mate to let the prisoners out and bring them up to the bridge. Five minutes later he was back. The Colonel didn't look like he was any worse the wear, but the woman was pale and evidently needed some support. Her injured hand was obviously causing her a lot of pain.

'Your weapons are over there, Colonel.' The Captain pointed to the corner of the bridge. 'I do regret the dramatics, but simply acted to prevent you making a serious mistake that threatened the success of our mission, and the safety of my vessel. I am sure that you will come to understand.'

The Colonel turned to retrieve his weapon, checking to see that it was loaded. 'That will obviously depend on the outcome of the rest of today, Captain.'

'Of course. We are only a couple of miles from our turning point. By my calculations we should have a metre or so underneath our keel going across the bar. The swell will make it much more difficult for the smaller vessel.'

The Colonel walked to the bridge wing and looked aft. The corvette was close enough to make out individual figures on the bridge. 'Will they try to follow us?'

'If I were the Captain, not in a lifetime. This vessel was designed and built for just such a contingency. His most definitely was not.' The Captain paused. 'He will try and disable us before he has to turn away, but he will have a very small window of opportunity. I also have a plan.'

'What is that?'

'All in good time, comrade Colonel. All in good time.' He turned to the seaman on the helm. 'Start manoeuvring thirty degrees either side of our course. Use the swell, and be aggressive. He will have his work cut out trying to keep tracking our rudder. Lady and gentlemen, I suggest that you hold tight.' His passengers reached for any handhold within reach as the ship commenced to veer and roll violently.

On the bridge of the corvette, the Captain had to be impressed at how the stern of the much larger vessel was charging back and forward in front of him.

'That is going to be hard to hit, Sir,' commented the XO. 'We risk putting a hole through the engine room as opposed to damaging his rudder.'

'If that is what it takes, so be it,' came the grim reply. 'See how Weaps is getting on tracking the gun.'

'Aye, Sir.' The XO turned and dropped down into the Operations Room. He was half way down the stairs when the radio came to life.

'Please, please, do not fire on us, do not fire on us!' A woman's voice, over-pitched and full of stress, but immediately recognisable as South African.

The Captain grabbed the handset and pushed the transmit button. 'Who is this?'

'Please do not fire on us. My name is Elizabeth. Elizabeth Dortmus.'

The Captain had faced any number of difficult situations through his time at sea, but nothing had prepared him for this. 'What are you doing on that ship?!'

'I was abducted in Cape Town. Held prisoner. They will hurt me!' The transmission ended.

'He is running for the shore!' shouted the lookout standing just inside the shelter of the bridge door. By now they were inside the squall line and the visibility was down to less than a mile in blinding rain. Clouds of white spume were being torn from the tops of huge swells.

'Follow him!' ordered the Captain.

'XO, aye.' The XO took over the navigation of the vessel while his CO fought to come to terms with the situation. 'Miles to the shallows, please Nav. Count them down.' He turned to his CO. 'Your orders, Sir?'

'The bastard. He had this planned all along. He knows there is no way that we can get clarification from Marcom now.'

'One mile to the shallows, Sir,' warned the Nav. 'Bottom is coming up. Five metres under the keel.'

'Engage!' ordered the CO.

'Engage, aye, Sir.' The XO turned and yelled down the stairs. 'Fire at will, Weaps.' The answer was the sound of the radar directed naval gun firing, but the XO already knew that it was too late. As both vessels approached the bar, the sea was building up to mountains against the shallow bottom.

It probably wasn't too bad for the much longer freighter, but the corvette was seriously at risk of broaching and rolling over. Although at point blank range, the stabilised and radar directed gun was firing shells alternatively into the water off the bows, or high over the top of the vessel that loomed in front of them.

The officer of the watch's voice from across the bridge was up a couple of octaves. 'Three metres under the keel, Sir.'

The Captain swore. 'Break it off, XO.'

It was a superb feat of seamanship on the part of the coxswain to time his turn across the surf that threatened to roll them over. There was silence as all on the bridge held on and watched the bows swing around, smash through the breaking wave that threatened to knock them down, and then continue around until they were pointing safely back out to sea.

'My God that was close,' said someone. It went without saying that everyone agreed.

'Radio, make to Marcom that we have had to break off pursuit. Nav, a position please. Send that the freighter is on the beach.'

'What about the hostage, Sir?' asked the OpsO.

'What about her? For all we know it was a trick.' The CO kicked the mount of his chair. 'XO, we will hold out here where we can keep a radar plot of the bay, but get us well out of this surf.'

'XO, aye.' He felt the disappointment as keenly as his commander.

The crew of the freighter were not celebrating, yet. At first, speed was a friend, as the water pressure between the flat underside of the ship and the gently shelving bottom provided an additional margin of buoyancy. The helmsman, and the other lookouts, were working as a team to pick the deeper stretches of water, and the first mate had his eyes glued to the depth gauge and the radar. There was one nasty moment when they kissed the bottom and the shock rippled through the ship, but then they were through and clear in the bay on the other side of the bar.

'Full astern!' ordered the Captain. The relatively flat water in the bay was almost surreal. He watched as the speed fell off until they only had just enough forward motion to answer the helm in the strong wind. The beach was only 500 metres ahead. In a manoeuvre that they had practiced many times, the crew aligned their ship perpendicular to the beach and eased her slowly inshore. At 100 metres the Captain ordered the giant stern anchors away. At 50 metres he signalled for the propellers to stop, allowing the wind and residual momentum to carry the vessel the final stretch until they felt her motion change subtly. They were aground. Soon the outgoing tide would leave them high and dry.

The Captain turned to the Colonel, and bowed slightly. 'Ready to disembark your cargo, Colonel.'

'Thank you Captain. Well done. We will wait just a little for the tide to go out.'

'Of course.'

CHAPTER 25

The mood in the watch room of the distant command centre was grim. The Naval liaison officer was desperately trying to defend the honour of his Service, with absolutely no information as to how what seemed to be a relatively straight-forward exercise had gone so wrong. Everyone in the room was aware that it only got more difficult from here.

The watch commander, an Army brigadier, eventually decided that the blood-letting had gone on long enough. He needed to get everyone focused on the next phase, so turned to his Air Force liaison officer: a young fighter Pilot, who would much rather be back at the airfield getting ready to climb into the beckoning clouds. 'How is the weather looking for the air strike?'

'Not at all good, Sir. There is an active front lying across the area, with low cloud base and heavy rain underneath.'

'Forecast?'

'Might be a clearance later in the day.'

'Right,' the Brigadier replied. 'Work on getting the strike in before last light. We don't want those weapons sitting on the beach all night, because one thing that I can guarantee you all is that they won't be there in the morning.'

'Wilco, Sir.'

'I want an update every hour, understood?'

'Every hour, Sir.'

The door slammed behind him as he went off to brief the General. Those that remained decided that they all had important things to do. The Air Force officer decided that it just might be time to get religion.

Elizabeth was praying quietly. The medic had given her another shot of pain killer, and, with the ship firmly attached to the beach, she was feeling physically much better. But she was sick with fear. The fear of not knowing. From the bridge she watched as two big tractors emerged from a hangar in the forward hold, and were lowered into the shallow water alongside, using the ship's cranes. One by one the containers followed, were connected to the tractors, and then towed up the beach until they were well above the high tide mark. Throughout the whole operation, the rain drove down.

Finally the last container was offloaded, and the men were winched back aboard in a couple of cargo nets. The tractors must be part of the deal, Elizabeth noted absently. She turned around only to find the Captain standing behind her.

'It is time for you to leave us, my dear.'

'What do you mean?'

'I mean that we are leaving all our cargo on the beach. That includes you.'

She looked for Victor down on the deck, only to spot him and his men being held high off the deck in one of the nets, well covered by the weapons of a couple of the ship's crew.

'This way please.' The Russian shoved her roughly in the direction of the companionway that led down onto the now-empty container deck. Her world shrank to just the next step, one step at a time.

Emerging onto the cargo deck, she was thrown roughly into the remaining cargo net and immediately swung over the side, accompanied by two sailors. By this stage the tide was coming back in, and she gagged and struggled as the heavy net dragged her under the water surging around the side of the ship, until rough hands dragged her free of its embrace and toward the beach. But her injured hand got caught in one of the supporting ropes and she

215

almost lost consciousness as the pain threatened to overwhelm her.

The other seaman threw her over his shoulder and carried her up the beach. He dropped her in front of one of the containers, tied her hands and feet to the locking mechanism, and then headed back to the ship without looking back. The tide was rising quickly, and they had no desire to be caught on this exposed, barren, shore.

The log would show that the ship was winched off the beach at 1500 hours. Empty, and with no ballast, the Captain did not have to wait long before there was enough water over the bar for a safe passage. As a precaution against any misplaced heroics, the Colonel and his men were locked in their quarters. The Captain had not yet decided how he would report their conduct on arrival back in Sevastopol.

As he expected, the busy little corvette was waiting for them as he cleared the shallows on the way out to sea. He also knew they would not have any reasonable cause to detain him now he was outside of the three mile territorial limit. He could, therefore, wind them up with relative impunity. He picked up the radio handset.

'Good afternoon little warship, it is very nice of you to wait around for us. It was quite an exciting ride across the bar. But we missed you in the lagoon?'

There was no reply, but then he would probably ignore the insults as well. He decided to raise the stakes a little and see if they took the bait. 'We have left your woman tied to a container on the beach. She is alright now, but I don't know how she will be in the heat of the day. What do you think?'

Again, no reply. He laughed, a hearty, relieving type of laugh. The members of his bridge crew joined in, although none of them spoke English. As the Navy were being so predictably boring, he simply turned and set heading for the equator. He decided to leave the KGB safe in their quarters, until they were at least a day further north.

What was it about a pretty face, that so completely screwed with men's minds? he asked himself. There might be a little extra money in it for him, if he chose to go down that particularly dangerous path. We will see, comrade Colonel Krakovsky, we will see.

The corvette was retasked to shadow the freighter, as far as fuel would allow. The Captain thought that the wording of the message from headquarters was perhaps a little more formal than was required.

As he worked over his initial report, he pondered the last couple of messages from the freighter. The trick was, he knew, to say enough, but not too much. Problem was, his squadron commander would be looking for things that he did wrong, rather than what he did right. The loneliness of command.

What did he say of the business with the woman hostage, or at least what sounded like a woman? What could he, or should he, have done better, or different? There were no easy answers. He went back up to the bridge and grabbed a steaming hot coffee, as they settled into the routine business of making sure the freighter continued north.

The XO came and leant over the rail alongside him. 'Bit of an interesting day?'

'You could say that, Ben.'

'What do you make of that stuff on the radio from a woman?'

'What do you think?'

'It sort-of sounded genuine,' his second in command replied. 'I had the comms guys run the tapes. The more I listen to it the more convinced I am.'

His CO took off his cap, and scratched his head. 'Right. Well, if you are convinced, send off an intel report to that effect. Can't do any harm.'

'Aye.' He paused, and then turned to the older man. 'He was very good, that guy. I have re-run the whole thing, and can't think of anything that we might have done differently.'

'Thanks Ben, but we both know that it will not be seen that way by the arm-chair warriors back in headquarters.'

Just at that moment the officer of the watch stepped out on the bridge wing. 'Captain. Distress call, from the freighter; *explosion in the engine room, on fire.*'

The conclusion was obvious. 'One of our shells must have done some damage!' said the XO, not sure whether it was more appropriate to sound elated, or concerned.

'Bring us up alongside her, Lieutenant,' ordered the Captain. All seamen are united by a deep-seated fear of fire at sea. 'And get a quick message off to Maritime Command.'

'Aye, Sir.'

It was not long before they were close enough to clearly make out the ominous dark smudge of the burning vessel. 'Get the damage control team together for a brief, number one. Radio, any other vessels in the vicinity that you are aware of?'

'No-one that has responded to the *Mayday* message, Sir.'

'Understood.' He peered through the binoculars, trying to get a better look at what was going on.

The corvette slowed as they arrived about half a mile off the stationary vessel. The weather was not ideal, with a good swell and a wind-driven chop running across it. Both vessels were rolling heavily.

The fire had taken the crew of the freighter completely by surprise. Elated that they had been successful with the mission against huge odds, it took a little too long to respond when the engine room alarms went off. The engineering officer assumed that it was another short in the troublesome fire-wire sensors, designed to provide an automatic fire-watch in the engine spaces not routinely manned. He could not have been more wrong.

One of the shells from the corvette had penetrated the engine room wall. A piece of shrapnel had grazed a high pressure fuel line, and it was only a matter of time before the weakened pipe failed. The explosive gasses built in the compartment until eventually they found an ignition source. Fortunately the automatic protection systems functioned as designed, immediately shutting down the engine, and isolating the fuel line, allowing the freighter's automatic fire suppression system to partially extinguish the initial flames. But the damage was done.

Rushing down from the bridge, the engineering officer moved passed the mess deck where Colonel Krakovsy and his men were being held, but acted on an impulse and unlocked the door. There was only a thin bulkhead separating this deck from the engine compartments, and he did not wish to have the soldier's deaths on his conscience.

The alarms were loud in the confined room, and Victor was the first to the door. 'What is going on?'

'Engine room alarm. Might be a fire,' the officer shouted over the racket. 'Get your men topsides, Colonel.'

It was well that the engineer did. When he opened the door to the machinery spaces, the residual superheated gases exploded in his face. He died instantly as the overpressure rearranged his internal organs.

With the fire now unconfined, the next compartment to go was the mess deck. Victor grabbed the intercom handset off the wall just outside the door off the cargo deck, and punched the button that put him through to the bridge. When the first mate answered he didn't waste any time with formalities. 'This is Krakovsky. There is a fire in the engine room and it has now reached the mess desk. My men will attempt to get some water on the blaze from the container deck.'

Almost immediately the ships loudspeaker system rang out. 'Emergency stations, emergency stations. Fire in the engine room. Fire in the engine room. All hands to damage control stations. All hands to damage control stations.' Up on the bridge the crew activated the fire fighting pumps in the forward section of the freighter to provide water to the damage control effort.

'Quickly,' Victor shouted. 'Get these hoses deployed.' The soldiers raced to unroll the big hoses, and, after what seemed an age, water shot from the big nozzles. The battle with the fire was on.

The ship lost two more men to the heat and smoke, but eventually the weight of water thrown at the flames robbed the fire of vital heat and oxygen. After a desperate forty minutes the fire was out. The Captain appeared from a smoky hole where there had preciously been a heavy door, and held out his hand to Victor. 'Thank you. If you had not acted as quickly as you did we would be in the embrace of the ocean.'

'What is the damage?' asked the Colonel, bracing against the rolling of the big ship as it sat broadside to the big swell.

'It will take a while to sort out the chaos in the engine room. At best we are going to have to limp home on the auxiliary engine. At worst we are stuck out here until we can organise a tow.'

'Mind if I go up and use the radio, Captain?'

'We lost the radio room power supply to the fire, Colonel. Maybe your Navy friends can pass a message for you.' The Captain smiled and pointed at the corvette that was keeping station by moving quietly around his crippled vessel.

'They might offer me a bath,' Victor joked, as the tension of the last few minutes unwound. Both men worked their way up to the bridge.

'The warship is signalling, Captain,' advised his first mate. The two senior officers moved to the bridge wing. The residual smoke was less obvious out in the fresh air.

'Do — you — need — assistance. Shall I respond, Captain?' asked the radio operator.

'Send: the fire is out and we are assessing damage,' the Captain directed, turning to Victor. 'No point in trying to disguise the obvious.'

Victor nodded. 'I might go down and check the stateroom.'

The Captain waved his dismissal, his attention on the warship pitching and rolling its weary way around his stern.

Down in the stateroom, Victor covered his face with a cloth against the almost overpowering stench of smoke and cooked flesh. He made his way across to the wall safe and in a few quick moves opened the door, reaching inside to retrieve a metal container about the size of a shoe box, and a matching pair of simple tanned-leather pouches. He placed the pouches in the ample pockets of his overalls, and took the container across to his desk and cleared the remains of his precious books.

Opening the container, he took what looked like a radio handset out of its padded surrounds and dialled a pre-arranged code into the counters on its the face. That done to his satisfaction, he flicked the guarded switch from 'Off' to 'Activate', and was rewarded with a flashing amber light above the switch. Clearing some of the books from his library, he placed the apparatus carefully out of sight. *How long?* he wondered, patting the lumpy pockets to smooth their contour a little, allowing himself to speculate for just a moment at the inconceivable wealth they contained.

High overhead the South Atlantic, a highly classified military satellite picked up his transmission almost immediately, and relayed its message across the constellation until it was received at a very secret installation at the base of the Ural Mountains. Minutes later a message was in the hands of the KGB. Not much later, tasking orders were broadcast back across the same satellite.

Not far off the coast of Namibia, a tiny communications buoy picked up the encrypted message and relayed it deep below the surface to the Russian nuclear powered submarine sitting almost stationary below.

There was a knock on the door of the deputy-Captain's cabin, and the message was passed. After reading it twice, the man rolled off his bunk and moved along to the operations room. 'Get the Captain.'

The deputy-Captain was hunched over the charts when the Captain arrived. 'What is it?'

'Flash message from fleet ops, Captain. We are released from patrol, and are to proceed to this position to take a KGB special operations team off a crippled freighter.' His finger indicated the position that he had just plotted.

'And then?'

'Sevastopol,' he smiled. *Home, or close to it, early.*

'ETA?'

'About three hours at patrol speed.'

'Make it two. The KGB was never very patient.'

'Aye, sir.' The deputy-Captain stepped through to the control room. 'Cut the buoy. Turn onto course 050 degrees and make your speed 40 knots.' The big vessel came alive as her twin reactors accelerated her through the water. 'Make your depth 250 metres.'

The crew felt the deck tilt under their feet as they came up to sit just below the thermocline, the temperature change in the water column that would deflect the majority of the noise of their passage down to the ocean depths. But at this speed they were basically running blind, and pumping an awful lot of noise into the water from their cavitating propeller.

They briefed the top-side party and boat crew. The boat crew were going to have to launch their inflatable boat, housed in the rear of the submarine's sail, and then get the KGB safely off the crippled freighter. The top-side party were warned out to expect a heavy swell. The most difficult part of the whole exercise would be retrieving the boarding party, and their passengers.

Just under two hours later, the navigating officer reported. 'We are in position for the rendezvous.'

'Very good,' acknowledged the deputy-Captain. 'Revolutions for 8 knots. Make your depth 50 metres.' The instructions were passed and acknowledged to ensure there was no possibility of a misunderstanding. The Captain stepped into the control room.

'Captain has the boat,' acknowledged the second-in-command. Easing their way up to 50 metres, they used the sophisticating sensor suite to check the area for surface contacts. Passive sonar could clearly make out a couple of noisy pumps on the freighter.

'Three pings please, sonar, just to check there is nothing else in the area.'

'Sonar, aye, Captain.' They waited for the pulses of energy to travel out through the water, and return.

'Sonar has two contacts, close together, bearing 035 at 6 miles.'

'Two contacts?' queried the deputy-Captain.

'Apparently our friends have company,' agreed the Captain. 'Never mind, our patrol is compromised anyway. Bring us up to periscope depth.' The submarine drifted closer to the surface, and the Captain raised the big surveillance periscope up through the waves. He already knew it was not a pleasant day on the surface, as his vessel began to roll around him. Submariners much preferred the quiet sanctuary of the ocean depths. 'A South African corvette, no less. Time to give him something for his log. Clear above. Surface the boat.'

'Surface, aye,' replied the control station.

Just fifty metres above them, both ships had reverberated with the short bursts of compressed sonar energy.

'We appear to have company, Captain,' remarked Victor, indicating the black shape emerging from the ocean depths a couple of miles west of his crippled vessel.

'So we do, Colonel. Am I to presume that they were invited?'

Victor saluted and then moved to organise his men. 'Always have a plan B, comrade. Always have a plan B.'

Well out into international waters, there was very little for the corvette to do but observe and report the quite extraordinary feets of seamanship as the huge submarine — twice the length of *Exetor* — took a party off the freighter in the open ocean and then slipped beneath the waves. 'That is one for your memoirs, skipper,' commented the XO.

'Never be allowed to tell the tale,' warned his CO. And then a thought occurred to him. 'Don't forget to send the message about the possible hostage to maritime command. Make it flash precedence.'

CHAPTER 26

A nod from the flight leader sent the four jets accelerating down the runway. With a maximum load of high explosive bombs, the first leg of the mission was the climb to rendezvous with the tanker that would shepherd their transit northwest. They would stay in loose formation with the big jet until they were cleared to proceed with the strike. That part of the mission was in the hands of the much slower maritime patrol aircraft, currently working its way up the coast towards the target, trying unsuccessfully to stay out of the worst of the weather.

The patrol aircraft Pilot came up on the intercom. 'Not looking good, Nav. As far as the radar can see it is socked in.'

The Nav was not quite as pessimistic. '85 miles to run yet, Skipper. Navy reports that there was a break over the target area, when they departed.'

'Pity they couldn't hang around,' remarked the Co-pilot. 'Shall I try and raise them?'

The Pilot gave a thumbs up across the cramped cockpit. 'Good idea. They should be well within range by now.'

The Co-pilot selected the appropriate radio frequency, and pushed the transmit button. 'Warship *Exetor*, Warship *Exetor*, this is *mike papa x-ray four-six* on maritime common, do you copy?'

After a brief pause, the radio operator on the warship replied. '*X-ray four-six,* this is *Exetor,* go ahead.'

'Currently en route up the coast to our tasked area. Strike package is approximately five zero minutes behind us. Request your current position and weather.'

'This is *Exetor.* Stand by please.' The aircraft crew chuckled. The radio operator would be sending a message for someone who was allowed to offer an opinion on the weather.

After a couple of minutes, the warship came up on the frequency. '*X-ray four-six* this is *Exetor,* do you copy?'

'Go ahead, *Exetor.*'

'Roger. We are currently some 25 miles north-west of your target. We have run back into the weather. Visibility is less than 5 miles with a cloud base of around 500 feet. When we left your target area, the weather was clear.'

'Good news,' answered the Co-pilot.

'Ask them if they have any further info about the target area that might be useful for the strike,' suggested the Nav.

'Containers will be clearly visible about the mid-point of the bay, on the beach,' came the reply. There was a pause in the transmission, and a different voice continued. 'This is *Exetor.* Be advised that there may be, I repeat may be, a South African national — female — hostage tied to one of the containers. We are trying to confirm details with headquarters.'

The Pilot signalled to his Co-pilot that he was taking over the radio. 'Confirm your last, *Exetor.*'

The transmission was duly confirmed.

'Ah, we acknowledge that *Exetor,* and will do likewise on our net. Have a good trip home.'

'Thanks. Good luck. *Exetor* Out.'

The radio operator came straight up on the aircraft intercom. 'Radio copied. I am on to it.'

'We may need to drop down over the target area?' suggested the Nav.

'Not very keen on that,' answered the Pilot. 'We are too slow and there is no knowing who is hanging around on the ground. Let's see what we can get from Ops.'

'My butt agrees with that, for sure,' confirmed one of the other crew members. They watched the miles to the target tick down.

About 10 miles out from the bay the weather cleared dramatically, and the pilots looked down at the barren stretch of coast below them. The beach was clearly visible on the nose. Just above the breakers in the middle of the bay, was a haphazard collection of containers. 'How much daylight have we got, Nav?' asked the Pilot.

'Fifty minutes.'

'Radio. Transmit the strike clearance message. Send in the jets.'

'Wilco, Skipper.'

'What about that report of a hostage?' asked the Co-pilot.

The Pilot looked at the line of surf below them for a moment. 'We have done everything we can, Rick.'

Elizabeth was barely conscious in the afternoon heat reflected by the sand around her, amplified by the walls of the containers. It was like being trapped in a slow cook oven. She was desperately dehydrated, had stopped sweating, and her core body temperature was dangerously high. In her more lucid moments, she thought that perhaps the sun would go down before she died. In her delirium, it was already very dark, but still just as hot.

Early on she had used valuable energy fighting against the bonds that secured her, terrified of being discovered by some hungry animal. In fact, this section of the coast was almost completely deserted and devoid of life. Just a few scorpions, snakes, and lizards that eked out a miserable existence on the edge of the dunes that ran inland. Late in the afternoon, the king tide had given her a good scare as the larger breakers ran up and around her, but the containers were well positioned, and the waves advanced no further. Her whole world consisted of the roar of the surf and the blinding light of the sun full on her face.

There was a knock on the General's door. 'It is open,' was his invitation to enter, if you were feeling particularly bold.

It was the Watch Commander, and he was not feeling at all sure about this one. 'Sir, I have a query from the strike overwatch.'

'What is it?'

'The *Exetor* passed a report that there may be a woman hostage on the beach, tied to one of the containers.'

'Really?'

The watch commander thought that his boss did not seem as surprised as he should have been. 'Affirmative. Supposedly her name is Beth Dormus, or something like that. It appears that this woman may have been held on the freighter, and then left behind when they offloaded the weapons.'

'Lucky, given what appears to have happened to the freighter.' The General looked at the papers on his desk.

'I guess so, Sir. But where does that leave the strike?'

Now too many people know, thought the General, wondering how his conscience let him get so far into this dark place. 'Abort the mission.' For a moment the other man did not respond. 'Abort the mission — hurry man!'

'Right away, Sir.' The Watch Commander raced down the corridor, bursting into the watch room. 'Air. Where is the strike package?'

The young fighter pilot looked at the clock on the wall and did a quick bit of mental arithmetic. 'About now they will be on descent into the target area.'

'Shit. Flash message to all units. Abort the mission.'

'Sir?'

'Don't waste time, man. Do it!'

The young man started to write out a message. One of the old hands in the watch room shook his head, and raced out the door and down to the communications centre.

Swabi had to shade her eyes as the sun went down over the lake. She was seated under one of the willows, praying and seeking solace in the familiar words of her favourite Psalms. Confused and hurt at the death of Roos, and then the sudden and unexplained departure of Daniel, she had finally relented late in the day to obey the quiet, but insistent, calling of her spirit.

Paul had taught her the importance of acting on those gentle prompts. Elizabeth was on her heart, and she poured out her soul for the safe return of her friend.

Descending into Springbok in a small twin-engine aircraft, Paul was similarly challenged to intercede for the woman he loved. He had a clear sense that he wrestled with dark and powerful forces, as he watched the parched landscape come up to meet them.

The flight leader took the four aircraft down from their high altitude perch, running through the checklists instinctively. As soon as they broke out of the cloud he pushed them out to their attack formation, turned to put the coast on his wingtip, and flicked the final master switch that armed his weapons and applied power to the trigger on the control column. He could see the containers on the beach ahead of him.

He entered a shallow dive to position the aircraft at the exact release point for the high-drag bombs attached to the ejector racks under each wing. 'Cobra Black is in live,' he transmitted.

Above them in the radio station of the patrol aircraft, the abort message was coming off the printer. At that moment, the Nav was working through the first few elements of the mission report with the radio operator, but the communications officer at headquarters had thought to insert a line of dashes at the front of the message, that made the mechanical typewriter in the aircraft shout out four urgent tones in Morse code. It immediately caught both their attention.

The Nav ripped the message off the printer and threw himself into the cockpit. 'Abort. Abort. For God's sake, abort!'

The Pilot simply pointed at the Co-pilot, who hit the transmit button.

Elizabeth thought she could hear a higher pitched noise that was different to the lower roar of the surf. She tried to look down the beach, but her eyes were closed by the effects of salt and heat. If she had been in better condition, Elizabeth might have just been able to make out four sinister black dots, just above the line of clouds to the south.

The flight leader eased slightly left to bring his bomb sight into the middle of the target. There we are. He was lifting the guard over the little red button on the control column when the earpieces in his helmet came alive.

'Abort, abort, abort. Cobra Black, abort, abort, abort!'

Elizabeth jumped as the jet screamed overhead, and then another, and another, and another. She was beyond understanding.

The flight leader pulled the nose of his aircraft skyward. 'Cobra Black weapons safe.' All this way for a split second call off the target.

'Black this is *X-ray four-six*. It appears that there may be a civilian hostage tied to one of the containers.'

'Black One, roger. Just in time.'

'Understood, Black One. Do you have enough fuel to cover my recce?'

'We can hang around for ten minutes. The tanker is not too far away.'

The pilot of the patrol aircraft turned his lumbering beast towards the target and put the nose down. 'Crew, Pilot, buckle up, we are going down for a look. Descent and tactical checks thanks Nav.' He decided that it was safest to descend over the dunes and then cross the target area heading towards the open ocean. That way if there were any bad guys on the ground, they were exposed for as little time as possible.

'Checks complete,' confirmed the Nav.

The wind around the airframe of the old aircraft made a distinctive whistle as they descended at maximum allowable airspeed. Approaching the containers, the Pilot closed the throttles to slow down as he levelled off at approximately 100 feet above the sand, and then applied just enough power to keep the aircraft in the air. It was perfectly judged, and the Co-pilot could clearly see an adult figure tied to the front of one of the containers. There was no movement.

The Pilot pressed the transmit button, '*four-six* is clear to seaward. We confirm the presence of one individual on the target. No other activity from what we can see.'

'Black One roger,' came back the strike flight leader. 'We are climbing to the south. Thanks guys, would not have wanted that on my conscience.'

'You are welcome. Safe trip home.' They were all quiet for a while as they climbed back to their cruising altitude and turned for home.

CHAPTER 27

Home was somewhere that none of the Operation Thunder battle staff were going to see that night. The whole team was present for the 1900 brief, but the feeling of defeat was in the air.

The General sat through the operations update, studying his bootlaces impatiently. As arranged, the watch commander handed over the brief to him.

'Not a good day, team. Not a good day.' There were few in the room who bothered to catch his eyes. 'But.' He got to his feet. 'But, from the situation reports that have come in so far we didn't do that bad, either.' The General looked around the hostages in the room. 'The presence of a civilian hostage made our job very difficult, if not impossible.' He gave them all a chance to digest that. 'So. To the airmobile operation tomorrow morning. How are we looking?'

'Not that good, I am afraid, Sir,' replied the Army Colonel in the middle of the room. 'The target is too far north for us to get the full package up there in one lift. It will take three lifts to get everyone and their equipment to the selected helicopter landing zone, and then they will be pretty much on their own.

'Alternatives?'

The Special Forces liaison officer stood. 'We could send in a light section and get the hostage out. Then the Air Force can have some bombing practice.'

'Anyone else?' there was silence across the room. 'Right. Work it up. Warn out the units concerned. I would like them on target as soon as possible tomorrow morning. This is now a race between us and the bad guys. Understood?' There were a few nods in the audience. 'Make it work. Outline brief at 0100 hours. Those not involved are welcome to stand down, at your section leader's discretion.' The General went to find some coffee. Another long night ahead, and he had yet to call Defence HQ with the obligatory report to the Chief of Defence. He was not looking forward to that conversation.

His watch commander met him in the kitchen. 'We do have one other option.'

'What is that, Rory?'

'Major Hogan and his team are on their way north, not that far from the border. They also have Rutter with them.'

'That is a pretty left-field option.'

'Yes, it is.' The General paused. 'But it may also be the best. The chopper would be empty departing base, so should be able to go out there with a full fuel load. They could get up to the target and be back before breakfast.'

'Check it out. Keep this between us, and don't mention Rutter to anyone.'

'Wildo Sir.'

'And Rory.'

'Yes, Sir.'

'Good thinking. That is why I have you on the team. For God's sake make it work.'

Peter's hunting patrol was laagered up for the night. Progress was slow and frustrating, following a couple of wanderers working their way across the semi-desert of this part of the High Veldt. They had to be very careful that dust from the vehicles did not give them away.

The radio operator disturbed their evening coffee. 'Boss, radio for you.'

'Thanks Corporal.' Peter got up and went around the back of the vehicle.

A few minutes later he came back to the carefully shielded fire. 'Got a minute, Daniel.'

Peter filled him in on the details.

'Elizabeth?'

'Apparently.'

Daniel shook his head, trying to get the reality into his head. 'No reason it shouldn't work. The unknown is how far away the bad guys are.' Daniel smiled. 'Only one way to find out.'

'Chopper will only have room for four.'

Daniel nodded, thinking on his feet. 'You, me, your medic, and your comms guy.'

'Bit light on the fighting side, isn't it?'

'If we end up firing a shot in anger, the chances are we will need the medic.'

'Comms?'

'I like the idea of someone else carrying the radio.'

Peter laughed. 'When?'

'Soon as the chopper can get here.'

That turned out to be 0430. Peter activated the patrol radio beacon for the big utility helicopter to home in on. It appeared out of the night sky as a noisy black hole, and the four men jumped on. They were quickly airborne, and headed north just under the scudding overcast. Their route took them to the coast, and then they flew just outside the surf line so as to minimise the chance of running into trouble before they had to. The weather did not make for a comfortable trip, but the white phosphorescent line of the surf was easy to follow, and the coastline itself provided few hazards. By the time they were running into the final turning point, there was an early morning grey flush on the eastern horizon.

'Ten minutes,' said the crewman, and moved to man the starboard side door gun.

Daniel positioned himself on the port side. 'Weapons check,' he yelled to Peter, as the pilot took them down so low that they were actually flying in between the surf that was rolling in of the Atlantic Ocean.

'Five minutes,' said the winchman, and moved to man the port side door gun. There was now more than enough light to pick out the details of the terrain out to their right.

'Hold tight!' was the final call, as the chopper banked steeply and flared, to arrive at a stationary hover alongside the seaward container. Nothing moved. Daniel immediately noticed that the container doors were open.

'Go, go, go!' yelled the crewman, and the four soldiers bailed. In a cloud of sand, the chopper was gone.

Daniel led them into cover. Nothing moved. Telling the others to sit tight for a moment, he checked the nearest container. Empty. They were all empty, and there was no sign of Elizabeth.

He went back to where Peter and the others were hunkered down. 'We are too late. They have already emptied the containers. Elizabeth's not here.'

'What now?' asked Peter.

'You go back, Peter. I will find Elizabeth. Send Lester north to meet us at the border in one of your vehicles. I have a feeling that he knows where to go.'

'You will have no communications, no support.'

Daniel patted his friend on the shoulder. 'So what is new?' They shook hands.

Daniel did not wait for the chopper to come back for the pick-up. He was already working his way down the beach at a steady trot, as it slipped past on the other side of the breakers. Right at that moment the Pilot was transmitting an initial report through to his command centre. Operation Thunder was dead in the water.

CHAPTER 28

Elizabeth had recovered a little in the cool of the night, and a couple of heavy showers had allowed her to drink from the runoff of the container. She lay as quiet as she could, hoping that the land breeze that blew every night in these parts would take her scent out to sea, away from any predators that might be working the beach for a meal.

Much later the last of the moon rose over her open-air prison. Gradually she became aware that she could hear vehicles toiling their way slowly up the beach. Then quiet. She became aware of her breathing.

Finally she could not stand the suspense any longer. They were going to find her anyway, whoever it was, so she might as well take what initiative was left her. 'Help me! Help me!'

Nothing. Just the steady wash of the surf on the beach out to her left. 'Please. I know that you can hear me. I am tied to one of the containers.'

Silence. The breeze had dropped away, and suddenly Elizabeth found herself sweating. 'Help me, please!'

The ANC patrol was fanned out in whatever cover they could find. Expecting to find the containers on a deserted beach, they were wary that this might be another trap.

'Aha, Jacob. The lady said please,' whispered the ANC patrol commander to his lieutenant. 'I suppose we should find out what she wants.'

'Be careful. Something doesn't smell right.'

Major John Sawka grinned. 'Just your clothes, Jacob. Wait here and keep me covered.'

The man sighed. 'The last time you told me to do that, I spent another month getting you out of an Army prison.'

'Just in time, too. The food was beginning to get to me.' The Major moved forward, carefully.

He found the woman at the front of the third container he checked. As far as he could make out there was no-one else. Even so, discretion was his survival code, and he stayed out of sight. 'Who are you and what are you doing here?'

Elizabeth started and turned towards the voice. 'Who are you?'

'I am sorry, but I am asking the questions, for now.' Major Sawka repeated the question, while scanning around him for any movement.

'My name is Elizabeth Dortmus. I was held hostage on the freighter that dropped these containers on the beach.'

'An interesting tale.'

'The Russians left me here. I do not know why.'

'I think I do,' he said to himself. The Major and his patrol had heard the unmistakable sound of the air strike going in the previous evening. Well to the south at that stage, and under the cover of the atrocious weather, it had still given them a good fright. They had fully expected to find their precious cargo scattered across the beach.

'Are you alone, then?'

'As far as I know. Yes.'

The Major gave a brief whistle, and waited until his men were in position around the perimeter. He moved forward and crouched down in front of the woman. 'You appear to be in front of my container, Miss.'

Elizabeth fought back the panic. 'Your container?'

'Well, actually what is inside.' He took out a wicked looking knife and leant towards her. Elizabeth's feet scrambled in the sand as she desperately tried to move away from her.

'Please. Please don't hurt me.'

He backed off. 'I have no intention of hurting you. But I do need to get this container open, sooner rather than later.' Behind her, Elizabeth heard the sound of the tractors firing up. She stopped struggling, and held her breath while the man reached around behind her and cut her bonds.

'Much better,' he said. 'There you are.' He issued a couple of quick instructions to his men and then guided her out of the way. 'Let me take you back to my truck. There is food and water there.' Her limbs refused to work, so she had to accept his support.

'Who are you?'

'It would be better if you did not know my identity, for now.'

'ANC?'

He didn't reply. They arrived at the vehicles, dispersed as best as the beach allowed. 'Make yourself at home, the driver will show you where the food is.'

Elizabeth accepted the help up. 'Thank you.'

He was gone. The driver pointed to a box full of military-style rations, and went back to his surveillance out of the top of the cab. For now Elizabeth just ate and drank, and tried not to let her imagination get too far ahead of reality. Trapped with a guerrilla patrol, on the edge of the desert, a long way from home.

The containers were quickly emptied onto the waiting trucks and the patrol prepared to move inland, careful not to take the same route back to base. It would be slow going over the uneven terrain, but they had to be as far away from the rendezvous as possible by dawn. Preferably, they also had to be in cover.

The ANC commander stepped lightly up into the cab. 'So Miss. Tell me how you came to be the reason why I now have a convoy full of arms and ammunition?'

There didn't seem any reason not to. Elizabeth told him in straightforward terms who she was, where she was from, why she had been in Cape Town, and events since her abduction. She left out, for now, the exact relationship between her diamonds, and his weapons.

'So you could say that you were in the wrong place at the wrong time?'

'I guess so.'

'I must say that you have come through your ordeal rather well?'

'The Russian Colonel looked after me as well as he could.' She remembered the photo in the breast pocket of her overalls, and withdrew it. 'He gave me this on the condition that I get a message to his family.'

The ANC man took it, and read the message on the back. It seemed that her rather incredible story had at least some truth to it. It would be easy enough to verify, when he got back to the base.

Elizabeth reached out to take it back. 'It was important to him. He didn't seem to think that he would make it home.' For a moment, the Major thought that he might keep it for a while, but saw a genuine sadness in the woman's eyes that moved him to return it.

'Thank you,' said Elizabeth.

The convoy rocked and rolled its way across the featureless terrain. Just before dawn they reached an ancient river gorge, where they would camouflage their vehicles and rest for the day.

Daniel was a couple of hours along the track of the vehicles, making good time along the beach, when he became concerned. The effect of the sun and sea breeze was gradually eroding the vehicle tracks in front of his eyes. If anything, they should be getting clearer, not the reverse. He was going the wrong way.

Decision time. He could continue to follow the diminishing trail away from the patrol in the hope that they were going back to where they came from. Or he could backtrack and start again from the containers. He kicked himself — such a simple error. He could only hope that it wouldn't make a great deal of difference in the end.

There was one advantage with returning to the containers: he was able to take a good look around the site. Daniel worked his way through each big waterproof steel box, building a general picture of what they had contained. No wonder both sides had been desperate.

He almost missed the prize. Leaning against the back of one of the last containers he checked was a trail bike, specially adapted for scouting ahead of military units. It still had traces of the anticorrosive plastic wrap, but apparently had refused to start. A quick check showed that it was fully fuelled and ready to go. It looked as if it had got pushed out of the way and then forgotten in the hurry to get away. 'So why won't you go?' Daniel asked, checking for the obvious things first.

It soon became obvious that there was no spark from the spark plug lead. A check of the wiring loom didn't reveal anything until Daniel traced the wires to the ignition coil. There was a tell-tail spark as he tested the big black wire to the frame of the bike — it looked as if the earthing strap was defective. A couple of minutes work with his knife and the bike roared to life. His day was looking up.

Daniel spent the next few hours roaring across the featureless landscape until the bike inevitably ran out of fuel. With more than a tinge of regret he abandoned it to the desert and went back to placing his feet in the tracks of the trucks that continued out to the east. At least he had made up for the mistake earlier in the day. But he also knew that he was going to have to find water before too long, or the wilderness would claim him before he got anywhere near Elizabeth.

The ANC patrol commander had told Elizabeth that it was not advisable to go too far from his vehicle, and she took him at his word. The majority of his men looked exactly what they were — hardened, seasoned guerrilla fighters who had seen far too much conflict, and not nearly enough of their villages, cattle, and families. That said, the patrol was well disciplined, and brutally effective at their particular mix of hit and run.

Major Sawka spent some of the afternoon discussing his guest with his loose ANC hierarchy, while waiting for confirmation or otherwise of her story. While tactically the ANC organisational structure was flexible and very difficult to interdict, he knew that it was not particularly effective at responding to this sort of information request. At the end of the day he was no closer to validating the woman's story. Two days from base. So be it. As the sun went down they freed their vehicles from the camouflage and set off into the night, using a minimum of illumination.

Daniel was actually close enough to hear the vehicles as they climbed out of the other side of the watercourse. But he might as well have been a continent away. With no option but to drop down and scavenge around the camp for clues, he did find a little discarded food. But first he needed water.

He reached back into the skills he had learned from his time living and studying with the Bushmen, finding a likely place to dig in the old watercourse. After half an hour of work, the sand was damp. Another ten minutes had a murky pool of water in the bottom the hole. He suddenly realised that he missed the companionship of Dktfec, and Marcus. Someone would pay for the death of so many of the little Bushman tribe, completely innocent of any part in the current conflict across the northern border region.

Daniel wondered where the guerrillas were taking Elizabeth. He knew that there were well formed, and well led, ANC groups, roughly equivalent to the Army units that opposed them. Then there were the quasi-criminal gangs on the fringes of the movement — like that sent south to create as much mayhem as possible through the Impala homelands. It was likely the group who were sent to pick up the weapons and ammunition were the former.

However, what took them two days was going to take Daniel three, at least. At the end of the second day of walking, Daniel had just made it to the springs where the convoy had paused at midnight the day before.

CHAPTER 29

Elizabeth was asleep when the convoy drove into the untidy camp that was their base. It was about a couple of hours before dawn, and the ANC Commander was pleased with their progress. The trucks dispersed into well disguised garages, and the men went to wake up their wives across the sleeping community. The Major took Elizabeth with him to the rough house that accommodated the single officers, and showed her to one of the vacant rooms. He didn't tell her that the previous occupant had been killed during a mission just the week before. Exhausted, Elizabeth was asleep on the rough canvas stretcher before he left the room.

It was the heat that woke her. Oppressive, claustrophobic in the airless room. She opened the door to find a soldier posted outside. He smiled through the gaps in his teeth. 'The Major asked me to take you to him when you woke, please Miss.' He walked off, expecting that she would follow.

'Guess there is nowhere else to go,' Elizabeth said to herself. On their short walk across camp, she could not avoid comparing it with home. Women and children were busy with the morning routine, but their clothing was threadbare, and the children looked hungry. There also seemed to be a large number of young men loitering around town. Empty eyes, without anything better to do, followed her progress. She was thankful for the shapeless overalls.

Around the corner was what she took to be a medical clinic. Here mothers with small children mingled with wounded soldiers, bandages bloody and crawling with bush flies. The smell was shocking.

Her escort hurried her along, and she was glad to go. She walked across an open area where a group of children were playing ancient tribal games, with sticks and a stone. They should have been in school, but Elizabeth suspected that she already knew the answer to that.

Crossing the market only confirmed the poor level of nutrition of the whole village. She realised that the soldiers must be living off the military rations they were provided to keep them in fighting condition. Their families, meanwhile, were weak and malnourished.

Eventually they arrived at their destination. The collection of military-style tents sat in behind a razor-wire perimeter, with two soldiers guarding the entrance. Elizabeth had a nasty feeling that they were mainly there to keep the locals out. She was taken behind the outer ring of tents and found the Major working at a desk, in the shade of a large knob thorn tree.

He stood up to greet her. 'Good morning, Miss.'

'Hello.'

'I trust that you are rested?'

'Better, thank you.' She took the offered seat in the shade, and noticed that her escort had slipped away. Her hand throbbed.

'Where is this?' she asked.

'Again, it is best that you do not know,' he replied. 'Reduces the risk of complications.'

'I see. Then you will let me go home?'

'I hope to be able to do that. But I regret it is not as easy as just calling up a taxi. You must appreciate that you are in a war zone, Miss.'

'Elizabeth. Please call me Elizabeth.'

'All right, Elizabeth. You can call me John.'

'Thank you, John.'

'There. The beginning of a rich and rewarding friendship!' He smiled, a warm, handsome, smile.

'A little premature, I think,' cautioned Elizabeth.

'Perhaps,' he replied. 'I prefer to look on the bright side.'

Without really thinking too much about it, Elizabeth challenged him head on. 'Then you should look at the conditions that your people are living in.' She was not at all ready for the reaction. The major looked devastated, clawing for a defence, then simply got up and walked away. She was left quite alone.

After a good half an hour sitting, waiting for something to happen, or someone to arrive, Elizabeth wandered back through the tents. As she walked through the gate, the guards saluted her with broad smiles. *Maybe they were only there to stop people coming in,* she thought. Wandering through the camp, she quickly had a group of children gathered around, competing for the place of honour at her right hand.

Later, Elizabeth would wonder who had been leading who, as they arrived in front of a single-room building and took her inside. There was no furniture, the roof was falling in, but at one end was a chalk board.

A pretty girl at her side looked up. 'Are you our new teacher?'

The other children picked up the theme. 'Misser John promised us he would bring a new teacher,' offered one of little boys.

Elizabeth looked around, comparing the dirt and decay to the beauty and relative plenty of the Impala valley. It moved her to tears. 'Where has your teacher gone?'

A third child responded. 'She got sick with the malaria, and died, Miss.'

'How long ago?'

'Very long time, many seasons, Miss.'

Elizabeth crouched down and looked in all of the dirty faces. 'I will talk with Misser John. I will see if we can get the building fixed, and find some paper and pencils.'

'What is a pen-cil, Miss?' asked a handsome young man just off to one side.

A new voice, rich in timbre, came from the door. 'This is a pencil, Goonah.' Suddenly Elizabeth was forgotten.

'Misser John, Misser John!' The children ran to greet the Major.

'Hello children. I hope you have been looking after my friend.' He looked up at her and winked.

'You found us a teacher, Misser John?'

Elizabeth pre-empted the reply. 'Perhaps for just a few days, children. Then I must return to my home.' A huge cheer went up, 'But Misser John will have to do something about the classroom.'

Away to the south there was a thunderclap that signalled the build-up of the afternoon showers. The Major smiled across the room. 'I will see if we can find some materials to fix the roof. The children can help you tidy up. Would you join me for a meal, Elizabeth?'

She nodded. 'Children. Meet me back here in one hour. We have much work to do to get ready for classes tomorrow.'

They walked across to the Major's room in silence. He showed her to a rough table that supported a selection of preprepared rations. 'Not the Hilton, but the best that I could do.'

'It is more than I deserve,' replied Elizabeth. She fixed him with her most devastating smile. 'I am truly sorry that I offended you, John. It was unfair.'

Her victim sat down before he fell down, and took a moment to collect his thoughts. 'You are a very interesting woman, Elizabeth. In my experience, the only time that a woman admits she is wrong is when she is after something.'

Elizabeth smiled. 'Exactly. There is much to be done.'

He laughed. 'I was right to be suspicious.'

'Very.'

'What? Very right or very suspicious?'

'Both, Misser John. Both.'

He smiled. 'We had better eat, then. It appears we have a busy afternoon ahead.'

Major Sawka was true to his word, setting a small army to work to repair the roof of the little building while the children worked below them. By the time the afternoon showers rolled in, the children were seated inside, and Elizabeth was conducting her first class. At one stage she felt that she was being watched, and looked up in time to catch John watching her. He smiled and moved out into the pouring rain.

Two hours later it was the end of class. The rain had stopped, and Elizabeth sent her new students off to their homes, but two of the older children lagged behind. 'Miss Elizabeth, would you like come home with us?' asked the girl.

Elizabeth didn't have anything else to do, so agreed. 'Of course.' They led her across town and out into the surrounding scrub. She was getting worried, but they reassured her and eventually they came across a small hut. 'Please come in,' said the little girl.

Elizabeth paused. 'Where is your mother?'

The children shared a glance, and then the boy spoke up for them both. 'Mother was killed by soldiers in the last big raid on the village. They hurt her very bad. She died a week later in the night.' The girl took Elizabeth's hand, and led her across the clearing. 'We hid in the bush. The soldiers wanted to hurt me too, but mother would not tell them where we were hiding. She is buried here.'

Although she suspected the answer, Elizabeth had to ask. 'Where is your father?'

The boy took up the tale. 'We do not know our father, Miss.'

'So you live alone?'

'No Miss,' he answered, firmly. 'We have each other.'

'You are both very brave.' She gave them both a hug, and they clung to her. Elizabeth realised that it was probably the first adult affection they had experienced since their mother had been killed — by soldiers who fought alongside Daniel, Peter, and Roos. 'Why do you not live inside the village, like the others?'

The boy answered. 'This is our home, Miss. We have nowhere else to go.'

She woke early the next day, although the camp was already up and busy. On an impulse, she decided to go for a walk, although not sure where. Her legs took her straight to the clinic.

At least, in the cool of the early morning, the smell was not quite as overpowering. The only ward was just rows of canvas stretchers, filthy from a collection of dirt and congealed body fluids. Some of the patients were fortunate to have mosquito nets. Others just ignored the ravages of the hungry insects. At least half of those present were soldiers, with terrible wounds typical of that type of warfare — missing limbs, festering bullet holes. Without even the most basic sanitation, it was no better than death row.

'Who is in charge here?' she asked of a woman who was trying to control the fever of a young woman on the bed.

'No-one, Miss.'

'Then who cares for these patients?'

'Their families, mostly, Miss. Mostly they just dig holes for when they die, mostly.'

Elizabeth went over to her. 'What is wrong with her?'

'Malaria, Miss.'

'Do you have drugs?'

The woman wept. 'There are no drugs to treat this, Miss.'

'O yes, there are,' Elizabeth said to herself, quietly. She looked around one more time, and then marched across to the Major's rooms, banging on the door.

'What is it?'

'It is Elizabeth. I need you to come with me, urgently.'

The door opened. 'Where?'

Elizabeth just turned and walked off. The Major swore and followed her. It was not long before he knew where they were going. She stood in the middle of the ward and turned on him. 'This is as disgrace! You must be aware of the need for basic hygiene, particularly in a ward like this.'

The Major sat on the end of a stretcher, and held out his hands. 'We have no medicines. For a while an international medical charity ran this clinic, but had to leave because it was too risky for them to get medical supplies across Army lines.'

'You could do much with basic hygiene. For a start, these cots need to be burned. All the beds should have a net. This woman has malaria. Everyone in this ward is exposed to the same mosquitoes that are feeding on her.'

'The people do not understand, Elizabeth.'

'Well, then teach them, John. You know, so they have a right to hear from you!'

The major got up and walked towards the door.

'Don't you dare walk out on me, not on this, John. This is as much your responsibility as fighting your dirty little war.' Elizabeth rose to her subject. 'What are you fighting for — the whole country to look and live like this?'

But she had gone too far, and he responded with a threat, his voice only just above a whisper, and full of violence. 'Be very careful, Elizabeth. It is solely in my hands whether you will ever return to your version of South Africa.'

He turned and walked out; however, he had underestimated Miss Elizabeth Dortmus.

She called to him from the dirt in front of the clinic. 'John, please. Your people need your leadership. I can do a little, but, with your support, we could have this cleaned up in a day or so.' He paused, so she offered something. 'I may be able to help with medicines, as well.'

He answered, but did not turn around. 'I tried to get some drugs and dressings included with the weapons and ammunition, but they didn't want to waste the space.' Now he turned. He was angry, but not at her. 'Do you like that, they didn't want to waste the space.'

'Help me to fix it, then?'

'Don't you have classes?'

'Yes. But there are a couple of hours before and after class every day. An American missionary doctor taught me a lot. For as long as I need to stay, I might as well make a difference.'

'What do you want me to do?'

'Clear out the ward. Burn the cots. Change all the dressings, and clean the wounds with water boiled with ash. Sweep out the building, and then put the patients back on clean cots. I will call in after class. Agreed?'

He looked across at her, nodding. 'I think that I can remember all that.'

'I am sure you can, John.' She went and stood in front of him. 'It is important.' She turned and left to tidy up before class.

'Oh, Elizabeth,' he called after her. 'I have found you some chalk.' She waved over her shoulder. 'But how do I get you to stay?' he asked of her back, quietly.

It was a credit to his character and leadership that by the time Elizabeth had finished class, the clinic was transformed. It had been emptied, scrubbed, the ward was full of fresh new stretchers, and each had a mosquito net over it. The patients had all been bathed, and had their bandages changed.

When Elizabeth arrived, there was a small army waiting for her to inspect their work. More importantly, two young women who had previously worked in the clinic had found their old uniforms, and were waiting anxiously to see if they could start work again. It was a very good start.

'You have all done so well,' Elizabeth told them. 'Thank you. This is very important for you and your families.' They all congratulated themselves, and a small, impromptu celebration started. It was during this distraction that a stranger slipped into town, unnoticed.

CHAPTER 30

After walking night and day in the tracks of the convoy, Daniel arrived on the outskirts of the ANC encampment. He spent some time ensuring that he could just about line up with the rebel troops, and not look out of place. That included acquiring a dirty, nondescript uniform out of a discarded kit bag, and cutting his hair very close. He knew that it was not uncommon for people from a mixture of ethnic backgrounds to move in and out of the loose communities that formed around the guerrilla units, so thought he could probably mingle with the local people with minimal risk of being challenged, at least for a time.

There was, of course, one person somewhere close who was sure to recognise him, and at that moment she was standing on the steps of what looked like a medical clinic, talking to a man that he thought he should know.

In fact, Elizabeth looked as if she was here on some sort of working holiday, full of energy and confidence. She went inside, and Daniel concentrated on staying inconspicuous on the edge of the crowd, but it started to rain, causing the crowd to rapidly disperse. Daniel knew if he stayed out in the open he was going to look out of place, so in typical fashion he simply jogged across the open area onto the small porch outside the clinic. After a quick look around he walked through the door, as if he was going to visit someone.

Elizabeth saw the man step through the door over the Major's shoulder. He smiled at her, and she was puzzled for a moment.

'Hello, Elizabeth. Fancy seeing you out here,' he said. The voice gave her such a shock that she stepped backward, nearly falling over the cot behind her. It took a huge effort to regain her composure and step around the Major to shake Daniel's hand, probably a little too formally.

Daniel didn't miss a beat, continuing forward to offer his hand out to the ANC commander. 'Daniel Roost. Freelance security. I was hired by the lady's family to find her.' The men shook hands, although only as a matter of form at this stage. 'You are?'

'Major John Sawka, Commanding Officer of the ANC regiment that is based here.'

'I have heard of you, Major.' That was true. In fact Daniel knew quite a lot about Major John Sawka.

'Then you have me at a disadvantage.'

'There is not much about me to worry about,' assured Daniel, making sure that his body language was relaxed. 'I was hired because I know my way around, but don't have a stake in either side of this nasty little war. My sole interest is in getting Miss Dortmus home, safely, and then being paid of course.' Elizabeth sat on an empty cot, trying to sort the situation in her own mind.

'How did you know where to find her?'

'Inside info passed to my clients. It was easy to track your vehicles from the beach.'

'Very interesting, Mr Roost.' The Major took a step towards Daniel. 'I have a strange feeling that I should remember you?'

'We may have met before, under different circumstances. I spent a little time in the Army, but must say that it didn't really agree with me. Too many rules, and not enough money.'

'Really?' The Major smoothly produced a pistol from underneath his bush shirt. Elizabeth went to intervene. 'Stay where you are please, Elizabeth,' he barked, and it hit her almost physically.

'How did you get to where we unloaded the containers, so quickly? They had been on the beach for less than 24 hours.' There was naked malice in his voice.

'Army helicopter,' replied Daniel, happily.

'Extraordinary support for a freelance security organisation, wouldn't you agree?'

Daniel shrugged. 'It suited them. I was to get Elizabeth out of the target area, so the air force could come in and finish the job.'

The Major had to admit that it fitted with what he knew. Good thing they had risked travelling just about 30 hours non-stop, to get to the drop in time.

Daniel decided it was time to pursue his slim advantage. 'I have to take my hat off to you, it was quite a feat to get out there, get the weapons loaded, and then get away before the authorities were able to intervene effectively.'

'The weather was kind.'

'Maybe.'

'You intrigue me, Mr Roost. I am definitely not ready to trust you. And I am even less inclined to let Miss Dortmus leave right now, with you or anyone else.'

Elizabeth took her opportunity. 'Am I not to have something to say about that?'

The Major turned to answer her, and Daniel used the momentary distraction to jump forward and disarm him in one easy, fluid movement. Abruptly, the roles were reversed. The patients that were able scrambled for safety.

'Please, Major. Calm your people. I am not here to cause any more misery than what they have already faced.'

Nursing a bruised wrist, the Major got up off the floor. 'And you are no ordinary freelance security man.'

'I just don't like having quite reasonable conversations at the point of a gun,' replied Daniel. His voice was absolutely devoid of emotion. 'Next time you produce it, mean it.'

With a smooth action he dropped the magazine out of the weapon, made sure that there was, in fact, no round in the chamber, and handed it back. 'I really could do with a brew.'

Elizabeth bristled with being relegated to tea lady, but swallowed her pride in order to keep the brittle truce between the two men. Her bandaged hand was beginning to throb, again.

Daniel decided to take a conciliatory position, for openers. 'I had forgotten how tough it is to survive out here in the bush. You have done pretty well, considering the odds.'

'We have friends who do what they can to get food across the frontier,' the Major answered. 'Lately, in fact, the Army has tended to let most basic supplies through, I presume for humanitarian reasons.'

Elizabeth chipped in. 'There is growing international pressure for an end to the conflict. It was all through the papers in Cape Town.'

'Newspapers, now when did I last see one of those?' commented the Major with a wry smile.

'Likewise,' added Daniel, keen to identify with the other man.

Elizabeth sat down across from them. 'But is it not interesting that the papers are feeling free enough to publish that sort of a story?'

The Major regarded her across the little table. 'You are very much your father's daughter, Elizabeth.'

Daniel watched Elizabeth intently for a response, well aware of Pieter Dortmus's longstanding relationship with John Sawka.

A strangled 'How?' was initially all that she could get out.

The Major got to his feet and walked to stand to one side of the flickering fire, weighing carefully what he was about to disclose. 'I met you several times, years ago, at your home in Cape Town. You were just a child. I was one of several young men that your father was developing through his businesses.' He turned to her and smiled, but there were tears on his cheeks. 'My father was a labourer in one of the storehouses. He died when the buildings were ransacked and burned to the ground. I only escaped because I was a little late for the shift change that night. I should have been there.'

Elizabeth stood and closed the distance between them. 'So you were one of the early refugees father took north on that first trip?'

'You knew of those?'

'Father kept the details to himself. But, from time to time, I would lie in my bed listening to my parents discussing how he was going to continue to support you all.'

'Yes. Your father's reserves were not going to last forever. It was a couple of years later that he met an old and dying prospector, who passed on the secret of the mine. Pieter worked that mine by himself to support us through the long and bitter struggles of the last decade.'

'That explains a lot of things,' Daniel noted.

'Such as?'

'Such as how your organisation knew of the mine, and only took action to try and secure it after becoming aware that Pieter had been killed.'

'The details of his death are not clear, but I assume that you are correct.' The Major paused, filing away the other information for later. Daniel and Elizabeth shared a glance.

'So I guess, Elizabeth, you can now see why I have treated you as best as I could in the circumstances. I owe your father everything. In the end he was the closest thing to family that I had.' The Major returned to his seat and Elizabeth did likewise.

'So, now we are up to date, where does that leave us?' asked Daniel, leaning back on his chair.

Elizabeth took up the challenge. 'It leaves me wanting to continue my father's work here, in my own way.'

'That would be dangerous.' Daniel leant forward. 'You could also find your name on the Government list of ANC suspects.'

But Elizabeth was not fazed. 'So be it. It is what father would have done. And God only knows the community here needs help, with just about everything apart from soldiering.'

Daniel turned to the Major. 'This is Pieter's daughter. Could you live with yourself if something happened to her?'

'I think that Pieter would want Elizabeth to make that decision.'

'Then you might consider reducing your overall risks.'

'How?'

'Well, as a suggestion, offer to cantone your heavy weapons under supervision of a neutral third party. Perhaps think about an undertaking to stop offensive operations for a period, in return for some security guarantees. In my humble opinion, Major, the big stuff is not your style, and you risk a massive retaliation from Government forces that would, frankly, wipe you off the map.'

'We have survived over a decade. What makes you think things would change?

'Right now you are still here simply because Government policy has been to limit the scale and intensity of the conflict. Use of your heavy weapons would make their continued restraint very difficult.' Daniel rose to his theme. 'John, third party cantonement means that you don't actually have to give up the weapons, and it brings a neutral party into the equation. It also gives you a voice in any negotiations over the future of this region.'

The Major was not convinced. 'Where did all this come from, Mr Roost?'

'Shall we say that I have had plenty of time by myself to think this through.'

'Apparently.'

'What do you think, Elizabeth?' the Major asked. 'Would such a step make it easier for you to stay on for a while?'

'I could almost guarantee to bring a Doctor I know up here,' she enthused. 'He is also very good in the classroom. And of course there would be fresh food.'

'I will need to put it to my officers, and to the community.'

'Of course,' Daniel replied. 'But I would not leave it too long. If I am not mistaken, somewhere south of us a sizeable force is being assembled. Their mission will be to ensure that you never get the opportunity to employ those new weapons.'

'They have no idea of our current position,' challenged the Major.

Daniel got to his feet. 'John. If I can find you, on foot, in the middle of nowhere — they can find you. Trust me, time is not on your side.'

Elizabeth joined him. 'He knows what he is talking about, John, that I can tell you.'

John looked at the other man. 'I still don't trust him.'

'If I were in your position, I wouldn't either,' observed Elizabeth. She walked over to where the Major was still seated. 'But the survival of this community may depend on him.' As if on cue, just at that moment a dusty vehicle drove into the middle of the village, and Mr Lester Ruston stepped out.

CHAPTER 31

The self-proclaimed last great white hunter jumped down from his vehicle and marched over to join them. 'John. Good to see you again.' He shook the Major's hand as if he were handling an old established client.

'Lester. What on earth brings you all the way our here?'

'These guys.'

The Major had the sense that he was rapidly losing control of his own destiny, if not command of his senses. 'How?'

'Long story. Short version is that the Army are at best a day behind me, in force.'

The Major swore, and turned on the messenger.

'Please.' Lester raised his hands, defensively. 'I had no choice. I could either come here direct, and risk that they simply followed me, or I could try and be a little more clever, and arrive in time to help dig your grave. What would you have done?'

'We will run north into the desert.'

Lester shook his head. 'They have a blocking force moving to cut off any escape. Right now that is all that is holding up the main body.'

John Sawka walked in circles when he had to operate under pressure. It was a disarming habit that disguised a sharp intellect. 'We will not surrender. There will be one hell of a fight!'

'That will end in disaster for you, and for the ANC,' Daniel assured him. 'There is still time for Plan B. Let Lester and I head the Army off and see if they are prepared to talk. You have a significant number of women and children here with you.'

Elizabeth stepped into the middle of the discussion. 'And me. Don't forget me. I will stay here.'

Lester looked to Daniel for an introduction. 'Lester, sorry, I am forgetting my manners. Allow me to introduce Elizabeth Dortmus.'

'Charmed, I am sure. I knew your father well. A fine man.'

Elizabeth was already beyond surprise.

'Daniel makes a good point,' said Lester, turning to the Major. 'A potential hostage could be useful.'

'Hostage, or supporter?' Elizabeth challenged them all.

'Let's play that one by ear, Miss Dortmus,' said Lester. 'No telling which tale will go down best at this stage.' He turned to the other men. 'We have no time to lose. John, it is your call. Things are changing across the country. This may be a time for a bold initiative.'

'I don't see that I really have a rational choice.' He shook Lester's hand. 'Get going, and good luck.' Daniel gave Elizabeth a hug and jumped in the passenger door of the already moving Jeep.

When they were gone Elizabeth turned to the Major. 'I think that you are doing the right thing, John.'

'Why do I have the feeling that ever since I picked you up off the beach I have, in fact, not been in control of the situation.'

'Well,' she said with a smile. 'Most women would take that as a compliment.' She returned to her room, leaving the Major with his nightmares.

Lester drove at a crazy pace across the barren landscape. After a couple of very close calls, Daniel suggested that he should slow down just a little, as no-one would be well-served if they crashed now. 'What I didn't mention back there is the air strike planned for first light, Daniel. I must let them know that Elizabeth is being held in the village.'

'How far are they?'

'Probably about six to seven hours, and then a couple of hours roaring around in the dark trying to find them.'

'Radio?'

'You know the Army. Bloody funny attitude about letting those things fall into the hands of the bad guys.'

'Right. So we make as much noise as we can, and hope they jump out in front of us.'

'That is about it, my friend.'

Daniel made himself comfortable. 'I need some sleep. Wake me up when you need a break.'

They ran into the scouting patrol at 0337 hours, and were quickly directed across to the group of vehicles in the next valley that contained the tactical headquarters. Daniel was out of the vehicle and moving before Lester managed to get it under control.

The night improved dramatically when Peter stepped out of his vehicle, and Paul came around from the other side. Peter called across. 'Daniel. Over here.'

'Good to see you, guys. Both of you!' He took a few precious seconds to give Paul a massive bear hug. 'Elizabeth is fine, Paul. Better than that, she has already reorganised the ANC community. I don't have time now, but I hope you are ready for a sabbatical in the middle of nowhere. We can catch up soon.' He turned to Peter. 'Who is running this show?'

'Here on the ground it is one of your old friends, Mack Slouter.'

'Great. Where is he?'

'Right here, Rutter.' The two men embraced like the old colleagues they were. 'Brew on over here. Anything that you can tell us about their disposition and strength will be welcome.' Paul and Lester hung back on the fringe of the group of officers.

One hand around a huge tin mug, Daniel gave a succinct outline of everything that he had observed, just as if he had been a formal part of the mission. He needed to build a rational and compelling picture for the decision that he was attempting to shape. Part of that was the number of women and children present in the target area.

'That would seem to mitigate against the air strike going in ahead of us,' the Colonel observed.

'And they are still holding Miss Dortmus as hostage,' Daniel noted.

Colonel Slouter stood up, looking out across the landscape he loved so dearly. There was a tinge of light on the eastern horizon. 'So you are telling me that softening them up with mortars before we go in is not on the cards, either.'

'You risk turning yourself from a hero to a villain.'

'Are there other options? Can we get a small team in there and rescue her first?'

'Unlikely. She is well secured in the middle of the village.'

'So, any other ideas?'

'See what they want to trade,' suggested Daniel, trying to make it sound as if it could really be Mack's idea.

'What do you mean?'

'Well, he knows you have him cold. Cornered, they will fight, and fight hard. You will inevitably take casualties, and they now have some serious stuff to throw back at you. Anti-tank rockets into a few of your vehicles would make your eyes water, I can assure you.'

'Go on.'

'Well. Arrange a meeting, and see if there is another way.' Daniel picked his words carefully. 'I don't think the Government wants what the international media would call a massacre, at this stage.'

'Can't hurt, Boss,' offered one of the company commanders. 'If they are not interested, then we can at least say we tried.'

A voice came out of the communications truck. 'Strike Lead is on the radio asking for an update of the target.'

'Tell him to stand by for a change of plans, Sergeant.'

'Roger, Sir.'

The Colonel looked around his assembled officers. 'Any other points?'

'The fighter boys have come a long way not to have a little fun,' Daniel offered, after a moment to allow any others to comment. 'Show of force might get the bad guys' attention, Mack.'

Daniel and Peter left them to their duties and found Paul, and Lester gathered around a small fire, brews to their lips, as the dawn sky threw fire across the stark but beautiful landscape.

Lester offered him a big steaming mug of sweet bush tea. 'Going to work?'

'Thanks.' Daniel took the steaming hot mug. 'You know, I just think that it might.'

Peter laughed, that easy, companionable laugh between men whose friendship has been tested and found true. 'What have you conjured up this time?'

Daniel filled the others in on the proposal, and then they pieced their individual pieces of their puzzle together. Peter had gone back to the Impala capital, after having sent Lester north as Daniel had suggested. Paul had arrived from Cape Town the same afternoon as Peter and his team. They had immediately decided to chase the action, and only ran into the Army units by accident the day before.

But at the end of the telling, the picture remained incomplete. There were just twenty-five days left to meet the legal challenge to the tribal claim over the mine.

CHAPTER 32

The ANC company was 'stood to' at dawn. The women and children were below ground, as safe as possible, and Elizabeth was with them. All they could do now was watch and wait. It was not long.

There was literally no warning. The jets came in at just a fraction below the speed of sound, at treetop level. As the pilots pulled the noses of their aircraft up over the camp, the airflow over the tops of the slender delta wings accelerated to Mach 1, and the resulting sonic booms crashed against the unyielding landscape. The noise was shattering and disorientating, but was over before the collective consciousness of the village had time to register what it was. The departing aircraft left behind a great cloud of dust, picked up by the jet wash.

The initial silence was almost surreal. Then, shock set in with the women and children, and the screaming started. It took a while for the reports to come in from across the village, and for their commander to sort through the noise. There was no damage. No weapons had been dropped. But the message was absolutely beyond doubt. Major Sawka could see it in the faces of his men as he went to check on the other members of his community. He found Elizabeth desperately trying to console a group of terrified children.

Catching the accusation in her eye, he turned away. 'Has it all come to this?' he asked himself, quietly.

He got back to his position just as a vehicle drove slowly into view, the same vehicle that Lester had been driving earlier. It stopped just outside of effective rifle range and a figure got out and waited. This was his cue, he presumed. He handed over to his deputy, and walked as boldly as he could out to meet his destiny.

It was someone that he did not know, that was clear as he got closer. Probably in the sights of a number of very efficient marksmen, heroics were out of the question. He stopped a few paces away from the man, and one of the strangest conversations of his life began.

'My name is Colonel Mack Slouter. I am the tactical commander of this task force.'

'I am Major John Sawka. I think that you know the rest.'

'I would like to avoid casualties, Major, and have a proposal.'

'What might that be?'

'Hand over your heavy weapons, your hostage, and we go away.'

The Major noticed the changing hues of the dawn as the sun touched the distant hills with fire. 'Just like that?'

'Just like that.'

'If I am not able to do that?'

The Colonel glanced over his shoulder. 'We will take them off you.'

'That will not be easy.'

'No, it won't. But the jets are up there with the tanker right now. A signal from me and they will level your village with more than just noise. I would have to sit here and watch.' The Colonel paused and leant on his vehicle. 'Frankly, Major, that prospect does not attract me. The blessed Air Force does not have to search through the resulting carnage for any survivors, or equipment that might be rescued. I would rather not put my men through that.'

'You make your point, Colonel. I would only be prepared to cantone my heavy weapons with a neutral third party, but would also give you an undertaking that my Company would conduct no further offensive action, for a period of time, if you will allow humanitarian supplies through.'

'An interesting proposition. It would take us some time to arrange cantonement.'

'It has been many years to get us to this conversation. Surely we could allow a few days to set up such a solution?'

'I would need to put this up the chain.'

'I understand. Quite obviously, I am not going anywhere.'

'Very good, Major. Shall we meet at 0800 and 1800 hours each day until this is resolved?'

'Agreed.' The ANC Major saluted the SADF Colonel smartly, turned about, and walked purposefully back to his position. He was not sure whether it was a good day, or a bad day, but for the first time in a long time he sensed the quiet music of the high veldt. Then, as he walked back into town to brief his officers and community leaders, he saw Elizabeth standing outside the clinic, a child on each hand. They waved to him.

The report from Colonel Slouter arrived on the General's desk a couple of hours later. After reading what was proposed, the General picked up the phone and rang through to Defence Headquarters in Cape Town. As he waited for the call to go through, he considered how this sat with the operational-level briefing he was working-up on options for de-escalating the conflict, as a first step towards encouraging the ANC to take a political route to resolving the underlying issues.

An hour later a very senior inter-departmental group was in the Minister of Defence's office, discussing the merits of constructively engaging one of the ANC's better and more moderate commanders, as something of a test case. Nothing ventured, nothing gained.

Right at that point the Minister could see considerable political mileage in the proposal, and intercepted the Prime Minister, who was just leaving for a state reception. The PM simply told him to make it happen, and happen well. It turned into a very good lunch, and the PM's guests noted that the pressure that he had been under for a number of months appeared to have lifted, somewhat.

As arranged, at 1800 hours that same day Major Sawka walked out of the village and met the SADF Colonel at the same place. This time there were a couple of seats in the shade of a tarpaulin rigged off the side of the vehicle. 'Good evening, Colonel.'

'Good evening Major.' They shook hands. 'Please have a seat.'

'Thank you.'

'A cold drink?'

'Yes, why not. Thanks.'

With a flourish and a smile the Colonel produced a couple of cans of ice-cold lager. 'Good news. I am able to advise you that your terms have been accepted.'

The Major paused with the can half way to his lips, not daring to move in case he missed a detail. For a moment, there was silence between them. Then John very slowly and carefully placed the can on the table so that he had both hands free to support himself. Somewhere out to the west a late afternoon storm rumbled. 'Just like that?'

Mack continued. 'A platoon of my company is to escort your vehicles, with the heavy weapons and ammunition, through to Upington, where there will be facilities set up for cantonement. Government is approaching possible third parties to supervise, but I am assured it will be resolved by the time your convoy arrives. Apparently there is likely to be considerable media coverage, both local and international.'

'At the end, so easy—'

'Makes you wonder, doesn't it?' The Colonel picked up his drink. 'I guess there are likely to be a few hurdles yet, but it is a start.'

'Yes it is, Colonel. A good start.' The Major decided that he trusted his hand enough to pick up the can again.

Pulling his seat closer to the table, the Colonel continued. 'As for your undertaking to avoid offensive action: I could have a brief letter drawn up for your signature?'

The Major took a deep draught on the ice-cold liquid, and savoured the moment. 'That would be fine.' The empty can settled back on the table. 'I will have the convoy ready to go, by first light tomorrow.'

'Good. The sooner we are on the road home, the better.' The Colonel got to his feet. On impulse, he decided that it was time for a gesture of goodwill. 'John, do your people have any other immediate needs?'

'Well Colonel, could you spare any medical supplies?'

'We can do one better. With your consent I could send my medical team into the village tomorrow, to conduct a medical clinic. They can leave behind anything the Doctor thinks we can spare.'

'Agreed. Thank you. That would mean a lot to my people, and dramatically help me sell things to the hard-liners in my company.'

'Good. I presume that you would guarantee their security?'

'Yes, of course.' They shook hands. 'Good night.'

'Good night. The escort will be ready to go at 0600.'

'Fine. Thank you.' As he turned to go, they were joined by Daniel and Paul. 'Major, this is Doctor Paul Tradour. With your permission, we would like to accompany you back to the village.' Paul and John shook hands. Daniel turned to Mack. 'Colonel?'

'Fine by me, Daniel.'

'Major?'

'Consider yourself my guest, after all much of the credit for what has been worked out belongs to you.' They walked off into the evening twilight, and Colonel Slouter made a mental note to mention Daniel's role in tonight's report.

Elizabeth was working by candlelight to dress the wounds of a soldier who would probably not last through the night. She found it miserably distressing. There were footsteps on the porch, and someone came into the ward. Elizabeth was expecting one of the two assistants, and asked for a fresh bandage from the table. It appeared in front of her, but the hand was not right. She looked up into Paul's smiling eyes.

'Paul!' She couldn't just drop the stump of the limb that she held, and Paul took advantage of her constraint to kiss her gently on the cheek.

'Hello Elizabeth. Can I help?'

'I hope you are ready for a long night, Doctor.'

'With you? A lifetime.' Paul helped her to wrap the horribly torn flesh, stinking from gangrene. The job done for the moment, she got up and reached for his arms. After a while enjoying the strength and comfort of his embrace, she took him by the hand and led him through the ward, detailing the condition of each patient. 'It is difficult. We have no drugs or supplies.'

'The Army has agreed to send a medical team into town tomorrow to conduct a clinic. I have already discussed what they can afford to leave behind with the medical officer.'

He smiled his best Uncle Paul smile, and Elizabeth melted from the inside out. 'You are such a clever man.'

'You should give Daniel at least some of the credit.'

'Where is he?'

'With the Major, helping to arrange for the convoy to leave tomorrow.'

'Convoy?'

'All the heavy weapons are being taken into Upington. It appears that we have avoided a catastrophe.'

'That is great news.'

Paul took her hand. 'Sore?'

'A little.'

'Let's have a look.' Paul had managed to put together a basic triage pack out of Army supplies, and he broke it open. Elizabeth sat down and started to unwind the dirty bandage. Paul washed his hands with disinfectant, and then took over. The stump of her finger was bruised and ugly, but appeared to have escaped infection, so Paul simply rebandaged it.

'So now there are nine and a half,' chuckled Elizabeth with a wry smile.

'Good thing it is not your wedding finger, then,' challenged Paul, and kissed her.

The evening brief in the Joint Operations Command Centre was just getting underway when the Chief Intelligence Staff Officer excused himself and slipped into his allotted seat in the second row of the Command Centre briefing room. He passed a folder forward to his Commanding General.

The General skimmed the main points of the intelligence summary, and then went back to the beginning and worked through the detail. The voices around him gradually subsided until there was an expectant hush. He stood and faced the assembled staff.

'Congratulations ladies and gentlemen. The ANC have agreed to cantone the heavy weapons, and one of their most effective regiments has formally undertaken to cease offensive operations.' He paused to allow the significance of that report to sink in. 'This is by no means the end of the fight, but it is a very good beginning.' The normal military protocol was briefly interrupted with a spontaneous round of applause, and the General went across to his Watch Commander. 'Well done Rory. It was a stroke of brilliance sending Rutter into the mix.'

'Thanks Sir. Just doing my job, as you know.'

'Rutter, and Hogan, have done very well,' continued the General. 'This should clear the way to fix the gross injustices done to a number of people involved in the earlier Impala shambles.' He turned to look for his resident secret service liaisons. 'Don't go away. My office in ten minutes.'

As requested, the three men were waiting when the General walked in. 'Right. There is one last, vital piece to this puzzle, and I think that you know what it is.'

They were, of course, professionally non-committal. 'Go on, General,' said the local man.

'If the ANC commander who has shown such courage and foresight is going to have any chance of surviving much past tomorrow, we have to move on what we know about our Minister who is playing on both sides.'

'I think we could agree with that,' answered the Brit.

'What it will take is to get the right information, in the right hands, at the right time. Your part of the picture will be necessary to do that. Agreed?'

The three men looked at each other. 'Agreed,' said the American.

These guys have got to be cloned, thought the General.

The summary situation report was added to a few other carefully tailored pieces of information and rushed to the executive offices of the Prime Minister in time for his late briefing. On top of the briefing folder was a separate sealed envelope marked for his eyes only. The PM dismissed his staff and opened it in the privacy of his office.

A few minutes later he walked into the cabinet meeting room. Assembled were most of the members of his Cabinet, called together for a special briefing on military developments out on the Northern border.

Rather than taking his chair immediately, the PM walked along the table and passed the envelope to one of his most senior ministers. He stood behind the chair. 'Read it.' The conversation around the table stopped.

The Minister finished reading, and then folded the two pages back into the envelope with the broken seals of the security services. 'You can't, and you won't,' the man sneered.

'Get out!' roared the PM. 'And leave your papers on the table.'

CHAPTER 33

The last of the daylight was fading as Elizabeth made her way out of the village proper to check on the two orphan children. She left Daniel and Paul planning the following day's activities with the Major, insisting that she wouldn't be gone long. In the growing shadows, however, the path was not as easy to follow as she had expected, and a couple of times she found herself confronted by an impenetrable wall of scrub. About the time when even her determination to check on the children was beginning to be challenged, she heard a muffled cry ahead, and then silence.

She froze in her tracks, holding her breath. Hearing nothing more, she crept the last few metres to the edge of the dirty clearing that surrounded the primitive hut. Movement off to one side caught her attention, and in the last of the available light she just made out a couple of dark figures carrying a struggling child into the thicket. She knew she should go back for help, but realised that whoever had taken the child would be long gone by the time an effective rescue could be mounted. She slipped over to the hut and furtively looked inside.

It was pitch dark, but her foot brushed against something right at the entrance. Dreading what she might find she reached down to discover a small foot, wet and already sticky. She knew that feeling only too well. Then the leg moved at her touch and she dropped to her knees to reach forward, to be rewarded by an almost inaudible whimper. It was the little girl, barely breathing. Elizabeth scooped her up in her arms and moved outside.

She did not see the blow coming.

Daniel reached for another bottle of water, courtesy of Army logistics, and noted for the first time that it was now fully dark. He turned to the others. 'I wonder what is keeping Elizabeth?'

Paul glanced up from the list of supplies that he was compiling. 'She has been gone for longer than I expected.' Both men turned to the ANC Major.

'I know where she went. Perhaps I should go and check.'

'We will tag along for the exercise,' offered Daniel and followed Major Sawke out of the lamplight. Paul, caught out by the sudden departure, found himself alone with no real idea of what direction they had left, so opted to sit tight for now.

The other two men worked their way across the village to check that Elizabeth had not just returned to her hut without letting them know, and then followed the trail out to the hut. Accustomed to the bush, they moved without difficulty in the starlight, walking a little carefully for the first few minutes until their eyes adjusted to the lack of light. Neither spoke of their growing concern.

The clearing was empty. Daniel moved quietly across the open ground, crouched and ran his fingertips through the dust at the entrance. The ground was freshly disturbed. He traced a number of different footprints, but then felt the blood, and whistled to John. 'Elizabeth appears to have been taken from here, by a number of big men.' He sniffed the air, and smelt blood and fear. 'They have not been gone long.'

'I need to get back to the village,' whispered the Major. 'This is not good.'

'Who and why?' asked Daniel.

The Major looked around the perimeter of the clearing. 'Not sure. Could be some of my men. Might be others.'

'Others?' asked Daniel, but he was talking to himself. His instinct was to attempt to follow the tracks, but his discipline and training counselled against it. If he was to have any chance of rescuing Elizabeth, he was going to need to even the score just a little. He jogged quietly back into camp, arriving inside the defensive perimeter just in time to avoid being shot by the ANC soldiers, who were still orienting themselves having been rudely dragged from their beds. He crossed to the HQ buildings, and found the company officers hastily assembled.

The Major looked a little embarrassed and agitated at Daniel's arrival, and went on the offensive. 'How do we know that these rebel guerrillas were not also part of your plan?'

Daniel crossed to where he could use his slight height advantage to good effect. 'By the very fact that I am standing here, Major.' He paused to allow the tension to subside just a little. 'What do you mean, guerrillas?'

John Sawke sighed, and looked around his assembled officers. He turned away and slammed his hand, palm open, against the supports for the roof, breathing deeply. 'So close. So close.'

'What do you mean?' asked Paul.

The major looked across the small group. 'You tell them, Jacob.'

His second in command took a small step forward. 'A few fringe ANC units were deliberately recruited and trained to employ terror tactics on the local people, in order to undermine support for Pretoria. They also have a sort of internal police role, to ensure that the more conservative regular units, such as ours, hold the line in the face of government direct action. They are accountable to no-one, and are allowed to keep all the spoils of their miserable activities.' He spat in the dust for effect. 'They are worse than criminals, living off the suffering of both sides in our struggle.'

Daniel replied very quietly from the other side of the group, but the raw malice in his voice was unmistakable. 'We believe it to be a fighting patrol of one of those units that massacred almost an entire tribe of Bushmen, and attacked the Impala northern outpost, causing considerable loss of life. We were tracking a couple of them who escaped.'

The Major found his voice. 'This will be their main body. We are almost certainly outnumbered, but even so they will be reluctant to confront us in strength. It is not their way of doing things.'

'They are after the weapons?' asked Paul.

'Probably, but they would normally have just walked into camp and demanded them.' Major Sawke shook his head. 'Their actions suggest that they know we have been negotiating with the government forces.'

'And that suggests they have been tipped off by someone,' commented Daniel, absently swiping at a moth that was teasing with the lamp.

'The information game works both ways,' acknowledged the Major.

'But the Army will be concerned, nevertheless. It is only a very small group of individuals who know of events here over the last twelve hours.'

Paul stepped in to the discussion, a little impatient. 'What about Elizabeth?'

'Correct. We must get to her quickly.' Daniel turned to the Major. 'You will want to stay and organise your defences. I am better off by myself, anyway. But can I borrow some equipment?'

'Of course,' replied Major Sawke. 'Take whatever you need.'

'And we need to get word to Peter and Lester — they will back me up.' Daniel turned to Paul. 'Can I leave that with you, Paul?'

'Of course,' he replied, pleased to have some active role.

The ANC agreed to make sure that Paul got to the Army lines safely, and Daniel got Jacob to take him to where the weapons were stored. In short order he was fully equipped with a variety of weapons, and a top spec set of night vision goggles. *That should even things up a little,* he thought to himself, setting off into the night.

He wished that Marcus was at his side, and Dktfec. Thoughts of his Bushman friend brought the bitter taste of revenge to his mouth, but he knew that for now he must stay focused on Elizabeth's rescue. He carefully stepped through his personal pre-combat drill, ensuring that every fibre of his being, and all his skills, were directed to the one aim.

Meantime the ANC party took Paul pretty-much directly to the small hollow where Peter and Lester were laagered up for the night, along with the balance of Peter's patrol, now caught up with their boss. Paul's unexpected arrival obviously did not bode well, and in short order the three of them were in Colonel Slouter's tactical HQ, working out their options.

'Rutter can handle himself for now, Mack, but at first light it would be good to be in a position to offer him whatever support we can,' assured Peter. 'It seems likely that the guerrillas will have not moved too far, given the magnet of those weapons.'

'I agree,' replied the Colonel. 'But my absolute first priority is to secure those weapons. I cannot allow them to fall into the wrong hands.'

'But Elizabeth —,' protested Paul.

Peter intervened, a hand on Paul's shoulder. 'If anyone can bring Elizabeth back, it is Daniel. I will take Lester and my patrol, and see if we can get into a position to respond if he needs us. If we act too early, we might only compromise his position.'

'And what should I do?'

'I suspect that the Colonel's medics may well need your skills, if and when the shooting starts, Paul,' Peter responded.

Mack Slouter nodded grimly, and left to organise his forces. At first light, he planned on moving up to occupy the village and secure the containers. He hoped that they would be well received — but should he warn the ANC of his intentions? One opponent or two — that is what it came down to. Anything that he could do to reduce the odds was worth it. He called for his driver.

Major Sawke was checking out the northern perimeter defences, when he was summoned across the village. A vehicle was approaching.

It stopped a sensible distance out from his forward posts. Nothing happened for five minutes or so, and then a familiar figure walked calmly out of the night, silhouetted by the headlights. *You are a very brave man, Colonel,* thought the ANC Major. *I wonder what you want?*

The Major shouted across the remaining fifty metres or so, 'Colonel, a little late for a social call?'

'Yes. May I come through your lines?' came the reply.

'Be my guest.'

The headlights went out, and a few tense moments later the two soldiers shook hands in the relative safety of a huge kiaat tree. 'Thanks. Got to admit that was a long walk,' said the Colonel.

The Major nodded, 'Rather you than me.'

'I hear that you have a problem,' offered the Colonel.

'I might, but nothing that I cannot handle.'

Colonel Slouter came directly to the point. 'That may or may not be the case, John, but let me be very frank: I will not let those weapons fall into the wrong hands.'

'What are you trying to say?'

Mack placed his hands on his hips and looked around. 'You have a choice. You can face two enemies, or one.'

'Meaning?' The Major had a nasty feeling that he already knew the answer.

'Meaning that it is my intention to occupy this village at first light, in order to secure the weapons.' The determination in the Colonel's voice was clear.

'That is not acceptable!'

'It is the only option left open to me. With my forces in the village, the guerrilla group will not dare attack. It secures your forces, along with the women and children in the village, and it guarantees the security of the weapons.'

Major Sawke shook his head. 'You expect me to effectively surrender to you on the strength of … of … just your word?'

'I was hoping that I had demonstrated enough good faith over the last day or so for you to have some degree of trust.'

The ANC Major paused, and allowed his eyes to take in the scene behind him. His village, his people, a life of hardship in pursuit of a cause. 'I will need to consult with my officers.'

Colonel Slouter looked at his watch. 'There are six hours to first light. I will need to start moving my forces up in three, so that we are in defensive positions by dawn. I intend to make as much noise as possible so that your guerrilla friends are well aware of what is going down.'

Major Sawke thought about that for a moment. 'Alright. Could we arrange a few fireworks to make it sound like we have put up some sort of resistance? That will confuse the picture for them.'

Daniel worked his way along the trail at a steady patrol pace that was perfectly balanced between the need for speed, and the need for stealth. He didn't expect to have to travel too far from the village before he ran up against the guerrilla rearguard, and could not afford to be detected prematurely.

After an hour of travel, the sharpness of the tracks in the dust convinced him that he was getting close, so he slipped the night vision goggles out of their protective pouch and placed them on his head. A flick of the switch and the gloom was transformed. An adjustment of the lens and everything came into focus.

Nothing moved, but Daniel opted to work his way off the trail to some high ground to his left. There was a shallow basin in front of him; the most likely place for a temporary encampment. The larger trees on one side suggested that there might also be a water source. It all made sense. Careful to stay below the ridge, Daniel moved across a slight spur that gave him a reasonable view of the feature.

Although the guerrilla force was practicing good illumination discipline, with the advantage of the goggles Daniel was able to make out most of the details of their disposition and activities. There were a number of vehicles loosely organised in the open area in the middle of the basin, and most of the force was resting around them. Those that had apparently been involved in the recce party into the village were gathered around one of the larger trucks. Sentries were posted at the obvious locations, and appeared to be alert.

At first, there was nothing to indicate where Elizabeth might be held, until the canvas backdrop on one of the trucks was lifted up and a huge man jumped to the ground. He was followed by a much smaller woman, carrying what looked like bandages. She hurried off into the shadows, while the man gathered a number of the waiting personnel around him.

If Elizabeth was in that truck, it was going to be a challenge getting close to her. Daniel did a quick calculation of the strength of the force based on those that he could actually see, compared with the number of vehicles and the amount of equipment that was visible. More than enough to prevent any serious consideration of the direct approach — just walk into camp and start shooting — although that did have some attraction, given his drive to avenge the slaughter of Dktfec's people.

But Elizabeth — all the trauma since that fateful day on the beach, when he had taken the life of her father — through to surviving the kidnapping, and then being left on the beach tied to a container, came down to the next few hours, and what he did or did not do. The mine, the diamonds, her inheritance, the future of the Impala, were now all focused on this one point in time and space. He knew he would have one chance to act, and one chance only.

He spent the next hour observing the routine below him, mapping out where the sentries were, the exact location of all the vehicles with reference to key parts of the terrain, and planning his next move. Daniel had to admit the rebel force was well organised, although at first glance what lay out in front of his high-tech goggles looked haphazard. The only thing that they might have got wrong, was that their defences were orientated on the obvious access — the rough track that ran into the basin from the direction of the village. Daniel slipped back from his observation post, and began to carefully work his way around the flank.

Elizabeth was nauseous with pain from the wound in her head. Any movement was agony, sending her head spinning. She lay still on the bare boards of the truck, the raw smell of her own vomit caustic in her nostrils. Her entire left side was completely numb, whether from the injury, or simply that she had lain there without moving for so long, she could not tell. The little girl moaned softly alongside her. A tear slipped down Elizabeth's face onto the dirty boards, and she lost consciousness again.

Peter and his patrol moved carefully across the broken landscape. Lester led the way forward, drawing on the skills borne of a life-time hunting across this rich but unforgiving landscape. There was very little ambient light, which made for slow going, but they dare not push the pace and so alert the rebel force of their presence. Peter checked his watch. Just about time for the fireworks. He hoped that Daniel was not going to be caught out when the show started.

After a hurried planning group over maps and photographs back at their vehicles, Peter and Lester had agreed that the most likely place for the rebel force to be was a series of small valleys and basins out to the northeast of the village. Apparently there was water there, and a rough road connected the two locations. But at this pace it was going to be another hour before they approached even their initial objective.

Peter caught up with Lester and they dropped into a quick huddle. 'We are going to be late.'

Lester looked up at the stars. Still no sign of the first light of dawn out to the east, but not long. 'Going as fast as I dare.'

'I know, but we are just not covering enough ground in this wretched light. The troops must be just about to move into the village.' Peter looked at the men gathered around him. Time to take some risks. 'As soon as the flares go up let's crack on; use the noise and illumination to make up some time. Hopefully the bad guys will be focused on what is going on over there.' He pointed over his shoulder.

'Right you are, old chap,' Lester replied with a grin.

They didn't have to wait long.

Daniel was about half-way around the perimeter of the basin, when the sounds of the mortars carried to him on the gentle breeze. He slipped beneath a handy bush and ripped off his night vision goggles, counting down the seconds until the big flares would turn night into day.

Not far from his temporary hide, the sentries also responded, runners fanning out across the encampment to rouse the fighters. This became much easier when three giant flares ignited out towards the eastern horizon. The sound of vehicles on the move carried across the scrubland, and then the familiar cadence of heavy calibre machine guns.

Daniel assumed the obvious. With the rebel force in the area, Mack had taken the only tactical option open to him. Get into the village and secure the containers. What a tragedy, but he forced the consequences from his mind, and concentrated on his immediate problem. The camp was now fully alert, with heavily-armed guerrilla fighters rushing to take up defensive positions.

He did, however, have one new advantage. The flares threw very sharp shadows, as dark as the night from whence they came, providing natural optical holes for Daniel to hide in as he moved quickly across the haphazard collection of vehicles and equipment. Soon he was close to his objective. He was about to run across the last strip of open ground, when the same huge man that he had noticed before, walked around the side of the vehicle he was lying underneath, accompanied by a handful of his men. Daniel recognised one of the two prisoners that they had released from the goat pen, back in the valley of the Impala. The big man, obviously the leader, was giving instructions. He held a heavy machine gun in his giant hand as effortlessly as a rifle, the dead weight of the belted ammunition draped casually over his shoulders.

Daniel could only catch a few pieces of the conversation over the noise of the firing out to the east, and in any case it was a dialect that he had not encountered before. He could do little but wait for the group to move towards the mouth of the basin, to observe the action. His opportunity came when gunfire erupted slightly south of the main access to their position, and the party rushed off to investigate. He crossed to the truck, and slipped under the heavy canvas awning.

CHAPTER 34

Peter's patrol was in trouble. Moving too fast, they had run into the forward picket of the guerrilla encampment without warning. Two of the patrol died on their feet, but brought the other ten men a few precious moments for their training to click in. They dived for whatever scant cover that was available, as a hail of bullets tore into the scrub and ground around them.

Lying on his belly in the shallowest of depressions, Peter knew that they had to get back into the gully about 20 metres to his right. The adrenalin was surging through his system as his special forces training and combat experience overrode the fear and panic of the initial onslaught. He looked to the sky. The first set of flares was getting low and the shadows longer.

'Sergeant! Gully to the south. On you. Go!' He got to his feet and emptied the first magazine in the direction of the incoming fire before sprinting towards the protection of the dry riverbed. In a drill they had practiced daily for years the rest of his patrol followed, alternatively laying down covering fire, and then moving. Magazines flew on and off their automatic rifles with instinctive precision as they ran. All but one man made it.

'Report!' bellowed Peter, breathing hard.

His patrol second-in-command came up alongside him, as the bullets continued to ricochet around their position. 'Three men down. Charlie and Rees are dead. Laces is out there somewhere, unknown.'

Peter realised that he had not seen Lester in the last few minutes. 'The hunter?'

'Not sighted.' Off to their left, their light machine gun had swung into action, and was having a noticeable impact on the number of incoming rounds.

'OK. We work our way down this feature until out of range, and look to come up on their flank.' *Any advantage of surprise is lost,* thought Peter, but he knew his depleted little force was in no position to launch a frontal assault on the well defended position. 'Tell the gunners to give us two minutes and then follow. Rendezvous is two clicks to the west, at this corner.' He circled the chosen feature on the map with his thumb. 'Pass it around.' The young officer moved off into the shadows. Another set of three flares ignited just beneath the early morning overcast. Closer this time. *Maybe the cavalry is on its way,* thought Peter.

Indeed it was. Observing the tracer from the patrol, hurried orders had been passed from the Army company command post to the platoon on that flank to pivot left and move up in support.

As soon as the illumination rounds were in the air, the mortar section was also retasked, and in a matter of seconds the rounds from the section of four mortars started to walk their deadly path down from the initial ranging shot on the ridge behind them, onto the exposed position of the guerrilla sentries. With nowhere to hide they took their chances in the open and ran, only to be met with a hail of bullets from the patrol's machine gun.

There was some satisfaction in the set of the gunner's face as he released the trigger. 'That one was for you, Charlie,' he whispered. The two men made their way down the gully to rejoin the rest of the patrol.

Peter had a decision to make. Wait for the reinforcements to come up, or continue to infiltrate the enemy positions. Mindful of how exposed Daniel and Elizabeth might be, he chose the latter, and led the way north out of the protection of the old river bed. But they were almost immediately greeted by the thump, thump,

thump, of a heavy calibre machine gun from the ridge in front of them, and high explosive rounds exploded against the ancient trees just in front of them. They had little option but to withdraw to the relative protection of the dead ground on the side of the gully, and wait for support.

It was not long before the mortar fire was redirected onto the bright muzzle-flashes coming from the ridge. One shell must have landed inside an ammunition container, because abruptly the early morning glow to the east was outdone by a spectacular display, as the individual high explosive and incendiary rounds cooked off from the heat from the exploding mortar round. The patrol ducked instinctively, as shrapnel screamed across the landscape. The effect on the rebel force closely grouped on the ridge was appalling.

'That one paid for itself many times over,' Peter commented to no-one in particular, as a temporary hush fell across the plain. He noticed movement behind him, and gave two flashes on his patrol beacon to identify their position.

Moments later he was joined by the commander of the advancing platoon. 'Major.'

'Lieutenant.' Peter replied, trying to keep the fatigue from his voice. 'Nice timing. Thank you.'

'No problems. Bit boring where we were, anyway. What next?'

'I think we give these guys time to absorb the reality of who they are facing. They are not generally inclined to fight man on man.'

'But as I read the ground, the only way out for their vehicles is back toward us,' observed the Lieutenant.

'Correct. Suggest that you set up either side of the road, where it crosses this feature. They will have to slow down, and there is good cover either side of the ford.' Peter paused. 'I will take my patrol around to cover any attempt to reverse back into the basin.'

'On my way,' the young officer responded, and moved off to set the trap. He well knew the reputation of these thugs and murderers, and had lost a number of close friends through the long years of the conflict. It was a fine day to be a soldier.

Peter gathered his depleted team together, and moved carefully towards the small ridge that defined the exit from the valley. He need not have worried about running into forward elements of the rebel force, as they had hurriedly withdrawn to load the most valuable of their equipment into their vehicles.

Daniel had found Elizabeth and the two children, as expected, roughly tossed in the back of the truck. He could not rouse Elizabeth, or the little girl. The boy, slightly older, was clinging desperately to the frame of the awning, as far out of sight as he could get, plainly terrified beyond his wits.

Daniel tried to make Elizabeth as comfortable as he could, ensuring her airway was not obstructed, and that she was not immediately at risk from loss of blood. He then took a couple of dirty cargo strops and lashed the two of them as tightly as he dared to the tray, deciding that the lad didn't look like he was going to let go of his hold in a hurry. That accomplished, Daniel moved out of the truck and around the darker side into the cab, carrying his weapons. As expected, there was a simple go/stop lever rather than any requirement for a key. He listened to the sounds of battle around him, and tried to judge the best time to act. Too early and he would not make it further than the truck ahead of him. Too late and the regular occupants of the truck would make the cab rather overcrowded. He decided to go around the back and check on Elizabeth.

Too early. His feet touched the sand just as the first of the retreating guerrilla forces came around from the blind side of the truck, and he was immediately spotted. There was nowhere to go. He froze and very slowly raised his hands, cursing his impatience. Moments later, he was stripped of all his equipment, and on his knees in front of their leader.

The first blow from the huge hands bowled him across to the feet of a couple of the rebels, who used their boots to send him back for more punishment. The second blow took him in the other direction, and his assailant followed him.

'You think you steal my truck. My truck!' bellowed the man in broken Afrikaans. 'Very bad. It is pity I have no time to play.' The man gave an exaggerated sigh and then reached out for a machete from one of the bystanders. He tested its blade with an enormous disfigured thumb. 'A quick death I no like.' He swung the weapon in a wide arc behind him. Daniel held his head high and looked into the eyes of his executioner. He noted the big blade reverse direction for the killing blow.

Lester Rushton, of the Upington Rushtons, had made his way discreetly up the ridge and then worked his way around the back of the basin, away from the fighting. He regretted leaving Peter and the patrol to their fate, but considered that he had a better chance of getting into a useful position alone. He observed Daniel's capture from a slight saddle in the surrounding terrain: about 400 yards away. Very carefully, so as not to attract unnecessary attention, he moved his father's rifle into his favoured firing position, assessed the distance and the breeze, and set the simple mechanical sight. He took aim very carefully, knowing he would only get one shot.

Daniel might have ducked, but pride held him still to observe at the critical moment a small hole appear in his assailant's chest. As the machete swung towards him, the balance of the dying man was just sufficiently upset that the blade took a neat slice of the top of Daniel's scalp, but the impact was enough to stun him temporarily. He dropped to the ground just ahead of the huge body that fell over the top of him. That saved his life, as it was assumed that the blow had, in fact, killed him.

Pandemonium reigned. Individual groups of rebels made for the vehicles, and a desperate escape. Lester added to the panic by methodically picking off any who paused in the open.

Daniel regained his senses and forced himself alert, as the truck behind him roared into life and moved away in a broad arc to head out of the valley. He struggled out from under the dead weight of the body lying on top of him. Partially blinded by the blood pouring from his head wound, he desperately tore a strip of cloth from his shirt and bound it around his forehead, at the same time tracking the progress of the truck. Using the dust and confusion to his advantage he ran a perfect intercept, opened the passenger side door and physically dragged the first totally surprised occupant through it.

The driver tried to accelerate away from the threat, but was boxed in by slow moving vehicles on either side. He made the mistake of assuming that Daniel would attempt to get through the same door, and pointed his rifle across the cab. The blow to his temple came through the driver's side widow, and moments later Daniel was at the wheel of the truck, cab empty. He wound up the dirty windows to reduce the risk of casual observation, and turned his attention to driving the wayward vehicle.

The trucks were forming up in a loose convoy. Daniel judged it best to work his way quietly to the rear, allowing anything that was able to, to move around him. Eventually the track narrowed to the extent that there was no longer room to be passed, and he was forced to accelerate, or draw further unnecessary attention to his particular vehicle.

He was fighting for control through waves of pain and fatigue. 'Must think,' he shouted to no-one in particular. 'Where are the friendly forces? Where are they?' He gasped for breath. 'Orient, decide, act!'

The vehicles in front cleared the choke point and accelerated. He raged at his greying vision. 'Decide Daniel, decide, for God's sake decide!'

Something was slowing the vehicles again, but through the dust he missed it until it was too late. As the back of the truck in front of him loomed large in the windscreen, he desperately swung the heavy steering wheel and careered off the track into the scrub. Instinctively, he shoved the accelerator to the floor, steering around the larger obstacles.

The truck survived for almost half a kilometre, until the old river bed swung in front of them. Daniel saw the edge of the drop ahead just in time, and hit the brakes. Lightly loaded, every wheel on the truck locked up, and they came to rest, miraculously, with the vehicle resting on its chassis, the front wheels hanging over a 5 metre drop to the sand below.

Not realizing that it was a long way down, Daniel dropped from the cab and fell heavily. It was only his parachute training that saved him from serious injury as he instinctively tucked and rolled to absorb the impact, but his ankle turned under him and he heard the bone break. Only absolutely dogged determination kept him conscious, as fresh waves of pain assailed his mental processes.

Peter and his patrol were barely in position, when the first of the trucks accelerated past in a cloud of dust. Most had the windows wound up to try and keep the fine powder churned up by the wheels out of the cabs. They could pretty-much see the entire track between their position and the ford across the old riverbed, and waited for the trap to be sprung. *Where was Daniel?* wondered Peter.

Suddenly a truck close to the rear of the convoy appeared to overshoot the slowing vehicle in front of it, turn, and charge across the broken ground in the direction of the village. But Peter knew what the driver obviously did not — that the river turned north and almost certainly cut off any escape option in that direction.

Now gunfire came from the other side of the ford, and the vehicles scattered in both directions, trapped in the gully. Many of the guerrillas bailed and tried to run for the bush. Some made it. Most did not. Abruptly, by some mutual signal, the fighting stopped. Those still alive lay face down in the sand. Some of the trucks were on fire, and would rot where they lay.

Almost disappointed, Peter noted that none of the guerrillas had attempted to run back into the basin. He stepped out from cover carefully, to see Lester jogging down the road towards them. Peter wasn't sure; Daniel trusted the man, but where had the hunter been for the last forty minutes?

Lester shouted across the distance between them. 'Peter. Daniel must be in one of the trucks. He is hurt.'

'Which one?' asked Peter, looking around him. He went to lead the patrol down the road at a trot, but was interrupted by three evenly spaced shots from the direction of the village. Things suddenly fell into place. Daniel, and quite probably Elizabeth. 'Quickly, this way.' He turned off the track and quickened his pace.

Daniel had managed to crawl back up the side of the gully, and retrieve the fallen rifle from the cab of the truck. He fired the internationally recognised signal for assistance, and then hobbled back to check on Elizabeth and the children. They were still there, but much the worse for wear from the journey.

The boy was exactly where he had been at last sight, and refused to move. Daniel desperately undid the cargo strops and moved Elizabeth onto her other side. There was little else he could do but wait for help to arrive. He lost consciousness just moments before Peter led his team around the corner of the ridge.

Peter was horrified by what he saw. 'Medic! At the double.' He joined in the effort to get the four of them out of the back of the truck, and then stood back to let the young man with the red crosses on his uniform make his assessment. He filled in the few spare moments by filing a quick report back to the Army tactical HQ. Off in the distance was the unmistakable sound of a helicopter. Peter fired up his patrol beacon and two of his team quickly cleared some loose brush away from a patch of open ground not far from their location.

Daniel regained consciousness as the helicopter flared for landing outside of the regimental aid post. Elizabeth was first out of the aircraft, and immediately into surgery. Although spectacular, Daniel's condition was not as critical, and he found himself in the triage tent, being fussed over by a couple of attractive young nurses.

About an hour later, Peter's face appeared around the corner of the tent. He had splashed a bit of water over his face, but could not hide the fatigue. 'Good to see that you are as bulletproof as ever, although seems like you do bleed, after all.' He drew a folding chair to the side of the cot and took a seat.

'They tell me that I will have a very impressive scar, and will probably have a bit of a limp.' Daniel patted his leg and added, 'at least for a while.' He looked in the direction of the small mobile operating theatre. 'How is Elizabeth, Peter? No-one seems able to tell me anything.'

'Still no word, but seems to be touch and go. Her head wound is the main concern.'

Daniel nodded, as Paul came through the door removing his surgical mask, shaking his head, his face drawn and tired. 'Morning guys.'

Both men spoke at once. 'How is she?'

Paul came around the other side of the bed. He sat down on the empty stretcher alongside them. 'Nasty head injury. Comatose and unresponsive. They are getting the chopper ready to fly her to the base hospital in Springbok for a scan. I have asked if I can go along.'

There was nothing more to be said, until a whimper from the other side of the tent attracted their attention and Paul moved over to where the two children were huddled together on the one stretcher, in spite of the nursing staff's attempts to keep them apart. One of the nurses joined him. 'They are OK — just cuts and bruises. A nasty gash on the little girl's calf.'

'But scared half to death,' added Paul.

She adjusted the light blanket that covered them. 'They are very undernourished. The wounds will take some time to heal.'

Paul crouched beside them. 'The real wounds are not physical. That is what will take time.' He turned back to the others as the sound of the helicopter starting up intruded on the eerie quiet of the morning. 'Time for me to go.'

Daniel reached out a hand. 'Race you back to the valley, Paul. There will be a brew on when you get home. God speed.'

They got a glimpse of Elizabeth's stretcher as she was loaded onto the chopper, and then it was gone in a cloud of dust and noise.

Daniel turned to Peter, switching frames with the clinical efficiency of his training. 'How did we do?'

'A number of casualties, good men. More letters to write to grieving families. But the guerrilla force is no more — just a handful of prisoners in various states of repair.'

Mack Slouter had stepped quietly into the tent. 'But the containers are secure, and we are already onto a number of community projects in the village.' He walked over to the cot. 'We had breakfast with Major Sawke and his officers. I think I would call this one a success.' He paused. 'Sorry to hear about Elizabeth, though.'

'She is strong, and stubborn,' replied Daniel. 'She'll pull through.'

Mack dragged a chair across and sat down opposite Peter. 'So, Daniel. Tell me more about these diamonds.'

PART 3

REUNIONS

CHAPTER 35

It was nearly two weeks later that two vehicles drove through the gates of the Impala capital, just before midnight, and went straight to the cottage. Daniel, Peter, and the newly constituted patrol were all exhausted from the long journey, and agreed to meet for a late breakfast the following day.

On the way back they had stopped briefly with Dktfec and the remnant of the Bushmen tribe, who were busy rebuilding their lives, as best they could. But the scars were very deep. Many members of the tribe were deeply distressed, sitting alone for hours on end, unable to climb back up the precipice of disaster. Daniel determined that he should return with Marcus and the children as soon as possible, in an effort to restore their souls.

As they unpacked Peter had one of those random thoughts. 'It is a shame that Shuka could not come back to see Swabi. I think he would have liked to spend some time out here making sure that she was alright before returning to duty.'

'He is?'

'Shuka was Roos's older brother, Daniel. Sorry, I thought you knew. I know that he was talking with Swabi about bringing his wife and children out here to visit, and possibly to settle. Swabi had offered to sponsor them all. The brothers were very close.'

Daniel dropped his kitbag on the porch. 'I just need to stretch my legs. See you in the morning.' He wandered off around the lake shore in the direction of the girls' lodges, on the off chance that Swabi was still up.

He discovered a number of the village women sitting on Swabi's porch over a cup of Swabi's best tea. About to slip away into the shadows, he was spotted by Marcus who came bounding down the path to greet him, almost knocking him over on his weak leg.

'Who is there?' Swabi called out.

'Hello ladies,' was about the best that he could do.

Swabi stood up and came down the path, stopping a couple of paces in front of him. 'Daniel, welcome back. But you are a late visitor?'

'I wondered if you had heard any news of Elizabeth.' Unable to read her face, Daniel wanted to run, but managed to hold his ground.

'Nothing more.' She paused to check the hem of her skirt. 'I heard the trucks. How are you?'

'Mending well. Just a few more scars.' He bent down to Marcus. 'Could have done with you along, boy.' The big animal whined in appreciation of the attention.

The tenderness of the scene prompted Swabi's anguish of the last few weeks to slip out before she had really had a chance to consider her words. 'You left in a big hurry?'

'Yes.' Daniel started to say something else, but couldn't put it into words. He stood up slowly, favouring his broken limb, and still stiff from the long days confined in the vehicles.

She shook her head. 'Why?'

'I … I didn't know that the man I saw you with —' He faltered, and tried again. 'I didn't know the man I saw you with on the night we left was Roos's brother. I got it all horribly wrong.'

Swabi nodded. 'I came looking for you that night, but you were asleep. I guess that I should have kicked you out of your cot there and then.'

'Perhaps, but it was not very adult of me to go and hide,' replied Daniel.

Swabi closed the gap between them, stopping very close. Marcus nuzzled his way between them. 'Roos is gone, Daniel. I know it is early days, but life is short.' Daniel could smell her subtle fragrance. She just stood there, arms at her side, and waited.

Eventually Ngashi could stand it no longer and walked down to join them. 'You are supposed to kiss the girl, Daniel.' He dropped his head, too embarrassed to do anything, so she hugged them both. 'I am exhausted, so will leave you two alone to catch up. Do everyone a favour and tell each other how you really feel, before there are any other grand misunderstandings.' She stepped away. 'If she were here, Elizabeth would approve.'

'Have you heard the news?' said Peter as he walked up the path to join them on Ngashi's porch. It was the following day, and they were gathered with the senior members of the court for a council of war, looking to decide how best to protect their interests through the impending High Court hearing.

'What news might that be?' asked Daniel.

'Just through from HQ. A member of the Prime Minister's inner cabinet resigned in disgrace yesterday, having had certain business dealings and links with organised crime exposed by the security agencies. At this stage it is not clear whether or not he will actually be charged.'

'That would be the Minister who was behind the challenges to our claim, and everything else?' asked Ngashi.

'The very same. I have asked for confirmation, but it now seems unlikely that any challenge to your rights to the mine will proceed.'

Ngashi got to her feet. 'This is extraordinarily good news, Peter.'

That set off a noisy discussion and celebration, which continued for the best part of thirty minutes as the group unpacked the significance of the news. Finally, Ngashi turned to Peter. 'What will you do now?'

'I have to leave today to make my report in person, and hopefully spend some time with my family.' He turned to his oldest friend. 'Daniel, I was told to invite you to come back with me. Your

Service record has been reinstated, in full, and there is some pretty impressive recognition coming for your role in the recent ANC reconciliation initiatives.'

Daniel was speechless. Peter went over to him and banged him on the shoulder. 'Your old job is there for you, if you want it, although I suspect that you have other things in mind.' He smiled at Swabi and everyone within earshot laughed.

'And you?' asked Daniel, head spinning.

'Promoted, and appointed to command the 5th Infantry Regiment,' Peter replied with a very broad grin. 'That, of course, includes my old Survey Company, so I will be able to bring Matty up from Dad's.'

'Well done!' Daniel led the line of people to congratulate him.

Swabi got to her feet and came over. 'Any news of Elizabeth?' she asked softly.

Peter took her hand. 'I spoke with Paul earlier today. Elizabeth's condition has not changed. She is still in a coma.' Realising that everyone had turned their attention back on him, Peter looked at the concerned faces, and raised his voice a little. 'He asked us to keep her in our prayers.'

Swabi looked at Daniel. 'I must go to her.' There was a passion and an urgency in her voice that could not be mistaken.

'So we go,' answered Daniel. 'If that is OK, Peter?'

At last light on a crushingly hot day the party drove into the car park of the Springbok base hospital, and climbed down from the big patrol vehicles. Without pausing, Peter led the way inside.

Marcus walked quietly at Daniel's side. He had simply climbed into the truck with them as they said their farewells four days before. Ngashi had smiled through her tears, 'I think he knows where you are going.'

The hospital receptionist was the first barrier, hiding from the enormous dog behind the glass screen. 'You simply cannot bring that animal into the hospital. No way.'

Daniel avoided the issue, for now. 'Would you please just call the ward for Doctor Paul Tradour.'

'Not until you get that animal out of my reception,' she insisted.

Swabi interrupted, 'Let's wait outside, while Peter sees if he can find Paul.' She led the way back through the heavy glass doors. Daniel made to follow, but nothing was going to budge the dog. He stood his ground, and a low growl escaped his massive throat.

Peter looked across at Daniel. 'I think that you should just call the ward, Miss.' The receptionist picked up the phone, but dialled the hospital security watch room. Moments later, two burly security guards appeared through the door to their left.

'Marcus, stay,' Daniel commanded as the security guards paused to take in the situation. He turned to them, 'Please do not move. He means no-one any harm, but there is a patient here who he believes that he must see. That is all.'

Peter decided that it was time to pull rank. 'I am Colonel Peter Hogan, Commanding Officer of the 5th Infantry Regiment. This is Sergeant Rutter. We have come a long way to check on a friend who was critically injured some weeks back. Please call Dr Tradour.'

One of the security guards took a pace towards them and Marcus immediately roared his defiance, but held his ground.

'Not a good, idea, believe me,' commented Daniel. The man stepped back towards the door.

But through an open window three floors up, Paul heard the commotion. Expecting their visit, he looked down into the carpark and spotted the vehicles. He sprinted down the stairs to burst through the doors on the other side of the reception concourse. 'Marcus. I thought that sounded like you.' Seizing the situation immediately, to the astonishment of the security staff, he walked straight across and embraced the big dog, who immediately reverted to a puppy. 'Hello fella.' He held out a free hand to greet the other travellers. 'Great to see you. Just let me make a couple of calls.'

It took a bit of doing, but eventually the hospital registrar relented, and the five of them were permitted to move quietly up to the ward, where Elizabeth was lying deeply unconscious, connected to this world by a number of tubes and monitors. Swabi was deeply distressed at how pale and drawn she looked.

'We are doing everything we can,' said Paul quietly.

'Has there been any change at all?' asked Swabi.

'Not really. Her wounds have healed fine, and she seems to be getting some feeling back in her left side, from what we can tell from her reflex response.'

Marcus had dropped behind obediently as they had made their way into the ward, but now gently pushed his way through to the side of the bed. Paul gently moved the drip line and life support sensors out of the way, as the dog placed his giant head gently on her exposed forearm.

After a few minutes of stillness Marcus grew impatient, and gave a couple of play barks. His rear end wiggled playfully. Daniel went to restrain him, but Paul had a flash of insight and shook his head.

The barks grew louder and more urgent, using every tone and inflexion Marcus could produce. When this did not elicit any response from Elizabeth, he roared, three times. It was so loud in the confines of the room that the people instinctively covered their ears.

Silence — the dog waiting for a response. It came in the pace of the pulse monitor, which suddenly jumped, drawing Paul's attention to the irregular rhythm displayed on the screen of the ICU equipment.

He leapt to confirm Elizabeth's pulse with his stethoscope. It was racing. 'Speak up, Marcus, speak up you big beautiful dog!' he shouted.

Marcus obliged with another volley of barks and growls.

A finger moved tentatively, and Marcus gave it a huge lick.

Paul leant forward and slipped the tube from Elizabeth's throat just as she started to gag. Outside of the room a ripple of excitement went through the hospital staff who had gathered to watch.

Swabi reached for Daniel's arms and they just held each other tight, as Elizabeth Dortmus, daughter of Pieter and Sarah, returned to them.

EPILOGUE

It was a few days later. They were all gathered in the little hospital room for the last time, before Peter and Daniel were to leave for the final journey back to base. It would be several weeks until Elizabeth would be strong enough to make the trip home, and Swabi had opted to stay with her and Paul.

Peter moved over to the bed. 'Duty calls.'

Elizabeth smiled, but there was a sadness in her voice. 'Seems that it always will.'

Daniel and Peter looked at each other and shrugged, but their farewells were interrupted by one of the nurses who knocked and then stepped into the crowded room. 'This letter was dropped off at the front desk earlier today, Miss. I regret that it sat around on matron's desk until I noticed it just now.' Paul took it and passed it across.

Her curiosity aroused, Elizabeth looked at the dirty envelope. It seemed to have travelled a long way, but there were no stamps or post marks. 'Strange,' she remarked, and slipped her fingernail inside the top cover to ease it open. Inside was a grainy black and white photograph, that bore a simple note on the back.

Nina and I with the boys, recently.

Tears of joy and relief streamed down her face, and she relaxed back on her pillows, eyes closed, the photo to her lips.

Glossary

CO   Commanding Officer
XO   Executive Officer, or second in command
OpsO   Operations Officer
Nav   Navigator
Weaps Weapons Officer